MW00440772

TURN

By
Jacqueline Druga

TORN
By Jacqueline Druga

Special Thanks to M. Rita Knits for her help and to Jane Dare
Cover Art provided by Steven McGhee

NATURE'S FURY

1 - ODD

May 3rd

"Buster!"

There was no answer to his mother's call.

"Buster," she beckoned again.

A bark was the response.

Sally sniffed.

It didn't take a bloodhound to find his scent. The overwhelming aroma was distinctive, and with a few good whiffs, Sally found her son. His very first words were actually a sound that mimicked the neighbor's barking dog, which earned the two-year-old the nickname of Buster. However, they should have called him Houdini because he had a talent for and the habit of disappearing. But his mother one-upped him; she always found him through her keen maternal instincts or the Buster neighborhood watch program.

"There you are," Sally scolded gently as she opened the cupboards under the kitchen sink.

"Cookie." Buster held up the dog biscuit.

"No." Sally took the snack from his mouth, and pulled out the child. "Whew, you smell bad. Are you trying to tell me something, Buster?" she asked.

The child giggled.

"First barking, now dog biscuits." She carried

him in the other room.

"Play."

"After I change you." She laid the child on the floor. "Stay."

Buster barked.

Sally rolled her eyes, smiled, and retrieved a diaper and wipes. She brought them over to Buster. "Okay. Soon enough we'll get you trained, right?" She took a deep breath, undid the diaper and then…Sally screamed.

***

A large cockroach was adhered to the center of the fecal-stained disposable diaper. When Sally called Bret's name that afternoon, she thought for certain that Sally was looking for her son. Never did she expect the frantic-sounding mother to burst through her back door holding a dirty diaper.

The petite woman, a mother herself, remained calm and prepared to tell Sally that Buster wasn't there, until Sally placed the diaper on her kitchen counter.

"I don't know what to do, Bret. I don't know what to do," Sally said hysterically.

People always considered Bret Long a sarcastic woman. Teetering on whether or not it should be laced with anger or humor, Bret assessed the situation, stepped back, pointed and said, "Tell me that's not a…." Before she could finish her sentence, she caught a whiff. "Aw, man, Sally. Get that off my counter."

"Look, Bret, look at it."

"I'm not looking at a dirty diaper."

"Please," she begged.

Hearing the seriousness and desperation in her voice led Bret to worry that perhaps there was something wrong with Buster. "Ok, show me," she said, not wanting to touch the diaper. "But could you please…take that off my counter."

Sally lifted the diaper and unrolled it.

To prepare for the aroma, Bret inhaled before the exposure. But she wasn't prepared to see the two-inch roach in the center of the mess.

"Bret, should I call poison control? What?"

Knowing Buster, no one would have put it past him to pick up that bug and eat it. However, even though cockroaches were expected to outlive man and be the sole surviving species on this earth, it was highly doubtful that the bug could have survived not only the chewing process, but the digestive acids as well.

It was still alive.

"Bret?" Sally beckoned for a response.

"He didn't eat that," Bret told her. "Look, the legs are still moving."

"Oh, my God. I don't have roaches."

"Well…Buster does." She winced at her scream. "Sally, just because you see a roach doesn't mean your house is dirty. However, if there's one in your house, there's.…"

"Stop." She held up her hand. "I have to throw up."

"You? Me." Bret gagged as she watched Sally in her frazzled state rewrap the diaper and run her fingers through her red hair so quickly that she didn't notice she had new highlights—remnants of her son's bodily functions.

"Should I call an exterminator?" she asked.

"Call your husband first. That's what they're there for. And Sally, you have…poop in your hair." Bret pointed.

Sally gurgled out a scream. It had Bret's attention for only a moment as it was soon drawn to her twelve-year-old daughter who blasted into the house.

"Mom!" Casper raced into the kitchen. Born Elizabeth Ann Malone, she fell victim to her mother's habit of nicknaming people by the age of three. She always seemed to catch a cold, and never was able to suntan, hence she acquired the nickname of Casper.

"Mom, you have to see this." She was as frantic as Sally. "Come outside."

"What is it?" Bret asked.

"You have to…why is Mrs. Rogers holding a dirty diaper?"

Nonchalantly Bret responded, "A cockroach climbed in it."

Casper snarled a look of disgust, and then regained her composure. "Mom. Please."

"What is it?" she asked again.

"Just come outside."

At that point it was obvious that getting into a verbal ping-pong match was unproductive, so Bret just followed Casper outside.

To those in the lower-income echelon this

neighborhood was considered suburbs, but those who were above middle class called it the 'poor' section of the school district. Although it had more concrete than grass, it was a quaint little borough a few miles outside of the city. Only a few feet separated most of the homes and everyone had a sidewalk. The sidewalk was the destination of Bret and Casper.

Before Bret could spit out, "What am I looking at?" she saw it on the sidewalk just in front of her property. Its identity changed with each closer look. A metamorphosis, if you will. At first glance, it looked like a man's brown shoe, then closer she thought it was coffee grinds…until the huge pile moved.

Nine inches around, at least six high, the dark brown mound shifted around in one spot.

"Are they ants?" Bret peered a little closer. "They are."

"Is that the grossest thing you've ever seen?" Casper asked.

"It's a toss-up between this and the shitty diaper." Bret was struck with awe over the mound as she crouched down to look at it. "My God. This is amazing. I've never seen anything like this. I wonder what they're eating." She stood up straight. "Casper, go get the camera."

"What?" she asked, aghast. "I'm not taking a picture of them. Why?"

"This is strange. Please? I'll go get a bucket of water."

"Fine," she flounced into the house. Bret followed.

Sally was still in the kitchen as Bret grabbed the bucket and started to fill it.

"What's wrong outside?" she asked.

"Get this…ants. A freakish amount of them," Bret answered.

"Great. Just great." Sally spun on her heels and opened the door. "Bugs are taking over." She barged out.

The dramatic comment made Bret pause. Then she finished filling the bucket and took it outside.

"I took their picture," Casper said holding the camera. "They didn't pose."

Bret snickered, "That was good. Step back." She held up the bucket, preparing to dump it. "I don't want you getting wet."

Casper stepped back.

Bret believed that the mound would wash away with whatever the ants feverishly devoured.

Her mistake.

The expulsion of water onto the sidewalk cleared nothing. It made matters worse. Horrified, she dropped the bucket and Casper screamed as the mound began to wash away.

Her head quickly jerked to the snap of a picture Casper took, then back to the sidewalk, where, like a river of mud, more ants poured from the crack in the concrete. An unstoppable amount oozed out as if washing away the mound opened a door to freedom.

"Shit." Bret leapt back. "Get the hose." With Casper closely behind her, she raced up the outdoor steps and grabbed the garden hose, yanking it with her in the rush back to the ants. "Casper, get ready to turn it on."

Bret found herself a safe place on the lip of a wall just before the sidewalk. "Full blast," she instructed, eyes locked onto the ants that kept coming. The once-normal sidewalk was brown. She held tight to the hose and squeezed the nozzle, trying to clear them off, drown them.

"Aim for the crack, Mommy," Casper said. "Aim there."

She did. Casper was correct. Power stream going, Bret blasted the crease for a good five minutes straight until there were no more ants. Then she squirted the sidewalks clear of the ones that moved and swam for their lives.

It was as if she was in a battle. Bret's adrenaline spiked and her breathing was heavy. She lowered the hose when Casper shut down the water.

The mother and daughter joined in staring at the wet property, waiting to see if the ants would return.

"Mom? Why were there so many ants?"

Bret shook her head. Never had she seen anything like it before, but there was a first time for everything. There was no explanation for it, only the excuse of a strange occurrence in an already strange day.

***

Mid-lecture, actually mid-word, the

dumbfounded, 'Huh?' made Professor Darius Cobb pause in his speaking. He chuckled as if the 'huh' was a joke, then he prepared to continue. Professor Cobb, whose age was never divulged, was somewhere around forty, but that was hard to tell. His slight yet toned five eight frame often made him look younger than his students—at least from a distance. Although he added highlights, he didn't attempt to cover up the occasional gray hair in his tossed, slightly long brown hair. He felt that it added an air of distinction to him, separated him from the students. However, one need not speak to Darius Cobb longer than a minute before the realization came through that the highly intelligent and often humorously arrogant man was not a child.

Of course, if Professor Cobb wanted respect based purely on his appearance, he could opt to dress less like his students.

Back to the lecture.

He heard the 'huh' from the galley, shook his head, and then opened his mouth. He paused again and pointed his pencil at the young man four rows back. "Tell me you're joking, right?"

"About?" the young man asked.

"The 'huh'. When I said the word Chernobyl, you said 'huh'."

"Yeah."

"You…you don't know what Chernobyl was?"

The boy of nineteen shook his head.

Just as Darius was about to explain, he saw hands rising. "I'm gonna assume none of you know about Chernobyl."

Silence and awkward nods.

"Figures. Ok." Darius walked around his podium. "Listen, go home and blast your parent or parents for me, please. This is a big part of world history here. Especially ecologically, and that's why most of you are in my class." He paced as he spoke. "Chernobyl plays a big role as an example. Therefore, when I said to you, technological and modernized impacts on our ecology such as Chernobyl, I was hoping that all of you would understand. Yes, Melinda." He pointed to a young woman.

"Wasn't that like a place where a nuclear bomb went off by accident," she said.

"Yeah," another male student said brightly. "China or something."

"What?" Darius laughed. "You have got to be kidding me. All of you got together and planned this joke. Okay. Stop. How many of you know about Chernobyl? Show me hands."

Darius scanned the room. Eleven of the thirty raised their hands, including the young man and young woman who believed Chernobyl was an accidental nuclear bomb that exploded in China.

In defeat, Darius set down his pen, walked to the white board, picked up a marker and wrote the word, 'Chernobyl.'

"Now," he continued. "Chernobyl is in Russia."

A group of 'ahs' emanated from the class.

"See, we're learning." He smiled. "In 1986, a nuclear reactor meltdown caused an explosion in a nuclear power plant, Chernobyl," Darius said. "This happened without warning, and the plant spewed radiation into...." he paused and looked up when the whap of paper, followed by a mumbled 'shit', caught his attention. Shrugging it off, Darius continued his lecture. "Spewed into the air. The radiation levels were estimated to be about 400 times stronger than the radiation released by the Hiroshima and Nagasaki bombs. But...." with excitement he lifted his finger. "Compared to bomb testing, Chernobyl's ecological effect pales in comparison to bombs tested in say 1970. When this...." Another pause at another 'whap' sound. A shift of his eyes and Darius caught a glimpse of one his students. Paying no mind, he went on. "The casualties primarily consisted of firefighters on the scene, then people began to fall ill from the radiation. The cloud itself spread and reached as far around the world as Europe. Contaminated areas...." Again he stopped; this time not only was the student swinging a paper but also jumping around. "Scott, problem?"

"Uh, yeah. Roaches," Scott said.

"What?" Darius asked.

"Cockroaches. First there was one, now shit!" he jumped up.

Darius moved up the few steps to Scott's seating level. "How do you like that?" Darius grabbed a notebook, and scooped up one of the seven roaches.

A female student winced and scooted away.

"Ironic." Darius held up the notebook. "We're

talking about radiation and this here, the cockroach, is supposed to outlive man when it comes to radiation. Its body is like a suit of armor." He stared at the roach.

"Sir," Scott said. "Why is my desk infested?

"Your desk is not infested. Probably the room is," Darius said nonchalantly as he turned and walked down the steps. He snickered at the cringes of disgust that rang out in the room. "I'll report it to environmental services. As far as this little fellow." After examining the roach, he let it dropped to his desk. "He may be immune to radiation. But...." With a slam he smashed the bug with the book. "Not to me." He stared up at his students who audibly groaned. "Now." He grinned. "Back to class."

2 - LIFE

The so-called 'ideal' housewife supposedly disappeared right after the women's liberation movement. However, in the Long home, Bret was stuck in a rut of modern working woman meets Donna Reed.

She didn't complain, especially when it came to her children. She was very grateful for the closeness, except when it came to dinner. Whether all of her children were present at the table or only half, it was a madhouse. It could easily be said that Bret hadn't eaten a hot meal, uninterrupted, since she became a very young mother.

It was a given that her oldest son, Perry, wasn't going to show for dinner. He rarely did since he proclaimed his independence on his eighteenth birthday, three months earlier. Of course, he was a free man until he needed food, laundry done, or a couple bucks to get him through. Bret wished he'd come home more often.

The other three made for a noisy supper. Luke, the second son, was upbeat, bubbly, and sixteen going on twelve. Blessed with twin daughters, Casper and Andi, Bret swore they hated each other. How many times did she hear from them, 'We shared a womb for eight months, that's enough for a lifetime.' They were only twelve. All the while Jesse, her husband, pretty much ate and listened, only speaking up when he had something funny or sarcastic to say.

That evening in particular didn't start out

much differently. Like someone from a 1950s sitcom, Bret was walking around the dining room table putting food on everyone's plate.

"Thanks. Looks good." Jesse peered up. "Perry not coming?"

"When does Perry come anymore," she said.

"Who knows. Thought for sure he'd be asking for money. It's been weeks. Where's Luke?" he asked.

Just as he inquired, the front door slammed and the sound of Luke rushing in could be heard.

"Sorry I'm late!" he hollered as he raced up the stairs. "I have to wash my hands. Wait until you hear this."

The bathroom door slammed.

"Must be big," Bret commented and took her seat. "How was your day, Jesse?"

"Fine." He shrugged. "Hot. Too hot for May. Did I ever tell you how much I hate Wal-Mart?"

Curiously, Bret looked at him. It was a well-known fact that Jesse wasn't always the brightest bulb in the bunch; it wasn't uncommon for him to say things that didn't make sense, and it was evident by the look on Bret's face that Jesse just uttered one of those things. "Wal-Mart?" Bret asked. "Why were you at Wal-Mart today?"

"I wasn't."

"But you said it was too hot and it made you hate Wal-Mart."

"My crew is by the brand new Wal-Mart. Where do you think the traffic was going? Made it impossible. Wal-Mart."

"Anyhow…." Bret folded her hands and

perked up with excitement. "Wait until you hear...."

"Check this out." Luke barreled into the dining room. "Oh, sorry, were you talking, Mom?"

"Yes." She nodded. "But go on, tell yours first. Something really weird happened to me and Casper today."

"No, mine's cooler," Luke said. "Go on."

"No way," Bret argued.

Andi, the other daughter, spoke up. "I had a weird thing happen. Can I tell?"

Everyone looked at her.

So sweet, so fragile, she consumed her food as she spoke nonchalantly. "Mrs. Rogers was showing me Buster's poop diaper and it had a roach in it."

Everybody grunted with disgust.

Casper dropped her fork. "Thank you for that."

Andi shrugged. "Sorry."

Luke was bursting and couldn't wait. "Ok, here is mine. Check this out. We see flies, right. Tons and tons of them, me and Ray. So, being the inquiring boys that we are, we went to this garbage can. Thinking, okay, maggots."

Casper groaned.

Luke continued, "So we look inside, and there's this giant rat. It's like eating this bird that's still alive."

"What did you do?" Bret asked.

"Well, Ray went and got his BB gun. He said to me, dude, you're the better shot, you do it. So I aim, right. Pow. I shoot. I miss."

"Then what?" Bret inquired.

Luke shrugged. "The BB ricocheted, flew up and nailed Ray in the head. We had to take him home. When we went back the rat was gone. Bird was there. Dead though. It was the coolest thing. It was my first real rat outside a pet store."

Bret paused, smiled politely, and then gained enthusiasm to tell her story. She told of how she and Casper, within the course of two hours, fought three times against a phenomenal number of ants.

"It's true," Casper said. "You should have seen how many."

"I called the police." Bret said.

Jesse laughed. "You what? You called the police."

"Oh, yeah. It was freaky. It was scary, Jesse. We have like, this infestation of gigantic proportions right outside our house."

"And what did the police say?" he asked.

"They told me to call an exterminator. I did. Exterminator said it was borough property so it's the borough's responsibility. I called the borough but they blew me off."

"So would I." Jesse shook his head "You called because of ants."

"Jesse, I'm serious. You should have seen how many there were. I swear to God there has to be the world's biggest colony living under our sidewalk."

"Bret, you know how ridiculous that sounds. It's May. And you tend to exaggerate...."

Casper gasped. "My mother is not lying. I

saw it. We took pictures. Quit being rude to her."

"Oh!" Bret snapped my finger. "We did. We took pictures." She nodded in a 'so there' manner. "Jesse, we have to do something. We have to. There's a gazillion ants...."

"A gazillion?" Jesse snickered.

For sarcastic clarification, Casper said, "Yes, that's a big word, I know. But it means more than a million."

Jesse looked at her. "Where is that attitude coming from? God. I know what it means. But I think that's a bit much. Bret, there weren't that many."

"Bet me." Bret was adamant. "I bet they are breeding under the sidewalk. Borough or not, I'm calling an exterminator first thing...."

"No. Bret. You will not. For ants?" Jesse shook his head. "Let me eat. I'll handle it."

"Jesse, there's a ton."

"They're ants, Bret." Jesse continued eating. "How many can there be? We deal with this a lot at work. I'll show you there's not a gazillion. We don't need an exterminator."

"We need something."

Jesse smiled. "You have me."

"What are you going to do?" Bret didn't receive a verbal response; she only received a glance that told her more than she probably wanted to know.

***

The country music played at an almost inaudible level in Darius Cobb's large classroom. Stacks of papers were in front of him; he tapped the pencil to the beat of the music as he read through them. His head bobbed slightly, shaking, all while he smiled.

"You're kidding me. No." He snickered and lifted the paper. "Scott, where were you when I talked about this?" He grunted, shrugged, then wrote down, "Man, I must be boring."

"And a bit insane. However...." The male voice entered the room. "Your sensuality, boyish figure, and boy toy appeal make up for that." A briefcase was set on Darius' desk. The fiftyish bald man with a healthy build smiled at Darius. "I'm happy to see that no exchange of sexual favors for grades was occurring. How are you, Dare-Dare?"

Darius set down his pencil with a laugh, "Only you and my mother call me that."

"Well of course, that was a wonderful time in my life. Really, she should have married me instead of that rodeo star."

Darius only glanced up.

"Who was it next, the...."

"Colin," Darius silenced him with a smile.

Dr. Colin Reye sat down on the edge of the desk. He did indeed date Darius' mother at one time, for five years. In addition, she referred to him as the youngster. Only eight years her junior, Colin genuinely was crazy about her, even if the package included a rambunctious, too intelligent for his own good teenager named Darius. But even the eccentric and wild Colin couldn't tame Darius' mother. Despite the break up, Colin remained close to him vowing to be the father figure he never had, and their friendship spanned over twenty years.

"I thought we were having lunch," Colin said.

Darius looked at his watch. "We can."

"It's six o'clock."

"Dinner?" Darius suggested.

"Can't. Have to try to make it up to Pittsburgh by eight."

"You should. We're only in Morgantown. I thought you were here all week as a guest lecturer."

"I am," Colin said. "But tonight, I want to try to catch the Matthews lecture at Carnegie Mellon on biological warfare. Wanna join me; we'll get a late dinner at the 'O'. Maybe…." he winked. "Hit Crickets and watch some aging strippers."

Darius laughed. "Can't. I want to finish grading these, and there's an open mike night at the café. I have a couple new songs I wrote. It uh…it starts at ten…." Darius raised an eyebrow.

"Lecture is two hours." Colin looked at his watch. "Sign up late, I can make it."

"Excellent."

"Can I do harmonies?" Colin asked.

Darius laughed.

"Helps in picking up the girls." Colin lifted his briefcase. "OK, I'm out of here. If I don't make it tonight to hear you…." He turned. "I'll catch you tomorrow."

"Sounds good."

"And so does a meal in the middle of the day."

"Lunch tomorrow." Darius held up a hand. "I promise."

"I'll hold you to it."

"Be careful."

"You, too." Colin began to ascend the stairs.

Darius, with a look of enjoyment over his visit with Colin, lowered his head to his papers. It immediately lifted when he heard the slam of Colin's foot.

"Roach." Colin scraped off his shoe. "Better call maintenance." He continued on up the stairs.

Shaking his head, Darius looked thoughtful and put down his pencil. Opening his desk drawer, he pulled out a guitar pick then extended a long arm to his guitar that perched on a stand. He lifted it to his lap, hummed a few bars, and then began to strum. Mid-song, he pulled back his hand and shook it. "Fuck." He looked at the back of his hand. Directly behind his thumb was a spot of blood. "What the...." He sprang up and dusted five roaches from his lap. "Holy shit." Quickly, his head jerked to the hand that held the guitar neck. Three roaches raced up his hand. Hurriedly setting down the guitar, Darius flung the insects from him and stomped at the same time. "What the hell is going on?" He turned to where his guitar had been perched all day. As he neared the stand, he could see more cockroaches scurrying around. Like an investigator, he crept over. The stand was next to a bookcase and as Darius arrived, the roaches flew behind the case. "So this is where you're coming from."

Grabbing on to the shelf, Darius slid it from the wall. When he did, his face went pale.

***

Jesse definitely could have been titled the 'Demolition Man'. He carried a large pick in one hand while toting a can of gasoline in the other.

"Jesse." Bret followed him. "What are you doing?"

"Taking care of the…ants."

"By what? Burning down the house?"

"Bret, the house is fifty feet away."

"Yeah, but those cars parked on the street aren't. We are so getting fined." She stopped on the top step, refusing to go further down.

Jesse stood on the sidewalk. "Where?"

"There." Bret pointed.

"Bret, I can't see. Tell me where."

As if courting danger, Casper raced down the step, pointed, and then raced back up.

"Thanks." Jesse grumbled then shook his head. "I see about ten ants."

"There's more," Bret said. "Underneath the sidewalk."

"Well, we'll find out. But first…." Jesse began dousing the section of sidewalk with gasoline, then ran a small trail away from it.

"What are you doing?"

"Bret, if there are gazillions of ants, I want to be ready when I lift this."

Bret didn't believe he was ready.

Curiosity brought her close enough to see him and prove him wrong. Jesse placed one end of the pick into the crack in the sidewalk, and his huge frame heaved up the section. The concrete slammed backwards onto the ground.

"Holy fuck," he exclaimed. "Bret, look at this. Casper, take that picture."

Bret inched closer; so did Casper. Remaining calm momentarily, Casper took the picture.

He repeated his earlier sentiments. "Holy fuck."

The small two-foot section exposed more than dirt. It looked like black moving quicksand underneath where the concrete once lay.

"Just tell me they are mixed with the dirt. Right?" Bret inquired.

"They have to be. Let's see." Holding the pick, he placed it downward. He didn't hit soil, it sunk. "Oh, my God," Jesse exclaimed. "They have to be at least two feet deep. At least."

Bret screamed when, thick and fast, the ants blanketed their way up the pick.

Jesse dropped it into the masses of ants, then jumped back and grabbed the gas can. He dumped gasoline as he diligently flung ants from his body. Faster than the ants, he cried out for the hose, lit a match and tossed it in the ant pit. He secured himself away from the flames, but not without his legs being covered by ants.

He remained unnervingly rational. Bret on the other hand couldn't even squeeze the nozzle on the hose. Luke took over in hosing down Jesse.

The street got quite the show. Bret, Casper, and Andi were screaming. A small roaring fire was ablaze on the sidewalk, all while Luke hosed down Jesse. Someone probably thought Jesse was burned, because the paramedics were there within two minutes.

The fire department showed up directly after and put out the little inferno. Just when they were about to chastise Jesse, they saw how many ants were on the sidewalk and floating about and changed their minds.

They looked into it further. They put out the fire Jesse started, but then after labeling it contained, they ignited more flames. Because the ant farm didn't descend two feet like Jesse claimed; it measured a depth of five feet.

***

Some would argue her case, but Bret stood firm that she was a hypocrite in the truest form. Dr. Jekyll and Mr. Hyde. Primarily, her grossly exaggerated self-description was based on her career. Three nights a week, midnight to five, Bret worked as radio talk show host on a huge Christian broadcasting station, delivering biblical advice and quotes to live by in regards to viewer problems and daily events. Did she know The Bible that well? No. She hada kick butt producer who was fast on the keyboard with an awesome Biblical program.

She wasn't the religious woman she

portrayed; she had a strong belief and faith in God, but just not staunch.

A mother young in life, she considered herself blessed. If asked, motherhood was the one thing she did correctly.

Her personal life…another story.

She divorced the father of her children when the twins were born but didn't meet Jesse until years after.

Jesse Long was, without a doubt, an oxymoron—in Bret's eyes. Long for a last name…short on thinking. He was big, strong, and at times almost handsome. His physical attributes were what attracted her to him right away, that and his weird sense of humor. It wasn't his level of intelligence. Jesse operated on a different level than most when it came to brainpower application. Reading wasn't something that he did. He never claimed to be an Einstein, which was an endearing quality. If a task was at hand, he thought obscurely and slowly before he did something. He listed things in his mind. Plotted them out. He tried to eliminate mistakes before they happened. Jesse's biggest problem in life was his tendency to speak before thinking. Bret claimed he never put that thinking cap on straight, because he'd spout forth or act on his emotions first.

Were they happy in their marriage? In a sense. They lived their lives as they should. Aside from her sons, the only other male that played a predominant role in Bret's life was Chuck. In fact, Jesse introduced them. Chuck worked as a newspaper reporter for the Johnstown,

Pennsylvania paper, but he was originally a disc jockey there. Chuck's career record wasn't the reason Jesse introduced him to Bret. Chuck was the brother of someone Jesse worked with. Since Bret was 'Divine', the top advice woman at a Christian station, this coworker asked Jesse if Bret could help Chuck. Chuck had recently lost his wife and two daughters in a car accident.

Jesse obliged in the introduction and the rest was history. The friendship was in its third year. Bret and Chuck didn't see each other nearly as often as they communicated through email and the phone. They had a strong friendship.

The ant incident left her itchy and unable to nap before work, and Bret was anxious to get to the station early to access the resources the radio station had. However, she got caught up in an online chat with Chuck.

"Shit," she typed. "I gotta go. Show starts in ten minutes."

"I'll be listening." He typed back. "I have to drive to Erie."

"Careful," she jotted, then quickly signed off as her producer entered the room. "Hey, David," she said.

David gave her a sideways glance and odd look. "You okay?"

"Yeah, yeah." Bret waved her hand. "Just had a really strange thing happen today. That's all. I wanted to look up some stuff on our resource center, but I got caught up with email."

"If you need me to help, let me know."

"I will. I'm probably going to mention it on the air. Maybe one of the listeners knows something."

"What is it?"

"Ants."

David snorted a chuckle. "Ants. Okay." He whistled. "I'm going in the booth." He pointed backwards then walked out.

Bret shrugged off his 'I could care less' attitude and planned what she was going to say.

The show started as usual: Music to news, then finally the actual 'talking' portion began somewhere around one AM. About that time of night, listener calls were minimal, and Bret was able to give attention to anyone who happened to be awake. Never did the lines illuminate with passion.

It was Monday, the slowest night of the week, and there hadn't been a single call. Bret glanced at the board, and all twelve lines were blank. Coffee in tow, she began.

"All right, and we're back. Before I started taking calls tonight, I want to share something with my listeners, in hopes that maybe some of you may have had similar experiences, or can explain this. Today…today was weird for me. I won't mention what led up to the incident, but wait until you hear."

Then Bret shared the horrific tale of her ant trauma and the outcome.

***

As promised, Chuck Wright had his radio tuned into Bret's broadcast. If asked, Chuck would always say that Bret brought a smile back to his life after his tragedy. She made him laugh the way she gave her Godly advice. Chuck knew Bret well which made the show that much more enjoyable. He found humor instead of finding God the way that his family had hoped. It helped him and his attitude was better than the 'God who?' outlook the forty-two year old man had when his world came tumbling down.

Chuck was multi tasking—as he called it—speakerphone on, driving, half listening to Bret, taking notes.

Chuck snickered.

"Who is that talking in the car?" George, on the phone, asked Chuck.

"That's the radio. My friend Bret. She's talking bugs or something." Chuck said. "God, I hope she doesn't dedicate another hour segment to lice again."

"Why? Make you itchy?" George asked.

"Me? No. I'm black. Black people don't get lice."

"That's right," George said. "Hey, don't you think it's ironic? She's talking about bugs, you're going to Erie for that story."

Chuck blinked and stuttered as he responded, "Um, yeah. Yeah it is."

"What is she saying about bugs?" George questioned.

"I don't know. I've been talking to you."

"Maybe it's related."

"Doubtful," Chuck said. "I mean we were just online fifteen minutes ago. She would have said something if it was that big."

"Why don't you listen? You never know."

"I can do that. I'll call you when I get to Erie." Chuck disconnected the call and reached for the radio. As soon as he did, he heard it.

"The colony goes down at least five or six feet deep." Bret said. "They haven't a clue how far width-wise. Can you believe that many ants?"

Chuck had to stop himself from slamming on the brakes as he drove down the highway. "Shit." He hurriedly hit the turn signal, while speaking out loud in the car. "Yeah, Bret. Uh, I would think that was something you would tell me." Shaking his head, he pulled over. Lifting the phone, Chuck dialed the direct number to Bret at the station.

David answered.

"David, this is Chuck Wright. Is it possible to speak to Bret, or to put me through to her show?"

"No can do, Chuck." David said. "Her lines are lit up. She has a ton of calls about this."

Chuck exhaled. "I thought so. Hey, do me a favor."

"If I can."

"Oh, you can. I know you type up the caller name, area, and reason for call. Can you save me a log of all that?"

"Why?"

Chuck grunted. "It goes with a story I'm working on."

"You're working on a story about ants?"

"Amongst other things."

"Does Bret know?" David asked.

"Nope, because she failed to mention this to me. Tell her I called and please save that log."

"Want me to fax it?"

"I'd love you for it."

"Why don't you give Jesse a call? He blew up the street."

"Jesse blew up the street?" Chuck laughed. "I'll call him tomorrow. He's probably sleeping. Thanks, David."

After hanging up, Chuck just stayed there on the side of the road. He lifted the notes he had taken during his call to George, then reached out to increase the volume on the radio. Three times, he glanced from his notes to the radio. "Man," he whispered in confusion. "What is going on?"

3 - THE CHANGE

May 6th ...

Scientists attributed it to enriched soil, perfect weather conditions, and immunity to pesticides, all of which built throughout the years, until finally...boom. It hits. That was the explanation for the sudden surge in the ant population that seemed to plague the Northeast United States. It didn't make sense to many, but it was accepted. After all, the scientific community presented it.

Bret's street looked like a war zone. They hit the pest lottery, and a huge ant colony was discovered existing under the street. Sidewalks were lifted, pavement and black top removed, all to uncover it. The borough worked diligently to destroy it. But every attempt seemed futile, and the ants returned in ten fold.

They dug twenty feet downward, closed off the street and suggested flooding the pit. Though it sounded insane, it was worth a shot, and to Bret anything that stopped her from buying all those round traps was a bonus.

That was one pest.

There was another not mentioned at all by the borough.

The cockroach.

There must have been something attractive to them about Buster's bowel movements, because the third roach was found in his diaper.

Though Sally had set traps and not seen a single roach in her house, she called an exterminator, the only one who wasn't overwhelmed with work and could promise he'd stop by within a week. The pest control business was booming, at least in Bret's town.

***

If Chuck didn't trust Bret's producer as much as he did, he would have sworn David was pacifying him about the fax. But David insisted he faxed the caller log twice. Finally, Chuck went to David's home and picked up the document.

The Erie, Pennsylvania story kept him there an entire day. When he returned the next, he spoke to Bret and David. Chuck was a man on a story mission, and before he finished the piece, he wanted more information and facts. Those were to come from Bret and David. Chuck didn't fear someone scooping him; the severity of the Pittsburgh ant incident was swept like bugs under the rug, and no one took it seriously.

The newest McDonald's creation dripped a ketchup mixture onto his lap, and Chuck only smeared it when he used the rough napkin. Car eating was always a sloppy task for Chuck, but he had no choice. At least he was parked.

Rolling the napkin into a ball, the red speckled paper snapped his mind back to the day before. He followed a name that came up twice in

Erie—a man he spoke to only briefly—and that trail led him right outside Canton, Ohio.

"Dr. Andrew Jeffers," Chuck requested of the soldier who was posted outside of the abandoned small church. "Tell him Chuck Wright, The Johnstown Tribune Democrat."

The solider nodded to another soldier then slipped in between the double doors.

Chuck took in the site. The small white building had several black cars and military vehicles parked outside. It was deemed the 'Temporary Office of the Federal Department of Agriculture.' As if Canton required the United States government to step in to help with their minor farming needs.

Chuck assumed that this extension had been quickly set up and was temporary. But why where they here?

The soldier returned and opened the door for Chuck, allowing him inside, but he was only permitted to go into the foyer.

He let his ears zoom in like the bionic woman, trying to hear what he could. Within seconds, Dr. Andrew Jeffers emerged in a secretive manner from the interior of the church.

"Before you thank me for seeing you…" Jeffers said. "Allow me to say you are fast becoming a pain in my ass." He ran his hand over his head and walked to a canteen. "Coffee, Mr. Wright?"

"No, thanks," Chuck said. "How, sir, am I becoming a pain in the ass?"

"Four calls yesterday…."

"Which you didn't return."

"One today. Two visits to Erie...."

"Well, I'm sure it's nothing compared to other reporters."

"What other reporters?" Jeffers fixed his coffee. "The way you're pursuing this, Mr. Wright, I'd believe I was some sort of big celebrity and you're the paparazzi."

"Exaggerating, don't you think?"

"No." Jeffers was polite, yet blunt. "Are you pining for a big newspaper job somewhere? Do you think you're on the brink of breaking of huge story?"

"Well, yes."

"Well…you're wrong." Jeffers raised his eyebrows. "There's nothing to tell. I'm sorry."

"The ants in that Pittsburgh community, the...."

"Mr. Wright." Jeffers cut him off. "Occasionally the earth gets a little too stuffed with nature, and it burps that little stuff out. That's it. No more. Happened before, will happen again."

"At this magnitude?"

"What magnitude?" Jeffers asked.

"An entire street, sidewalks and all, removed, a huge lake hole dug into it."

Jeffers laughed. "The work of overreacting and neurotic borough workers. That's it. Your information is also grossly distorted. I believe that street that was dug up was only a twenty by five foot section." He spoke nonchalantly. "Hardly lake-size."

"What about Erie?"

"Smaller than that Pittsburgh community incident. Two bug mishaps do not a story make." Jeffers smiled and walked to the double doors. "Mr. Wright, may I give you some advice?"

Chuck nodded.

"Let this go. Save your paper the expense, yourself the work and humiliation. There is nothing happening. We had two freakish incidents. That's it."

"Only two."

"Yes." Jeffers opened the door. "Now, if you'll excuse me."

"One more thing."

Jeffers huffed, and gave a polite smile. "Yes."

"If they were freak incidents, and only two in Erie and Pittsburgh, then why, Dr. Jeffers, does the United States government have an agricultural office, complete with military guards, set up in Canton Ohio."

Dr. Jeffers didn't respond; he slipped back through the doors.

That was it.

With another bite of his cold McDonald's sandwich, Chuck closed that memory and meeting. He glanced down to his phone, and lifted it. "Come on, Bret. What's taking you so long?"

***

A day off. A complete day off for Bret. She

even forewent getting some sleep to enjoy the day. Got the kids off to school, cleaned her house, then settled on the porch for a while to watch the construction workers and fire department flood that huge gaping hole in the street that was fast becoming James Avenue Lake.

She thought of Jesse while she was on the porch. How it could have easily been him out there working on the street, because that was the type of construction he was doing. In a way she felt fortunate he wasn't, because her days were hers. She enjoyed watching other sweaty construction workers—her sweaty husband was not the vision she wanted to see.

She stayed out for a short time; the progress was slow, and it was a bit boring. The only excitement came when occasionally someone would yell out, 'Fuck, these things won't die.'

Inside she booted up the computer, a task she was supposed to do an hour earlier but forgot. Her plan to attempt—again—to send Chuck the pictures from the street was thwarted momentarily when Jesse walked in the door. She glanced at her watch, then at him.

"What are you doing home?" she asked. "It's only eleven o'clock."

"Why?" he retorted.

"I asked first."

"We're not working today. It's raining."

Immediately, Bret stood up, walked to the door, opened it, and looked out. The sun was bright and warm. "Oh, yeah." she said sarcastically. "It's pouring." She shut the door.

"Jesse, there's not a cloud in the sky."

"It was raining."

"When?"

"This morning. We waited for it to stop. It didn't."

"Right. You called off on purpose, didn't you?"

"Yes, I did." He shook his head. "No, Bret, It was raining. Feel." He grabbed her hand and laid it on his thigh. "My jeans are still wet."

"Ew." She shook my hand. "Probably sweat."

He just stared.

"Fine." She turned from him.

"Fine?" he chuckled. "It's fine that I'm home. Thanks for permission. You act like I'm in the way or something."

"You are."

"Of what?"

Smug, Bret cocked her head. "My day. So there. I'm not making you lunch. I cook for you enough."

"Bret, I still have my lunch from this morning."

"That's foul."

Jesse gave up. After giving his stock, 'whatever', he headed up stairs.

"You're not going to sleep are you?" She yelled up.

"No. But so what if I am. I'll be out of the way of your day." He yelled down.

"I just made the beds. Don't sit on them."

"I'm taking a shower."

"OK, but I just used the Daily Clean. So

squirt the doors when you're finished."

The closing of the bathroom door was his only response. He was either going to follow her instructions, or he was just ignoring her. She banked on the latter and returned to the computer.

Her message to Chuck was simple: 'Okay, routed from your mother. Hope you get it this time. I can't believe you haven't received these pictures yet.' After attaching the photos, she hit 'send' in her fourth attempt to electronically reach Chuck.

***

Chuck laughed in complete enjoyment, gloating—as if anyone was around to see it. "Yeah, right." He said to himself in his car. "This is nothing." Laughing aloud, he viewed via his phone the pictures that Bret sent him; pictures that had gotten lost in the electronic universe for some odd reason. "Thank you," he said then typed it in as a reply.

He put the phone in the glove compartment, checked the tiny recorder, and opened the door to his car. A good whiff of the spring air lifted his chest and a grin crossed his face as he took a good glance at a building on the grounds of West Virginia University.

Chuck glanced down at the call log in his small notebook and made a check mark as he proceeded to the building. The door was open, and he followed the directions hand-written on that sheet.

Empty corridors struck him as odd seeing how it was the middle of the day. Though some classes were done for the summer, surely there had to be students remaining. He saw them about campus.

Another turn of the bend, and he caught glimpse of the yellow 'do not cross' tape that plastered the set of double doors.

It had to be the room. It was.

The room number and name matched the information Chuck had. Mini-cam tucked in his chest pocket, Chuck snapped a few pictures and then reached for the handle.

"May I help you?" A female voice called out.

Chuck turned around. "Hi, Chuck Wright, I'm a reporter with the Johnstown Democrat."

She didn't recognize the name of the paper; that was obvious.

So Chuck lied. "And also with People Magazine."

The woman smiled brightly, "Yes. How can I help you?"

Chuck pointed at the doors. "Professor Cobb. Where can I find him?"

She shook her head. "I haven't a clue."

"Do you work here?"

"Yes, I do. I'm Assistant Dean."

Chuck snorted a laugh. "And you don't know where he is. He's the head of…." He reviewed his notes. "Geology?"

"Ecological Studies. And I don't know where he is."

"Did he just leave? Vacation? What?"

"They took him."

"Who?" Chuck started to take notes.

"After the incident, he and Dr. Reye...."

"Who is Dr. Reye?"

"Colleague, friend." She answered. "They took them by ambulance."

"Both? What happened?"

"Don't know."

Chuck paused in writing.

"Seems Dr. Reye called emergency services for help, but they took them, and before I knew it some government services were in here sealing off the room."

"Can I go in?"

"We're supposed to keep everyone out." She said innocently. "I'm sorry."

Turning on the charm, Chuck gave her a smile. "Come on. Just a look. Aren't you the least bit curious as to what happened in that room?"

She titled her head. "Well, yeah."

Chuck winked. "A peek."

After exhaling, she reached for her keys. "A peek. But hurry. The soldier went for a soda."

Chuck laid his hand on her wrist as she went to unlock the door. "Soldier."

"Military, yes," she said. "I told you the government came in."

"Thank you for this."

"Not a problem." She inserted the key.

A clearing of a throat made her pause.

Chuck looked up and whined. "No."

Dr. Andrew Jeffers walked down the hall with two soldiers.

"Now, who's following who?" Chuck asked.

"You mean 'whom'." Jeffers corrected. "Ms. Withers, can you excuse us."

"Certainly," The woman rolled the key into her hand, gave an apologetic glance to Chuck, and backed away.

"Mr. Wright" Dr. Jeffers walked closer. "You are fast becoming a pain in my ass as I said before." He reached forward snatching the camera from Chuck's chest pocket.

"Hey." Chuck snarled. "Fine. Forget it. I don't need that. I have other proof."

Snidely, Jeffers held up Chuck's phone. "You mean this? Now you have nothing." He handed that to a soldier.

"You went in my car." Chuck said. "What the hell?"

"I told you to drop this."

"What are you doing here?" Chuck asked.

"I'm doing my job."

"So am I," Chuck responded. "And you won't hold me back. I got proof once, I'll get it again."

Jeffers slowly turned. "No you won't." He gave a nod to the soldiers.

Before Chuck could question, his arms were grabbed.

"Take him," Jeffers said, and then walked away.

***

Jesse took quick showers. Not like most men

who took extremely long showers and used the excuse, "I had to wash twice" as a cover up for the fact that they were jerking off. Jesse was in and out. Bret had enough time to send Chuck another simple message when the water lines squeaked— Jesse was done—and Sally yelled in through the back door.

"Bret, you have a few minutes?" she asked.

Bret turned from the computer. Sally was in the kitchen with Buster. "Yes, what's up?" she met up with Sally. "Hey, you, Buster."

Buster giggled and reached his hand out. "Bug. Big bugs."

"Yes, I know." Bret glanced to Sally. "Did you find another?"

"No, the exterminator is here. Can you…can you come over. He looks like a rapist."

"Bug guy rapist." Buster kicked his legs.

Bret chuckled. "He looks like a rapist?"

"Yeah, like your husband when he works on the yard."

"Jesse doesn't look like a rapist."

Buster repeated, "Jesse rapist."

Sound traveled. Jesse heard. His loud, "What was that?" made them hunch. His feet barreled down the steps and he came into the kitchen.

"See." Sally pointed at Jesse whose dark, curly, hair was wet and tossed about.

"What are you teaching Sally's kid?" Jesse asked.

Bret waved her hand at him. "He's repeating. The exterminator is at Sally's. She said he looks like a rapist and I'm going over."

"Oh." Jesse nodded.

"In fact." Bret sang her words. "She said he looks like you. Hmm."

"Sounds about right, last week I made it on the post office wall for parking meter fraud." Jesse gave a pat to Bret's head then kissed her. "If you need me.…"

Bret snickered. "Well, you are the undercover bug expert."

Jesse grumbled and Bret left the house with Sally and Buster.

To say Bret was insulted was putting it mildly. Sally thought the bug guy looked like her husband? Bret wondered if Sally was looking through rose-colored glasses and if the entire neighborhood viewed Jesse as some overweight, sloppy, pudgy-faced, formerly bad-skinned man. To her the only thing that they had in common was the hair. That was it. The bug guy didn't even have the same color hair as Jesse. In fact, he was much shorter than Jesse's six four frame.

"He doesn't look like Jesse," Bret said irritably to Sally, then cringed as the bug guy bent over, exposing his plumber's crack. "God."

Buster pointed. "Bug guy."

"Yes," Bret nodded. "Bug guy."

"Bug guy sex Bret. Jesse said.…" Buster yelled. "Thank you!"

Over his shoulder, the disgusting bug guy peered at Bret.

She flashed an annoyed smile and through gritted teeth spoke to Sally, "Your son has a big mouth."

Sally shrugged.

The bug guy cracked his head as he reached for a tool.

"What's that?" Sally asked.

"Oh, state of the art…probe." He grinned at Bret.

Bret rolled her eyes.

"This here goes in the wall," he explained. "I made a small hole and this lets me see inside. Gives that true in-depth look." He disappeared under the sink again. "Now.…" He grunted. "I'm…oh, yeah. Got a nest. Big one…shit." He paused.

"What? What?" Bret asked.

He came out from the sink. "I have to pull out some of the wall. That okay? I can't reach the entire nest. Kind of extends."

Sally looked horrified. "You have to break my wall."

"No, no," He shook his head. "Who ever put this kitchen in put a removal panel over the pipes. Not a problem. Just got to pull it off."

"Then what?" Sally inquired.

Simply and matter-of-factly he stated, "I kill the nest."

Sally exhaled. "Go on. Please."

They stepped back further toward the kitchen wall.

"Play." Buster kicked out his legs. "Play."

"Sure." Sally set him down. "In the other

room. Okay?"

Buster took off for the living room.

Bret and Sally waited and watched. The bug guy continued working under the sink. However, it wasn't the sound of the panel breaking that made them look at each other.

A hiss.

A loud hissing, cracking sound emanated from under the sink.

"What . . . . What was that?" Bret asked.

Under the sink, the bug guy didn't respond…at first. Then, "Holy Mother of God!" He screamed in horror, and as his body squirmed out there was a thump.

He started to cough, sounding as if he were choking.

"Hey." Bret inched with Sally. "Are you okay?"

Just as they neared the sink, nearer to the shaking bug guy, the hissing grew loud, and then suddenly, like a river, the roaches scrambled out. There were so many there was no distinguishing a single roach from the thick black mass.

As they screamed, the bug guy scurried out for his freedom. Face purple, he held onto his throat and reached out for help as cockroaches crawled at a rapid pace from his mouth.

They were everywhere. Bret tried not to scream but couldn't help it. Repeatedly, she yelled out, "Jesse!" hoping her husband could hear the commotion next door. Her hand extended toward the bug guy, and roaches flew up her arm. There had to be fifty. Then others started up her leg.

"Oh, God." Bret tried flinging them. She felt the pinches, the pain. "They're biting me." She shuddered, shook, swept them off, but they just kept coming.

Sally was crying, her hand frantically wiping the bugs from her legs. Bret looked quickly toward the bug guy. He was gone, buried beneath the roaches. The second she heard Sally whimper 'Buster', Bret grabbed her arm and they flew to the living room.

The crunching was as bad as the bugs, but not as bad as the scream.

Buster cried.

They made it to the living room; cockroaches crawled up the walls, the furniture . . . everywhere, then the front door swung closed.

Buster ran outside.

Bret cleared the cockroach from her eyes with a shudder of disgust and a swipe of her hand over her face, and out the door she bolted with Sally.

"Buster!" Bret called out. "Jesse! Help!" she screamed as she made it to the porch.

"My baby!" Sally's voice raised in hysterics. "Oh God, my baby!" Over and over, she screamed it as she raged past Bret, nearly sending her sailing into the porch railing.

Bret turned—a flash of Sally and then…Buster as he ran to the street.

Sally chased him. In hysterics, Buster kept running. The huge gaping hole filled with water was in his path.

The construction workers seemed clueless and Bret cried out, "Someone grab the baby! Get the baby!"

It seemed to happen in slow motion. Like she was in a dream, her legs couldn't move fast enough to get her off the porch. Her heart pounded, ears burned, as she hurried. Sally was almost there, her hand extended, begging Buster to stop. He didn't.

Everyone rushed to him. A fireman close by caused a short-lived sigh of relief. Everyone was certain he had Buster. Certain. They even stopped running.

Suddenly, the tiny two year old, almost embraced in the fireman's hold, sank into the depths of the sluggish water-filled twenty-foot death trap.

Sally jumped in after him.

Both sunk.

All human beings are equipped with the heroic drive. In some, it kicks in automatically. A construction worker had it, and he dove into the pit with all that he had.

Bret was hysterically focused on the lake in the road and never noticed when Jesse emerged from the house. He grabbed on to her asking if she were okay, but her attention was focused on the pit as yet another worker jumped in.

Jesse's hands were all over Bret, diligently attempting to clear the cockroaches. His eyes never left his wife, nor did he stop brushing off those roaches, despite all that was going on around them. It seemed he didn't know or care about what was happening at the pit.

"Buster. Sally," Bret murmured.

Jesse's hands paused. "They fell in?"

She whimpered. At that instant, her body began to tremble out of control. She thought Jesse was going to leave and join the four others that had leaped into the hole. But the fireman, angry and shouting, drew everyone's attention. "No more!" he yelled. "Stop." He reached out and grabbed the arm of another who was heading in. "It's like quick sand. Can't you see?!" he shouted. "No one's coming up or out."

No sooner did he say that than a set of arms whooshed from the water. They rose high, holding a motionless Buster inches above the level of the ant bath.

Everybody rushed forward.

Then the arms sank. So did Buster.

Silence.

The thick sluggish mixture of ants and mud was still. No sound at all.

***

Bret asked for a Valium. No one had any to give, so she settled for a bottle of bourbon while she sat on her front porch and waited.

The day trudged on, the sky grew dark, and the street was lit by flashing emergency worker lights. They brought in fishing nets to pull through the hole, but it was tedious and slow. Still, she watched.

The kids weren't allowed to return home. Jesse went down to the school and took the kids to

Bret's mother's house before returning. It was debatable who was more an emotional mess, Bret or Jesse. Physically, Bret was bad. Her body ached, but the alcohol aided in numbing that.

She couldn't stop crying. It was like a war zone. The fire department executed a well-controlled torching of Sally's house. When they went in to help the bug man, the fireman said there was nothing left. After Bret questioned the freakishness of it all, the fireman claimed that cockroaches feed on anything.

Even on a bug man. The bugs got their revenge.

Sally's husband stayed right at the edge of the hole. Her other two children were taken to a relative's home. The street was a spectacle. Hundreds came to watch as they dragged the hole. Everyone gasped when they pulled something out. A dog was in there, two cats and many squirrels. There were many rodent carcasses that began to pile up.

"Cigarette?" Jesse extended one to Bret.

She had quit but took it anyhow.

"How are you feeling?" he asked.

"Exhausted. What's happening, Jesse?"

"I don't know. I think they're gonna evacuate."

Curiously, she turned her head his way.

He continued, "Just rumors. I heard the cops talking."

"I would think if they were going to evacuate, they would have done so. What are they waiting for?"

The loud sounds of trucks caught their attention, and if the street didn't look like a war zone before, it certainly did after military truck followed by military truck rolled in.

Both Jesse and Bret slowly stood.

Soldiers marched in. The leader pointed, waved and the battalions spread out.

Bret swallowed. "This is frightening."

"No," Jesse shook his head. "*That's* frightening." He pointed to a crew of four wearing biohazard suits.

Bret watched as they approached a fireman, and to her surprise, the fireman pointed in her direction.

"Jesse," she whispered and grabbed on to his arm. The group of military moved their way. "Jesse?"

"It's all right." He pulled her into him.

The first of the four walked up the steps, followed closely by soldiers. "Are you Brettina Long?" he asked.

"Yes," she answered apprehensively.

"I'm Dr. Jeffers with the Center for Disease Control." He gave a nod and two of the armed soldiers moved forward.

"We need you to come with us," Dr. Jeffers said.

Bret shook her head.

The soldiers reached out for her.

"Hey!" Jesse yelled, and grabbed Bret away.

"I don't wanna go. Jesse?"

A soldier seized Bret.

"Get off my wife!" Jesse blasted then ensued

in a struggle over his wife.

It was a tug of war, one that ended with the quick aim and point of an M-4 directly at Jesse.

"Back off!" The soldier ordered. "You'll be informed shortly where she's going. This is for her own good." The soldier calmed some. "Please back off."

With eyes that conveyed his apology, Jesse slowly lifted his hands away. "I'm sorry, Bret." He leaned to kiss her.

They wouldn't let him. Before she knew it, a damp, cold blanket was flung over her. It covered her from head to toe and she couldn't see a thing. It was black, confusing. All she knew was that she was being led somewhere, and before long, taken away.

4 - THE WARD

The sight of a face can help so much. Bret had to judge only by the voices that spoke to her. She couldn't see a thing and only knew she had been placed in the back of a truck or van.

"I'd feel much better," she told them, "if I could see."

Dan, a soldier who gave his name said, "The blanket is treated. It's for the best. We'll be there shortly."

"I saw this movie, you know."

"What movie?"

"The Stand."

Dan chuckled. "There isn't a virus taking over the world."

"I feel like there is."

"Hey, Bret. Can I ask you a question? It's gonna sound weird but there's something I need to know."

"What's that?" she asked, buried in her black wrapping.

"Are you 'Divine'?"

"Yeah, I am."

"I thought I recognized your voice."

"Who's Divine?" another asked.

Dan answered, "She's a DJ on a local station."

"Shit," the man said, and then hustled forward.

Bret tried to scope in on the muffled voices.

Something was happening. Her being a DJ made a difference, whether good or bad remained to be seen. Who knew?

She thought that maybe having a celebrity status would pay off, even if she really wasn't a celebrity.

The vehicle picked up speed—as if it wasn't going fast enough--and the trip to the destination didn't take long. Ten minutes maybe, then she was rushed from the van, lifted onto a cart, and laid flat on her back.

"What's going on?" she asked as the cart rushed about.

"Vitals?" a woman questioned, ignoring Bret's quizzing.

Someone replied to her request. "BP 110 over seventy. Heart rate 72. Respiration normal. All good."

"Any convulsions?"

"None."

"Signs of distress?"

"None."

"Time frame?"

"Eight hours."

"We're still good," she spoke quickly.

"What's going on?" Bret asked out loud again. "Someone, what's going on?"

"Shh," She whispered comforting. "Just bear with us."

Bret was wheeled away quickly and the cart made sharp turns; to Bret it was like some kind of medical Disneyland ride. Turning, speeding, careening in blackness.

The woman continued the blurting out of questions, "Placements?"

"Four. At quick glance. Can't be positive."

"Any count?" she asked.

"Not yet."

"In here."

Bret felt the cart slam into something before coming to a halt. Suddenly she was lifted—blanket and all—and lain on another table.

"I need a team STAT," the woman ordered out. "Nurse, ready?"

"Ready," another woman said.

"I need this patient out and quickly."

"Out? Quickly?" Bret questioned out loud. She wanted to scream; her pleas for answers were ignored.

"On my call."

A pause.

"Now!" she ordered.

The blanket was whipped open and Bret was greeted with a blinding white light. Trying to make heads or tails out of everything, she raised her hand to shield her eyes, to try to see what was going on. Her hands were grabbed and secured without hesitation. In defense, she squirmed over their hold. Everything was happening so quickly that her head spun in confusion. Within a few seconds, she felt the pinch to her thigh. She had been injected with something. The serum moved through her blood with a burning sensation. Her chest immediately felt heavy and Bret gasped for air. The voices that surrounded her slowed down, sounding demonic and fake. Then, just like with the blanket, she was in the dark again. Everything went black.

***

If someone had taken the time to say, "If you don't come with us for help, you'll die," there would have been a lot less resistance and confusion on Bret's part.

Evidently no one thought the few seconds could be spared.

She was alone when she came to—or so she thought. A white curtain surrounded her bed. There was some dizziness, but she wasn't restrained at all. Slowly she sat up, swung her legs from the bed, allowed her head to stop spinning, and stood. Sharp pains shot up her thighs, but they subsided. Her face felt tight and slightly numb. Reaching up, her fingers touched upon a small bandage just under her eye.

Not dressed completely, and not caring, Bret reached for the curtain.

She envisioned a nurse's station, with a few clueless and lunching women there. She quickly realized the slim chance of that when moans carried her way, lots of them. Painful cries, aching groans, wet coughs, they melded like an orchestra of painful music. Bret pulled open the curtain. She wasn't in a hospital at all, but a warehouse. Huge, white interior, and for as far as the eye could see, cots—filled with patients—lined up throughout the inside.

Her hand gripped the curtain. "My God, this *is* the plague," she muttered as her fingers went numb. Controlling her eyes was a difficult task; they began to roll as everything spun. Two women in hospital scrubs rushed her way, but then all went black again to Bret.

***

They counted seventy-two cockroach bites on her body. Seventy-two. Bret didn't even recall being bit that many times. The nurse informed her that ninety percent of those in the quarantine were suffering from a fatal illness called hantavirus. Pneumonia, a SARS-like respiratory illness they acquired through the cockroaches. Cockroaches carry diseases; this particular one was running rampant amongst the rats, and it seemed the violent roaches were finding an interest in the rats as a dining pleasure. Carrying the germ all around, and then infecting those they bit.

Unlike Bret, those ninety percent hadn't a clue that they didn't have the flu. She was fortunate; they were able to monitor her, clean and scrub her wounds, and deliver antibiotics. They were hopeful she wouldn't get ill.

However, hantavirus wasn't the urgent situation. Again, she was fortunate that through the latest cockroach experience and bites, medical professionals learned that female cockroaches were finding nesting spots…within their bite victims. Laying up to eighty eggs in an area no bigger than a pimple, they'd nest behind their ears, nose, head, eyes and legs. Before the victim could possibly know they were a breeding ground, the eggs would hatch. More often than not, the roaches would crawl into the human body, and make—or rather eat—their way out.

Those unfortunate victims weren't around anymore to tell their tale.

There were three nesting spots on Bret's body: One in her eye, another behind her ear, and the last between her fingers. They were able to spot them and remove the nests.

It wasn't the repercussions of the cockroach bites that baffled her; it was the number of incidents and victims. It made her wonder: A warehouse full of people, most of which were dying? How bad was the cockroach epidemic, and how long had it been going on?

"Less than a week," Dr. Jeffers explained to her as he sat at her bedside. "This set-up was initiated three days ago. You're one of the twenty that we expect to release in good health. You're showing no signs of HV. Of course, tomorrow morning will confirm."

Bret sighed out in relief. "When do I get released?"

"That remains to be seen."

"On?"

"You." Dr. Jeffers said. "You're the media. The press."

"I'm a Christian Broadcasting DJ."

"You reach the masses," he stated matter of factly. "There are certain things we wish to keep quiet until we can figure this all out. We want to withhold this story from leaking and curb any worries or panics."

"So you're going to keep me here."

"In three days, four tops, we should have a grip on what is going on and be able to release an explanation if news of the incidents is leaked to the public. Unfortunately, there's nothing we can do until we have a course of action to take. I would like to ask for your silence."

"Can you tell me what you know?"

"Do I have your silence?"

She chuckled. "Dr. Jeffers. My family is foremost. I give advice. I have no designs on being a story breaker. I believe I have a funeral to attend in a couple days. I'd like to be there. You have my silence."

"Thank you." He inched closer. "Well, it doesn't take a genius to look around you and see this isn't a freak incident that you experienced."

"Is it just here?"

"No." He shook his head. "Entire northern region. You can say we are a migration destination."

"I don't understand."

"In a layman's explanation, the earth is heating up. But not atmospherically as you would think. Internally."

"The core?"

He nodded. "Volcanic activity below sea level, shifting of plates, magnetic impulses, we don't know. Whatever the cause, earth's subsurface temperature is raising…slightly. Our friends who live below the surface, such as the ants, are coming up because it is too warm for their nests. The ants are forcing other insects to another direction; they in turn are forcing animals to migrate. Chain reaction. Nutshell. All these creatures are pushing to one area. The Northeastern United States and Southeast Canada are plagued right now. It's peaking. Overcrowded masses of insects, they have nowhere to go but up."

"To us."

"Exactly. Their survival is limited. The strongest will survive. They're fighting one heck of a fight. Right now, we're watching, being quick when the incidents are reported."

"So our entire city is infested?"

"No." he replied. "We just need to find the pockets. In Pittsburgh, your borough is a pocket. We're lucky; your street has had the least amount of casualties. No other reports nearby have come in."

"But all these people…."

"Ohio, West Virginia. The bigger this gets, the harder this story will be to contain."

"So why not let it out?"

"And tell people what?"

"How about what you told me?" she asked.

"They'll want a solution." Dr. Jeffers said.

"You have one. This."

He snickered humbly, "My dear Mrs. Long. This is not a solution. This is a band-aid on the wound created. A solution would be finding the nests and destroying them."

"Are they able to do that?"

"They say they're close. A couple more days. They believe they'll be able to pinpoint the nesting areas soon because they're growing."

"Oh my God," she whispered. "This has to be huge."

"It's a natural phenomenon. Yes."

"Well, once they find them they'll be able to destroy them, right?"

"We believe so. Then it will be over." He nodded. "Yes. If we can do this without the general populous being the wiser, all the better. If not...." he paused to shrug. "We just need media silence and are doing everything right now to ensure we get that." He started to leave, but stopped. "Brettina Long."

Bret looked oddly at him. Why was he repeating her name? Obviously, he knew it.

"Are you familiar with a Charles Eugene Wright?"

"Who?" she asked, then her eyes grew wide. "Chuck. Yeah, Chuck. You threw me. What about him. Wait...." She snapped her finger. "He was following the story. He didn't say much. I don't think he knew much."

"Hmm." Dr. Jeffers nodded. "I just needed to check."

"Check on what?"

"If you were the one and the same Bret."

Bret gave a curious look. "Have you spoken to Chuck?"

"Yes, we have. Several times," Jeffers replied. "He was working on a bug story."

"Have you seen him lately?"

"Yes. Today."

"Where is he now?" Bret asked.

"I believe…." Dr. Jeffers smiled. "He's working on this story."

***

The eight by eight room wasn't cold, nor was it dirty; it was part of a newly constructed county prison awaiting its opening. Alone in the room, Chuck was left wearing only his underwear and given a thick blanket which he had wrapped around his shoulders. There was a pencil in there and a single sheet of paper. No light.

Chuck would write small. He'd make the best of that piece of paper. After all, he hadn't a clue how long he'd be held prisoner. And that's what he was—or at least felt like.

He heard someone walking outside his door, the mumble of voices; not many, which led Chuck to believe there weren't many in his section.

No one else said anything, argued, nothing, unlike Chuck who had done nothing but argue with anyone he could for ten hours. He'd shout out to anyone who walked down the hall.

Just as he planned to do when he heard the footsteps.

He jumped from his bunk to rush to the door.

"Food," a male voice said as a tray was slid

through the tiny ten-inch by four-inch opening.

"Wait." Chuck hurried and grabbed the tray. He peered out the small opening only to catch glimpse of a soldier. "Great. Just great." He sniffed the food. "Hey!" he aimed his voice through the hole. "How long am I supposed to be here? Answer me! I'm not under arrest! I didn't do anything wrong! Hello!"

"Shut up!" someone shouted.

"Fuck off." Chuck blasted back.

"No, you fuck off. I'm tired of hearing you shout at the guards! There's nothing you can do. We're stuck here!"

"Where is here?" Chuck asked. "I know I'm not arrested. I want clothes! I have my rights!"

There was a moment of silence, then the same male voice chuckled a laugh that rang with an eerie echo effect. "Rights? Hey, don't you know we have no rights when it comes to the United States government trying to keep a secret?"

Chuck was verbally humbled, and his unseen neighbor made a point. Holding his food, Chuck carried the tray to his bunk where he just sat down in defeat. Momentarily, that was, until he could figure something out.

5 - MOVE

May 8th ...

Two days. Sixty phone calls. Two hundred miles on his car, and Jesse finally hit gold. They kept missing each other because she was as busy as Jesse. He called her, and then gave up. Middle of the night, she returned the call and Jesse found some hope via Chuck's mother who was out of town…looking for her son.

"Do you think they are together?" Hazel Wright asked Jesse.

"Absolutely not. The military took Bret," he replied.

"Don't you think it's odd that they're both missing?"

"My wife is not missing. Just well hid."

"Maybe it has something to do with the email she sent me to forward to Chuck."

"What email?"

Again it was never claimed that Jesse was the brightest, neither was Hazel, so when it dawned on them both that perhaps Chuck was working on a story connected to Bret, pieces started to fall bit by bit into place. Perhaps it wasn't unlikely that they were together.

The two in the morning phone call brought

Jesse to Johnstown, Pennsylvania, and he and Hazel began a search of Chuck's apartment. They spoke to his editor at the paper who claimed Chuck was laundering his story for fear he had uncovered something big. The editor passed Chuck off as paranoid, but not before he was able to pass on to Jesse and Hazel the name of the person that Chuck's story and notes came through.

His name was Pierce Leonard. But he didn't get his story from Chuck; he got the story via another man who got it from another and so on.

Seven people were in an email chain created six hours before Chuck's disappearance. Though the story never changed, one name kept popping up as Chuck's target, a name Jesse found familiar.

Dr. Andrew Jeffers.

Jeffers, if Jesse remembered correctly, was the one who came with the military. He was the one who phoned Jesse to simply state: 'Your wife is fine. We'll be in contact.'

That wasn't good enough for Jesse, hence his plight. Where was his wife? He came to the determination that if he found Jeffers, he would find Bret and, hopefully, Chuck. Though Jesse was teetering on believing the Hollywood-ish plot that Chuck was dead—he knew too much.

George, the editor from the Johnstown Press, tried his hand at contacting Jeffers. The Centers for Disease Control stated he was out of town working, but wouldn't give his whereabouts. Classified.

His home number wasn't unlisted, but Jesse had an idea. After thinking about what it would take to give up his wife's classified whereabouts, he made the call.

"He is out of town working," Mrs. Jeffers stated.

"Do you know where?" Jesse asked.

"Well, yes, but I can't say."

"Uh huh. Well, if you decide to say can you give me a call back. I just found a stack of pictures. All of them your husband Andrew having sex with my wife and I'd like to find him and kill him."

Obviously this was not something new to Mrs. Jeffers because she had no problem believing Jesse. She gave up her husband's location in an instant. It may have wrenched a bit of guilt from Jesse because he was messing with someone's marriage, but he justified it: Jeffers was messing with his.

He hoped. He could have been wrong. His gut said he wasn't.

On the outskirts of Morgantown, West Virginia was a small village quarantined for ants. The CDC mobile set up was just on the town limits, and Jesse found Dr. Jeffers with ease. He was amazed that it wasn't more difficult. A simple request for the doctor along with his name brought out Dr. Jeffers.

No hello. No greeting. Jesse just spat out, "You came to my house. You took my wife. Where is she?"

Irritated, Jeffers huffed out. "We called you and told you that she is fine. She'll be home in a few days."

"Not good enough. Where is she?"

"I can't tell you. She'll be home in a few days. I assure you, Mr. Long, this is for her own benefit."

"Not good enough." Jesse repeated

Jeffers huffed again. "Fine. Those roaches that attacked your wife are carrying a deadly virus. Fortunately, your wife was not infected. She was, however, nested. Meaning the roaches implanted eggs within her. We are hopeful that we got the nests, but time will reveal if that is the case. End of story. She is resting, well, and waiting."

"Not...."

"Don't." Jeffers held up his hand. "Don't say, 'not good enough'. It's the best I can do."

"No, the best you can do is let me know for sure that my wife is fine."

"Follow me." He turned. "I'll get her on the phone."

"No...." Jesse smiled when Jeffers stopped. "I want to see her."

"Impossible. Now, since you've turned down my offer to speak to your wife, good day."

"Jeffers," Jesse called out. "I'm tired. I haven't slept in two days."

"Get some sleep then. Perhaps you'll be more reasonable."

"I don't think you quite understand." Jesse stepped toward him. "When I get tired, I get irritable; when I get irritable, I get angry. When I get angry, I get unreasonable and I act before I think." Another step. "Now don't doubt for one second, I won't pick you up and throw you through a fucking wall way before one of these soldiers can do a thing about it. I want to see my wife."

"Don't threaten me."

"I'm not." Jesse said reasonably. "I'll ask one more time. If I get turned down, I cannot guarantee what I will do. Ready?" Jesse smiled. "Will you take me to see my wife?"

"Fine, you can…see…your wife."

Jesse should have been more specific. Of course, that was to Jeffers' misfortune. When he brought Jesse to an observation window, stated, "See, she's fine. That's all. Let's go," Jesse grew angrier. However, when Jeffers claimed that he held up his end of the bargain, and he allowed Jesse to "see" his wife, Jesse lost it.

He had Jeffers by the throat and chest lifted two feet from the ground and proceeded to bang Jeffers into the glass window repeatedly as a way to break the glass.

After four hits into the window, three soldiers showed up. Their weapons and force didn't stop Jesse; he was a husband enraged and determined. His big body shucked off a soldier while he tossed Jeffers into the second soldier. The third one barreled into Jesse, and during the struggle, Jesse grabbed hold of the M-4, crashing it backwards into the window and smashing the protective glass.

Bret screamed. But she got to see her husband through the glass…briefly. There he stood, and there he wasn't. He sailed sideways to the ground when tackled by more soldiers.

Mission accomplished. Jesse sat in a small room with his wife. As a precaution, he couldn't touch her. Bret made him keep true to that; after all the kids needed him back at home.

The door opened and Dr. Jeffers walked in. "You nearly broke my collarbone, you big ape. Thank you very much."

Jesse stood.

Bret closed her eyes "Jesse, sit."

Jesse did.

"You know, this surprises me." Jeffers said with attitude as he tossed a tablet down to the small table that separated Jesse and Bret. "You spent eight years in the United States Marine Corps, so you of all people should know and respect the importance of all this. We have a highly volatile situation that we must keep tight. This behavior doesn't help. Of course you left the service, so you may have lost respect and importance.…"

"Hey!" Jesse stood up again.

"Jesse!" Bret yelled. "Sit!"

Jesse roughly plopped down to the chair.

Smug, Bret said, "Jesse didn't leave the service. He would have stayed. He had an asthma attack and was discharged."

Jesse groaned. "Thank you, Bret, for telling

him our business."

"I can care less," Jeffers said. "I'll leave you with your wife for a few minutes. That's it. Then she must leave. We're taking her somewhere else…that…I will tell you. Enjoy your few minutes." Jeffers opened the door. "And for God's sake don't touch her. All we need is you in quarantine." He left.

Bret, seeing Jesse reach her way, inched her chair back. "Don't."

"Fine."

"How are the kids?"

"They're good. They miss you."

"I miss them," Bret said. "How are things in the neighborhood?"

"What neighborhood."

"What do you mean?" Bret asked.

Jesse shook his head. "The whole place is barren. There's not a soul in town."

"The whole city?"

"No, just our neighborhood."

"They really evacuated you all."

"Everyone. Ten thousand people. Where in the hell do you put ten thousand people?"

"Since you were there and I'm here, you tell me."

"They have our neighbors spread out all over the place. Gymnasiums. Hotels. You name it. We're staying with your mom. I had to go buy new clothes for us all."

"You're kidding."

"Nope. Stores were offering refugee discounts. Then you have the places that are giving away clothes for the kids. Can you believe this?"

Bret snickered. "Refugee? I'm gonna take it the news broke."

Silence.

"Jesse?"

"Bret, sweetie, if the news broke would I be breaking in here to find you, and would Chuck be missing in action?"

Bret's eyes widened. "Chuck is missing?"

Jesse rolled his eyes. "Jeffers knows where he is. He assured me Chuck was fine."

"Jeffers asked me about him." Bret shook her head. "So if the news didn't break, how do the stores know to offer refugee discounts?"

"They saying there was a chemical leak. We were asked not to say anything until tomorrow. It's almost clear. We can go back. But…they took all the furniture out of every house. Every stitch of clothing, anything that contains fabric. They burned it, Bret. It was an amazing sight. You could see it for miles."

"What are we gonna do?"

He grumbled. "We can buy what we want or take what they give. Honestly, I'm taking what they give us until you come home, whenever that will be. Hey…the station called; they need to know if they should get a sub for your show."

"It's Friday. I have until Sunday. I wanna come home."

"I know." Jesse said. "We miss you."

"I miss you guys, too."

Jesse paused, then: "How's the food?"

Bret laughed. "Actually, it's not bad. Hey...." She softened her voice. "Any word on Sally and Buster?"

Jesse paused.

"Jesse? What's wrong?"

"You...you didn't mention them because I mentioned food, did you?"

"What? God, no. Why would I...." It hit her. "No. Jesse, tell me the ants didn't eat them. Did they?"

"Put it this way," Jesse replied. "They did find them. So I heard. Yesterday. What was left of them."

Bret's mouth dropped open, "Oh my God."

"Sally's husband said he'll plan the funeral once he gets back home."

"So you've talked to him. How is he?"

"Grateful for his other children to keep his mind occupied. I'll let you know about the funeral. I know you want to be there."

Bret sunk deeper into her chair. "That's if they let me leave at all."

Jesse probably knew more than Bret did. Escorted out, Bret was left alone with a 'Buffy the Vampire Slayer' video in a room for hours. The television picked up no stations; if it weren't for the visit by her husband Bret would have been left to deduct the world had ended. Bret talked to only two nurses and Dr. Jeffers. Jeffers did, however promise that Bret could call Jesse once she was moved a last time. She did not have hanta virus.

The final move took her to an older hospital in Morgantown. Two or three days, Dr. Jeffers promised, then without a doubt, she could go home. They were just making sure that they had gotten all the eggs laid within her system. No surprises. Bret believed that she would go home on Sunday.

She was given clothes, the first non-hospital garb in days, and escorted through the semi-vacant building. There were some people moving around, mainly moving equipment. She walked to an elevator, then to the sixth floor.

She thought for sure she was in some bad science fiction movie when she saw the old and faded sign: Psychiatric Ward.

Bret resisted. "I knew it." She fought. "I knew it." She shook her head as they guided her to the locked door.

"Hush now," the guard told her. "You're overreacting. This is just an abandoned building we're using to keep you guys from the press and the public."

That not only made Bret stop her resistance, but also question, "Us guys?"

The guard told her no more.

After checking her in, giving her a room and a couple of days' worth of clothes, Bret was told she could freely move about the floor. Paranoid, she still wanted proof that she was going to emerge alive and that people would see her again. They let her call Jesse.

Feeling somewhat better, but not completely,

she ventured out. The sound of music caught her ear and she began to follow it. The corridor was long and hers was the last door. She moved slowly and inconspicuously, peeking in the rooms. The first one she passed was definitely vacant; the second looked as if it contained someone, and so did the third. As she moved onward, a voice calling her name made her stop.

"Bret?" he called out.

First looking over her shoulder, Bret peeked back, then when she saw him in the hall, she spun and raced to Chuck with a loud shriek.

He bellowed, "Oh my God" and grabbed her in a big hug. "You are the last person I expected to see here."

"I was gonna say the same thing. Were you attacked by roaches, too?" she asked.

"Roaches?" Chuck pulled from the embrace. "No, I was arrested and detained over the ant story. They just moved me here this morning. Is that why you're here?" he asked. "Were you attacked by roaches?"

Bret whistled. "Was I ever."

"Oh, this is so great. Let's go back to my room and talk." He took hold of her arm. "You have to spill your guts, because after I'm out of here, I'm gonna spill my guts about this whole goddamn thing. My editor will love it."

"Do you really think…." a voice called out from the other end of the hall. "That's a good idea?"

As both Bret and Chuck turned around, two men and a woman wearing street clothes approached them.

Darius moved closer. "It's not, you know."

"Who...." Chuck crinkled his face. "No one asked you. Why were you eavesdropping anyhow?"

"We weren't." Darius said. "We heard a scream. We thought the new woman was being attacked."

"By me?" Chuck laughed.

Darius shrugged. "Hey, none of us have met you. You haven't left the room. We don't know."

"Do I look like the type to attack someone?" Chuck asked.

Colin stepped forward in a lighthearted manner and spoke quickly, with a smile. "Absolutely. But we won't hold that against you." He extended his hand to Bret. "Colin Reye. How are you?" He then shook hands with Chuck. "And you two are?"

Bret replied innocently. "Friends."

Darius closed his eyes and chuckled. "He meant your names."

"Yes," Colin said. "Names. Not that my friend was insinuating you made a dumb blonde comment or anything like that."

Bret's mouth dropped open and she swung a look at Darius. "That was really rude."

"What?" Darius backhanded Colin. "Quit starting trouble."

After a scolding glance, Bret turned pleasantly to Colin. "Brettina Long. This is Chuck Wright."

Chuck nodded, but kept eye contact with

Darius.

The quiet woman with long auburn hair slipped into the pack. "I'm Virginia. Nice to meet you. I got here yesterday."

"Are there any others?" Chuck asked.

Virginia shook her head. "Nope. We're it. Your quarantine buddies." She was pleasant enough.

"Nice to meet you all." Chuck clenched Bret's arm. "Now if you'll excuse us, we have things to discuss."

Darius huffed.

Chuck stopped. "Man, what is your problem?"

"My problem is, that you want to get all the information you can out of this woman so you can break a story," Darius said. "I don't think that's such a good idea."

Colin interjected. "Mr. Wright. Instead of picking only this woman's mind, why don't you join us in the other room, hear all of our stories. We're all in here for similar reasons. I mean, in case you were confused, that isn't acne on Darius' face, those are roach bites."

Darius rolled his eyes.

Colin continued, "Get his story. But don't tell it. Not yet."

"When?" Chuck asked. "This is news. I can't believe it's being capped."

"It's being capped for a good reason," Darius said.

"Who are you to make that judgment call?" Chuck asked. "You work with the government?

FEMA? What?"

"No, I'm a teacher." Darius replied.

"Well, thank you, but your opinion as a teacher isn't reason enough for me to withhold news." Chuck began to turn Bret. "Excuse us."

"Actually...." Darius called out. "I'm head of Ecological Studies at West Virginia University, and my *expert* opinion tells me that something bigger is headed this way, something worse than the bugs. *That* is the reason to cap the story...for now." Darius saw he had Chuck's attention. "Just...talk with us. I think that after you do, you'll see why."

Chuck stared at Bret for a moment then they moved. Not toward his room, but in the direction of the recreation area.

The smell of coffee was overwhelming, and while Chuck went to the small circle of chairs set up by the television, Bret went to the coffee pot. She grabbed a cup, poured coffee, and brought it to her nose to sniff.

"We...." Darius walked up to her. "We didn't have the proper introduction. Brettina, I'm Darius Cobb." He extended his hand to her.

"You can call me, Bret."

"Nice to meet you. And I wasn't calling you a dumb blonde." He gave a partial smile. "Colin, he just likes to instigate. It's his way of being funny."

"I take it you two are friends. Is this a new thing?" Bret said as she fixed her coffee.

"God, no," Darius said. "I've known him since I was a teenager. You...you look as lost as Virginia did yesterday." He pointed back.

"I feel lost," she said. "Shuffled here and there, like a refugee. Kept in the dark. Lost."

"We all felt that way. Not too much anymore." He ran his finger over his goatee. "If you came from the Ward. Sip that coffee. You need to. It's Starbucks."

Bret chuckled, sniffed, sipped, and then looked at Darius. "You were in the ward too?"

"We all were. Good, huh?" he referred to the coffee.

"Yes," She nodded. "Thanks."

"So, tell me, Bret. What do you do?"

"For a living?'

"Living, career." He shrugged. "Some don't make a living off of their career choice."

She smiled. "I'm a talk show host and DJ for a Christian Radio."

"Ah." He nodded once, then stepped out of the way for Colin who approached the coffee pot.

Colin said as he reached for the coffee pot, "She's married. Look at the ring."

Darius briefly closed his eyes. "I'm not hitting on her. I'm making conversation."

"Uh huh." Colin poured. "Really, Dare-Dare, idle conversation at this point would be to ask how badly she was attacked by roaches."

"Dare-Dare?" Bret questioned.

Darius waved off Colin. "I was getting to that."

"Bad," Bret said. "I had seventy bites."

"Only seventy?" Darius whistled. "Someone must have been helping you. Nestings?"

"Three."

"I had fourteen."

Colin chuckled as he stirred his coffee. "Cockroach bite competition. When do you stop?" He shook his head at Darius and walked to the chairs.

Bret laughed. "He's funny."

"No, he's not."

Smiling, Bret asked. "So with so many nestings, I take it they are watching you for hatchings?"

Darius winked. "That's the reasoning. I think otherwise. Please. Join us. We don't bite. No pun intended."

Gently, he took her by the arm and led her to the circle where she took the chair next to Chuck.

"We heard they were bringing in two new people," Darius said. "We were waiting."

Chuck aimed his finger at Darius, Colin, and Virginia. "So, all three of you, like Bret, were attacked by cockroaches."

He received nods.

"Were they big?"

Virginia shook her head. "Not too much bigger than average. How many times were you bit, Bret?"

"Seventy." Bret replied.

"What!" Chuck blasted in shock.

She lifted her sleeve. "These aren't prong marks. They're roach bites. This here looks like a scratch." She pointed to her eye. "One of the places they laid eggs."

"Oh, my God!" Chuck was flabbergasted. "Virginia?"

"They counted ninety-five bites, ten nesting on me. I'm gonna take it Bret had help, that's why they didn't nest as much as they did on us."

Bret nodded. "My husband was wiping them off of me." She shuddered. "I can still feel them."

Chuck lifted a hand. "Why and how were you attacked?"

Bret answered. "I was at a friend's house. The exterminator uncovered them."

"Same here," Virginia said. "Only it was my house."

"Did your bug guy die?" Bret asked.

"Oh, brother." Virginia nodded. "Just dying would have been humane for him."

"Wait," Chuck called out. "How about you two?" he asked of Colin and Darius.

Darius explained. "I was in my classroom playing my guitar. Roaches crawled out. Now we had seen a few that day, but when they came out of my guitar, I figured I knew where they were coming from. When I pulled out the bookshelf, bam, I was hit."

Colin added, "That's where I came in. I was just visiting him, left, but just as I was leaving, I felt bad for choosing the lecture over his open mike night, so I went back. When I did, Dare-Dare was covered with roaches. I called 911, but my preoccupation with that call left me vulnerable. I was covered as well."

Darius shook his head. "I blacked out."

"Me, too." Colin said.

"Whoa." Bret interjected. "You guys are lucky. The bug guy asphyxiated on them before Sally and I could help him."

"I was," Darius said. "They found a nest in my lungs. How I don't know. See." He pulled down the collar of his shirt.

"Oh, we're not hitting on her." Colin said sarcastically. "Now he's exposing himself. Perhaps I should tell her husband."

"Stop that," Darius raised the collar of his shirt. "Anyhow, with all the people attacked, and there were a lot, why are us five here? Isolated. We aren't the only survivors. That question popped into my mind when Virginia arrived, and then we heard two more were coming. Bret is a DJ. It fits, if you think about it."

"That it does," Colin commented. "Not what I expected, but still she goes along with Chuck."

Chuck lifted his hand. "Excuse me. Can I ask what you are talking about?"

Darius answered, "I couldn't figure out why they had Colin and me in here alone when there were others that had beaten the bites and nestings, until they brought Virginia. I'm head of Ecology. Colin is head of Geology, Virginia is Head Astronomer at Beachit Institute."

"Earth and space sciences," Chuck muttered. "Where do we fit in? Neither Bret nor I are scientists."

"No," Darius said. "But like us, you have the means to get the story out."

Bret spoke, "What if he just has us here to

make sure we're quiet until the government releases the story. He told me they were when they figure out what they're gonna do."

At that, Darius chuckled. "And tell the masses what?"

"Well," Bret said. "The earth is heating up, and some bugs came up. They have found the nesting and…." she stopped talking when Darius shook his head. "What?"

"His explanation is weak at best. Freak bug migrations? He told me that, I laughed. Please. The earth heats up, bugs surface, go crazy and eat people? Colin, tell her."

"It's not feasible," Colin said. "The earth's internal temperature has risen before. Never have we experienced anything like this. No, they have us here to keep us quiet until the United States government gets a division of the scientific community to explain these isolated attacks with an explanation the masses accept. Once they do…we're free and clear. No one will want to hear what we say."

"Or will they?" Chuck spoke in discovery as he slowly stood up. "What if…what if Jeffers put us in here with you three on purpose? Figuring, hey, we're gonna spread the story; why not spread the story with another believable angle. An angle learned from you three," Chuck paced, "because he can't get a decent explanation from his people. That's possible."

Virginia shrugged. "It is possible."

"Have you guys been discussing this?" Chuck asked.

Darius answered. "Nonstop. However, we don't have data to view. If we did, I think we could solidify some theories. Now all we can do is toss unfounded theories about."

"Can you get your hands on the data?" Chuck asked. "Information you need?"

Colin replied, "Yes. Once we're out. Until then, we're in a theory phase. Trust me when we tell you we want the story out, but we want it out when it is correct and has scientific backing."

"Can you hold off?" Darius requested.

"How long?" Chuck asked.

"Days. Weeks. Months." Darius shrugged. "Who knows."

Chuck laughed in ridicule at that. "Bugs attack hundreds of people and you want me to sit on the story until you can scientifically prove why it happened?"

"No," Darius shook his head. "The government will take care of that. We want you to sit on the story until we can figure out where all this is heading. The bug attacks. They aren't some freak things. They aren't the end result of some strange phenomena." Darius grew serious. "They are only the beginning."

6 - SHUDDER TO THINK

May 10th ...

"I hate him," Chuck unlocked his car, and opened his door. He slid into his car at the same time as Bret. "Did I mention I hate him?" His hand frantically reached into the ashtray before he even shut his car door. "Fuck."

"Who?"

"What?"

"You said you hate him. Who? We just left three different men."

"Oh." Chuck glanced up. "Jeffers. Fuck! None."

"What are you doing?"

"I need a cigarette. I thought I had a butt in here that was doable."

"Just stop at the store."

"I don't have any money. They mailed my belongings home."

"Oh." Bret sunk back. "I don't either."

"Well, this doesn't help, see." Chuck closed his door, and turned over the engine. "We'll never make back to Pittsburgh on no gas. One would think...." He raised his voice. "Jeffers would have helped us out."

"We didn't ask."

"Still he should know. They took my belongings and brought you with the clothes on your back. I hate him."

"I know." Bret brought her finger to her mouth. "Oh! Got it. Beep."

"Why?"

After grunting, Bret reached over and beeped the horn.

"What are you doing?" Chuck asked.

Across the parking lot, Darius and Colin stopped walking. They turned around and looked.

"Darius is from around here," Bret said. "I'm sure he has access to money. I'll ask him to loan us…."

"No." Chuck shook his head. "I hate him."

"I thought you hated Jeffers."

"Him, too."

"Well, you want to get home, right. And you need a cigarette." Bret opened her door. "I'll be right back." She waved her hand, shut the door, and trotted over to Colin and Darius.

Colin stepped to her. "Is everything all right?"

"Yes. Well. No," Bret said, "They sent Chuck's personal items home. I arrived with the clothes on my back, we have a long trip home and no gas or money." She gave a humbled look. "Any chance we can borrow a few bucks. Colin, I can give it to you…."

"Shit," Colin snapped. "Shit."

"What?" Bret asked.

"I'm screwed, too." Colin turned to Darius. "They took my wallet. My money card is in there. Did they take yours?"

"I never carry a wallet," Darius replied. "Bret, can you and Chuck follow me? I can hit the money machine for you."

Bret sighed out. "That would be great. Yes. Which is your car?"

Darius pointed to the blue pick-up truck.

"Thanks, Dare-Dare. We're right behind you." Bret smiled and hurried back to the car.

Colin grinned. "Ah, the good Samaritan in you emerges. Warms my heart. So, like, can you help me out, too?"

"Absolutely not," Darius said. "She just called me Dare-Dare. Thank you very much." Darius walked to his truck.

"Not a problem. We'll just bond some more." Colin followed. "I'll stay with you. How's your couch?"

"Fine. I'll get you money." Darius arrived at his truck.

Colin smiled.

***

Bret accepted the cash as she stood by the open car door. "Say thank you," she instructed Chuck.

Chuck leaned with a raised hand. "Thanks, Dare-Dare."

Darius slightly rolled his eyes then nodded. "I'm killing you, Colin." He grumbled and laid his hand on Bret's door. "Be careful. Stay in touch. I mean it. I want to keep this thing going, okay? We can't make progress if we aren't all in it together."

Bret nodded.

"Oh, she'll stay in touch," Colin said. "We'll even get into it further over lunch, right, Bret?"

"Right." Bret closed her car door. "See you Tuesday."

"I look forward to it." Colin leaned for a second in the window, gave a glance of farewell then backed away.

Chuck put the car in gear, waved and pulled out. "Jesse will have a fit."

"About what?" Bret asked.

"Lunch with Colin. You spent days with this man. Jesse isn't gonna be happy about that. You know how he is. Now you're having lunch."

"We've bonded."

"I'm staying clear," Chuck said.

"Oh, stop. I'll just explain to Jesse what we're doing."

"And what exactly are we doing, Bret?" Chuck asked. "They're the scientists. What can we possibly do except break the news?"

"Research," Bret replied. "That's what my part is."

"Research."

"You know Chuck, if you paid attention...."

"I paid attention." Chuck put on the turn signal and pulled over into a convenience store parking lot. "What kind of research?"

"I'm supposed to see if I can find out if things like this happened before in history. Just to see if maybe flukes like this occurred before and history is just repeating itself."

"And if not?" Chuck parked the car.

"Well, then, we stick to proving one of the

many theories we tossed out. That's Colin and Darius. They have lot of research; it'll take time and money. They said that's not a problem."

"And they are researching what?"

Bret huffed out. "Changes in the earth. God, pay attention."

"It's the lack of nicotine," Chuck said as he opened his door. "I'll be back."

"Chuck?" Bret questioned. "Why do you seem so disinterested? One would think...."

"It's not disinterest, Bret."

"What is it?

"Doubt."

Bret gave a curious look.

"We've had some freak occurrences, really bizarre things. What if it is just the beginning, but not of strange earthly phenomena? What if it's something else, really out of our control."

"Like what."

With a hint of sarcasm, Chuck said. "Gee, I don't know, Bret. You work as a messenger for God. Think about it."

After the car door shut, Bret immediately began to do just that...think about it.

***

"Kids." Darius picked up a ball that sat on his walkway and tossed it to the neighbor's yard.

"Your grass needs to be cut," Colin said as he followed him.

"It does?" Darius peered around. "I guess." Scratching his head, he moved toward his door. "But doesn't it strike you as odd?" he asked then stopped at his door. A huge stack of mail flowed in front, and Darius kicked it aside as he turned the key on the lock.

"What?" Colin picked up the mail. "That you just kicked your mail."

"No." Darius opened the door. "Strike you as odd. As...ah, man." His hand shot to cover his mouth and nose.

Colin stepped in. "Tell me, does your house normally smell this foul?" He shook his head with a wince.

"No." Darius immediately opened a window. "God, what is that smell?"

"I'll just leave this door open," Colin said.

"Please. I wonder if I left food out on the stove." Hand still covering his mouth, he walked to the kitchen of his single-floor one-bedroom home.

Glad to find the couch under the abundance of papers, books and notes, Colin sat down his briefcase. "Was it food?" he asked in reference to the sound of Darius in the kitchen.

"No, maybe it's milk gone bad," Darius called.

"Well, check, will you? Do you have any air freshener?"

"I don't know."

Colin mumbled. "He doesn't know. Go figure." He bent down and lifted a newspaper from the table. An entire half of a pizza was glued to it. "What are you doing in there?"

"Looking for the source of this horrible smell."

"Maybe it's an accumulation of odors over time," Colin suggested, pacing about Darius' living room. "How long has it been since you cleaned in here?"

"I don't know. Can you boot up my computer please."

Speaking softly to himself, Colin said, "If I can find it." He stepped over the coffee table. "Ah, yes. There. I see it."

"My house isn't that bad." Darius banged about in the kitchen.

"Yes, Dare-Dare it is," Colin replied. "I think I'm gonna open more…." Colin stopped speaking when his foot caught onto something.

Darius came out of the kitchen. "Maybe the neighbor has a sewage problem."

"It's not the neighbor, Dare-Dare, it's your smell."

"What?" Darius chuckled.

"I found the odor." Colin glanced downward.

Darius walked over to Colin. "Aw, man." He whined as he looked down. "My cat died. Fuck."

"You'll have that when they don't eat for a week. The humane society is gonna love you."

"Let them register the complaint with Jeffers." Darius shook his head and walked back toward the kitchen. "I really liked that cat."

"Where you going?"

"To get a garbage bag." Darius said.

"A garbage bag." Colin whispered. "Wow.

You really did like that cat."

"Ha. Ha. Ha. Funny." Darius emerged with the bag.

"You aren't gonna just toss it in the garbage are you?" Colin asked. "Of course the garbage men wouldn't know if you mixed it in with all of your other stuff."

"No, I'm not gonna put her in the can. I'm putting her in the bag so I can bury her."

"You're not gonna make me sit through a major production funeral like you did when you were sixteen and your guinea pig died."

"Shit." The bag dropped from Darius' hand and he flew from the room.

"What? What did I say?"

After briefly disappearing, Darius returned from the bedroom. "My hamsters are dead, too."

"Hamsters, as in plural."

Darius nodded.

"Before we proceed with the mass grave thing, are there any other pets that you possess that may be deceased at this moment?"

Ignoring him, Darius picked up the garbage bag and handed it to Colin. "Here. I'll be back. Start with her. I think she might be stuck."

"Me?" Colin questioned. "Dare-Dare." He inched his foot into the dead cat. "She's stuck alright. We may need a jackhammer." He turned his head; Darius was gone. "Really, if we just shuffle the mess no one will know the cat is here. The smell will dissipate in a few days."

"You know...." Darius poked his head from the kitchen. "This isn't funny. I'm upset. I loved my pets."

"Are you getting another bag for the hamsters?"

"No, tongs. I'm just gonna flush them." He withdrew into the kitchen.

"Oh," Colin said with a single nod. "Flush the hamsters. That's love of pets alright." He nudged the carcass of the cat. "I'm in trouble when I die, aren't I, cat?"

***

Colin was too apprehensive about drinking anything from a cup that came from Darius' cupboards, so he opted for a can of soda. Not really his favorite.

"You realize," Colin said as he shuffled to join Darius at the computer desk. "This house it's…it's deplorable."

"It's not that bad." He replied.

"Really? Health department catches wind of this…you're shut down." Colin wiped off chair and sat down. "Does your mother know you live like this?"

"Fortunately for me, no. Of course, I haven't heard from her in six months."

"Really?"

"Really."

"What kind of guy is it this time?" Colin asked.

"Weatherman."

"Figures."

Darius just looked at Colin then returned to the computer. "Nothing."

"What?"

"Not even on the net. I did a search, yeah, little ones."

"Are we looking for new pets to kill?"

Darius gave a scolding glance. "No. News of what happened."

"I don't understand."

"Remember when we were walking in the house I told you it was odd."

"I thought you were referring to the house."

"No," Darius said. "I was referring to the fact that nothing is mentioned in the news, the paper, nowhere."

"Well...." Colin popped the tab to his can. "I guess the government accomplished what they wanted. They got their story out, people are satisfied, move on with our lives." He wiped off the can before taking a drink. "So, now that you've looked on the net, wanna go get that food now?"

"One more thing. I want to post on my science club."

"Excuse me?" Colin asked. "You have a science club?"

"Not me personally. I belong to it. Harvard runs it. You have to enter your teacher information and doctrine stuff before they allow you to join. Everyone's legit. You should join. It's fun."

"Fun? A science club is fun? No, no thank you. I'll pass."

"Suit yourself," Darius said as he typed.

"What exactly are you posting?" Colin asked.

"The way I figure, if there are any earthly changes, weird occurrences or phenomena being discovered, it will be here. Trust me. In addition, if it's not, my post should send them scurrying to look. This is fascinating enough that they'll research it themselves with vengeance."

"Ah...." Colin nodded. "Have all the bright minds out there do your hard work for you, then you piece it together and take credit."

"Exactly."

Colin smiled. "I knew I raised you right." He lifted his soda can with a grin.

***

It amazed Bret how much remained, or rather how little remained in her home after the government seized and disinfected it.

The computer received a nice dust job, but other than that and anything else hard, it was gone. Anything with cushion, foam, or feathers...removed for fear of hidden nesting. She was grateful her clothes—with the exception of a few sweaters—were still there. The new furniture was cheesy but free. So were the bedspreads for that matter.

It was evident that Jesse worked hard on the house. Having been told by a remaining neighbor that the authorities pretty much showed zero respect toward property, the house could have been destroyed. Or not there, such as Sally's home and the house to her right. Both were gone, set aflame by firemen to kill the infestation that was out of control.

And what of the ants?

The hole was filled in, paved again, and with the exception of the two new vacant lots, and scattered 'for sale' signs, Bret's street was back to normal.

Though the consensus was that Bret needed to get home and get some rest, such was not the case. She insisted she had enough rest while quarantined, but she desired good food and computer access.

That was until Jesse warned her about her email. Days without checking, and a message sent out to the Christian listeners of Bret's show brought nearly 3,000 emails of well-wishes and prayers her way. Everyone in the family volunteered to pitch in and help reply to those emails.

But Bret first. Settled with a cup of coffee, Bret opened her email. The most recent of which was bold and top. One from Darius.

"What's he want?" she asked aloud.

"What was that?" Jesse called from the kitchen.

"Darius sent me an email."

"Who?"

"No one. Some guy from quarantine," she said and clicked on the mail.

A thump-thump of his shoes brought Jesse to

the dining room. "Why does some guy you were quarantined with feel the need to email you now? You just left him."

"The sex was great." Bret said.

"Excuse me?"

"Oh, he wants to get together and have coffee when I meet Colin for lunch on Tuesday."

"Who's Colin?"

"Another guy from quarantine."

"Bret, why.…"

"Jesse." She spun her chair to face him. "They're scientists. Okay? I'm helping them with something."

Jesse laughed and walked away.

Bret snarled, "Like that's funny." She shook her head, returned to the computer and replied, stating that she'd like to have coffee and would bring the money he lent her.

7 - NEW MOON

May 11th ...

Coffee bar latte in hand, Darius toted books under his arms; they, of course, had papers sticking out. Over his shoulder was a book bag and he sipped as he walked down the corridor to his classroom.

"Morning, Professor Cobb."

Darius gave a polite smile to each student that greeted him and to the three that waited outside his classroom door. "Last I looked we still had close to half an hour until class," he said as he handed his coffee and books to a student. He lifted the key to his door and unlocked it. "Thanks." He took his stuff back.

"Had to take the early bus." Scott followed him into the class. "Don't know about them. How are you feeling? Is it safe to come in here?"

"Fine and yes," Darius replied then walked down the step. He turned on his computer before placing his armful of items down.

"Anything we can start on?" Scott asked.

"No Just relax. Talk." Darius took another drink of his coffee, eyes glued to the computer.

"We should have known something was up with them bugs." Scott sat down. "Dude, I could have been you."

"Any of you could have." Darius saw the

'ready' screen and began to type. He was focused, and attention to the early birds in his classroom was just about nil.

He logged onto the Internet and then to his Harvard site. "Now let's see," he spoke softly to himself typing in his information. "What is this?" he asked of the line that read 'URGENT', and then he clicked on it.

***

Like Darius, Colin arrived early to his classroom. He had a lot to catch up on.

"Dr. Reye, how are you, sir?" Roger, an intelligent, less-than-attractive boy approached the desk holding a box.

"Fine, thank you."

"I heard you were ill."

Colin glanced up from his work. "Yes, I was."

"What was wrong?"

"Brain tumor. Very sad. Deadly. They got it though."

"Whoa."

"Yes." Colin returned to his work.

"I was camping and found some specimens, I was wondering if you could look at them."

"Wouldn't be much of an educator if I didn't encourage you to find out for yourself, now would I?"

"Yeah, but I looked," Roger said. "I can't find them. Can you?" he reached into the box. "This one here...."

Colin's cell phone rang.

"Your phone is ringing," Roger said.

"Yes, I know." Colin lifted it. "Hey, Dare-Dare. What's up?"

Roger extended the fist-sized geological specimen to Colin.

"Are you near a computer? Can you go online?" Darius asked.

"Yes; why?" Colin replied.

Again, Roger extended the sample a bit further. "Sir, if you can just…."

Colin only raised his eyes then turned back to the computer. "I'm looking at my computer. What now?"

"Go where I tell you," Darius said and proceeded to give the information to Colin.

Colin typed.

"Dr. Reye?" Roger called his attention.

Darius said, "Now my user name and password."

"What am I looking up?"

"Are you in?" Darius asked.

"Yes." Colin replied.

"Click on Urgent."

"Done." Colin said.

"Dr. Reye?"

"Hold on Dare-Dare." Colin faced the boy. "Can't you see I'm on the phone?"

"Well, yes, sir, but I thought I you could tell me quickly what this is, then I could research it before class."

Grunting, Colin nodded. "I can."

"And?" Roger asked.

"It's a goddamn rock." Colin spun his chair and when he did, he saw why Darius called. His eyes skimmed as he read. "Holy shit."

"Exactly," Darius commented. "Now the question: Do I go or not go."

Colin sat back in his chair and took in the words. "Go."

***

"Reading about it, worrying about it, isn't going to do you any good," Jesse told Bret while getting ready for the funeral.

"But what if it happens?" she asked.

"Nothing is going to stop God's end, Bret. If there was something that could do it, don't you think there would have been a little mention of it in the Bible?"

"Yeah, the chosen...."

"Bret, stop." He took the Bible out of her hands. "God's not ending the world."

"I didn't say he was."

"Enough. For today…enough."

She simply nodded, promising to place it out of her mind.

She shouldn't have. The Biblical ramifications of all that was happening should have been forefront; if they were, Buster's funeral would not have been one of the most difficult experiences of her life.

Her eldest son Perry stayed in the car, appearing out of respect, but declining because the thought of a little baby in a coffin was too much to bear.

Luke didn't handle things well at all. Buster was a toy to him, and he babysat and played with the toddler often to help Sally. Luke also went to school with Buster's big brother.

Casper and Andi went with Buster's sister. They were all connected somehow, and it hit Bret's family extremely hard.

Silence in a packed family automobile was usually an impossible objective. Not that day. Bret was ill-prepared for what she'd face. They had both Sally and Buster's coffins in the same room, and she just couldn't handle seeing that tiny coffin. A tradition in Pittsburgh is an open casket. However, in the case of Sally and Buster, both lids were closed.

Jesse stayed in the doorway of the funeral home and spoke to Sally's children who were holding up remarkably well. Not John, Sally's husband. John was drunk. The smell of bourbon was strong on his breath as he greeted people. He hid his intoxication well; it only became slightly evident once the funeral was over.

Bret joined him in a few drinks. Seeing photos of Sally and Buster brought back memories of that day, memories that only she had. It didn't dawn on her until she and John sat on the back porch of his mother's house.

People were mingling, eating, talking.

"What was her mood? What was she doing?" John asked. "Was she happy, sad? Did she bitch about me?"

"No. Sally was in a good mood. She said Jesse looked like the bug guy. And...." Bret chuckled. "She said they both looked like rapists."

"You're kidding."

"Nope. Then a few comments were made, and Buster...." Bret sniffled. "He repeated something he heard. He told the bug guy I was going to have sex with him."

John laughed. "He was something, wasn't he?"

"I never met a child like him."

"I keep thinking he's alive. He's gonna show up. We never could find him when he wandered."

"I still think our neighbor Bill took him and moved him about."

"I thought that too." John said. "I miss them. Do you think...do you think they suffered?"

"No." Bret replied. "That pit was so thick with ants; I think they both went fast."

"If you could have seen what was left of them...." He paused. "Bret, the ants ate them."

She closed her eyes.

"Ate them?" He chuckled in disbelief. "I didn't think ants were carnivorous."

"They aren't by nature. Some are though."

"What's next?" He shook his head. "Something is up, some weird government experiment."

That caught her attention. "Why do you say that?"

"They took you away and wouldn't say anything. The military came and got you. Why? You were there. You saw the cockroaches, how many there were."

"I also had nests in me."

"Yeah, what if there was something about those nests that they had to keep secret."

"I don't think it's the government, John." Bret said. "It's something, I don't know what, but it's not the government. If they're guilty of anything, it's hiding what they know."

"Bugs are natural. What happened isn't."

Bret nodded her agreement.

He continued, "We are at war against Nature, Bret. My family suffered a casualty of that war." He took in a silent moment and then, "Me and Sally fought that morning. I wanted to wait for my friend to fit us in, but she called that bug guy. My last words to my wife were that she was such a horrible housekeeper that the roaches were her doing and we were probably infested beyond belief."

Bret sighed out. "She knew better."

"I suppose."

"You know we all have fights, John. We all say things we don't mean."

"I realize that. I loved her, Bret. Seventeen years I loved her. So make me a promise, okay?"

"Sure, what is it?" she asked.

"Never, *never* let your last words to Jesse be something you will regret. Even if he's going to the store, to the car, just…. Promise that. Because you never know." He gripped on to her hand. "You just never know."

***

It was something out of a sci-fi movie. The television picture in Bret's home looked as if an old foil antenna were used rather than the premium digital cable she and Jesse paid so much for. She had to work later on that evening and sitting back relaxing was just not happening.

Jesse hit the cable box twice.

"What are you doing?" Bret asked.

"What the fuck is wrong with this picture. We have squiggle vision."

Bret chuckled, "Squiggle vision?"

"Yeah, look at the picture."

Bret winced when Jesse hit it again. "You think that smacking the box will do it."

"Yeah."

"Fine." From her chair, Bret stood, stopped, and cocked her head to the playful screams outside. "What are they doing out there?"

"Seems the kids have the entire neighborhood in some demented game of release."

"Why are you calling it demented?"

"Them screaming like that is demented." Jesse raised his hand to hit the box again.

Bret grunted. "Do you think maybe it's not the box but the signal?"

Jesse only looked at her.

"Maybe not." With the full intention of going to get a cup of tea, Bret paused when there was a knock at her front door. "I'll get it."

"Thanks," Jesse said focused on looking at

the box.

"Chuck?" Bret said with surprise when she opened the door.

Chuck stepped inside. "Did you know your kids are running around in the dark screaming?"

"They're playing Release."

"With a stick?"

"As long as no one gets hurt." Bret shut the door.

"Hey, Jesse." Chuck greeted. "Something wrong with the box?'

"I think our box is broke, look at this picture." Jesse replied.

Chuck paused to check out the picture on the television. "Looks like you aren't getting a signal at all. Maybe it's not your box."

Bret added, "I told him that." Seeing that Jesse wasn't paying any attention to Chuck, Bret waved her hand. "So what brings you by?"

"I was on my way down to Morgantown."

"For what?" Bret asked.

"You're kidding. Right?" Chuck asked and waited. "You're not. Ok, have you checked your email tonight?"

"No; why?"

"Just about right now...." Chuck glanced down at his watch. "Darius should be lifting off for Africa."

"Africa." Bret said, shocked. "Why?"

"That...I don't know. Can I smoke?" he pulled out his pack.

Bret nodded.

Chuck continued. "I got a call from Colin to

meet him. He wanted to know if I could go to Morgantown, hit Darius' house, and pick up some documents Darius had put away. Colin can't go. I said I would."

"What documents?"

"Just items pertaining to this trip and things he's dug up."

"Why do you have to get them?" Bret asked. "Does Colin need them?"

"Get this. Colin wants to copy them and have them put in safe places. He doesn't think anything is that important, but down the line, some sort of readouts Darius did may be."

"So Colin doesn't need them, he just wants them in safe keeping."

"Exactly," Chuck said. "I guess they aren't taking any chances. I mean, they locked me up, kept us tight in quarantine, right?"

"Right. So you think you and I can make heads or tails out of these papers you're picking up."

"If we can't, Colin can."

Bret nodded. "Good point. So why was I checking my email."

"Darius said he'd email you."

"Did he say why he was going to Africa?"

"He was vague." Chuck said. "Only that something occurred there that he felt was going to end up covered up."

"Hence our securing his findings."

"Yep."

"You think it's a plague? A lethal virus?" Bret asked. "You know Africa is famous for them."

"Could be a number of things. Colin said he'd explain what he knew when he met us for lunch tomorrow. He also said it isn't much."

Bret rubbed her chin. "This…this is weird."

Before Chuck could say anything, Jesse did. "Tell me about it."

Bret gave a motion of her head backwards. "He probably is talking about the television."

"No," Jesse said. "I'm talking about this conversation you two are having. Chuck's going all the way down to Morgantown for papers to hide. Papers that he hasn't a clue what they are, all because some wacko takes a trip to Africa on a whim."

Bret gasped. "Darius is not some wacko. He's a very brilliant scientist."

Jesse rolled his eyes. "I don't even think he went to Africa. Let's all just drop what we're doing and run for Dare whatever his name is."

"Darius." Bret corrected, "And yes, we will. He knows things. Why are you being so cynical? You should take this more seriously."

"Like you?" Jesse asked.

"Um, yeah."

Chuck intervened. "Jesse, though I think the man is an arrogant ass, he makes sense. This is serious."

"Tell me why." Jesse requested.

"Because," Bret was adamant. "Darius followed this to Africa. This is serious because this is about surviving."

"Surviving what, Bret?" Jesse asked.

"Whatever is happening to our planet."

"And you don't think these two men and you two might be taking it too far?"

"Not at all. I'm not a scientist; they are. If they're right, this is just the beginning of a long line of strange things that will take place." Bret said.

"Strange things?" Jesse questioned.

Bret nodded. "Yes, like the ants. The roaches. They are strange."

"And he thinks they are leading to what?" Jesse asked. "Chuck, do you know?"

Chuck shrugged. "Specifically, no. We will."

Jesse breathed out. "Things have been quiet. Maybe it's over, or it died down."

At that instant, Casper flew into the house. "Mom. Hurry. Come outside. Bring the camera!"

"What's wrong?"

"The moon's on fire." She flew out the door.

Bret looked at Jesse then the three of them quickly followed Casper outside. The entire brigade of neighborhood children stood on the front lawn peering up at the sky. At her first step it couldn't be seen, but as soon as Bret moved down the stairs it was in view.

The moon wasn't ablaze, but it looked it. Gone was the whitish-yellow color; it hadn't even the hint of red a summer moon often projects. It was orange. The roundness of it was distorted and encircled by a strange cloud of gasses. The mist absorbed the new color making streaks across the sky, like shooting flames. With the background of a clear dark sky, the moon looked like the reflection of the setting sun on rippling water.

A remarkable sight.

"Jesse," Bret whispered, then swallowed the lump in her throat.

"I'll get the camera. You can send it to your science buddies." He spoke dazedly, staring up. "Because this would be one of those strange things you were talking about, right?"

She didn't know and was silent.

"Chuck?" Jesse beckoned for an answer.

"I don't know either, man," Chuck said. "I mean, it could have been an optical illusion. But whatever it is, I don't want to look anymore." Chuck turned. "It's too ominous." Without saying any more, he opened the door and walked inside.

8 - REVELATIONS

May 12th ...

The hour and a half trip to Morgantown could have been more productive for Chuck had someone not ransacked Darius' house. Of course, that was what he initially believed until he placed a call to Colin.

"Is the place totally trashed?" Colin asked.

"Man, whoever was here tore this place apart." Chuck said.

"Uh huh, and is there a petrified pizza on the coffee table?"

Pause.

"Yeah, why?" Chuck asked.

"I don't believe his place has been ransacked. That's the way Darius lives."

Chuck was appalled. But just as he'd been told, the important documents along with the disk were located under the newspaper on the coffee table—which ironically was under the petrified pizza.

He retrieved what he needed, made copies, secured several of them in different spots, wrote his assignment story on some old lady and her dog, caught some sleep, and was at the restaurant only five minutes late.

He beat Bret there.

"Coffee, thanks," Chuck told the waitress as

he took a seat. "Colin." He extended a hand across the table. "You're dressed differently than I expected."

"It's my 'get down with the people' look," Colin said of his black button down shirt and tan pants.

Chuck snickered. "You wear that as a teacher?"

"No, I don't have classes today."

"Oh." Chuck nodded, and then looked up when Colin lifted from his chair, greeting Bret.

"You look lovely." Colin extended his hand to her.

"It's the lipstick," Bret said. "Remember you saw me without any make up."

"Have a seat." Colin motioned his hand. "Coffee?"

"Yes, please." Bret sat.

"Coffee for the lady, and we'll have these menus." Colin told the waitress.

Chuck kissed Bret on the cheek. "You look tired. Didn't you sleep?"

Bret's mouth dropped open. "You know, Colin complimented me. How come you downplayed it?"

Chuck shrugged. "You look tired."

"I didn't sleep after work last night." Bret shrugged. "I couldn't. Last I heard from you, Darius' place was ransacked."

Colin chuckled. "It wasn't."

Chuck shook his head. "No, Darius just doesn't clean. And his place smells."

"Really?" Bret asked surprised. "He doesn't

strike me like that."

"Slob," Colin said. "Always has been."

"Did you get the stuff?" Bret asked.

"Yes," Chuck pulled out an envelope and handed it to Colin. "Do you know what that is? I peeked at it; it only looks like numbers and abbreviations."

Colin lifted the contents of the envelope slightly, "Ah…. Yes. Readouts. Figures and such. I'll go through these and let you know how they break down."

"What are they?" Bret asked.

"Geological readouts. Odd changes other scientists have noted. Things that will play an important part in figuring out what is happening and where this is going. You know, watch the pattern, figure out what's next sort of thing."

Bret nodded. "What about that lady, Virginia. Has anyone spoken to her?"

"Yes," Colin answered. "She wants to get together in a couple weeks. Says she too has some findings she's following up on."

"Why all the secrecy?" Chuck questioned.

"Take no chances." Colin closed the envelope. "If we by chance discover Mother Nature is about to throw a hissy fit that will totally disrupt the world, the government is not gonna want that information getting out."

"Why?" questioned Chuck

"Would you?" Colin asked. "If nothing can be done, why say anything. Let people go. Let them live out the rest of their lives without chaos, panic, riots, fear."

"Oh, my God." Bret gasped. "You mean we all could die."

"No, no." Colin shook his head. "Absolutely not. No."

"But you just said...."1

"For the layman." Colin lifted a finger. "We will be informed; therefore, we will prepare. Therefore...we will live."

"Even if nothing can be done to stop what might occur—whatever that is?" Chuck said.

"Just because you can't stop it," Colin said, "doesn't mean you can't work around it." He winked. "Besides, I think we'll get a better grip once Darius checks in. He's following something that either, A, is nothing along our lines, or B, follows our lines and Virginia's at the same time."

After looking at Chuck, Bret looked at Colin. "I am so lost."

Colin explained, "A post appeared on the Harvard site for Darius' attention. See, Darius posted that he was looking for strange natural phenomenon that would be consistent with permanent geological changes and shifts—along with other things. This post appeared and he followed it. Now...it could be nothing along the geological lines at all, or it could be. Virginia has a theory that actually helps fill in the pieces."

"What theory?" Chuck asked.

Colin shook a finger. "I hate discussing theories before we get some backbone. Darius can get that."

"But it could be bad?" Chuck asked.

Colin nodded once. "Could be, yes. But

nothing we can't work around." He smiled.

Chuck asked, "What did this post to Darius say?"

"Merely told of this section of Africa where nineteen people have died and seventy five are failing fast. Gave their symptoms. Sounds like plague, but it could be something else, there were no known plague cases in the village at all."

Chuck was confused. "What does plague have to do with geological changes?"

"Keep in mind that Darius is ecologically oriented, how our environment works and things that affect us. That is him, no matter what. Plus, there were some other environmental changes that occurred that flagged it. The CDC says it's nothing, but he went anyhow."

Bret sat back. "It sounds scary."

"Yes, it does," Colin said. "Now…enough gloom and doom. I'm starved and I have to stay upbeat. I have a book-signing this afternoon."

Puzzled, Bret glanced at him. "You wrote a book?"

"Yes, I did. Have a signing for it. Ladies' tea signing."

"What's it about?" Bret asked. "I love to read."

"It's called Passion and Vengeance." Colin replied. "It deals with the fury of woman." He smiled. "Mother Earth."

"So it's nonfiction," Bret said.

"Exactly."

"Wait. Wait." Chuck interrupted. "Are these scientific women that are coming to this tea?"

"Nope, not at all," Colin replied. "More than likely, they're everyday housewives."

"For a geological book?" Chuck quizzed then laughed. "And you expect to sell to these women?"

"I not only will sell to these women, but others in the store. In fact...I'll sell out." Colin pulled out a cigarette.

"You think?" Chuck laughed. "Fifty bucks says no way."

With an arrogant smile, Colin held out his hand. "You're on."

***

"I have to go to the ATM machine," Chuck whispered in Bret's ear.

Bret peered up from the book. "What was that? I didn't hear you. I was," she held up a copy of Colin's book, "so intrigued."

"I said I have to go to the ATM so I can pay off the bet."

"You think he's gonna sell out?"

Chuck looked over to the long line of women waiting to greet Colin. "I'd say so. God, how is he doing it?"

"The book is good."

"It's about geology." Chuck retorted. "And...." He snatched the book from her hand. "What is up with this cover?"

On the front of the book were a man and a woman entangled in a passionate embrace.

"This indicates nothing about geology," Chuck said.

"Colin said it is symbolic of the earth changes. Water, air. See?" She held it up "Plus, he says everything in everyday terms. It's like reading a love story."

Chuck grunted, "And have you heard him? He's lying to these women."

"He is not."

"Is too. Come here." He took hold of Bret's arm and pulled her toward the table. "Just listen to him."

Perturbed, Bret folded her arms. "Then can I go back to reading?"

Again, Chuck grunted.

Colin opened the cover to his book. "And who should I make...." He glanced to the large woman before him. "My God, don't think me forward but that is the loveliest shade of green I have ever seen. Very earthy."

She tilted her head with a blush. "Thank you."

"Same color as the mist on the cover of my book. Did you notice?" Colin asked.

"No," she said brightly, "I didn't. Wow."

"Great sweater."

"The book looks great."

"Thank you." Colin replied.

"Is it a true love story?"

"It is a beautifully true love story." Colin answered. "Intense."

"Like the cover and title. I love the title. Sounds like there may be a little tryst in there as well."

Colin only winked. "Your name?"

"Mary Beth."

"Very nice name."

"Thank you. You know it's a shame it isn't a mystery. My daughter would love it and you're such a nice man."

"Why thank you. And…there is a hint of a mystery that runs through it." Colin closed the cover after signing.

"Really, well…." She reached and took a book from the stack. "Can you make this one out to Sue?"

"Absolutely," Colin raised his pen.

"See?" Chuck inched Bret away.

"I think you're just sore because you have lost the bet and owe him fifty bucks."

"Yeah, I am sore."

"Go to the money machine."

"I am. He drives me insane."

"I thought Jeffers and Darius did."

"They all do," Chuck spoke dramatically.

"Well." Bret snickered sarcastically. "You're in trouble if the world does end, because you're stuck with Darius and Colin."

"You think?" Chuck raised his eyebrows. "If the world ends, there are no more laws. No more laws, I can kill them to make my life more tolerable."

"Ha!" Bret laughed. "You don't have it in you."

"You're right, you're right." Chuck smiled. "I'll just tell Jesse you had an affair with one of them and he'll handle it. See ya." After a pat to her cheek, Chuck walked away.

***

Even though it was close to sundown, the heat was still unbearable. Riding in the open jeep helped, adding a slight breeze that blew through Darius' hair. But he was stuffed in the jeep with six others. Their body heat added to his discomfort.

He hadn't slept, not since leaving the United States twenty-four hours earlier. He was briefed on the private jet about the situation, but the briefing was just that…brief. Not much was known. As they moved from location to location, clearance for the team of scientists came through, and in a caravan that consisted of two jeeps and a truck, they rode to the infected area.

They were told that the Center for Disease Control group was already there, along with scientists from the World Health Organization. Darius was invited by a group of Ivy League minds that went from place to place, under private funding, to investigate strange natural phenomenon. On the surface, the outbreak didn't appear unusual, with vomiting, diarrhea, lesions of the skin, general malaise and death. But underneath the surface, it was a different story.

Not a single strain of virus was found in the bloodstream. Nothing.

Why were these people so sick?

Darius prepared to put on his surgical facemask. Though he hated them and it was hot, it would help with the smell from both the village and the jeep.

He put it on one mile outside the town, as instructed. His mask was the only protective clothing he had. That and gloves.

He would work alone, but report as a team. They worked that way. He could go alone to uncover his findings, but he had to share—like everyone else—at the end of the day. Darius didn't mind that. If by chance he couldn't figure out the cause someone else would. Science more often than not is selfless.

Carrying his backpack complete with his testing equipment, Darius disembarked the jeep directly after it stopped. Several of his senses were aroused when he did so. An enormous number of flies swarmed about creating a symphony of buzzing. His sense of smell was muffled, but his sense of touch was not. The heat felt weird on his skin, almost burning; Darius chalked it up to his imagination.

When his group arrived, most of them followed in a pack. Not Darius. He pulled out a camera and immediately began taking pictures. The sound of coughing flowed through the air. There were no children running around, very little movement at all. In fact, Darius would have sworn the town was dead had it not been for the sounds of illness.

One of his crew, a man named Jameson, caught Darius' attention. He had walked into the hospital while Darius still photographed the sites of the street. Almost immediately, Jameson flew out the door of the single-story frame building. He barely made it off the porch before he vomited copiously. For some strange reason, he tried to catch it in his hand; it didn't work. The vomit splashed out violently.

Darius took a picture, 'mind filing' it as a great action shot. Some would call it demented; Darius called it curiosity. Holding his camera at the ready he went into the hospital. He lifted it to shoot but stopped. People were on the floor, on beds put together...everywhere. All of them were discolored and covered with sores; vomit seeped from their mouths, and their backs and bottoms were encircled in fresh and dried blood. He swallowed the impulse to vomit that formed in his throat and lifted the camera.

"She is with the CDC," Darius heard a man say. "Got ill three days after getting here."

Darius zoomed in on the conversation.

"Fourth case," he continued, "What is it? Obviously, it's contagious."

After a few pictures, Darius couldn't take anymore and lowered the camera and left.

Outside all he wanted to do was remove his mask and inhale a long, deep breath of fresh air, but he couldn't. He could only walk away. Just a little way, he figured, away from the pandemonium and death.

In the distance, a water hole caught his eye. Not that he would drink from it, but it seemed isolated and no one was there. Reaching into his backpack Darius pulled out a bottle of water and uncapped it. After lifting his mask slightly, he took a long, deep swig, swished it in his mouth, and then spit it out. Looking down, wiping his mouth, readying to take another drink, it caught his eye. Darius walked ahead a few feet then crouched down.

Black.

His fingers ran against the dirt on the ground, and it was black. He rolled his fingertips together and it smeared like charcoal. He stuck his fingers into it and the black dirt extended down not only four inches, it encircled out that much as well.

"What the fuck?" he wondered aloud, then stood up. Pivoting his body, he allowed his eyes to gaze around. While he searched he saw that the black spot wasn't the only one. For a moment, he stood there dumbfounded. Were they burning bodies? Were they burning anything? Just as he went to lower his mask again, he felt the heat sizzle on his brow. With widening eyes Darius fumbled in his bag and pulled out a small hand-held unit. He clicked it on, and aimed it around. "Shit. Shit!"

He whacked the side of the unit and watched the digital readout. "Shit!" he called out, then raced back toward the main section of the compound. "Dr. Waters!" he called out. "Dr. Waters."

Dr. Waters emerged from the hospital. "Dr.

Cobb, where is your mask?"

Darius shook his head. "We need more than masks right now, sir."

"What do you mean?" he asked.

"These people don't have a plague or viral infection. They have radiation poisoning." He handed him the unit. "Take a look. We're standing at fifty rads. In another four hours we'll all be sick."

"Good Lord." Waters brought his hand to his head and wiped away the sweat. "What in the world is causing that much radiation?" As he removed his mask for a breather his head tilted back and he paused as he stared up.

"What?" Darius asked.

"Our cause." Waters said.

Baffled for only a second, Darius glanced to the same location as Waters. He peered up to the bright and shining…sun.

9 - The Pull

Memorial Day - May 25th ...

It was a letter to her Uncle Alistair that told Virginia that she and the others would be getting vital information: A letter from Darius, dated two weeks earlier. He called her when he received it and she called Colin.

Colin was relieved; he hadn't heard anything from Darius at all and calls to Harvard, posts on the net, and even contact with government officials, bred nothing. Darius had arrived in Africa. That's all that was known. The short letter from Darius was all that they had.

What was going on?

"That's all it says," Virginia told him on the phone the day before. "In fact it was written on half a sheet of paper. There are some partial equations on the back, but I can't make heads or tails out of where he was going with them."

"Were those equations for us?" Colin asked.

"I don't think so. I think he used the back of the paper." Virginia said. "You mentioned something about statistics. What did you make of them?"

"Nothing conclusive. I do however see changes, and it's indicating it may have something to do with magnetic fields."

126

"Really?"

"Yes, why?"

"Well, I was theorizing polarity shifts. Sporadic incidences, popping up like acne, forming a head then bursting in various spots."

Colin chuckled. "I like that analogy."

"Thanks. Anyhow . . . what are you doing tomorrow?"

"Since all government agencies are closed on Memorial Day, I'm doing nothing."

"Feel like taking a ride to Beaver County?"

"Why, what's in Beaver?" Colin asked.

"A sister center to my facility. It deals with the environment. They have a nice monitoring station that shows magnetic pulses as they occur, along with weather changes. I thought I'd go and sit for a while. You know me, I'm the solar gal. Since most of our occurrences are happening just before noon...."

Colin chuckled. "Thinking it's the sun?"

"Maybe. What do you say?" she asked.

"Well, since you're riding in from Akron, I'll come up from Pittsburgh. Sort of meet you halfway."

"That's better than no way."

"Hey, that's a Partridge Family song," Colin said.

"Love the Partridge Family."

"Now, see, you are much too young to know them, aren't you? I'll have to guess reruns."

Virginia snickered. "You flatter me."

"I try. Virginia...." Colin took a serious pause. "Thank you. I needed to take my mind off my worries. I love Darius as if he were my kid. In fact, I view him as my only kid."

"Then I know how you feel. If my son was lost out there, I'd go crazy, too. I'll email you the directions."

And she did.

Colin had them on the counter, right on top of his briefcase. He was going to grab a bite to eat then head out. It was a little over an hour drive to Beaver County.

The microwave beeped at the same moment the door bell rang. Foregoing the removal of his food, Colin walked from the kitchen down the long hallway to the foyer of his home.

"Chuck?" He opened the door. "This is a surprise."

"Can I come in?" Chuck asked.

"Absolutely." Colin opened the door wider.

"Glad I caught you."

"You almost didn't. In another fifteen minutes, I was leaving." Colin turned. "Come to the kitchen. I was just about to have my lunch," he spoke as he walked. "Can I fix you some?"

"No thank you."

"A drink?"

"Nah." Chuck shook his head. "Now you mentioned the name of this scientist thing was the Harvard 'I' team?"

"Yes. Why?"

"I had my information correct, then. Anyhow.…" He paused as he watched Colin open the microwave. "You're having hot dogs. You don't strike me as a hot dog guy."

128

"It's Memorial Day. You're supposed to eat hot dogs on Memorial Day."

"On a grill."

"Minor detail." Colin proceeded to fix his food.

"Back to what I was saying. I have been checking the AP newsfeed. Nothing is coming up or has come up with anything unusual going on in Africa. I have a reporter friend who has an in with the CDC. Check this out. The CDC does have a team in that location along with the WHO."

"This is good."

"But…they are denying an outbreak. In fact, they are deeming it educational.…" Chuck said with a raise of his eyebrow. "So I thought. Hey, Darius' reason for being there, right? Educational, Harvard. So I asked. I asked about the Harvard 'I' team."

"And?"

"They didn't know what I was talking about. I then clarified, in case they weren't using that name. But the CDC contact said there are four people down there. Two from the CDC and two from WHO. Educational purposes only."

"So that leaves us with the question."

Chuck nodded. "Is there really nothing going on, or are they covering up?"

"That wasn't the question I was thinking," Colin said. "I was thinking, where is Darius Cobb?"

***

To be taken by immediate, utter surprise, rendered speechless and placed in a temporary state of disbelief. If asked, that would be Bret's definition of shock. Following that, she would say she was not one easily shocked. Frightened, yes, surprised a little—that too. But to be shocked is another story.

Twice she had been completely shocked. The first time occurred two years after she married Jesse. He told her about this great truck a friend of his had for sale. The price was good, parts would cost little, and it needed little if any bodywork. It was the deal of the century. As far as repairs went, Jesse could handle those. Admittedly, to her the price was right at seven hundred dollars, and she knew nothing about trucks. She let him handle it, and after weeks of bragging and 'I love this truck' comments, Jesse brought the truck home.

Now, on that particular day, Bret was in the living room when she heard a bang. Immediately, she wondered who had wrecked. It wasn't a wreck; it was Jesse putting the truck in park. A few noises, not a problem, but when she saw the truck, she almost died.

Could it even be called a truck? It looked older than any living person that she knew. A cross between a flatbed and a pick-up truck, it had no front end and was a hideous shade of maroon.

"Nice, huh?" Jesse smiled. "I love it."

"What is it?" she asked.

"A truck. 1965 Ford Econoline." Jesse nodded.

"Looks older than that."

"What do you think?"

"I think you got ripped off. No wonder it only cost seven hundred bucks. It's ugly as hell."

"Come on now," he said offended then hugged that truck as if she insulted his best friend. "It's a solid piece of transportation."

"Are you really gonna drive that? Jesse, do they even make tires for that anymore?"

"Bret, look at her."

"Her?"

"Betsy."

"You named it?" she asked.

"Not me. Ray's father did. It was his truck."

"And did it belong to Ray's father's father?"

"She's not that old."

"It gives new meaning to May-December romance, Jesse."

Jesse shook his head, smoothed his hand over the truck door. "Everyone will be jealous."

Bret rolled her eyes. "Oh, yeah, we'll be the envy of all our friends."

"See." He gloated. "You see it now?"

"Are you fixing it?"

"Fixing what?"

"The body."

"It's in perfect condition." Jesse lifted a finger as he instructed her. "They stopped making them."

"I see why. It has got to be the most God-awful vehicle I have ever seen."

Jesse's mouth dropped open. "That is so wrong. You know what? Take a ride." He opened the door.

"Ha!" She scoffed. "Get into that. No way. Where are you parking it?"

"Right here."

"I don't think so. That truck is the type people drove to the food line during the Great Depression."

"So much you know. People who were poor didn't have trucks like this back then. So there." He nodded.

"Yeah, well, people who are poor have trucks like this now. So there." She nodded back. "Move it to the alley."

"Bret."

"I hate it." With folded arms Bret walked away. But his showing up with that truck wasn't her shock. She ended up loving that truck. *That* came when Jesse decided it was too much of a pain in the ass to park that behemoth of a vehicle and sold it…to a collector for eight thousand dollars.

That was shock number one. The second came two days before Memorial Day in the mail. Mail she didn't get when Luke grabbed it, and without thinking, carried it to his room. There it stayed until she collected his empty soda cans on Monday.

There were reasons it was a shock. Things seemed back to normal ecologically. But mainly, why was it mailed to her? Finding that envelope

132

was a sign.

In her hurried state, trying to get the house cleaned, macaroni salad done and the kids gathered so they could head to her sister's picnic, it was a normal holiday.

Three soda cans in hand, she spotted the stack of mail on top of Luke's television. "Oh, here's my cable bill. I'm killing him." she said as the large golden brown envelope caught her attention. Getting a grip on the mail, she saw the return address. Africa. 'D. Cobb'. Immediately she took the envelope into her bedroom. Jesse was in there getting dressed.

"What's that?" he asked.

"From Darius." Focused, she opened the envelope. "Feels like pictures."

"Is he back from Africa?"

"This is from Africa." She slid the contents out onto her bed. The exposed edges indicated there were indeed photos in there. Also inside was a sealed white envelope addressed to Bret and a hand written note clipped to the pictures.

The handwritten one read: *You will find these disturbing. But they are a must see for our cause. I need you to research. Is this out yet? More in my letter. Darius.*

Perhaps she should have read the other letter first. She gasped when her eyes set upon the first picture. Mounds upon mounds of bodies, men, women, children. They all looked the same; though the pictures were black and white, clearly their skin was unevenly toned, blotched. Their eyes were wide, their mouths agape, and dark

133

tears, as if blood, flowed from their eyes.

Plague. A new virus? That was the first thought that hit her.

She couldn't help it. She stared at each picture, growing more frightened by the moment. Gasping, whimpering.

"What the hell is he sending you?" Jesse snatched the pictures from her hand. "Something is not right with this guy."

"Jesse, please."

"No, Bret, please. What is this? It's morbid."

"It's reality." She peered up with sad eyes. "This is where he went. This is happening there."

"What? What happened?"

She shook her head, and then with a trembling hand grabbed the envelope and opened the other letter.

It wasn't the plague at all.

His letter read: "Bret: I hope that you opted to open this letter first; if curiosity got the best of you, I apologize. These pictures are deathly vulgar, but they speak a truth. I hope the envelope arrived intact. When I received the call about this situation in Africa, I was able to investigate because it deals with my field of specialty. Never did I expect the magnitude I witnessed. Obviously, the situation had decayed in the mere two days it took me to reach the town. Right now, as I compose this—well protected from what took the lives of those in the photos—another fifty have passed on. They are dropping like flies on a daily basis. On those lines, so are the birds, monkeys, and any other air-breathing creature. By the time you receive this letter, I am certain I will be preparing to return home, leaving a dead area, and witness to over five hundred lost lives. I give thanks to God that this area is remote. What killed these people wasn't an illness of nature, but nature itself. Radiation poisoning...."

Darius went on to say how it wasn't an explosion. In laymen's terms he told of how the radiation had made its way through a vulnerability brought on by a current magnetic reversal our world was experiencing. It hit instantly, the radiation of fifty Hiroshima bombs detonating without the explosion.

An isolated area.

He also explained why he sent her the envelope. She had no scientific background or association with a university. Just on the chance the Africa incident was meant to be kept a secret, her mail was the safest and stood the least chance of being scrutinized.

He included sheets of data that he'd collected. He requested she make copies of everything, secure a set, and distribute the rest to Colin, Chuck and Virginia so everyone could review and contemplate them. Bret was to find out if the story had leaked at all to the public. Darius called it their evidence, and ended his letter with a line that would forever stay with her.

If it happened here...it could happen anywhere. This is scary, Bret. I believe we are in trouble.

***

Bret's mind wasn't on the family picnic at all. Her actions, her lack of speaking gave it away. That and the fact that she snapped out, "Kiss my ass, Jesse." As they walked into the backyard of her sister's home and walked in separate directions, she kept true to her word to John and yelled out, "but I love you."

Jesse gave her an odd look, thought she was being her usual sarcastic self and kept walking away.

How many times did she hear, "Are you okay? You aren't talking." How many times did she want to reply, "No, I'm not. I think the world is ending."? Her family thought her crazy enough; she didn't need to add fuel to their fire.

That envelope didn't leave her side. Luke commented she looked ridiculous wearing the backpack, but all the copies were in there. Though Jesse wouldn't let her drop off copies to Colin, she was able to convince him to go to the copy store en route to the picnic.

Why was Jesse so angry? She wondered.

"It's Memorial Day, Bret!" he shouted in the car. "Not fuckin' death day. Drop it!"

End of that discussion. She vowed that unless it had something to do with work, kids, or keep her promise to John, she wasn't speaking to Jesse.

He was so bitter about it all. Bret had her theory. Jesse was angry because he was frightened. Life was finally going his way, and there she was with some influential scientists stating that the world neared extinction.

Bret rambled. She rattled with enthusiasm, between 'quit hitting your sister,' and 'I can't wait until the meeting'. What started out as a simple conversation where she was trying to impress Jesse with her budding scientific mind turned into a heated moment that could have exploded far worse than any volcanic eruption.

"Cosmic radiation," she explained to him.

"What's that?"

"It's when the rays of the sun make it through the protective layer of our atmosphere."

"Like the hole in the ozone layer."

"Sort of. But the cosmic radiation rays found a weak spot. Darius says there are lots of them now. The sun is what's causing this."

"Causing what?"

"What's happening to the earth. Virginia is convinced it's the sun. Solar flares."

"Dude," Luke poked his head between the front seats. "I saw this show once about a solar flare. It zapped out earth. Burned it completely. But that was right before the sun went nova."

Bret whistled. "If the sun goes nova we're all in deep shit. But we wouldn't know about it."

"So all those people in Africa," Luke asked, "were killed by radiation?"

"Yep." she answered. "Darius says it will happen again. Anywhere, any time."

"What else?" Luke asked.

"The bugs, this is the beginning."

"To?" he questioned further.

"He has a theory. Many. The data collected now will confirm one of those theories. I don't even want to start thinking about them until they know for sure which way we're headed," she said. "Once they figure that out, we'll be able to know what's coming up."

"Are you gonna talk about this at your meeting?" Luke asked.

"Yes."

Jesse mumbled. "Doomsday meeting."

Bret shrugged. "Possibly."

"Can I go?" Luke asked. "Can I sit in?"

"I don't see why not," she replied. "I'd prefer not to take the girls. Casper, Andi, you don't mind, do you? I can fill you in, though."

Casper responded. "Um, I don't think I want to know what's going to happen, Mom."

"Me either." Andi added.

"Suit yourself," Bret said. "Me and Luke will be there. It'll be fun."

Jesse's foot hit the break.

"Is something wrong?" Bret asked him.

"Fun?" he said. "Fun?" his voice raised more. "This end-of-the-world talking is fun?"

"Well, I...."

"Listen to you. Do you hear yourself?"

"It's those pictures," she defended. "They got me excited."

Wrong choice of words.

"Excited?!" he shouted.

She hunched. "In a bad way. Bad way. Geez. Are you sure we can't go to Colin's? He doesn't live far from...."

"No!" Jesse yelled.

Bret closed off her ear. "Yell, why don't you?" she muttered.

Luke snickered.

"No, Bret," he ranted. "Cosmic radiation. Solar flare-ups."

"Flares."

"Whatever. You're scaring the kids. Stop it."

Bret snickered. "The kids could care less. They aren't scared. I think I'm scaring you. Today...." That was all she spoke. Jesse shouted out the line that brought forth total silence in the car.

"Today is Memorial Day. Take a break. Drop it."

She did.

***

"You remember Chuck, don't you?" Colin asked Virginia when she met them in the parking lot of the weather station.

"Of course I do." She smiled politely, shook Chuck's hand, and led them into the plain gray concrete building.

A simple check-in with a normal security guard came first, then off to an elevator that took them down three stories.

"Why the basement?" Colin asked. "Seems kid of weird for a weather station to be underground."

"It was a bunker at one time." Virginia answered. "Of course we could have it upstairs, but we wouldn't be able to track incoming missiles as well. What better place to be."

After a brief look at Chuck, Colin shrugged.

Virginia opened the door. "Here we are."

"Nice set up." Chuck commented.

The large room had two men working. Computers were set up at various workstations. They viewed maps on large-screen monitors. At least ten monitors lined a counter while the printing of data continuously filled the air like background music.

Virginia explained, "The images continually switch. Every ten seconds." She pointed to one monitor. "Like…." The image switched. "Now."

"What if you want to see one?"

"Just pull it up." She replied.

Chuck's finger swirled around the screen. "The multi colors, are those weather patterns?"

"Actually, right now, on these four screens." Virginia said. "Stew here is monitoring polarity. Like here…." She pointed. "This red area is switching."

"Looks like a cyclone." Chuck said.

"It'll be gone in a second."

Virginia was right. The red circle was gone, and she said, "It's Mother Earth reacting to the sun. Change in magnetic fields are normal."

Stew, the tech, spoke up. "This isn't."

Virginia rushed past three monitors. "What do you have?" she asked.

"Northern Canada." Stew replied. "Check it out."

"Whoa." Virginia commented.

"Whoa." Colin repeated sarcastically then turned to Chuck "Whoa would be her scientific reaction to this very large red circle that takes up half of Canada."

"Now what would be happening there because of this?" Chuck asked.

"Good question," Virginia answered. "Stew, anything?"

Stew shook his head. "We have a sub up in that area. Nothing coming in."

"Got something now." Bill, the other technician, spoke. He ripped off a piece of paper. "They sent a watch." He typed in the coordinates.

"Bring it up over here." Virginia requested.

Stew did. "Okay, our area."

Colin observed. "Ohio, West Virginia and Pennsylvania. I'm not up on this, but I see nothing."

Virginia appeared puzzled "Strange. Bill? Anything else? That's a large area."

Bill shook his head. "I'm not seeing what they're talking about. Things are clear as a bell, even on weather...." his head jerked to the right to the three printers spewing out data. "What the hell." He peered at the headers. "From three other subs."

Stew just shook his head. "What are they saying?"

"What's this black dot?" Chuck pointed. "It's moving."

"Glitch?" Colin suggested.

"Cloud?" Chuck guessed.

Stew shook his head "Not the right color. I'll

zoom in." With a few clicks, he brought the image closer. "This is a large mass…shit. It's in the air."

Virginia aimed her voice to Bill. "What are they saying?"

Bill's head slowly shook. "Can't understand. This doesn't make much sense."

Stew added, "This one dot isn't alone. Look…one here and here.…"

Bill slid the papers Stew's way then looked at the monitor. "Those are the areas we got reports from."

"What are the masses?" Virginia asked.

Colin laid his hand on Stew's shoulder. "Can you concentrate on one? This one here." He indicated. "It's close to Pittsburgh. Give me a general area, and get in close."

"I'll try." Stew replied.

"May I?" Colin reached for the papers and lifted them.

"Whatever this mass is, it's slowing and looks like it may stall south of Pittsburgh." Stew said.

"How far south?" Colin asked.

"Five miles."

"Let's call Bret," Colin said. "To see if she sees anything. Something that large is gonna be visual very short.…" his paused, looked at the paper, then to the screen again. "Shit. Magnetic field disturbance." He laid down the paper and lifted his phone. "I know what that is."

***

The pickle protruded from the edge of the hamburger bun. It caught Bret's eye and she found herself staring at it. Round, off edge, sort of like the earth was.

"Something wrong with the pickle?" her sister Aggie asked.

"Huh?" Bret snapped out of her daze.

"Bug?" She snickered. "Whoops. Wrong word."

"Ha ha ha. No. The pickle is fine. I was staring at it and the burger."

"Can I ask why?"

"It's there."

"Okay," she said.

"You know, ground meat alone doesn't really hold together."

"Not well. You need eggs, bread crumbs."

"True," Bret said. "We take for granted when we buy a hamburger that there is something inside of it that will make it firm and stay together," she rambled. "But say the cook starts taking out a little of those bread crumbs and eggs each week, just a little. We won't notice the gradual change. Before we know it, eventually he'd omit all the eggs and breadcrumbs and the hamburger will...fall apart."

Aggie just stared.

"So many questions over this," Bret said.

"The hamburger?"

Bret nodded. "Could we have stopped it if there was a way? On the other hand, had it progressed too far before we had a chance to notice it? Is the hamburger salvageable? If it isn't and there's no way to save it, can we still eat the hamburger? Yes, but it isn't a hamburger anymore. It's just ground beef. However…if it forever stays that way, generations to come will never know the hamburger the way we know the hamburger. Make sense?"

Aggie exhaled, stood up, and aimed her voice across the yard. "Jesse! Bret is really gone." She walked away.

Her eyes strayed to where Aggie darted. The kids were across the yard, diving in and out of the pool. Bret was chilled, and swimming was not an option.

"I understood, Mom." Luke sat down.

"You did?"

"You were making an analogy to what's happening."

"Yes, I was."

He nodded and winked. "A little advice. You have to let people know you're making an analogy or you won't make sense."

Bret started to laugh but stopped when her phone rang. "You have a point," she said and grabbed the phone. "Hello?

A high-pitched whistle, like feedback, rang out.

Bret cringed, pulled the phone away and then heard her name.

"Bret. Bret."

Bret returned to listening, but only the clicking sound of the call breaking up flowed through the receiver. "Hello."

"Bret. This is Colin."

"Colin. Bad connection."

Empty air. Static. Then: "Reason. Are…outside."

"Am I outside? Yes, why?"

"Get…. Understand? Get…side…now. Magnet…cause…direction…bad. Sat…lite picked it up. Centered…area."

Bret shook her head. "Colin." She started to snicker. "Are you joking with me?" Covering the mouthpiece she looked at Luke. "That Colin is so funny. Where you at? Wanna join us for burgers?"

"Bret odd…am it."

Bret's head cocked back; something about the tone got her attention. "Colin, is something wrong?'

"Duh."

That came out clear as a bell. Bret glanced at Luke, "He just said duh to me."

"What aren't you understanding?"

Bret shrugged and tried to communicate with Colin again, "You want me to do what?"

"Get…side."

"Get inside?"

"Yes," he spoke, rushed.

"Why?"

"Swarms. Attack. Magnet…. Direction."

"Oh, my God." Bret stood up as she figured it out. She hurriedly spoke to Luke. "We have a swarm attacking."

"How's he know?" Luke asked.

"Colin, how do you know?" she asked.

"Sat…lite at Virginia…station…."

"Oh." Bret sang out knowingly. Then…. Pause. "Satellite? God, it must be huge to be seen

145

on satellite."

"Huge. Possibly deadly."

"Are they bees? Hornets?"

Nothing.

"Colin."

Silence. A dead phone.

Thump.

Phone sliding slowly from her ear, Bret looked for the noise. Not one foot from her lay a dead bird.

"Shit," she said.

Luke stood. "Flock. Not swarm."

"Everyone in the house!" she screamed "Get in the house now!" She scurried for the kids. "In the house!"

Does it ever really work? Screaming out something and having everyone immediately halt their actions and follow the dictate?

No.

Everyone looked at her as if she were insane.

"Bret?" Jesse called out. He stood up from his seat poolside. "What the hell is the matter with you?'

Squawk.

Swooping down like a torpedo with precision—it even sounded like one—the bird sailed fast and furiously straight into Jesse. The beak nailed him in the head and knocked him off balance.

One bird. It started with one bird. Bret screamed, the kids screamed. In the moment of confusion, it happened.

Aggie whispered out, "Oh my God."

The word swarm truly was the best description. So many birds, squawking, squealing, meshed together so there was no way to distinguish individual sounds. The bright Memorial Day sun was suddenly blacked out.

Then it started.

"Grab the kids! Get in the house!" Bret shouted.

Jesse, blood dripping down his face, scooped up Andi. Aggie grabbed her youngest boy. Luke grabbed his three-year-old cousin. The oldest nephew, ten, jumped from the pool and was the number one target. Twenty, thirty and even more birds raged after him. He ran, swinging out his arms as his dad, Greg, aided in the battle.

Greg then came under attack.

Was it Jesse? Luke? Bret didn't know. Someone grabbed her arms, but she couldn't move. Her eyes were focused on Casper. She didn't get out of the pool; she dove underwater.

Crying out for Casper, Bret felt a peck on her cheek, then her arm. She was engulfed within moments, blackened by the birds that landed on her like a loaf of bread.

Everything happened too fast. Bret, pulled and confused, fought both the birds and the person trying to help her

Suddenly the bird noise was muffled, and it was replaced with crying. She was in her sister's house.

The kids were hysterical. Aggie was asking, "Is everyone okay?"

It was chaos.

"What the hell is happening?" Greg yelled out. "What's going on?"

Breathing heavily, Bret scanned the room. "Casper." She wasn't there, so Bret dove for the door. Jesse blocked her.

"Let me go." Bret fought him. "Casper!" Her call carried out.

"Bret!" he barked, trying to snap her out of it. Grabbing her face, he made her look out the window. "She's in the pool."

The black and brown avian-covered yard exposed only one recognizable thing, the underground swimming pool. The birds flew around it but avoided it.

"Birds can't swim," Jesse said. "She knows that. She's smart. She's safer there. If we go out and get her, we put her and ourselves in harm's way the second we get her out of the pool."

Even though she was safe, Bret felt helpless. How frightened Casper had to be. She stayed in the center of the pool, her head exposed, showing the scared expression on her face as she shifted her eyes back and forth quickly, watching, shivering. When they came for her, she dived down.

Some birds showed no fear; they shot into the pool like rocks. They were kamikaze pilots determined in their mission. Casper was the mission of every bird out there.

In a state of suspense, they all watched out the window. The birds were preoccupied; they didn't come for the house.

The ringing tone made Bret nearly jump from

her skin. Still clutching the phone, she answered it. "Hello?"

"Did they hit?" Colin asked.

Her hand pressed against the pane of glass. "We were attacked."

"Is everyone all right?" Colin questioned.

"A few scrapes. But... no. Colin, my daughter is out there. She's in the pool."

"Then she's safe; birds can't swim. Is she staying mainly below the water?"

"Yes."

"She'll be fine."

"But for how long? How long will this last?" she questioned with desperation.

"Last satellite image showed it breaking up. A few more minutes, Bret," he said. "It won't be long. It'll be over."

Bret took some comfort in Colin's words. Nevertheless, even though a few minutes wasn't really a long length of time, it seemed like an eternity as she watched her child—alone—avert the danger that pounded relentlessly at her.

***

Blain Davis had just pulled on the Pennsylvania turnpike heading east when the call came through. Mouth full of take-out, he used the hands-free method to take the call.

"Hey, Mom."

"Mom?" The woman on the other end spoke. "I know I'm older than you, but I don't believe

149

I'm old enough to be your mother."

Quickly Blain checked out the number on the phone. "Sorry, I thought you were someone else."

"Obviously," she said. "You still have my cameraman, or did you ditch him on a highway."

Blain lifted his head to the rear view mirror. He gazed by his own young, handsome reflection to the complete contrast in the back seat. Doug Swanson, Vietnam vet with long hair, was highly intelligent, but he always acted as if he were stoned.

"Depends," Blain replied. "He's physically here. Sleeping right now."

"Good," she said.

"Why?" Blain asked.

"I know you're headed back to New York." Shirley McConnell answered. As head Story Editor, she had achieved the nickname, 'Shit' McConnell amongst the younger reporters at the highly-regarded Central News Station. Blain never knew why, but he was about to find out.

"Yes, I am," Blain said.

"Do you like Hitchcock?"

"Um…uh.…" Blain stuttered. "I guess, why?"

"Good. Get off at the next exit, turn around and head back to Pittsburgh," she explained. "They just relived one of his old classics."

***

Like an ice cream jerk, Chuck scooped Blain

Davis. Big time, too. Not only was Chuck present at the satellite center, he had close personal contact with a family who had experienced the bird attack first-hand. Not to mention the cool video Aggie took. That, Chuck sold to the highest bidder.

Blain was not happy about that, but he was not giving up. He did a small piece but was informed by Shirley to stay and follow up.

"Not here," Jesse said, hung up the phone, and held the rag to his head. "Reporter. How'd he get this number?"

Chuck shrugged. "It's listed."

"Where's the duct tape?" Jesse asked.

"He needs stitches." Chuck pointed.

"I know," Bret said. "But duct tape works well, too."

"Back to work," Chuck tapped a pen on the sheet of paper. "I have to get this and those pictures to the AP. Pronto. What do you think?"

Bret lifted the sheet of paper, and then glanced down to the photos which were taken from the video and satellite center, photos of black clouds which were large flocks of birds. Bret read out loud: "The attack was centered in one area in the metropolis of Pittsburgh. At one point, a six-block section of town was completely encompassed by the birds." Bret nodded. "This is good," she said, then read silently, finishing the last line aloud. "It was something straight out of Alfred Hitchcock. And as with Hitchcock, the bird attack stopped without notice and flew off, leaving Pittsburgh waiting and wondering would it happen again?" She laid the paper down. "Very good. Can it?"

"Happen again?" Chuck clarified.

"Yeah."

"Colin said unlikely."

"Did he say why?" Bret asked.

"Simple. Birds were migrating early from the north to the south. Not for weather changes, but for food."

"Wait. For food?"

"Yeah. With the ground temperature warming, the attacking insects suddenly became dead insects. Eggs and larva, along with the adult bugs, couldn't survive the slight temperature increase. Without the bugs, rats, mice, squirrels, and birds had a hard time feeding; so they searched for other sources of food?

"Us."

"Well…." Chuck tilted his head then went on to explain what Colin informed him: The migration would have taken the birds south without incident, except the recent solar flares—not uncommon—caused magnetic stress and electromagnetic pulses. Birds work on the magnetic pull of waves of sound. Their sense of direction was lost. In fact, their entire perception was lost. Starving birds became confused, scared, and disoriented; then they suddenly became violent.

The poolside attack was just one of many. Casper was a shivering mess when the birds finally flew away. A few scratches graced her face, nothing major. They commended her on her quick thinking, attributing her common sense to saving her life. She attributed her fear to that, saying she was just too scared to get out of the pool that she didn't even think about the birds not being able to swim.

Bret was in a mesmerized state listening to Chuck. So much so, that when Jesse laid his hand on her shoulder she jumped a foot in the air with a shriek.

"What the hell are you telling her?" Jesse asked Chuck then showed Bret the phone. "Can you please talk to this guy?"

"Am I allowed?" Bret asked Chuck.

Chuck glanced at his watch. "Yeah go on, I'll send it now." He scooted over and opened his laptop.

After a breath, Bret took the call. "Hello?"

It wasn't a long conversation. It started out with her asking his credentials then making him wait while she watched CNS for a few minutes to see his report. Then she spoke to him. She agreed to meet Blain Davis within an hour to share the story. Bret was a star in it all because she was being called by the media the 'Attractor', first the bugs, then the birds. The fact that she was a DJ didn't hurt.

When the call was finished she informed Jesse that she was meeting Blain; he made Bret promise to take Chuck.

Not a problem. But where was Chuck? He had slipped out onto the front porch and Bret found him standing at the railing staring out.

"I agreed to meet Blain. Jesse says you have

to come."

Chuck nodded.

"Something wrong?"

"Listen," he said. "Just listen."

Bret folded her arms and stepped closer to Chuck. "I don't hear anything."

"Exactly."

"What do you mean?" Bret asked.

"Quiet. No sounds. An eerie silence has taken over the world—or at least our part of it," he said, nearly dazed.

Bret sighed out heavily. "I didn't notice."

"Do we ever? We taken them for granted. You know something is different, but you can't put your finger on it. This is it."

"The silence."

"Yep." He nodded once then looked at her. "It's scary. A world without birds, rodents, and insects is not only a silent world, Bret, but it's fast becoming a dying world as well."

***

The four-day trip returning from Africa required nothing more than a bed for Darius to sleep on. He was tired of hard ground, and though sloppy, unmade, it didn't matter, he wanted his bed.

He wasn't a firm believer in signs, although occasionally he'd admit to receiving them.

From the moment he left Africa, he was bombarded with signs. He ignored them, but admitted he should have paid closer attention. If he had he would have been ready for when he arrived home.

They were attacked by rebels en route to the city, then the small plane ran out of gas and they had to crash land.

The crash landing was followed by a truck ride full of soldiers who'd spent forty sweaty days in the jungle. Finally a plane out of Africa brought him to the United Kingdom where he went through a twenty-four hour quarantine for typhoid.

A comfy seat on the way back to America was the only positive thing. They served ham—a dish Darius hates.

Three times he called Colin, once from the UK, and Colin assured him he would be there at the airport to get him.

After a two hour wait and with no answers from Colin's phone, Darius realized Colin was a no show. So he took a cab.

The fare was high, although not a problem; he had enough cash on hand to cover it. He unloaded from the cab, walked up his path and stopped.

'This is a joke.' Darius thought when he saw the white sheets of paper plastered all over his windows and door. Was someone protesting him?

The month old stack of mail was falling out of the screen door when Darius pulled it open. Like a flood through a broken dam the letters rushed out and the return addresses and emblem for University of West Virginia caught his attention.

Believing it was important—it looked official—Darius opened it before even going in the house.

"What?" he said aloud upon reading the letter. "Since I failed to reply to their final attempt to talk to me…when?" Darius peered down, ran his foot through the stack of mail and saw several other letters from the university. "Oh, there they are." Further examination of the envelope in hand, brought the surprise appearance of a hefty check. Darius whistled. "At this point in time, the severance works." He tilted his head, smiled, and tucked the envelope in his back pocket—check and all.

Perhaps he should have read one of the many white letters posted on his house. Had he done so, the padlock on his front door wouldn't have been such a shock.

Ripping the notice from the screen door, Darius chuckled. "Condemned. Figures." With a 'well' spoken in stride, Darius stepped back, set down his bag, and looked at his house. "Good thing I don't have much." After examining his car and determining it was big enough to lug his belongings, Darius went around to the back of the house and broke in.

***

Class was back in session the next day, and Colin wanted to get to sleep early. The day had been horrendous, the news reports on CNS kept him up way past when he wanted to slumber. Plus he had this overwhelming feeling that he was forgetting something.

He discovered what that 'something' was when his doorbell rang.

"Shit!" Colin yapped when he opened the door. "I forgot to pick you up."

Darius smiled. "Yes, you did."

Colin peeked out. "Did you drive all the way up here to bitch at me?"

"No, can I come in?"

"Absolutely." Colin widened the door for Darius.

As Darius stepped in he saw Colin ready to lock the door. "No, don't. I have to go back out and get my things."

"Are you staying the night?"

Darius set down his guitar. "And some. I'm living here now."

"Excuse me?"

"I lost my job," Darius said. "Failure to report."

Colin cringed. "You should have seen that coming."

"I did. Not a big deal in the scheme of things. And...my house was condemned while I was gone."

"You should have seen that coming, as well. You didn't...you didn't by any chance purchase more pets and forget about them, did you."

Darius stared at Colin.

"You did!" Colin whined. "Ah, Darius, learn some responsibility."

"Ha!" Darius laughed. "Responsibility. You forgot about me at the airport. How responsible is that?"

"Well, not very, but I had a good reason."

"Which is?" Darius asked.

"Birds attacked Pittsburgh," Colin waved his hand. "I'll get into it later. Come to the kitchen; I bet you're hungry."

Darius followed him. "Birds attacked Pittsburgh?"

"Yeah, all over the news, too. Your little friend Bret is the focus."

"No way." Darius nodded. "Was any one hurt?"

"Not seriously. Hot dog?" Colin opened the fridge. "I have some left from today's Memorial Day feast."

"Yeah, sure." Darius slid on a bar stool. "Was it magnetically related?"

"Bingo." Colin popped open the microwave. "Solar flare…sun spot thing."

"The frequency will increase," Darius said. "We know this. Has anything been said at all about…."

Colin shook his head. "Not a thing."

"It has got to be on everyone's mind. People have to be wondering what the hell is going on."

"Basically, I don't believe people are wondering what's going on. I believe they just want a scientific explanation they can accept, believe, and then they move on."

"Only one problem with that," Darius said.

Colin nodded his agreement. "If we give them our scientific explanation to believe… how *can* they move on?"

THE BLAIN REPORT

May 26th ...

'Thank you, Brenda. If the word 'mayhem' was derived from a crazy month of May some years ago, then this past month certainly reiterates that. From multitudes of rising ants across the northeast, birds in the 'burg, to what you see behind me. For the past two hours, hundreds of students have gathered on the campus of this West Virginia University to protest the firing of Professor Darius Cobb, who was officially released this morning from his head of Ecological Studies position. Professor Cobb is nowhere to be found; however, these students are making their voices heard. Carrying signs, promising candlelight vigils, and chanting, 'Bring back Darius Cobb'. One student even told me that they'll stay as long as it takes. Officials here at the university are citing just cause in releasing Professor Cobb from his contract. He disappeared a couple weeks back for Africa and other than a simple phone call today, no one has seen or heard from him. What makes it all so interesting is that Professor Cobb disappeared at the beginning of the month too, taken under the watchful eye of the CDC when he was attacked in one of the freak cockroach incidents. This is Blain Davis, live from West Virginia University, Morgantown. Back to you, Brenda.'

10 - SHIFTING

May 27th ...

Bret wasn't a rocket scientist, nor did she need to be to figure out who 'DC' was when the call was placed to her station while she was taking listener calls on the topic of depression.

"The answer you seek will be found," he said cryptically.

Bret looked at her producer, then at the screen which revealed why he called. Simply typed in was one word, 'answer'. Figuring they must have really been desperate for calls if they let such a vague one through, Bret prodded.

"Answer? What answer?"

"To it all, to the end, to the beginning, who knows."

Just as she began to think, 'what a fruitcake', she looked the name. "DC', the ever so slight hick accent that laced the voice like a country singer, she shook her head. "So, uh, DC. What's the answer?"

"Tomorrow. Two. Catch it at the Rye."

Click.

Bret put it together. Rye. Reye. Colin's house, the next day at two. After murmuring, 'what an asshole,' she pressed the next line. "Next caller, Jeanie. You're live with Divine."

The cryptic Professor Cobb didn't answer her

call or email, and contacting Colin only bred, "He's an idiot. Yeah, he wants to meet here."

So Bret went.

She took Luke for the trip. Having met Colin mainly in public places, it was the first time she had seen his impressive home. She even commented as she pulled in the driveway, "A man who lives alone shouldn't be permitted to have a house this big." She stopped. "Scratch that. Bet me Darius is homeless now and moved in."

"How can you tell?" Luke asked.

"His car is packed. He hasn't unpacked it," she muttered on the way to the door. "He's probably been here for days."

She rang the bell.

Brightly, Colin answered the door, "Ah, Bret. You're early."

"A little. I was curious. Colin, this is my son, Luke."

"Luke." Colin greeted him with handshake. "And…why aren't you in school?"

"Oh, my mom let me cut out for this." Luke nodded proudly.

Responding to Colin's grumble with a 'hmm', Bret waved her hand at him. "Anyhow. Do you know what's going on?" she asked.

"I wish I did." Colin finally shut the door. "Trust me; he's been as secretive with me as he's been with everyone else." He led them down a hall. "I've known Dare-Dare since he was Luke's age. He always has to be the first and he always has to be right. Want something to drink?"

"God, I'd love coffee. I worked last night.

But…I'm sure you knew that." Bret said. "Dare-Dare called the station."

"He's an idiot." Colin poured her some coffee.

Luke said, "So you don't know what's happening with the earth. That's what he wants to meet us for, right?"

"Correct," Colin replied. "He is finalizing his figures. I know which way he's going, but I promised I'd let him reveal since he's the one who came up with it. And…he has me and Virginia pulling verification material. That's what he's doing now in his wonder world."

Bret looked quizzically.

"This way," Colin said and opened a door adjacent to the kitchen. "He's gone overboard. But then again, that's our Dare-Dare."

Bret and Luke followed Colin down a flight of stairs, and after Colin knocked once on a door, he walked in.

"Dare-Dare. The first of the team is here."

Without turning around, Darius said, "Is it Bret?"

Colin smiled sinisterly. "How'd I know you'd ask for her first?"

"Whoa," Luke commented as he stepped in.

"Whoa is right," Bret too commented on the former family room. It no longer looked like a place to dwell and watch television, but rather a sophisticated computer lab. Images of the earth, maps and so forth graced each computer screen while readouts from noisy printers continuously flowed out.

163

"Colin," Bret said in awe. "Is this all yours?"

Colin pointed to Darius. "His. He's been buying it since yesterday. Hasn't been to bed yet. Hence why he called late last night on your program."

"I got it all in synch now. Just printing up," Darius said.

"I thought you were unemployed." Bret commented. "How did you afford all this?"

"Well, I was gonna use my money," Darius clicked away at the computer, eyes on the screen. "But I'll need that. So I just used the credit cards and applied for more. I have lots of it now. Instant credit. You have to love it."

"If you can get it," Bret said. "How are you gonna pay for the cards?"

"I'm not worried about it," Darius replied. "What the hell is seventy thousand? Probably be more later," he spoke nonchalantly.

Bret gasped. "Seventy.... Well, if you have that attitude, let me borrow one of those cards, I need a new TV."

Seemingly without thinking, Darius reached into his back pocket, pulled out his wallet and blindly handed it to Bret. "Take the platinum one."

"Wow. Thanks."

"Mom," Luke scolded. "You can't do that."

"He gave it." Bret spoke tough clenched teeth. "We need a new TV. Jesse beat the other one too bad."

"Dare-Dare," Colin finally spoke up. "Bret brought her son, Luke. He was allowed to cut school for this."

"I would have let him too," Darius said. "In fact...." Finally he turned and faced everyone. He ran his fingers through his hair and smiled. "I'd just take him out now."

"Yes, dude." Luke clenched his fist. "I like this guy."

Again, Darius smiled then just rattled off. "I mean, it really doesn't matter, and there probably won't be any school by the end of the summer anyhow. Left to go to I mean. Maybe." He shrugged and faced the computer again. "Latest October."

"What?" Bret asked. "Darius, that's not funny."

Over his shoulder, Darius peered at her solemnly. "And neither is what's about to happen."

Virginia and Chuck arrived, and they all took a seat around Colin's glass dinette table.

Darius—as expected—started things off. He held a bag. "I have a gift for each of you. Call it cheesy, but it's part of my demonstration." He walked around the circle handing out his black treats and continued speaking. "I know we've all worked on theories as to what is occurring. I believe we've collected enough data to make educated guesses. I want to share mine. My gift is my introduction."

Bret looked down to the object placed in her hand, a compass.

"Mom?" Luke called her attention as he tapped the face of the compass. "Mine is broke."

Bret pulled out her compass. Oddly, the needle bobbed, and when the compass was turned the needle barely moved. "Mine too."

"They aren't broke," Darius said. "They represent what is going on with our world."

Luke turned his compass and played with it. "The world is going in a wrong direction?" he questioned.

"In a sense, yes. My trip to Africa confirmed my fears. At first, I believed Earth was tilting on its axis. Colin believed we were finally feeling the effects of global warming."

"if you believe in global warming." Colin interjected. "I believed it was the misalignments of the planets and the fact that the moon is now ten more thousand miles away. I was looking astronomically at the geological changes. That is where I went. OK, so I was wrong. Don't rub it in, Dare-Dare, you're living in my house. Then again, I still don't know what you're building to."

Darius cleared his throat. "Yours was a good theory. I'm not rubbing anything in. My thinking should have been there as well. It wasn't. Yours helped me though. That's where Virginia came in—sort of."

"I helped?" Virginia asked with surprise. "I didn't think I did anything. I thought Colin thinking in the right direction."

Colin gave a smug look.

"He was." Darius nodded. "We needed a tie-in. Something that connected both theories, mine and his."

"Oh." Virginia sang out. "That. Okay. It was simple."

Darius smiled. "Elementary."

"Then I must be in kindergarten." Bret raised her hand. "Space? The solar system is causing this. And how in the world did the moon drift ten thousand more miles away."

"We don't know." Virginia answered. "But I only suggested what tied magnetic reversals to the solar systems."

"And as you saw by my basement...." Colin added. "Dare-Dare more than likely worked out the fine details."

Up went Bret's hands in defeat. "Then why am I here? Chuck, too."

Darius answered. "Research and supportive information."

Chuck finally spoke. "Excuse me?"

"You guys are research. I need both of you; while we're working on the other aspects, you two have to put together a list of every freakish geological event and natural disaster that has occurred recently."

"Why?" Chuck asked.

"Because watching what happens lets us see the path of what is going to happen. Also, you two are the voices. You can get the word out."

Colin snapped his finger. "And don't forget that big CNS reporter who's been snooping around. He did a wonderful piece on you, Dare-Dare."

Bret, lost, shook her head. "What are we

gonna get out? You said you know what's happening. You know what's going on."

"I believe I do." Darius replied. "But to get there, many other things must occur. Collecting data, information, can help us predict the when and where of such events."

Virginia added. "Predicting the when and where's will help in saving lives and getting people more prepared."

Colin spoke, "But we need to build a concrete case, present it to our government, so they can do something about this."

Quizzically Bret glanced at Colin. "I thought you didn't know what was gonna happen."

Colin shrugged. "I don't. But no matter what, my phrase fits. Whatever it is has to be big. Right?"

"Right. But . . . ." Bret questioned. "Whatever it is, can it be stopped?"

Darius shook his head. "Hardly. We can't stop it. We can only prepare for it, and figure out a way to have as many lives as possible."

Annoyed, Colin huffed out. "Now that you've gone around it a million and a half times, quit being melodramatic and get to the point. What is going to happen? Please."

Slightly irritated, Darius asked, "May I explain to Bret and Chuck what has happened first?"

Grumbling, Colin agreed.

Darius went on, "When I went to Africa, my revelation of cosmic radiation, and the documented cases, confirmed that a window

168

opened up in our magnetic shield, a window big enough to let the cosmic rays through. We're fortunate; anything stronger could have scorched Earth." Darius pointed to the compasses. "The reason the needle is bobbing so predominantly is because the world is experiencing magnetic reversals."

Luke perked up. "Oh, dude. I heard about that. North will be south. South will be north. Things shift around."

"Yes," Darius replied. "Takes tens of thousands of years to reach the full point. That is where we are. What causes this? Solar flares. Solar flares cause magnetic disturbances. Virginia?" he pointed at her.

Virginia answered, "When Darius asked me about recent sun activity, I was shocked. Our sun has been producing an enormous amount of flares, ranging from small to large. Though this is common, lately it's been out of the norm, but so gradually that we didn't notice."

Colin added, "Solar flares cause not only the magnetic disturbances, but electromagnetic pulses, EMPs. These effect electricity. Cause storms, blackouts, and power surges. You name it. They also cause magnetic fluxes within our earth and atmosphere. These are pockets of simulated magnetic reversals without getting into the full-blown reversals. Understand?"

Bret nodded. "Like an outbreak of the flu in Paris, is a simulation of a full blown epidemic."

"Yes," Colin said. "In an odd analogy. Instead of it being worldwide, only patches occur in certain area."

Darius added, "Ecologically, these patches cause the radiation poisoning that we saw in Africa. The bizarre hurricanes starting already."

Luke asked. "The ants and roaches?"

"Ah," Darius smiled. "Yes. Pockets or patches. The shift in some magnetic fields and disturbances brought on by solar flares causes earthquakes, volcanic eruptions. But the shift of tectonic plates are occurring underground."

"The earth heats up." Luke said. "The ground is hot, the bugs come up."

"Exactly," Darius pointed with a smile. "The bugs can't live, those animals who feed on them search out other food. Everything up north, because of these changes, is dying. The birds as Colin explained were just hungry, and then an EMP occurred, and magnetic flux, they lost their direction and sense. Hence the attack."

Bret spoke to get clarification, "So these fluxes as you call them. Magnetic shifts, solar flares, they are just causing earth disturbances. We're to expect more?"

"Lots more." Darius said. "See, this is just the beginning. Eventually, these teases, the fluxes and pulses will generate enough disturbances to cause the full blown magnetic reversal, and when that happens…." He whistled.

Quickly, Chuck looked at Bret. "He just . . . whistled. Is that a scientific term?"

Bret nudged him.

Colin explained. "He whistled because he knows."

"Knows what?" Chuck asked.

Darius replied, "What magnetic reversals can do. You cannot have magnetic reversals without magnitudes of destruction. We can monitor where the natural events occur and watch. It will eventually form a pattern that we can follow as a path to what is next. We'll soon be able to predict what will happen, when it will happen and the severity. It's gonna be like a guessing game."

"What kind of things will you predict will happen?" Bret asked.

"We're in for a rough ride," Colin said. "Magnetic reversals cause shifts."

"More than that." Darius took over. "These disturbances build up and up until we have a complete magnetic reversal. The compasses indicate that it is happening now. Magnetic reversals cause earthquakes. Tsunamis. Super storms. Breaks in protective fields like that experienced in Africa. Major underwater volcanic eruptions. These volcanic eruptions are the final occurrences. They will heat up earth's surface while causing enormous water loss in our oceans. My stats now allow me to predict that we will lose at least thirty percent of our oceans in a short span of time. Two months. Two months from the start puts us in September-October. Weather is cooler."

"Whoa. Whoa. Whoa." Colin stood up. "No. I see where you're going with this. This is nuts. It's a prediction of centuries."

Chuck's head spun. "What? I'm lost. You?" he asked of Bret.

She only shook her head.

Colin was adamant. "No way, Dare-Dare. No way."

"Yes, yes way." Darius insisted. "Think about it. Solar flares cause disturbances, storms, earthquakes volcanic eruptions. Volcanoes heat the earth; we then have melting up north. Glaciations. Meaning glaciers shift and move. The underwater volcanoes heat our oceans, kill our fish, and the water then evaporates." With a snap of his finger he pivoted his body. "Luke, where does the water go?"

Colin mumbled sarcastically, "Ah, yes, let's ask the boy who doesn't go to school."

Ignoring Colin, Luke answered with awe. "Up. Into the atmosphere."

"Basic law of Newton." Darius said. "What goes up must come down."

"Dude," Luke sat back. "If the ice up north is melting, the oceans evaporate and go into the sky, then all that water…Noah's ark all over again."

"Fuck." Colin whispered.

Bret's eyes widened. "Is he right? No."

Colin covered his eyes.

"Luke, that's a very good deduction." Darius patted Luke's back. "It would be one hundred percent correct if…if this all began in January. This is going to come full circle in the fall. Temperatures drop. When water is cold, it no longer is rain."

Colin interjected with a fake crying whine. "Three inches of rain equals thirty inches of snow."

Arrogantly, Darius smiled. "Snow. Correct.

Nature has a way of irradiating things. Making changes. Like clockwork every twenty-six million years magnetic reversals occur. Oddly enough, coinciding with these reversals are mass extinctions. We're at that twenty-six million year mark. We're in the midst of another reversal. This means we're in the midst of facing another mass extinction. What we're experiencing right now is nothing less than events leading up to a good old fashioned...." Darius paused and smiled smugly, "ice age."

THE BLAIN REPORT

June 4th …

"If you are having difficulty hearing me, that's because the winds here are gusting at times up to 75 miles an hour. This morning, they exceeded over a hundred. We have been advised to stay indoors, as have all the folks here in Charleston, WV, which I plan to do as soon as I finish this broadcast. But, I'll tell you Brenda, the rain, the raging river, one would not know this little city was so far inland. Experiencing Hurricane Daniel in Charleston…I'm Blain Davis. Back to you."

11 - PLANS

June 8ᵗʰ ...

Trying to get out of his car—which he hoped he parked close enough—Chuck fumbled with his camera, recorder, and paper all while listening to Bret. "Bret, just…."

"What will we become? I've been thinking about this. Have you?"

"Um, yes, but right now . . . ."

"The next woolly mammoths? Art work on a museum wall millions of years in the future? A viewable anomaly that the strange new breed of humans gawk at and say, 'We looked like that'?"

"Good Lord, Bret. Now you're overreacting. Haven't we decided that we will not become a statistic? The human race will go on, if we're smart and well-prepared. Isn't that what you're doing? Aren't you there yet?"

"Almost," she said. "I was driving and thinking. How about you? How's Albany?"

"I'm here. I'm not seeing any press…yet. In fact, I see only locals."

"Have you seen it yet?" Bret asked.

"Closing in on the crowd . . . wait. Shit."

"You see it."

"No."

"You can't see it?" Bret questioned.

"Bret, damn it," Chuck complained. "Did you

tell him again?"

"Who?"

"Blain Davis."

Silence.

"You did," Chuck said.

"Well.…"

"Bret, fuck," he griped. "This is mine. He scooped me on the Charleston bit. Darius is giving me the heads up on his finds. I'm the geo boy, remember. Not him. I'm the first here. Not him. Darius is the only one able to figure out what's going on, and he's giving me the info first. It's not intended for Blain Davis, CNS superstar."

"Chuck, please. He asked where you were."

"Why couldn't you tell him Cleveland or something?"

"All I said was Albany."

"In which he asked why I'm in Albany?"

Bret stuttered. "He uh…well, yeah."

"I'm not telling you anymore. When Darius sees an area stirring, I'll wait."

"Ha. Darius tells me."

"Well, then open your mouth one more time and I'll tell Jesse I think you have the hots for Blain, that's why you're giving him info."

"Ha, ha, ha, again." Bret said. "Jesse saw Blain. Met him. Sees no threat. Won't work."

"OK, he hasn't met Darius or Colin. What can I make up about them? Plus the fact you aren't telling Jesse it all."

Silence again.

Chuck laughed.

"Tattletale."

"Bye."

"It's only a crack in the ground, Chuck."

"Bye." Chuck disconnected the call, put his phone away and walked through the hordes of people. His main destination was Blain Davis, and he'd almost reached it when he saw the reason for his Albany visit.

The main street of Albany had lifted. A huge crack was not only on the surface of the street, but it went deep within the earth, like an earthquake had hit. Darius told him about the shifting in that area, even the fact that seismology was indicating something big. But thus far the only big thing was the crack in the street. Which…was pretty phenomenal.

"Chuck Wright?" Blain extended his hand.

Chuck showed his full hands. "Can't or I'd shake. What are you doing here?"

"I heard a big geological occurrence is gonna happen."

"Was." Chuck corrected. "It did. See the crack in the road? Now you can go. No big deal."

"I know you're getting information from Darius Cobb."

Chuck only stared.

"Come on, Chuck. Brotherhood of journalism here. What's up?"

Shrugging, Chuck shook his head. "Don't know. This is it. Take a picture. Not much. Darius was…."

Before he could finish his words, a slight rumble sounded followed by a vibration beneath their feet.

"Get back!" a fire fighter called out. "People step back."

"Did it lift?" Blain asked. "It doesn't look like it lifted anymore."

"I have to find witnesses," Chuck said. "See if anyone felt anything when this happened."

"No, the two men one block away having a beer only saw it when they left the bar." Blain spoke. "They...."

He paused when another rumble hit.

Blain continued, "They were shocked."

"Maybe they were half-crocked." Chuck started. "I bet this one registered a 5 on the Richter scale which is pretty big."

"No one felt it."

"Bullshit." Chuck snapped. "You're lying because you got a story."

"You're lying. There was no 5 on the Richter."

"Was too." Chuck said.

"Was not."

"I'm telling...."

It knocked him off his feet. In fact the jolt was so strong that the fifty people standing around bobbed, swayed, fell like dominoes.

"It's lifting!" an emergency worker cried out. "Back. Back up!" His arms and those of others shoved the crowd back.

Chuck raised his camera. "Holy shit."

The left side of the street lifted higher; then with another shake, the ground opened wider.

Blain backed up, staying close to Chuck. "It's like...it's hell reaching up to us. Oh!" he whipped out a recorder and held it close to his mouth, all while the ground shook. "The mouth of Mother Earth," he spoke in his recorder, "right here in Albany is opening wide. And it's as if Hell is reaching up for us."

Chuck gave a disgusted look to him. "Why you have to be so dramatic?"

"It's the news. I'm the news."

"You're a fool. Hell reaching...." Chuck grabbed on to Blain and yanked him back further. "Oh my God you're right."

Blain, who had been turned from view point, looked at Chuck. "What do you mean?"

"Hell unleashed. Let's go!" he charged and pulled Blain with everything he had. They ran with the masses and headed directly to the car, trying to break ahead and free. They couldn't stop. They couldn't take a chance on even hesitating. Especially when fire—thick and lava-like— spewed forth furiously like a fountain from the gaping hole in the ground.

***

Colin's handheld pocket-size television showed vivid, immediate shots of the emerging small volcano in Albany New York. Outside a parked car, he and Darius hovered over it watching.

"There are tectonic plates everywhere," Darius said. "You know they can appear."

"Who would have thought Albany?"

"Not me." Darius shrugged.

"Now, tell me…." Colin pointed at the screen. "How did Blain Davis know to be there? I thought we were giving all scoop to Chuck."

"We did. Bret told him."

"Bret," Colin grumbled.

"Someone say my name." Cheerfully, Bret approached the pair as they stood outside of Darius' car. "I'm sorry I'm late."

Colin looked at his watch. "Right on time. We don't have to be there until two."

Bret looked at Darius. "You said one thirty."

Darius nodded. "Chuck said you're always late, so I compensated. Get in." He opened the back door for her. "Winslow lives three blocks up."

"You want me to just leave my car here?" she asked.

"Looks better if we arrive all together." Darius replied.

Bret slid in, and waited for Colin and Darius to do the same. Immediately, Darius started driving.

"You look very nice," Colin complimented. "Thank you for dressing up."

"Darius said this was important to the cause." Bret leaned between the seats. "What role does it play?"

Darius simply replied, "Our survival."

The car turned the corner in the section of town where only the elite could afford to dwell.

"Second house," Colin instructed with a point.

"Whoa." Bret poked between the two men. "Why are we here? And don't give me the melodramatic answer."

Darius turned the car into the long and winding driveway. "To survive we have to implement a survival plan more than staying warm," he said. "To do an effective plan we need funds, lots of them and more than Colin and myself have."

"So we're coming to this house, to ask whoever lives here for that money."

"Some if not all," Darius answered. "Jacques Winslow has no family and seeing that he's older."

"How old?" Bret answered nearly interrupting.

"How that makes a difference, I don't know." Darius replied.

Colin snickered. "It could. He could die before he gives the money, or right after and we'd not owe him anything."

"Oh my God," Bret whisper as the car stopped. "Tell me he's not in a wheelchair."

Both Colin and Darius looked at her.

She peeped a shriek. "He is. I saw this in a movie. An end of the world movie, *When Worlds Collide*, and they got funding from this lonely, mean old man."

Darius nodded his head to Colin. "He must have seen the same movie. He told me he got the idea from that."

"Not entirely," Colin defended. "Mr. Winslow funds many things at the university."

Bret tapped Colin on the shoulder. "Was it the movie where the two planets were ready to collide and...."

"Hey," Darius halted her. "We have to go convince this guy."

"Wait a second." Bret stopped him before he opened the car door. "You two are the scientists. Why am I here?"

"To convince him." Darius stepped out.

Bret hesitated. "How?"

"Let me fix that skirt." Darius reached down for Bret's garment right at the door.

Colin covered his smile. "I can't believe you made her wear a dress."

"Whatever works." Darius grabbed the waist of the skirt.

"Hey." Bret snipped. "You're lifting it. It's already...."

"Needs to be shorter." Darius tucked it. "There."

"What is this guy, a pervert?" Bret looked down.

"Yes," Darius answered. "Don't touch it. And keep in mind," he moved her hand from the skirt, "he's a little out there."

Jacques Winslow was a seventy-year-old man

who was confined to a wheelchair. With an inherited fortune from coalmines, and with proper investments, Winslow had the means to help.

The huge double oak doors parted slightly, and a frail elderly man dressed in a suit walked out. He spoke slowly, and articulately. "Mr. Winslow...will see you...now." He nodded then stepped away.

Darius gave a courtesy knock on the door and stepped inside, whispering to Bret. "Don't say anything, please keep all answers limited to two words or less. Be nice."

Bret's mouth went agape in offense.

Colin stayed close to her. "Ignore him."

"Am I only for show?" Bret asked.

Colin smiled.

The motorized wheelchair spun around from the big window and into the desk. Jacques Winslow was a thin man, balding, and not quite as old as someone that would be dying shortly. "Awful shame about that volcano in Albany."

Colin sighed out. "Awful shame."

"Hear they're spreading like wildfire."

Colin shrugged. "Possibly."

"Oh my God," Bret whispered. "He looks just like the man...." She jolted when Darius grabbed her arm firmly and led her closer.

"Gentlemen," Winslow spoke in a dignified manner. "And...."

"Bret." Darius introduced.

"How do you do?" Bret extended her hand, still within the clutches of Darius.

"Better now. Thank you. Have a seat."

All three of them did.

"Professor Cobb," Winslow said. "Dr. Reye. I saw both of you on the news."

Darius smiled politely. "And hence the reason we're here."

Winslow looked directly at Bret. "Are you married?"

"Yes," Bret answered.

"Ah," Winslow nodded and returned to Darius. "Go on."

"May I?" Colin asked. When he received acknowledgement he stood. "Look, Mr. Winslow. You have been an integral part of funding for the university. Basically you're a man worth quite a bit of dough. Now . . . how can one spend that dough wisely if . . . if . . . no," Colin shook his head. "When . . . the world ends."

Darius groaned. "Can you be any blunter?"

Darius and Bret jumped a foot when Winslow slammed a hand on the desk.

"Silence, blunt is best. I hate beating around the bush," Winslow said crassly. "Go on Dr. Reye."

"Can you answer the question?"

Winslow paused in thought. "When the world ends? You can't."

"Exactly. Now . . . take that same scenario and . . . ."

"Are you married?" Winslow asked Bret again.

"Yes," she replied.

"Ah." He nodded then returned to Colin. "You were saying God . . . ."

"No, nothing about God. Scenario." Colin explained. "Answer this question. How can one spend tons of money wisely if he knows ahead of time that the world is going to end?"

"Use it to save his life," Winslow responded.

"Bingo." Colin smiled. "We're off and running. Would you?"

"Use tons of money to save my life? Yes," Winslow said.

"Good. Now . . . ."

"Wait . . ." Winslow sang the word. "Wait . . . are you? Are you telling me that you need money to stop the end of the world?"

"Actually, I'm . . ." Colin tried to answer but Winslow interrupted.

"Are you a prophet?" Winslow asked Colin.

"No, I'm . . ."

"Are you?" He questioned Darius.

"No, I'm . . ."

"You?" He went to Bret.

"Some say I am."

"Ah," Winslow nodded. "So you have had this vision of the end of the world. Has God spoken to you?"

Colin chuckled. "Sir, really if God gave Bret the message the world was ending, could money do any good?"

"No," Winslow said. "God can't be bought; neither can good judgment. Plus, money can't stop it." Winslow slammed his hand again. "Goddamn Russians, are we back in the Cold War? Are we gonna build a doozey of a bomb shelter?"

"Close." Colin said.

"I hate the Russians."

"Sir," Colin tried again. "The Russians have nothing to do with this. Although if you wish to blame it on them, I'm sure some experiment they pulled in the seventies might have had repercussions on what we're facing."

"Are you married?" he asked of Bret.

"Yes."

"Ah." Winslow nodded again.

Colin continued, "What we're dealing with basically isn't a man made issue. It's out of our hands. It's earth and space."

"Earth and space." Winslow repeated. "Can it be stopped?"

"No." Colin shook his head.

"We can't use the nukes to do any good?"

"No."

"Send a few men out into space and…."

"No." Colin lifted his hand. "We can't. It will happen. We can only prepare."

"Earth and space . . . ." Winslow stared out. "Earth and space. Prepare. You mean for survival."

"Yes, we may not be able to stop it, but we certainly can get ready. However, getting ready costs money. Things need to be constructed. A place to go, a transport there…."

"And you need me to fund." Winslow asked.

"Yes," Colin answered.

"How much?"

After a clearing of his throat, Colin said. "Eight million."

Bret sprang up in shock. "Holy shit. Eight

186

million dollars!"

Darius tugged her back to her seat.

Colin remained composed and repeated, "Eight million."

Fingers tapping, Winslow peered. "Doesn't sound like much. To build a station, transport and so forth. Supplies as well?"

"Yes," Colin answered.

"Doesn't sound like much." He grazed his finger tip over his top lip. "Will there be oxygen at this place we're going."

Colin responded, "Yes. Plenty. It'll still be cold, but not frozen."

"How will we grow our own food then?"

"Greenhouses."

"And there is oxygen? You're sure?" Winslow questioned.

"Positive."

"Hmm. Air samples, have you taken them?"

"We can."

Bret looked curiously at Darius who just flung his hand at her to be quiet.

Winslow continued, "Sounds like minimal to be able to live." He faced Bret. "And you are married."

Irritated, Bret answered, "Yes."

"How long?"

"Four years."

"Not long." He shifted his eyes to Darius. "If women become scarce, would you have a problem sharing her?" He gave a twitch of his head to Bret.

"Nope, not at all." Darius said.

Bret's mouth dropped opened.

Colin interjected, "As you know, Mr. Winslow, in desperate times, when women are few, a good husband should always be willing to share his wife. Professor Cobb knows this. He wants to share Bret." He winked. "Trust me."

Before Bret could say anything in her shock, Winslow spoke, "Okay then. I'll invest that and some more if you need it. Only I want a guaranteed seat on this spacecraft."

Colin winked. "You got it."

"How long will the journey take?"

"Depends on conditions."

"Very well." Winslow backed up his wheelchair. "Contact me in two days; resources will be set up for you."

"Thank you," Colin said then hurriedly escorted Darius and Bret from the office. He beckoned their silence until they were out of the house and en route to the car.

"A spaceship?" Bret asked insulted. "You allowed that man to think he was going on a spaceship."

Darius answered, "More than likely he thinks he's going to another planet."

"I'd guess that," Colin added. "Especially with the oxygen questions. He may have seen the same movie."

"Wait." Bret interrupted. "You can't let him think he's going on a spaceship."

"Why not?" Colin asked.

"He's not."

Colin fluttered his lips. "He may not live through the cold process up here."

"And if he does?" Bret asked.

"Well, we'll knock him out with Thorazine; he'll never know he wasn't on a spaceship. We'll tell him leaving the atmosphere did that to him.'

"You two are wrong," Bret said. "First saying you'll share, then allowing him to believe he's going to space. All for eight million dollars."

"That's right." Darius commented. "Eight million. We need that. You need that. Hell, I'll tell him we're going in a time machine if it means getting the money. Because we're not lying about the end result. The outcome for all of us will be the same, and that's what matters. Surviving."

THE BLAIN REPORT

June 9th ...

"The Humane Society and other animal lovers gathered around with glee when the Coast Guard arrived. The reports of the strange oceanic find spread like wildfire, and anyone who wanted to be a witness to this arrival flocked to the Hudson Bay. The excitement began yesterday when the Coast Guard reported finding a life raft with six kittens floating aimlessly seventy miles offshore of New York. A bag of food, one blanket, no water. Experts are saying these kittens may have been floating at sea for up to two weeks. How they survived is nothing less than a miracle. The New York Humane Society is already reporting an outpouring of adoption requests for these fine feline sailors. It's a story with a happy ending, and after the week of bizarre occurrences this reporter has seen, it is a welcome change. Blain Davis, CNS News."

13 - READINESS

June 11ᵗʰ ...

It wasn't a twenty-four-hour government station, although Virginia wanted to increase monitoring to 'round the clock'. She didn't have the manpower, and unless she herself moved all her belongings and gave up her husband and children, it would never be 'round the clock'.

But she arrived early, as she always did, just after five, never away for longer than seven hours. Her six-year-old daughter was curled up sleeping on the small couch in the computer room, while Virginia, alone with her coffee, pulled up the night's images. Usually it was uneventful, and any changes noted were slight and an indication something was about to turn. Nothing ever that alarming; after all she had left there at midnight.

The five a.m. images clicked in seven second intervals as Virginia scanned them visually. Four images, three a.m., Virginia hit 'stop'.

"Oh, my God." After a few clicks, the images of the sun zoomed in, and Virginia manipulated the color. "This can't be right." She went back an image, then skipped ahead. 'It is." Blindly, she reached for the phone and dialed. "Did I wake you? Sorry. Anyhow, go to your station," she said. "I want you to look at your images, and I'm sending you the ones I have."

A pause.

"Darius, I need you to confirm. I know…I know this isn't your specialty, but it doesn't have to be if I'm correct. What do I need you to confirm?" Virginia sighed out. "Whether I'm wrong, or whether we're really in trouble."

***

The Krispy Kreme was a safe house, unlike the Burger King, where Chuck couldn't order his Whopper without feeling it. He started to notice when he stopped for a latte. He could feel it when he paused at his office; by the time he picked up his early meal, he was positive.

Even though he looked he couldn't confirm it, so he decided to play decoy.

There was a Wal-Mart located outside of town, and Chuck, after parking, went inside. He made a maze of his movements, until finally he arrived at his destination.

Women's lingerie.

It was between the padded bra rack and underwear rack when Chuck's suspicions were confirmed. Acting as if he didn't see him, Chuck slipped by the girdles, and reached out his hand, grabbing his shirt.

"Hey. Hey." Blain pulled away.

"Why are you following me?"

"Following you?" Blain chuckled. "Does it look like I'm following you?'

"Yes."

Blain fluttered his lips. "Please don't flatter yourself. In fact," he straightened his clothes. "I was going to comment on what a coincidence this was."

"Coincidence?"

"Yes, that we're at the same Wal-Mart."

Chuck scoffed. "Yeah, right."

"It's true. I was buying something for myself."

"I see. It makes sense." Chuck folded his arms. "Of course you would come to a Wal-Mart way out of your way. Where else could you purchase women's underwear without drawing attention to the Big CNS reporter?"

"Shit." Blain quickly looked around.

"Cut the bull. You're following me. Why?"

Blain sighed out. "You're getting either really expert tips or psychic tips. Either way, you have the scoop I want."

"Sorry. Bret not talking?"

"No. Look, I can make a deal. You tell me and I'll do something for you."

Chuck laughed. "What could you possibly have that I want?"

"A chance at CNS."

Chuck shook his head.

"You don't want to be on CNS."

"Do I have the face for it? " Chuck asked sarcastically.

"Well, yeah, you…no." Blain shook his head. "But don't you want to claim credit of writing for them."

"Don't need it."

"Surely the exposure...."

This made Chuck pause. "Exposure."

"Yeah, national."

Thinking that the national exposure wouldn't be a bad idea when it came time to get the truth out, Chuck nodded. "I will think about . . ." he stopped when his phone rang. "Hold on." He answered it. "Hey . . . , What's up?"

Pause.

"When?" Chuck asked. "Can I ask why?" he nodded. "Not a problem. Call me then. Yeah, I'm on my way." He hung up.

"Going somewhere?"

"As a matter of fact," Chuck smiled. "I am. See ya." Chuck took off.

Blain did follow, as best as he could but just as assurance, he placed a phone call to Bret.

***

Darius looked more like a NASA engineer rather than the college professor he was. Earpiece in his ear, he spoke not only on the phone, but to Colin as well—who also had an ear piece.

"S5." Darius said as he looked at the image on the screen. It was of Earth and a red spot lingered like a cloud above a small section of the US. "Got my image?"

"Yes," Virginia answered.

"Four a.m. Next . . . . " Darius clicked. "Five. Next . . . six. "See the changes?"

"It increased."

"Exactly."

Colin's finger pointed to the screen. "What is this one here?"

"Seven a.m. S3." Darius answered. "It increased up until nine a.m. when it peaked. But…it only peaked for seven minutes, and hit an S5, over this area of Missouri and Kansas. It's leveling now."

Colin nodded. "But what about at S4?"

Darius nodded. "Some problems. It'll look more like food poisoning."

Virginia asked. "Did you let the airlines know?"

Darius laughed. "You kidding me? When you showed me this I immediately went to them. They got a warning from NASA. But it's nothing major."

"Nothing major?" Virginia barked, "S5 is nothing major?"

"Ah," Colin interjected. "It wouldn't appear to be nothing major if they were looking like we are looking. Correct? And they aren't. We're searching for it. They are merely doing their jobs."

Virginia exhaled over the line. "So it's a wait to see if you're correct."

"Oh, I'm right." Darius said. "When I noticed the area increasing more than the others, I immediately contacted the FAA. Luckily Colin knows someone there. Three flights went through the area at the time it peaked. I have Chuck arriving right before one of those planes do. In fact…I wouldn't be surprised if everyone is feeling it now. It's a minor version of Africa.

We're just lucky it stopped at S5."

Virginia asked, "What was Africa?"

"The solar scale only goes up to S5. If it went higher, I'd say an S10."

"Whoa." Colin commented, "And look at the time. I have to meet Bret." He lifted a folder. "Good luck. Keep me posted." After removing the ear piece he began his farewell.

"Oh, Colin?" Darius called out. "Don't give Bret details about this. OK?"

"Why?" Colin asked.

"Because she'll tell that reporter. Chuck wants an exclusive." He got agreement, watched Colin leave then returned to the computer screens. "Speaking of Chuck," he said to himself and Virginia. "Where are you?"

***

"Quit following me!" Chuck barked, walking at a quick pace through the main terminal of Philadelphia's airport.

"You're rushing. You speeded all the way here; I almost lost you." Blain said.

"Too bad." Chuck turned and kept on walking.

"Are you leaving the country?"

"Does it look like I'm leaving anywhere? No." Chuck moved fast, and made it as far as security would let him. "You lost your camera man."

"I let him go. I figured I could follow you...."

196

"A-ha!" Chuck pointed. "You are."

"OK, I am. I'm ready." He lifted the camera.

"You are unreal." Chuck pulled out his identification and walked to the security desk. "Charles Wright, Johnstown Journal. I have media clearance."

The security man skimmed the page. "I'm not seeing . . . hey . . . ." He smiled brightly and snapped his finger. "Ain't you Blain Davis?"

"Yes, I am." Blain answered bashfully.

"Sign here, gentleman. But I need to check that ID again," He said to Chuck.

After a grumble, Chuck complied.

"See." Blain pestered as they walked though to the main terminal. "I'm good for something."

"You have that camera linked up to the network?"

"All it's gonna take is a phone call. I figure, I'll shoot my footage, then do my story."

"What story?" Chuck asked.

"The one you're rushing to get to."

"I am not rushing to get to . . ." Chuck's words were interrupted when a barrage of medical people barreled past him.

A siren blared from a security cart, and three of them zoomed down the hall of the airport.

Chuck took off running.

Sure enough, Gate 47B, the one where he was supposed to be. It was swamped with police, airport security, and medical personal. Through the windows, Chuck could see ambulances pulled up to the plane.

A woman was moving people back from the

gate, and Chuck approached her. "Chuck Wright, reporter, what's going on with Flight 766?"

"I'm sorry, sir, I'm not at liberty to say."

Chuck tried another, while Blain filmed the hysteria.

A policeman.

"Sir, Chuck Wright with the Johnstown . . . ."

"Out of my way." He scolded.

Chuck jumped back and made yet another attempt. His mouth wasn't even open when an official in a suit barked out, "Someone get this reporter out of here!"

"Fuck," Chuck stepped back.

"May I?" Blain asked.

"May you what?"

"Here, hold this." He handed Chuck the camera. "Just press this button and . . . ."

"I know how to use this. Who am I filming?"

"All this and . . . ." Blain grinned. "Me." He reached into his pocket, pulling out a remote microphone and earpiece. He hooked it to his ear, checked the remote connection with the camera and stood straight. "Ready?"

"I'm not filming you. Forget it." Chuck snapped.

"Wanna story?" Blain asked. "Yes or no. We can scoop this."

"Ha." Chuck shook his head. His body was a billiard for those scurrying about. "You think you're all that. Mr. CNS reporter. No one's gonna talk. Not yet."

"They will to me."

"You think?" Chuck asked.

"Wanna bet?"

"Yeah, I'll bet. I'll bet you strike out."

Cocky, Blain said, "And if I don't, we work together on this. Because I have a gut feeling something big is gonna happen with this world, and you know what that is."

"I'm a Johnstown reporter."

"With some mighty influential friends. Deal?"

"Deal."

They shook.

"Give me a second," Blain pulled out his cell phone and dialed. "It's me." He turned his body and mumbled the conversation. "Thanks." He hung up and faced Chuck. "Ready?" Blain asked.

Chuck lifted the camera. "You're on."

Blain smiled.

THE BLAIN REPORT

"This is Blain Davis, coming to you live from Philadelphia International Airport, where a distressed plane has just landed. Emergency crews have gathered in hordes, and ambulances in incredible numbers are racing to the runway. As you can see pandemonium has gripped the airport, and this reporter along with Chuck Wright, Johnstown Tribune, were on site when it all went down. With me now is FAA administrator, Harold Evens. Harold, what's the situation?"

"Right now we're not sure. Emergency personnel are removing passengers from the plane."

"What's going on?'

"Seven minutes prior to landing we received a distress call from the pilot aboard 766. His description of the situation was patchy. All we know now is there are cases of severe vomiting, diarrhea, and delirium."

"Could it have been food poisoning?"

"Negative on that there, Blain. We've ruled that out. There are unconfirmed reports of skin lesions."

"Could it be gas? A terrorist attack of some sort?"

"We cannot determine that at this time."

"Any confirmed deaths or only illnesses?"

"We've not received word of deaths; we don't believe it is that severe. However there are reports of unresponsiveness."

"Thank you."

Harold backed off.

"That was Harold Evens, FAA. Now, Sam, we are told that there are some one hundred and fifty-three people aboard that plane. What their individual conditions are remain to be seen, and pending notification of family, all names are being with held. The cause at this time is unknown, and the question of the hour is, what happened on board flight 766? More later."

Pause.

"Blain Davis, with Chuck Wright, CNS news. Back to you, Sam."

14 - Cold Truth

Bret bit her nails, and sat like a child, knees close watching the television. The phone was to her ear. "I'm seeing this, Virginia. This is amazing."

"It's fucked up." Jesse commented on his way through the living room. "Fuckin' terrorists."

"It wasn't a terror attack, asshole." Bret said then returned to her call. "Sorry. So Darius saw this coming?"

From the kitchen, Jesse mumbled. "Fuckin' Darius."

Bret ignored him. "What's Colin's take? Yes, he's coming over later. He called this morning. I suppose he forgot that I worked all night. He said he and Darius were finishing up on a small proposal. Do you know what that is?"

"Not really, they said they had one for me too." Virginia said.

"Strange. He wanted to know what would be a good time to stop by." Bret dropped her voice to a whisper and covered the mouthpiece of the phone. "He asked when Jesse would be home. I figure he wants to avoid my husband."

"Why are you whispering?" Jesse yelled from the kitchen.

"Why are you eavesdropping? Go out or something; geez. Anyhow . . . ." Bret continued. "I was specific. Jesse's doing night road work and . . . ." Her head cocked when the doorbell rang. "Hold on." She walked to the front door. "Let me call you back. Colin's here. Man."

"Who's at the . . . ." Jesse paused. "Door."

Bret exhaled as she let Colin into her home. Jesse and Colin had never met face to face.

"Uh, Jesse, Colin. Colin, Jesse," she introduced.

Colin seemed pleased, extended his hand, and brightly smiled "Nice to meet you finally."

"Same here. So you're?" Jesse said.

"Yes, he is." Bret intervened. "And Colin has something he needs to discuss with me."

"Actually . . . ." Colin ran his finger over his top lip. "I need to speak to Jesse."

"Me?" Jesse asked.

"Him?"

"Yes," Colin said. "I believe you have an expertise that will come in handy with the ice . . . ."

"Tea." Bret blurted out. "Ice tea." Nervously, she spun to Jesse. "I've been telling Colin about your famous ice tea."

Blushingly, Jesse tilted his head "It's not that great. But I do get raves."

Colin chuckled. "Is that so?"

"Secret is in the length of time you steep the bags."

"Would you like some?" Bret asked. "We have some. Jesse, get some for Colin."

"I would love some. After that we can discuss the emerging ice . . . ."

"Tea contest." Bret said. "The one they're having in West Virginia. Geez, I forgot to tell you, Jesse."

Jesse looked puzzled, "An ice tea contest. That's strange. A new one."

"Age." Colin said. "Age." He shook his head.

"Thirty-two." Jesse said. "Does that matter?"

Bret snickered. "No. I don't think. Does it Colin?"

"What in the world?" Colin asked.

"I'll get that tea," Jesse said. "Then you can tell me if it's contest material."

"Jesse, stop." Colin called out. "Wait." He reached over and covered Bret's mouth, then said. "I'd love some tea. It sounds wonderful. I'm here to discuss the ice . . . ."

Gasping, Bret removed his hand, but before she could respond, Colin covered her mouth again.

"Age." Colin completed his sentence.

"Ice age?" Jesse asked.

Bret cringed.

"Yes." Colin nodded. "The ice age."

Fluttering his lips, Jesse shrugged. "Can't be more than a day old, we have a maker that pops out cubes every so often. Plus, the kids are always using it. So it's fresh."

Bret knew she was in trouble when she saw the stare on Colin's face.

Cover. Try to cover. Quickly, Bret shrugged as if she were embarrassed by her husband's lack of understanding.

The corner of Colin's mouth raised in a smile. "Jesse, I'm not talking about the age of the ice in the fridge, I'm talking about the Ice Age."

"Movie?" Jesse asked.

"Reality."

Jesse looked lost.

Colin blinked several times in that arrogance he often displayed. "Hasn't your wife mentioned it?"

"The movie?" Jesse asked.

"No, the reality." Colin repeated. "The entire predicted outcome of all the odd occurrences going on. The reason we've been talking, meeting . . . ." He rattled on, perturbed, then it hit him. "You . . . you don't know."

"Know what?" Jesse asked.

"You don't." Colin turned to Bret. "I cannot believe all this time, all these talks, our meetings, lunches, and you didn't tell your husband about the ice age that is coming?"

Bret winced.

"Wait." Jesse held up his hand. "You've been talking back and forth with him, and not only that, you've been meeting with him?"

Reluctantly, Bret nodded. "That's where I've been going, when . . . ."

"When you told me you were heading to knitting class." Jesse finished the sentence.

Colin laughed. "Knitting class? For weeks? Did the fact that she never bought any yarn, or made anything even tip you off?"

"Fuck." Jesse blurted.

Colin raised his eyebrows. "I guess not."

"Colin," Bret snapped. "Shut up. You aren't helping."

"Me?" Colin continued in his typical instigation. "You're the one that's lying to your husband about us."

Bret cringed.

Jesse flared.

"Whoops." Colin said. "Wrong word choice?"

Before she could say, 'yes', Jesse went overboard. Without warning or hesitation, he squared off and nailed Colin straight in the cheek.

***

Colin started coming to almost immediately. The ice to his cheek helped. He jerked back when it touched his skin.

"Sorry, he hit you," Bret said.

"That's alright. How long was I out?" he asked.

Bret would have explained right there and then that he wasn't out long, had the children not walked in the house, daughters first.

Casper stopped cold. "What happened to him?"

Kneeling by Colin, Bret replied, "Jesse hit him."

"Figures." Casper said. "Violence, Mother. Does that give you enough reason now to get rid of him?"

Andi gasped. "That isn't very nice to say."

"Well, neither is hitting someone." Casper defended. "Like *he's* a threat to Jesse." She paused, looked left to right. "Wait. Maybe he is. Where is he?"

"Gone." Bret answered.

"Why did Jesse hit him?" Andi asked.

206

Bret replied, "I suppose he thought I was having an affair with Colin."

Colin sat up. "He didn't seriously think that, did he?"

"Hey," Luke walked in the house. "What happened to Dr. Reye?"

Bret sighed out, "Jesse hit him."

"For no reason?"

"Jesse thought he had reasons. I am so sorry, Colin." Bret faced him. "I can't believe my husband hit you."

"It was a mistake. Now is not the time to be petty." Colin breathed out. "I came here for a reason. I'd like to get to that reason. Since the family is present, perhaps they should listen up. That is unless . . . unless they haven't a clue about it either."

"No." Bret said nonchalantly, as she helped him to his feet. "They know."

"Good. Now if you can just call Jesse . . . ."

"I can't; he's gone."

Colin looked at her sideways. "What do you mean, gone?"

"Gone?" Luke asked. "For real?"

"Gone?" Andi questioned. "Seriously?"

Casper clenched out an excited, 'yes'.

Bret shrugged. "Gone. He said he was leaving. Gone. Said he reached the end with this. Muttered something about having an affair with you and you can have me."

"Very nice of him. But like I said, I have a reason for being here," Colin said. "I need his help with the construction aspect of our shelter here.

You said he was a contractor before doing roadwork."

Bret nodded. "He was. Good, too."

"Great." Colin sighed. "Now I have to rework my plan."

Bret waved him off. "Don't worry about it. He'll be back."

"And if he doesn't come back?" Colin asked.

"Don't worry about," Bret said. "I know a perfect company. But it's a moot point. Jesse's mad. He may be gone from the house," she spoke assuredly. "But trust me. Jesse will be back."

15 - Building the Dream

June 12th

Jesse didn't come back.

He failed to return the evening he left and failed to answer his phone.

The next morning he placed a call to Bret telling her he couldn't take all the new men in her life, nor the 'end of the world' paranoia, and he just wanted out.

Plus, Casper hated him.

Bret thought it was a phase until Jesse emptied out the bank accounts, leaving her only a dollar.

"Remind me to thank Darius again," Bret said, getting into the car. "If he wouldn't have lent me that money everything would have bounced."

"Somehow," Colin said. "Dare-Dare isn't too worried about repayment. All good with the bank?"

Bret nodded. "Said there was nothing they could do. It was a joint account."

"I figured as much. How are you?'

"Fine. Shocked." Bret shrugged. "Numb. Not understanding."

Colin turned the wheel of the car and out of the bank parking lot. "Now, let's take your mind off of it. We're moving on the plan. Did you call them?"

"Yes," Bret answered. "I didn't tell him anything, only that I had a project proposition for him."

"Can you give me the run-down on this business?"

"Absolutely. Bruce Weiss started his own contracting firm when he retired from the service." She stated the facts. "Retired infantry. Tough guy. Very smart. Don't let him fool you when you see him. He dresses up well. His son works with him. Former cop. Was let go from the force for racist comments."

"Really?" Colin asked. "Hmm. And they're good."

"Oh, my God, yes. They built the crooked house by themselves. No other contractors and did it fast too."

"No wonder why it was crooked."

Bret snickered. "It was supposed to be that way. They were in the architectural digest."

"How do you know him?"

"Jesse and he used to hang out all the time. It was Jesse who knew him. They stopped. I guess life got in the way. Oh!" She pointed here. "Turn here."

Colin did. In an inner city neighborhood, they traveled down a side street until they came to a building at the end.

It looked like a small storage warehouse; a big parking lot housed heavy equipment that appeared in need of repair or cleaning.

The 'Weiss and Son Contracting' sign with red lettering was faded. The garage door was boarded up and a few windows broken.

Colin stopped the car. "Are you sure they're still in business?"

"Yeah, I just talked to him. He said they were in all day."

"Do they even have business?"

"They do now," Bret said brightly and opened the car door. As soon as she did, the front door of the building opened.

Colin paused. He looked as if he were thinking of getting back in the car when he saw Bruce.

About fifty, Bruce was fit, his head bald, face worn but handsome. He wore a pair of camouflage pants, black tee shirt, a shoulder harness containing a revolver, large hunting knife in hand, and instead of combat boots, he had on rubber fishing boots.

"Good God, it's Rambo." Colin whispered.

"Bret!" Bruce grinned, tucked the knife into a sleeve and the M-4 behind his back as he made his way to her. "My God do you look good." He embraced her. His voice was country, almost too country for being inner city.

"So do you." Bret smiled. "Bruce, this is Colin Reye."

Bruce gave a firm handshake. "Pleasure."

The smile dropped from Colin's face as he withdrew his hand and looked at it with a studious stare.

"Sorry," Bruce said and wiped his hand on his

pants.

"What is that? Blood?"

Bruce chuckled.

Colin pulled a handkerchief from his suit pocket and cleaned his hand.

Bruce, hands on hips, stepped back and looked at Bret. "Always said that Jesse is one lucky fella. How is he?"

Bret shrugged. "We broke up."

At first Bruce grinned, then turned serious. "Sorry about that. Well, I knew it was only a matter of time before you found out about Kyomi."

"Who?" Bret asked.

"Oops."

Colin shifted his eyes. "Oops? You say oops to her. What does that mean?"

"Oops." Bruce shrugged. "Means I made a mistake."

"Who is Kyomi?" Bret asked.

Bruce exhaled. "His little side girl. I swore I thought you knew. Didn't you wonder why him and I stopped hanging out? I couldn't take that he was being like that with you. Always liked you, Bret. I never bought his reasoning for the girl."

"And what was his reasoning?"

"You didn't . . . well, you know." Bruce shrugged.

"Be that as it may, I work night turn. Geez." Bret huffed. "How long?"

"A year."

"Oh my God." Her hand went to her head. "I was with him at least three times this past year."

Colin mouthed 'three times?'

"I have to get checked," Bret said. "For disease."

"Probably not," Bruce said. "Jesse bragged she was a virgin when they met."

Colin asked. "Virgin. How old is this person? Twelve?"

Bruce crinkled up his face. "Nineteen now. Maybe."

"I'm . . . I'm speechless," Bret said.

"So am I," Colin added. "Your husband left you because of your friendship while he carried on a pedophilic affair with a teenage Asian virgin."

Bret shifted her eyes to him.

"Sorry." Colin hid his snicker.

Bruce reached out and gave a squeeze to her arm. "On to better things, Bret, right?"

"Right."

"So tell me what brings you here?" Bruce asked.

Before Bret could answer, the door to the shop opened and Bobby walked out.

"Bobby!" Bret smiled widely, peeking around Bruce to the well-toned, fit and tall thirty year old black man who emerged, dressed identically to Bruce.

"Bobby?" Colin asked. "This is the 'and son'?"

Bruce nodded.

"Yes, I see the family resemblance."

"May not be blood," Bruce said with a slanted smile. "But no less my kid. Raised him all his life."

213

After a hug to Bret, Bobby stepped back. "What's up, Pop?"

"Bobby, meet Mr. Reye." Bruce introduced. "He's here for business."

"Mr. Reye," Bobby nodded politely with a shake of his hand.

Bret corrected, "Actually, he's Professor Reye, a scientist. And his stature is one of the main reasons he's here. This project has to do with his job."

"School job?" Bruce asked.

Colin shook his head. "No. Private. I'm head of Geology at Pitt. And the project is imperative. There is a lot of . . . shit going on and this needs to be done. You look like a realistic man, Mr. Weiss. And although I brought this briefcase full of data, somehow I think there's going to be a suspension of disbelief over the geological event of great proportions I'm here to tell you about."

"You don't say." Bruce swished his mouth side by side.

Colin formed a 'T' with his hands. "May I pause for a second and ask why you two are dressed like you are when you're contractors?"

Bruce nodded. "Sure can. Swamp Rats."

"As in some sort of reunion or birthday ritual for the Ranger squad."

After a chuckle, Bruce shook his head. "That's good. But no. Swamp rats."

"Like the rodent?" Colin asked.

Again, Bruce nodded.

"They're only prevalent in South East Australia."

Bruce fluttered his lips. "I don't know about South Australia. I just know they're here. Tons of them. Killed...." With one eye closed, he looked up. "Sixty-three, last count. Bobby? You?"

"Forty. Don't rub it in. You're good with the knife." Bobby said.

Bret asked. "Swamp rats?"

Colin repeated. "Swamp rats. I wasn't aware that swamps were a big thing in Pittsburgh."

"Not usually," Bruce turned and waved his hand. "Follow me. Watch your step."

Bret and Colin followed Bruce and Bobby through the building to the back.

"Near as I can figure," Bruce said as they walked to the back door. "It's being this close to the river. But . . . sure looks like a swamp to me. What do you think, Earth guy?"

Bret scurried, screamed and leapt back when a rat raced across her foot.

There were rats all right. Everywhere, crawling, but that wasn't the sight that took Colin aback. It was obvious the back property at one time was a good bit wooded and green. But instead of a yard, the fertile area, once flat, had sunk like a pit, as if a meteor had hit. It was at least ten feet deep within a circumference of nearly fifty yards. The tool sheds and garages erected on the property were tilted and partially collapsed. The bottom of the sunken area was filled with dark murky water, a pool that the rats splashed and ran through.

After blasting a rat with a quick shot from his pistol, Bruce turned to Colin with a smile. "Now what was that you were saying about me not believing this geological event of great proportions?"

***

Colin made a typical sarcastic comment to Bruce, that since the area was isolated from neighbors, instead of all the hard work of shooting the rats, why not try gas.

He didn't think Bruce would oblige.

After a, 'you know, that's a good idea', Bruce stood up, had a huddled talk with Bobby, then suggested that Bret and Colin return in a half an hour.

They did.

Carcasses of rats sprawled out everywhere.

"We'll clean them later," Bruce pulled out a chair at the table and joined Colin and Bret. "Now where were we?"

It didn't take much convincing, or much data at all. Bruce nodded, listened, read what he could, stated that he didn't understand some of it. But he grasped the concept and took it seriously.

"As you know," Colin said. "We can't stop the ice age. We can only brace ourselves, prepare and make moves. South is the only direction we can go. Winslow Funding has given us the funds needed to start. I seek hands now. Virginia and her husband will be checking out prospective land and vacant installations in Texas to make into our new community. We will go south, which is where you

216

come in. Bret has told me you and your son are the best."

"And we're pretty quick, too."

"Excellent. When this thing hits, it will it without warning, it will hit fast and hard. Everyone will be heading south at the same time. We cannot. Why? Mass hysteria will cause impassable roads to be blocked even more. Cars will die out, people will freeze. What we have to do is wait. Wait until all movement south has ceased; then those of us here in the north will make our move. So we need a special shelter for this waiting period." He handed Bruce a stack of papers. "Darius and I aren't architects, but this is basically what we need. We did a rough drawing, scaled the size and needs. It needs to be done ASAP. We've got a location. I think."

Bruce scratched his head as he flipped through the document. "Looks pretty feasible, but I think there may be flaws. Mind if I keep this, look this over and so forth?"

"Be my guest," Colin said. "So you can build it."

"Piece of cake. Structure is done."

"Wonderful. You may have to hire on . . . ."

"Nah. I doubt it."

Colin paused. "It's a pretty big job, are you sure . . . ."

"So was the crooked house, Bruce stated. "Let me see what we can do. Work it out for a week; then see our progress. We're pretty fast."

Colin smiled. "You wouldn't happen to know someone that works fast on cars."

"You mean like a mechanic?" Bruce asked.

"No." Colin shook his head. "We're wanting to enhance our transportation. Didn't know if you knew someone with those skills and your work ethic."

Bruce grinned and looked at Bobby.

Colin nodded. "Somehow, I thought the solution to the vehicles would be here."

"Yes, sir, we're your men. As long as we're along on this survival thing . . . ."

"Absolutely," Colin said. "My God, your skills will be needed after as well."

"Got yourself the best contractors in the country." He shook hands with Colin. "May need to hire on if one of us is working on the vehicles. But . . . don't know. We'll see."

"I have every faith." Colin's still blackened eye twinkled in his smile. Phase one of preparations for survival were underway.

16 - PULSE

June 14th ...

In her base lab, Virginia jumped back with a wince, when the seldom seen temper of Colin Reye reared its ugly head for about three seconds. He slammed paper with a mighty force, while blasting the word, 'Assholes!' as loud as he could.

Virginia blinked.

Darius snickered.

After a sigh, Colin ran his hand over the side of his hair, and stepped back. "Food poisoning my ass," he said. "What's the point? Someone want to tell me what is the point of lying to the public?"

Calmly, Darius answered that question. "Why not?"

"Huh?" Colin looked at him.

"Face it, Colin, people know. We aren't the top minds in the world. If we figured out what's happening, surely someone else has too. So . . . knowing this . . . and knowing nothing can be done to stop it, why cause people to panic?"

"They'll have to say something sooner or later. The word will get out." Virginia added. "We're letting it out."

"And when?" Darius asked. "We aren't letting it out until we're close. Bet me that's what the government is doing as well. Keeping people calm."

"While we're collecting books," Colin said. "Which I'm late for. Why am I the one collecting books? No, wait, scratch that. If I am responsible for finding the text books that will shape our future young minds, I know it will be done correctly. I don't want that to be in Dare-Dare's hands. Hannah Gives Head will be top the Accelerated Reading book list."

Darius' mouth dropped open. "Where is that coming from?"

"Frustration. Virginia, will you be okay monitoring alone?" Colin asked.

Virginia flung out her hand. "I'm good here. If I need you, I'll get a hold of you. Go, I'll keep both of you posted. Chuck is waiting for you, Colin."

"Am I gonna have that Blain fellow too?" Colin asked.

Virginia shook her head. "No, Blain is coming here. Remember, you promised you'd fill him in tonight."

Colin huffed. "As long as he keeps his mouth shut and adheres to our plan."

Darius added, "Yeah, last thing we need is for the word to get out. If that happens, those books you and Chuck are getting will be scarce. Everything we need to buy, build, you name it will become difficult. Thank God he didn't let word out about the radiation sickness. I mean, all we need is for the populace to think they'll die riding a plane; there goes the airline industry."

"Speaking of which . . . " Virginia said. "Shouldn't you be getting Bret. You guys have that plane to catch."

"Ah, yeah. Packed up and ready. We're flying…" Darius snickered. "Light." He stood. "In fact, I'd better go." He gathered up his things. "Call me, text me, if anything arises."

"Will do." Virginia responded. "I hope this is it. I hope this is the place you're looking for. We couldn't fully see inside and below, but the markings were on the floor as stated. So…."

"I'm positive that's it. If it has the markings, it has to be." Darius smiled. "And you found it. I appreciate you guys taking off to look."

"That wasn't a problem," Virginia said. "It wasn't just complex hunting, it was a day away from the kids. Oh, there's a great steakhouse right next to the hotel. You have to try it. My husband loved it."

"Husband." Colin snapped his finger. "You're fortunate, Dare-Dare."

Darius stopped in his dash out. "Why's that?"

"See this?" Colin pointed to his black eye. "If I got this over lunch, good thing for you her husband left her for a teenage Asian virgin. You're taking her to Texas."

"Timing is in my favor, then . . ." Darius smiled.

"You aren't planning to bed this woman? Dare-Dare, she still mourning…."

"God! Colin, stop. No. I'm not planning to bed her."

"Good. You haven't seen her in two days. She's hit that angry phase."

Virginia nodded knowingly, "I don't blame

her."

"So a bit of advice," Colin said. "Don't mention 'Chinese' and 'innocent' in the same sentence."

Darius left. Colin watch the door close, then turned to Virginia. "He's thinking sex fest. Trust me." He winked and then walked out.

Virginia shook her head with a laugh.

***

"Why are you packing items in a diaper bag?" Luke asked Bret.

"That's what Darius said to do. He said minimal, pack what can fit in a diaper bag. He'll buy me clothes there if need be."

"You're gonna be owing him a lot."

"I know. But . . . you can spend money you don't have to pay back." Bret said. "Done."

"Why a diaper bag?"

Bret shrugged. "I don't know. Keeps it light. We'll be gone one night." She tossed the diaper bag over her shoulder and murmured. "Wallet."

"Am I in charge?" Luke asked.

"Yes. You live here. You're the oldest, I won't be gone long."

He followed her down the stairs. "Don't you think the airlines are gonna think it's odd that you're carrying a Disney diaper bag when you don't have a baby?"

Again, Bret shrugged. "I'm late . . . ." she set the bag by the door. "Okay. You have everyone's numbers, right?"

Luke nodded.

"Bruce is coming by to buy Jesse's tools before Jesse comes and gets them. If Jesse comes by and causes a fit.…"

"I know. I know. Call the police then Bobby Weiss."

"Who says he has plenty of frustration and is more than willing to come over," Bret said.

"But . . . like, is it right to sell his tools."

"Was it right to wipe out the bank account for that child bride?"

"I don't know."

"You're so male. You would say that." She looked out the door. "Oh, here he is now. Call if you have problems."

"I will."

Bret gave her son a hug and kiss. "I love you. Be good. Okay?"

"Call me when you check in."

"How about I call you when we land, we're supposed to go directly to the real estate office."

"That works."

"See ya." Bret opened the door, mouthing the words, 'I love you' once more, as she walked out.

Darius waited in the truck and reached over, opening the door for her.

Bret stepped inside the truck.

"Everything okay?" he asked.

"Oh, sure, all's fine." Bret reached down for her bag to place on her lap. She stared at it while

Darius pulled out. "Darius?"

"Yeah?"

"Why *did* I have to pack in a diaper bag?"

"The airlines only allow you one carryon. But you're allowed one personal bag if it's small."

"One carry on each."

"Yes, that's the policy," Darius answered.

"I don't have a carry on," Bret said.

"I brought one for you."

"You…you packed me clothes."

"Actually no," he replied. "You'll carry one bag, I'll carry another. I packed…I packed parachutes."

Her loud 'what!' caused Darius to wince.

"Bret, please."

"Parachutes. As in jumping out of a plane, parachutes."

"Yes, in nice neat little bags," Darius said.

"Why in the world would we…oh my God."

"What?"

"Oh my God." She began to panic. "You think the plane is gonna crash." Bret began to ramble fast. "You think we're crashing, that's why you brought them. Huh? The plane is . . . ."

"Bret, calm down."

"I can't calm down. You brought *parachutes*."

"As a precaution only," he said calmly. "Trust me. Precaution. The plane is not going down."

***

"Don't panic," Darius turned his body toward Bret in the first class of the plane. "But . . . the plane is going down."

"What!" Bret snapped.

"Shh."

Everybody turned around and looked.

"Check it out." He held up his cell phone. "From Virginia. Read."

"Why do you have that on? The pilot said to turn it off."

"Well, it's a good thing I did. Look."

Bret read the display of the text message: EMP SIX MINUTES. YOUR WAY.

"Oh, my God."

"Listen. We have five minutes, maybe less. Calmly stand up, put the diaper bag over your shoulder and follow my lead. Calmly. Nod."

"Are we gonna be alright?" she asked.

"If you do as I say and follow my lead. Okay."

Bret nodded. Then she shook her head.

"What?"

"I don't think I can do this."

"You don't have a choice."

"Oh my God."

She reached under the seat and grabbed the diaper bag.

"Stand." He instructed. When she did, he allowed her to stand in the aisle and he reached for the overhead compartment.

"Here comes the air police."

"Huh?" he looked. The stewardess approached.

"Sir," the stewardess said. "You have to leave the luggage up there."

"I'm so sorry. My wife's medication is in one of our bags and I want to get it out," Darius said, his voice sweet. "She needs to have an injection and I need to take her to the back to administer it. As I am sure you understand."

Bret gasped.

"That's fine. I do understand." The stewardess even aided in the compartment hunting, allowing Darius to retrieve the two parachutes.

"Thank you." He smiled.

Again, Bret gasped.

"What?" Darius asked.

"You disgust me. Flirting. So male."

"I'm single."

"Not on this flight, mister."

"Then not for long." After taking Bret's hand he led her through the first class.

"Where are we going?"

"Just follow."

"Fine."

Darius looked at his phone. "Three minutes." He moved quickly.

"Oh, shit."

"We'll be fine." He pulled her along.

In the back of the plane they stood by an emergency door.

"Are you gonna be able to open this? Bret asked.

"I hope." Darius strapped on her pack. "Latch that tight," he instructed, then pulled on his. After the final snap, he manipulated his phone.

"What are you doing?"

"Taking out the batteries. We'll need this." He shoved them in his pocket. "Ready?"

"No."

"Too bad. Count to like ten, I guess, and pull this." He showed her.

"Count to *like* ten? You guess? You don't know?"

"Not really."

Bret peeped.

"Shh." Darius looked beyond her. "Shit." He pointed.

"Excuse me," another stewardess approached. "What are you doing?"

"Leaving," Darius replied. "In about...." He looked at his watch. "ten, nine...."

"You gonna jump out that door?" she asked.

"Pretty much."

"Oh, I don't think so," she said smug. "Take your seat or I get the Captain. Your choice."

Darius laughed and grabbed on to Bret. "At least we have a choice. I don't believe you do."

"Excuse me?" she asked, confused.

Black and quiet.

At that second, all the lights aboard the plane went out and the engines stopped.

"Now." Darius, holding on to Bret, turned the crank on the door.

The stewardess peered around confused. The plane instantaneously started to drop.

"Hold tight!" he instructed Bret.

"Oh my God. Oh my God." She grabbed him and the bar near the door.

"Ready?" Darius opened the door. He was aware of the dynamics of pressurized spaces, and how the opening of the door was an invitation to be sucked out. He was ready, so was Bret. The stewardess wasn't. She flew by Darius and Bret, right out of the plane, screaming the entire way. "Oh."

"Oh?" Bret asked.

Darius waved out his hand and spoke over the wind noise. "She was a goner anyhow. Jump." Without taking a chance on Bret's hesitation, he grabbed her arm and tugged her out of the plane right along with him.

***

Against the original grain of plan, instead of heading to Virginia's monitoring station, Blain figured it best to stay close to Chuck. After all, Chuck was the story to follow. However, Blain wasn't aware as to why Colin drove so fast to his house, and moved with the rush of emergency inside.

The computers in Darius' make shift lab beeped out of control. "Chuck, hit the mike. Remove the screensavers."

"Got it." Chuck said making a motion around the room.

Colin pressed a button on the phone. "Tell me you're there."

"I'm here," Virginia said. "We weren't affected."

"Where are we at?" Colin sat in front of the computer. "I know I missed it."

"By forty seconds. Its impact is just being felt now. My God . . . ." She paused. "Screen two. It's rippling."

"Fuck," Colin whispered.

"What's happening?" Blain asked Chuck.

"Look at this mother." Colin sated. "Texas, West Louisiana, Northern Mexico.…"

"I don't think it made California. Parts of New Mexico though," Virginia said.

"Were you able to hack into FAA?"

"Yes, coming your way now."

"Got it," Chuck called out. "Over here. Looks like a video game."

Blain added "A bad seventies one. The dots are disappearing."

"Colin," Virginia said sadly. "They're just dropping from the sky. One, two five, ten."

"What? What's dropping from the sky?" Blain asked.

Chuck answered, "Planes. Electromagnetic pulse. Everything running died."

"Where are they falling to?" Blain asked.

"Where ever they land." Chuck ran his hand across his face. "Oh, shit." He looked at his watch. "Bret was in the air."

Virginia interjected, "Got the text to him."

"Maybe their plane wasn't hit," Colin suggested.

"I have their flight number.…" Virginia

paused. "She's on the screen. Look. 425B."

"Found it." Chuck said. "She's still…."

Pause.

"Gone." Chuck's head dropped. "Their plane just dropped from the sky."

Blain turned left to right. "Is this real? Is this really happening? All these planes. People. And these on the ground. Is it real?"

Colin nodded, "Yes. Make your call, Blain. Be first on this."

Blain agreed, but slowly, in shock as he grabbed for his phone.

Chuck buried his face in his hands. "I'll have to call Bret's kids."

After a heavy sigh, Colin regained his composure. "No. Darius was prepared. He really was prepared for this to happen."

Chuck looked at him. "Did he know?"

Virginia spoke, "No, but he knew the probability with the increased sun spots. He was prepared. He got the text."

"But the question remains," Colin said. "Did they get off that plane?"

***

Thump. Grunt.

Thump. Grunt.

Darius landed first, with Bret not far behind or away from him. They'd opened their parachutes, and the graceful downward float to the ground enabled them to watch not only their plane fall and crash to the earth, but two others as well. The explosions sent smoke and flames billowing in the air, especially from one. Though at a distance, it was clearly seen to have crashed dead on into a town.

Darius was coming out of his roll, and he did it quickly, peering to the sky, just to make sure nothing was falling on him. He turned in a search and saw Bret standing, the straps of the parachute tangled around her.

He unlatched the chute, and headed to her. "Here," he said. "Are you all right?"

"Yeah, fine. Thanks. That was a jolt."

"Tell me about it." He undid her chute.

"Thanks. Hey. Look." She showed the diaper bag. "I still have it. Boy, I'll tell you I held onto it for dear life."

Darius chuckled. "I would think you would have held on to your chute. The diaper bag was not that important."

"You don't think? I'll have you know I have my toothbrush, tampons and ibuprofen in here. It is God."

Darius couldn't help but laugh, then he sighed out. "Wow." He looked about. "We're lucky."

"What do you mean?"

"I mean, a fifty foot patch of clearing surrounded by trees." He whistled. "We could have easily landed in the trees."

"I guess." Bret stared around. "But it looks like we're in the middle of nowhere."

"Nah, we're in Texas. That's somewhere." He chuckled. "I need you to start folding your parachute. We may need it for the elements if we're stranded." He headed back to where his parachute lay on the ground.

"Stranded? You mean there won't be a rescue chopper?"

"You're kidding, right?" Darius asked. "You're not. Bret? How? Pretty much everyone thinks we're dead. Planes fell from the sky. If that EMP extended into the metropolis, phones are down, cars won't run if they were running when it hit. No electricity."

"For how long?"

"Forever, or until they replace the components killed by the EMP."

"Oh man." Bret swiped down and grabbed the chute. "What now?"

"Now, first we get the chutes folded and put in our packs. Easier to carry. Then . . . " he lifted the cell phone, "Try to get a signal so we can at least let someone know we're alive. Where we are, I haven't a clue."

"Then there's no way for someone to send help."

"Not right now, unless they have an idea where we went down." Darius explained. "Our best bet is to try to find our way to civilization and get help."

"How long will that take?" Bret asked.

"Who knows. But…." Darius smiled brightly. "All is not lost. I was ready. Each of our parachute bags has a parachute survival pack in there."

"How did you know?"

"I didn't. But knowing we were going to be

hit with EMPs and knowing we hadn't yet, I figured, if it was gonna happen, it would happen while I was in a plane. Because I have a fear of flying."

"You didn't prove that by me. So what's in the packs?"

"First aid. Matches. Meals Ready to Eat pack. Which you and I can extend over days."

"Days!" Bret blasted. "We can be out for days?"

"We're in the woods, Bret." Darius said.

"You're like the outdoors guy. That's your work. Can't you get us out?"

"I'll try. I figure we stay one direction, we're bound to emerge. Right?"

"Right."

"And...." he reached into his bag. "We have a compass...shit."

"What?" She stepped closer.

"Look." He held it up. The needle spun.

"It won't stay put long enough to get direction."

"I know. Shit." He smacked it off his hand.

"Did the EMP do that?'

"No, the magnetic reversals. Oh, well. We just follow the sun."

Bret raised her eyes to the sky then gave a 'you think?' look to Darius.

The clouds were obvious. "Maybe not. Well, we always have the North Star, right? So...." He raised his voice. "Let's get our gear, pretend we're on a hike, and get out of here."

"Can we? Do you think we can?"

233

"Oh." Darius scoffed. "Absolutely. Without a doubt. But first, before anything." He slipped the battery into his phone. "I know we have a bunch of people worried about us. If we can only reach one."

"That's if we get a signal."

Darius turned on the phone. It beeped and he smiled. "We have one."

THE BLAIN REPORT

"What . . . (sniffle) has happened today isn't only an American tragedy, but a world tragedy. At three twenty-two Eastern Standard time today, forty-three planes fell out of the sky. Countless cities are without power and communication. The mid to south west are in scattered disarray . . . forgive my emotions, but this reporter witnessed it firsthand. Being at the center for solar investigation, we had first view of the flare that caused an Electromagnetic Pulse that struck without more than a seven minute warning. I . . . was and still am shocked. More so, I am saddened. Two dear friends of mine were aboard flight 425B. God be with them. More later. This is Blain Davis."

17 - Relieved

Colin mumbled, "We had it a minute ago. What happened?" As he and Chuck worked across the room on a printer.

Blain closed off his one ear while he spoke on his phone. Between the arguing of Colin and Chuck, along with the steady beeping of Darius' station, Blain was not getting the reception he needed, or able to hear.

"What? What do you mean it didn't show?" he blasted. "I did the segment. I thought my report aired live. We . . . ."

Do-da-beep-beep.

Crinkled brow, Blain's head cocked. "What was that? I'm sorry, go on." He nodded. "Responsible journalism?" he chuckled. "You're kid . . . ."

Do-da-beep-beep.

He lowered the phone. "Hey, there's a phone ringing."

Do-da-beep-beep.

"Someone. Doesn't anyone hear it?" He shook his head. "I was exercising responsible journalism by reporting about the EMP. It's not responsible to . . . ."

Do-da-beep-beep.

"The phone some one!" he shouted then continued. "It's not responsible to withhold the truth from the public."

Do-da-beep-beep.

He huffed. "Colin! Anyhow, what? Wait for

what?"

Do-da-beep-beep.

Blain turned to the phone that lay on the counter. "Waiting for conf . . . ." his eyes widened when he saw the digital display on the cell phone.

Do-da-beep-beep.

"Shit. Hold on." Dropping his phone, he snatched up Colin's. "Hello? Shit! Missed it! Redial. Redial." he hurried and pressed the button. "Nothing. Son of a bitch." he reached down and picked up his phone. "You still there?" Pause. "Fuck!"

"Good Lord." Colin walked to him. "What's going on?"

"Bout time I got your attention. I was on the phone with my producer." He handed Colin the cell. "By the time I saw who called . . . it was too late."

Colin peered. "Oh my God. We've got to try to call back."

"I tried. No luck."

"Who?" Chuck asked. "Who was it?"

Colin smiled. "Darius."

***

A pin could have been heard dropping; it was that quiet in Bret's home. Casper and Andi sat on the couch, Luke—head down—in a chair, even Perry, Bret's oldest, was there pacing.

Every once and a while, they'd all raise eyes to the ceiling at the sound of a bang or two from

Jesse.

Casper huffed. "Who called him anyhow?"

Luke shook his head. "Not me."

"Me either," said Perry.

The three of them looked at Andi.

"Okay. God! I called him; the airlines needed an adult next of kin."

Casper pointed to Perry. "What is he? He's an adult, next of kin."

"He's . . ." Andi pointed up, "her husband."

Casper rolled her eyes. "Debatable. Someone get him out of here. He doesn't have a right."

"And," Luke added, "he won't let anyone up there."

"I don't want him to go with us to the airport," Casper said. "Perry can drive us."

Jesse called down the steps. "Do we know where your mother's hair brush is?"

After a sniffle, Andi answered. "She probably took it."

With a slowly shaking head, Perry walked to the stairs and aimed his voice upward "What about…what about a hair band?"

It took a moment for Jesse to respond, and he did with a muttered 'thanks'.

They waded through a few moments of silence until Jesse's thunderous footsteps came down the stairs. "Let's go."

Luke stood up. "Why do they need a hair band of Mom's?"

"They need her hair," Jesse answered. "For DNA."

As if programmed, all of Bret's kids lowered

their heads.

"Let's go." Jesse reached for the door and opened it.

Luke paused before leaving. "Dr. Reye. Chuck?"

Jesse had a look of shock on his face, but it was nothing to the expression of surprise Chuck had when he saw Jesse in the doorway.

"What are you doing here?" Chuck asked.

"Not you, too," Jesse said. "The airline needs the families of those on the planes. I'm still her family. I'm her husband."

Colin choked as he held back a snicker. "Sorry." He cleared his throat. "I'm sure your Asian tinker toy loves hearing you boast that."

Chuck winced. "Colin."

Luke stepped forward, intercepting their glances between Colin and Jesse. "Chuck, Dr. Reye, are you guys here about my mom?"

"As a matter of fact," Colin replied. "We are."

Jesse said, "We're on our way to the airport. If you'll excuse us."

Colin held up his hand. "Then I'm glad I caught you. You don't need to go. They are requesting the families of those killed." Colin said as he and Chuck just made their way into the house. "So . . . Jesse . . . the spending fairy that is dancing in your head. That little kimono you have your buying sights on . . . ." he winked. "Drop it. Hate to put a damper on the insurance policy collecting day, but, sorry. I got a call." He held up his phone. "Bret is alive."

***

Child dragging behind her, Virginia flew into the Darius' world of computers. "Tell me nothing's happened, and you screwed it up," she said to Blain who stared at a screen, his hands to the side of his face.

"No," Blain answered.

Virginia exhaled. "Good." She turned and instructed her daughter to have a seat and not touch anything.

"Why are you here?" he asked. "I have it under control."

Virginia stared.

"No, seriously, I do."

"OK, if you do, then why the face?" She pulled out a chair and took a seat next to him.

"Oh," Blain grunted. "Life sucks."

Virginia blinked in surprise.

"My piece I did on the planes dropping. Dumped. The FAA or something has capped all stories regarding this."

"Are you more concerned with the fact that they capped the story or someone else is going to end up breaking it?"

Blain stood up. "Planes dropped from the sky, Virginia. Dropped. What are they waiting for? To see maybe if a few more drop?"

Virginia lifted her handheld unit. "If they're waiting for that, they'll wait a while. Things look calm right now."

Blain peeked at the unit. "Where did you get that?"

"Darius."

Blain shook his head. "His spending alone should tip people off." With a chuckle he sat back down. "Planes dropped. How can they keep covering up the natural disaster phenomena that are occurring?"

"They can't for long. And really , , , ," She snickered. "Think about it. How can they even remotely cover up this? This will get out. Planes dropping from the sky? No," She said. "There's no way around that one. Trust me."

***

"In what has been called 'one of the worst aviation terrorist strikes in history', President Greene is vowing to find who is behind…."

Colin shut off the news, and shook his head. "Terrorist attack. High altitude nuclear burst." He grumbled. "They did it. They found an out." He was more engrossed in watching the news than anything else. Chuck had left to drive Perry back to his place. Jesse was gone, and Colin was hanging out with Bret's kids until Chuck returned to get him.

"Play it again, Dr. Reye," Casper asked enthused. "Please play it again. I want to hear my mom's voice without Jesse around."

"With pleasure. He did kind of crowd the moment." He held up the phone for Bret's family to hear the speaker. It played, "*First message. Today, 2:45 p.m.*" Static. "*Goddamn it! I got the voice mail*."

Bret's voice spoke out, "Maybe they're busy, just leave a message."

"Fine," Darius said. "Hey! We weren't killed. We're alive. Fine. But lost. Right now we're headed south . . . ."

The message stopped.

Colin hit save.

"Can I hear it again?" Casper asked. "I was crying so hard."

"Absolutely." Colin handed her the phone. "I can imagine the torment you went through. I know what I felt when I believed Darius was killed. But they're both fine. Lost in the woods somewhere, but fine."

Luke asked. "So what now?"

Colin shook his head. "I don't know. I don't gather they'll be home tomorrow like planned. In fact . . . they're going to more than likely have to find their own way from where they are to civilization."

Luke nodded.

"I have an idea," Colin said. "You guys may or may not want to do it. We don't know how long your mother will be gone now. She's fine," he reiterated. "But with things they way they are, I certainly would feel better and I know your mother would if you guys stayed with me until she returned."

"Is your house big?" Andi asked.

"Very."

"Do you have kids?" Andi asked again.

"Darius, but he's with your mother."

Casper questioned. "Pets?"

"Not with Darius around. He tends to kill them."

Both girls cocked back in shock.

"Sad truth." Colin slowly shook his head. "What do you guys say?"

Luke shrugged. "I'll go."

Casper asked. "Can we swim in your pool?"

"Without a doubt."

"Oh, then I'm in, too," she said.

Colin chuckled, reached out, and rubbed her head. "Then let's pack our bags."

With apprehension, Luke spoke, "Dr. Reye, our mom, she's gonna be okay, right?"

Colin paused before answering. "She's with Darius. So very assuredly I can say . . . absolutely." He produced an affirmative look. "If he doesn't drive her insane first."

***

The air was stifling and carried a choking smoke that tickled Darius' throat as he walked. It was becoming bothersome, but not as much as the beeping behind him. "Will you . . . ." He turned and took the phone from Bret. "Stop. Please."

"I was playing the game."

"You're wasting battery power."

"It passes time as we walk."

"How about trying something else."

"Like?"

"Talking," Darius suggested.

Bret shrugged. "Sure." She took a few steps to catch up to him. "Can you not walk so fast?"

"I'm not walking fast. You're walking slow."

"Is that a dig because I'm small?"

"No," Darius defended.

"Oh, so it's because I'm a woman."

"Bret." He stopped, looked back. "No."

"All men are alike. They only . . . ."

"Bret," he cut her off.

"What?"

"Is this going to be a rant about your soon to be ex-husband."

"It . . . it might be."

"Save it." Darius said then saw the dejected glance she gave. "We . . . we may need conversation later."

"Oh. Okay. I'll stew it."

"Stew it?"

"Yeah, you know, hold it inside, think about it, get really pissed and then build up a good rant."

"You do that."

"I hate him," Bret declared.

"I understand." Darius kept walking.

"It's hot."

"I know."

"Do you think we'll have to walk at this pace, in this heat, on this terrain for very long?"

"Bret." Again, he stopped with a snap to his tone. "Are those tampons in the diaper bag as a precautionary measure or do you need them." He turned and started to walk.

It took Bret a second and she understood his insinuation. "I am not menstrual or premenstrual. I like to be prepared and I don't appreciate you making it out that my period is the reason for my bad mood."

"I apologize."

"So typically male."

Darius grumbled.

"So what is that yellow thing in your hand?" she asked, trotting to catch up to him.

"Your tone changed."

"Yes. I feel better now. I got some out of my system."

"Oh my God. You're a roller coaster."

"Pretty much," Bret shrugged. "So. You didn't answer."

"You confused me. What was your question."

"What's that thing in your hand?"

Darius held it up some. "A navigator. Helps navigate by putting in coordinates."

Bret nodded. "And you think that might help us find our way?"

"I don't know." Darius said. "It could be screwed up."

"Doesn't look like it makes sense to me." She peered over his shoulder.

Darius stopped. "Do you have another way?"

Bret pointed upward.

Chuckling, Darius shook his head "We established, following the sun isn't going to help. You can't see it."

"Not the sun. Why can't we see it?"

"The smoke."

Bret smiled.

"What? I'm lost."

"You're pretty smart, Darius, but . . . ." She pointed to her temple. "Think about it. We follow the smoke. Where there's smoke, there's fire, and where there's fire . . . ."

Darius grinned and finished her sentence. "There're rescue workers." With a grin, and a tug to her arm, Darius moved them more enthusiastically in the direction of the smoke.

***

So much for the theory.

It took two hours for Darius and Bret to walk the distance. The heat hammered at them and the smoke thickened, making the walk a struggle. But not as much as the sight of a body part here and there.

"Keep walking," Darius instructed. "But make a mental note. The rescue workers will want to know where the body is."

"Why don't you mark a tree or something," Bret covered her mouth.

"Good idea."

"I'm joking," Bret grabbed his arm again, and they continued on.

Both of them thought it wouldn't be much farther. They lightened the looming mood by encouraging each other with the thought of seeing rescue workers, paramedics, perhaps even some water so they wouldn't have to touch their supplies.

And Bret actually stopped bitching. Darius

supposed the sight of the bodies did that. They picked up enthusiasm the closer the noises drew.

But they realized that the crackling sounds were the only sounds they were going to hear.

Nothing.

No one. Nothing. Blackness. Fire.

Where were the workers?

"You have got to be shitting me." Darius exclaimed. He held out his arm blocking Bret. "This is the end of the line."

"What do you mean?"

"Nothing is here. No one." He inched them back. "Let's go."

"Wait . . . what about waiting."

"If they aren't here by now, they aren't coming. Fuck." He gave a twitch of his head. "EMP pulses. Fire trucks may not be working. Communications. Nothing." He took hold of her arm and led her in another direction. "We can't stay here. We'll get sick. We have to keep on moving."

"Where?" Bret asked.

"Who knows. East. West. Anywhere." He looked back at the devastation. "Anywhere but here."

***

Chuck had a seat on the grass, and pulled at the collar of his tee shirt. Using two fingers he swiped a bit of perspiration and ran his hand around to the back of his neck. "Feels hot." He shook his head. "Maybe it's my imagination. Would be odd."

He looked up at the sky, shook a finger at the sun, and then lowered his head. "OK, here's the deal, Mary. Forty-two? Yeah, no. Forty-some planes dropped from the sky today. Bret was on one, but she managed to parachute her way to safety. How do you like that? Darius knew, and they were prepared. I saw it coming. I saw her plane number leave the screen. I know . . . I know . . . ." He held up his hand. "How do I know all this? Well, the world see, is going to shit." He nodded. "Mother Nature, God had enough, time for a change. Like with the dinosaurs. Right now, there's some sort of reversal going on, caused by the sun. And get this, when it's done, this huge storm is gonna dump snow and ice on the northern hemisphere. But it gets better. Not just snow and ice. Hundreds of feet up north. Here in Pittsburgh maybe a hundred. For the first month, snow will extend all the way to the Florida state line . . . about."

Chuck paused to snicker.

"They say, after the destruction, the solar flares, earth quakes volcanoes, people are gonna know something is up. It'll be more than likely be explained as the reversal, nothing more, but we know better. After the destruction, after the reversal is complete, the storm will brew. They think we'll have a twelve-hour warning before the snow starts to come. When it does, four to six feet an hour. During which periods of freezing, instant freezing will occur."

248

Chuck played with the grass.

"Everyone is gonna try to head south. So our crew is making arrangements to set up here. Wait until the migrators leave or die off. More than likely, freeze and be buried. Then we'll head south. OK. Not we. Some view this as a bad thing, me? I view this as a great thing."

Chuck reached out and ran his hand over the flowers that decorated the base of the tombstone, a stone that held the engraved names of his wife and daughters.

"When the snow falls, I'm staying. Shh. No one knows this. In fact, no one knows I'm just gonna go out in it. One of those instant freeze things." Chuck snapped his finger. "It'll be over. I've missed you guys so much. My life is empty. Nothing. This isn't the end of the world for me, Mary. It's a new beginning." Peacefully, he touched Mary's name on the stone. "I'm coming home."

***

The small fire cracked and popped; Darius poked in to keep it going. He could see the edges of the MREs melting, folding a bit from the heat, where they rested close to the fire.

He had taken one of the parachutes and built a tent, make-shift, but something that would keep the elements from them for the night. But at that moment he waited on Bret. She had taken long, and Darius was almost at the point where he was going to worry.

The he heard the 'snap' of a twig.

He looked up. "Feel better?"

"Yeah, thanks. I've always had a hard time peeing around people. Hell . . . ." Bret sat down, "I get stage fright when someone walks into a public restroom."

Darius snickered. "Stage fright is a guy thing."

"You would say that."

Darius cringed. "Sorry. I am really trying to steer clear of male-related topics or implications.

"Yeah. I know. But aside from a guy thing, it's also a Bret thing. And look, I didn't use too much water to brush my teeth." She held it up. "Conservation."

"We'll be fine," He nodded. "We'll be in civilization by tomorrow."

"You think?"

"I know."

"Please don't tell me that smell is our food."

Chuckling, Darius shook his head. "It is and it isn't." Using the stick, he removed the packet. "Since we don't have anything to heat the food, I kept it near the fire. Should be good. No plates, we'll have to share."

"The same bag? Like a soda"

"If you want to say that. Why?" Darius paused. "Do you have a problem with eating in front of someone too?"

"No, I got over that in my teenage years"

Darius reached down and picked up the pouch. "Want to share . . ." heturned it over and read "Chicken a la King."

"Sounds good."

Just as he opened the pack with a small pocket knife, both he and Bret were startled by the ringing of the cell phone.

Both of them dove for it.

"Excuse me," Darius grabbed it. "Mine?"

Bret gasped.

"Colin," Darius said instead of hello.

"Dare-Dare. It's good to hear you. How are you?"

"Fine. We're both fine. Camping until morning."

"Tell him I said hi." Bret said.

Darius ignored her.

"You're breaking up," Colin said. "But I wanted to check. I've been trying the phone every fifteen minutes."

"Maybe we'll have a better connection tomorrow. I'll shut off the phone tonight to conserve the battery. We should hit civilization by then, get a car and go to the real estate place. Although I don't know if they're gonna sell with all that's going on."

"They'll sell. In fact you probably can get them down in price right now."

"Probably."

"What's he saying?" Bret asked. "What's he saying?"

Darius waved out his hand to her.

"Dare-Dare, rent the car for a while. FAA suspended all flights."

"Shit," Darius said.

"What?" Bret whispered. "What's going on?"

Darius turned his back to her.

Bret gasped.

After a few minutes of conversation, Darius ended the call with 'Shit' and put down the phone. "Connection died."

"Serves you right," Bret said. "You were rude."

"I was rude? You were rude. I was on the phone."

"Yeah, and you should have shared that phone call. So because you didn't," she tossed the foil food pack at him. "I didn't share the food. Night." She stood up and went to the makeshift tent.

Darius stared at the nearly-empty foil package. "She ate almost all of it. Shit." He looked up. "She ate the food." After glancing at the tent, Darius tossed the foil packet and summoned up a smug look.

THE BLAIN REPORT

The bright morning sun behind me doesn't brighten the gloom of yesterday's attack. It's a sad day for Americans, in fact the world, as experts estimate the loss of life due to the terror attack to be somewhere around six thousand. That would include those lost in the planes and on the ground. President Greene is expected to address the nation later today and still no one has come forth claiming responsibility for the attack. The FAA has suspended all domestic flights until further notice. You know, it is amazing, Dana, the outpouring of help from that has come in from around the globe, and right now experts are working hard to restore power to the northeast part of Texas. They're saying, because the loss was caused due to the electromagnetic pulse from the atmospheric burst, it is quite conceivable that it could take months, years before the power is restored. On Route to Texas via bus, this is Blain Davis. Back to you, Dana.

18 - A New Day

June 15ᵗʰ ...

It just had the feel of early morning to her. The sun wasn't too bright. But of course that could have been brought on by sky shrouded in smoke from the previous day. But it just had that feel.

The chilled air against her body was not alleviated by the parachute she used as a blanket/sleeping bag. Bret would have shouldered up the cloth had she not felt it.

Actually several parts of her body felt it. A pressure against her lower back, heaviness on her hip and a warm breeze swept past her ear...very close.

Fuck, she thought, and shifted her eyes down.

Darius' hand rested on her hip and that could only mean the warmth against her ear was his breath and the pressure against her back . . . .

Eyes wide, mouth screaming 'Fuck!' Bret flung off the covers and scooted quickly out and to her feet.

Darius, oblivious to what she meant, opened his eyes, and squinted. "What?"

"What do you mean, what?" Bret huffed. "What were you thinking?"

It took a moment, but Darius caught his bearings. Then he snickered.

254

Bret gasped. "You laugh?"

"Serves you right." He fussed with his hair and sat up.

"Excuse me?"

"You ate all the food. Steal the covers? I thought I'd share."

"You did more than share." With a growl, she stormed from the tent area. "I need coffee!" she shouted.

A few moments later, Darius emerged from the tent. He still had an amused look on his face. "Admittedly . . ." he said, "I didn't intend to end up snuggling with you. That just happened. In all honesty, I was just sharing the blanket."

"And you accidentally snuggled?" Bret asked with disbelief.

"Well, yeah."

"How does one accidentally snuggle?"

Darius shrugged. "I rolled, maybe?"

Grunting, Bret ran her fingers through her hair. "I'm telling."

"Telling who?"

Raising her eyebrows, Bret nodded. "Colin. He warned me that you might maybe try to take advantage of me in my vulnerable state."

"Vulnerable? You? Doubtful. Colin was just starting trouble."

"So what. I'm telling him that you not only snuggled, but you…." She dropped her voice to a whisper. "Snuggled hard."

It took a moment. Darius paused, and then he shook his head. "I did not."

"Did too. I felt it."

"Thanks." He smiled.

Bret turned and because she had nothing else to do, started gathering things. "I want to walk out of here."

"Bret," Darius made his way to her. "I'm sorry. I really didn't mean to snuggle." He took her arm. "And I especially didn't mean to snuggle . . . hard." He cleared his throat. "Even though I don't think that's the case."

"Why do you not believe me?"

"Simple, if I did…" he motioned his eyes downward. "It's only been a minute, where is it now."

"Those things can happen."

He scoffed. "Hardly. But I understand if you are confused on that matter."

"What do you mean confused?"

"That you may have thought you felt what you felt, but didn't because…."

"What?"

"Let's just say from what I heard, you may have forgotten."

"Forgotten?" A pregnant pause and then Bret gasped hard. "Oh my God. Are you implying I don't have sex?"

"That's what I heard."

"From who?"

"Is it true?"

"From who?"

"Your husband. I mean, ex."

"When?"

"When?" Darius thought. "When he sent me that threatening email telling me that if I was thinking of having an affair with you, don't, you don't put out."

"You're lying."

"Why would I lie?"

"True."

"And it is?"

"OK, enough talk about penises and sex. This conversation is getting gross."

Darius laughed.

"What?"

"Gross?" he whistled, then mumbled as he turned. "If sex is gross to you, no wonder he found the Asian chick."

"What was that?"

Darius shook his head. "Thinking. Anyhow . . . you said you wanted coffee."

"And I'm sure you'll produce some."

Darius reached to his backpack and opened it. After rummaging he tossed a small packet to Bret, while still holding a similar one in his hand. "Enjoy." He stood, zipped his bag and grabbed the make shift tent.

"What am I supposed to do with this? It's instant coffee. It's powder."

Darius smiled then held up a pack. "When I was in the Army." He ripped it open, and dumped the entire packet in his mouth. He grinned, and chewed.

Bret huffed. "That's gross."

"Instant caffeine fix."

"That's so gross."

Darius chuckled and returned to his task of packing up their camp.

***

The building stood seventeen stories high. Firm and solid, a structure built in the mid 1940's. At one time it was huge loft style apartments, which was before it was turned into storage, and then finally vacated.

The exterior was golden brick, arching around the huge windows that were boarded.

Inside, Bruce and Colin walked the tenth floor. Papers rolled about the dark interior as their feet kicked the garbage about.

"I have to tell you, Bruce, this is much better than the structure we had picked out."

"I thought so, too. Once I sat back and was looking at what you wanted, I thought of this place. Let me show you what I was thinking… I'll put the third divided wall here." Bruce indicated to the far right. "Both floors five and six should be where we all bunk down . . ."

"And you think it's our best bet to avoid the top floor?" Colin asked.

"Well . . ." Bruce titled his head. "I'm no expert. You are. But I was thinking it may get way too cold up there. Snow is insulation. Better safe than sorry."

Colin nodded. "Makes sense. Will it be shut off?"

"No." Bruce shook his head. "In case of emergency, you know, I don't think it's smart to shut off any means of escape to another floor."

"I have to tell you," Colin said with pleased look, "this is perfect. The fireplaces are still semi-operational. Heat was my big concern."

Bruce chuckled. "Uh mine, too. But this place needs only minimal work. I can get things going real fast . . . .   I was also thinking of using the bottom floor for wood storage. We're gonna be sealing the first ten stories. So that should stay dry. Plus, we're gonna have a ton of wood from when we break down the storage walls."

"Supply storage?" Colin asked.

"According to," Bruce made finger quotes, "The Plan."

"Which isn't etched in stone, mind you. We still have to meet when Darius returns to finalize."

"Still. Our supplies up here are limited, and should be. We can't travel with much."

"Speaking of traveling…." Colin said. "You told me on the phone that you worked out a plan."

"I did." Bruce pulled from his back pocket a sheet of paper. "After visiting this site a couple times, and remembering what you said about souping up them Humvees, I came up with my own modifications, specifications. Big words huh?" he winked and handed Colin the paper. "Plus, if you turn it over I've solved your other dilemma."

Colin received the paper and opened it. "Nice diagram. Other dilemma meaning where to store them."

"Yep, and it isn't a concern. Turn that over."
Colin did.

"We keep them here." Bruce said. "Right

smack with us."

"You're going to create a garage, here?"

"Yep. Pretty ingenious, don'tcha think? We construct a ramp on each floor. Attach them to the arch windows, big enough to take a vehicle though. As the snow piles up and is firm, we drive out, drive around, up the next ramp to the higher level."

"Holy cow, that's brilliant."

"Yep," Bruce said proudly. "Me and Bobby worked on that."

"Can it be done?"

"Piece of cake."

"And you have it worked out on how to get the Humvees in here in the first place."

"Got it covered, don't you worry."

Colin smiled. "Somehow, I don't with you." At that second, Colin's phone rang. He reached down to silence it but stopped. "It's Darius," he said brightly, then answered. "Dare-Dare."

"Hey, Colin, we got a signal!" Darius said. "We cleared a portion of the woods."

"And you're heading where?" Colin asked.

"Civilization."

"Well, let me know where that is, I may have to drive down there to get you. I can probably leave...."

"No, no need. We'll get back. I'll rent a car," Darius said.

"If you're sure."

"Yeah, I just wanted to make sure you know we were fine."

"And Bret?"

"Fine." Darius dropped his voice to a whisper. "Bitching."

"Are you behaving?"

"Yeah, but this morning she claimed I hit her with my erection."

"Excuse me?"

"I was sharing the blanket. Said I poked her with it."

"How would she know?" Colin asked.

"That's what I said. She got pissed."

"Dare-Dare, just behave and be careful."

"I will."

Another exchange and Colin ended the call. He held it near his face.

"You got that proud papa look on your face," Bruce said. "All is fine?"

Colin nodded. "Fine and safe."

"Good."

"Of course...." Colin sighed out. "Darius is showing her his erection, but other than that, they're making progress." He put his phone away, turned and started to walk. "What's this over here?"

Still spinning from Colin's comment, Bruce shook his head, snickered and followed Colin.

***

"I'm not understanding why they are sending you down there," Chuck said, talking on the phone while in the convenience store. "Damn it, I didn't see mustard."

"Huh?" Blain asked.

"Nothing." Chuck found the packet and opened it with his teeth. "Why?"

"Why are they sending me to Texas?"

"Yeah."

"They aren't. I asked to go."

"Okay. Why?" Chuck asked as he walked to the counter and waited for the clerk to ring him up.

"I'm a pretty big news celebrity."

Chuck paid, all the while bobbing his head and rolling his eyes.

"I have an obligation to keep this 'end of the world' thing a secret."

"When did that change?" Chuck asked.

"When I became part of the survival plan. You and I have book duty this upcoming week. Next week we are water boys. You think if this thing breaks we're gonna have all that easy of a time hoarding water?"

"No. We won't. Hoarding laws will go into effect."

"Exactly. And I want to hoard before that happens. We have a complex to stock. A wait house to get ready. It's not gonna be long before this thing gets out anyhow. Hell, it's probably already on the net. But until the governments confirm or deny, it's purely speculation. And while its speculation, we can prepare."

"Makes sense."

"Plus," Blain continued, "If I find Darius and Bret down there, my resources can help."

"Okay, you got a point." Chuck walked

outside and to his car.

"Darius and Bret surviving that crash. That's big news. It's a miracle. However…I need to get there and I need to cut it off at the pass."

"Oh, yes, sure, to scoop the story."

"No man, not at all. To save Darius."

Chuck laughed. "What? Save Darius? I think he's fine."

"You think," Blain said. "The government, the world, they're calling this EMP hit a terror attack, right?"

"Yeah." He opened his mouth to take a bite of his hot dog.

"No one's come forward. Man, if it gets out that Darius was on a plane, that he had a parachute and he survived, that he saw it coming. How long do you think it will take before Darius…is the fall guy. And all of us…and our little end of the world survival group? Part of his terror cell?"

Chuck had no more to say. He couldn't even eat. Blain had made a valid point.

***

"Triple Grande latte, please." Colin ordered his drink, then turned to Bruce. "And you're sure I can't get you anything?"

"Nope. I'm good." Bruce held up a bag. "These books will help me understand the weather and so forth."

"I could have given you any information you needed." Colin interrupted his talk, thanked the coffee shop clerk and returned to Bruce.

"In all due respect, as much as that is gonna help with questions, I kind of like to gather my info on my own."

"Makes sense."

The newest voice, "It doesn't to me," entered into the conversation.

"Bobby," Bruce said with a smile. "Glad you can meet us. We're heading to lunch."

"I'll pass," Bobby said, "I just came to get that new rat extermination handbook."

"Are they back?" Bruce asked.

"Tenfold today."

"Goddamn it." Bruce shook his head. "Where the hell are they coming from and why our swamp?"

Colin interjected "Perhaps we should test the water there. See if it contains anything out of the ordinary."

Bobby said. "It's river water."

"Yes, but perhaps there is some sort of gas leaking that is causing a problem," Colin said. "With all that's happening with the earth, you never know."

Bruce added, "Check this out, Bobby. I got some books so we can better understand the temperatures we're gonna have to deal with. I have this idea about sealing up the lower floors and creating a ventilation system. I'll get you to draw it up later."

Bobby nodded. "I still don't buy this, Dad. An ice age? Snow that's gonna pile up without warning in twelve hours?"

"We don't know. We have to take the word of the experts, here. I know that what's happened to our back yard ain't normal."

"And," Colin said, "there will be some warning on the snow. We'll see the storm clouds forming which will give us warning to get to the Wait Center."

"I know, Dr. Reye, you're an expert and all," Bobby said. "But it sounds far-fetched. I find it hard to believe."

"I can see that," Colin said. "As much as I find it hard to believe you lost your job as a police officer for being racist."

Bruce nodded. "That is true, though."

"I'm curious." Colin tapped his chin. "Was it racist against blacks, whites…."

Bruce answered. "Arabs."

"Ah."

Bobby winced. "Why are you telling him this stuff?"

"Well, son, what difference does it make? We're all gonna be living together forever real soon."

"Plus," Colin added. "I just find it hard to believe because you don't strike me as a racist."

"What makes one look like a racist, Dr. Reye?" Bobby asked.

"Being white," Colin answered then held up his finger when his phone rang. He answered it. "Chuck? Yes. Go on." All expression dropped from his face. "I can't believe we didn't think of that. Right away. Thank you." He hung up the call. "Can you gentlemen excuse me for a second?"

"Everything OK?" Bruce asked.

"Oh, yes, yes. Just a slight change in plans." He began to dial. "I have to call Darius."

***

They had just hit a side road and were having a liberal versus conservative bickering session with every step they took when a truck driver pulled over.

He asked if they needed a ride and informed them to 'hop in'.

They did.

"Whew." Bret said. "It's nice and cool in here."

"Thank you," Darius said. "We appreciate it."

"Didn't expect to see people walking," The truck driver said. "Not in this area."

"We didn't expect to be...." Darius stopped and answered his phone. "Hello."

"Who is it?" Bret asked.

Darius waved her off. "Oh, hey."

"Who is it?"

Darius ignored. "Yep. We just got picked up. A ride. How do you like that?"

"Darius."

Darius covered the mouth piece. "Do you mind? Thank you." He returned to his call, despite her huff. "Battery is almost gone so we have to make his...." he silenced and listened. "Shit. I didn't think of that. Yeah. Thanks. Bye." He hung up.

"I hate when you do that," Bret said. "Who was it?"

"Colin."

The truck driver cleared his throat. "So . . . just out of curiosity, what are you guys doing up in these parts. How long you been here?"

Bret answered. "Since yesterday morning."

"Are you aware of the plane crashes?" he asked.

"Are we ever." Bret said. "We . . ."

"Saw two go down." Darius interrupted. "Right in front of us."

"Hey!" Bret said. "Don't you want to let him know we . . ."

"Almost got hit with debris," Darius said. "It was freaky."

"What were you doing in the woods?" he asked.

"Walking," Bret answered. "You wouldn't believe this. We were . . ."

"Looking for the tillandsia recurvata. Which is a moss found in these parts. No luck." Darius said. "Then we got stuck. Because all the smoke and stuff."

"It's been a hell of a tragedy." The driver said. "Terror attack you know."

"You don't say," Darius said. "Really? Oh my God."

Bret huffed. "No, it was . . ."

"More than that, yes." Darius tapped her knee. "You're right dear. Sad."

A final grunt and Bret faced Darius "Why the

hell are you doing that?"

"Doing what?"

"Stopping me from talking."

Darius couldn't tell her that they couldn't divulge they had survived the crash. He had to come up with something. "Because . . . because . . ."

"Because what?"

"Because you're being typically female and hogging all the conversation."

"How . . . dare . . . you. You male chauvinist pig headed liberal!" Bret blasted, and then started into a rant. The driver hunched and winced at the loud vocal explosion that ensued in the cab of his truck.

***

"As a protective measure," Chuck said to Colin. "It works. But they're in Texas. How are they going to eat? Get a room? Rent a car? Dead men don't pay."

"Ah . . . but they do." Colin pulled out the keys to his house and aimed the key to his front door. "See, the credit cards will likely be denied if we inform them that Darius is dead. We'll do no such thing. As long as we don't try to claim insurance money or sue the airlines, we'll not draw attention to ourselves. We're not going to say he's dead, we're just not going to tell anyone they are alive."

"Won't they figure that out when charges are

on his card?" Chuck asked. "I mean, the airline is going to look into every person aboard."

"And Darius and Bret will not come up as terror suspects. If they come to me and ask, I'll simply tell them that some thief must have found the card and used it. After all, the plane did drop from the sky. It is conceivable his credit cards flew about."

Chuck winced, showing his slight disagreement. "I'll let you handle that and . . . this."

Colin walked into the house. "Does something smell like it's burning?"

"Like someone's trying to cook."

Colin set down his briefcase and closed the door. "If that's my maid I may reconsider her employment."

"No need," Mrs. Wilson, Colin's maid, hustled to the door. "I came on to your home because you had no children. It was bad enough when Mr. Cobb moved in, now this. No. They burned ramen noodles. Never heard of anyone who burned ramen noodles. You can send me my check. Good day." She opened the door and walked out hastily.

"There you have it," Chuck said.

"I never liked her pot roast anyhow. Burnt ramen noodles sounds better." He walked to the kitchen.

Chuck laughed, following Colin to the kitchen. He was amazed at the lack of surprise on Colin's face as Andi and Casper sat at the breakfast counter eating ramen noodles. Luke was nowhere to be found; the kitchen was a mess and Colin just smiled.

He asked Casper if she'd make him some ramen then took a seat at the counter with the girls. He informed them, as if it were nothing, that he needed them to be the best actresses they could and pretend their mother was dead.

***

"Do you think maybe . . . you could have told me?" Bret snapped at Darius. She stopped, fixed her shoe and then her backpack. "Or else maybe we wouldn't be walking."

"Oh, okay, let me get this right. I was supposed to stop you in the middle of your sentence and tell you that we can't say we survived that crash because it would look suspicious."

"Yes."

"Yeah, right." Darius scoffed. "That's real smart."

"Are you saying I'm dumb?"

"You aren't acting bright at this moment."

"Asshole."

"Thank you for that." Darius shook his head. "I would have thought you would have caught on. Or at the very least, saved your bitching for when we got to town."

"So it's my fault that the truck driver kicked us out."

"Yes." Darius answered adamantly. "You bitched."

"You started it."

"You screamed."

"You did, too."

"Listen to us." Darius sighed out. "I probably would have kicked us out as well."

"No you wouldn't have," Bret said. "Neither would I. I would have told us to quit, or shut up. I wouldn't have made us walk in this heat."

"True."

"We're both too nice for that."

"I agree."

"He wasn't a nice man," Bret said. "I could tell."

"You know what? I picked that up as well." Darius adjusted his bags. "See, we can agree on some things."

"I never said we couldn't. We're just in a bad spell."

"Which we'll get out of."

Bret laughed.

"What? What's so funny?"

"I'm just thinking we're in trouble if we don't. We're the future of society."

"It'll be a long end of the world."

"Just like it's a long hot walk," Darius said.

"Could be worse. A freak storm could brew."

They both stopped and looked at the sky.

Sunny.

They walked on.

19 - The Purchase

June 16th ...

Darius didn't mean to see her naked. It just happened that way. The plush hotel room had two doors to the bathroom, and Darius wasn't even thinking they led to the same one. He went in to shower. She was enjoying the bath.

Bret was so exhausted that she just released a slight 'peep', slid down in the bath, and accepted his apology. Darius himself didn't realize how tired he was until the apple he was eating revitalized him.

The shower would do wonders.

After the long walk, they arrived in some small no-name town which had been pummeled into blackness. A nice older gentleman driving a pickup truck – without air conditioning—offered to take them into Austin, or anywhere nearby. That's where he was headed to stay.

They vowed not to argue and were silent during the ride.

They were off on their calculations of where their plane crashed. They were a bit more south, but not too far south, as the trip to Austin took a couple hours. Highway driving became crowded the further south they rode.

"That's the only place with power," the kindly man said. "South Texas. Most folks would think it's the apocalypse without power."

"Why are you headed there?" Darius asked.

"See my son."

As long as the man didn't mind, they took the ride all the way there. Little did they know how many people would be flocking south.

The only hotel available was one that cost over three hundred dollars a night, and the presidential suite was a grand.

"We'll take it. At least two nights," Darius said without hesitation.

He would have paid two grand a night the room felt so good.

Bret didn't take a long bath. He wanted to tell her that he had heard from Blain who was arriving via chopper – brave man. The bus ride down proved too troublesome and the high-class reporters took the offer of a chopper.

Colin gave Blain the number.

Before Darius could tell her, Bret staggered from the bathroom wearing the thick, huge, complimentary robe and dropped face first on the bed.

She was out in seconds.

Darius let her sleep just like that, on top of the bed. And surprisingly enough, when he woke up the next morning, she was still in the same position. Only her wet hair had dried.

That made Darius laugh.

The coffee pot in the room brewed its last drop and the aroma filled the air. He poured a cup for himself, then one for Bret. Carrying the mug he went into her room, set the mug on the stand

and crouched by the bed.

"Wanna get up?" he asked. "Blain will be here shortly."

Bret's head cocked immediately as if she was startled that she was sleeping. "Doesn't he understand we want to get some sleep?"

"Sure," Darius said. "He arrived a few hours ago and already started things for us. I made coffee." He stood. "By the way, nice hair."

"What?"

"I never thought anyone's hair could look like that, but then again, yours dried in that position."

"Fuck." Bret sat up, trying to pat down her hair. "It dried sideways."

"I'm sure you have fix-it stuff in that diaper bag."

"I have a brush." She swung her legs over the bed and grabbed the coffee. "Thanks."

"No problem." Darius began to walk, but stopped. "Hey, uh, since you and I were clothes-less, I called down stairs; I told them to send something up from the clothes shop. Comfortable. Everyday. Stuff we can sight-see in."

"You told them to send tourist clothing?"

"No, no." He shook his head. "I just didn't want them to send formal wear. Shorts. Tee shirts. Underwear. That type of stuff."

"Thanks" Bret stood. "I'm going to go into the bathroom, in case you are thinking of going in."

Darius chuckled. "No, I'll let you have your privacy. I'll wait...." he smiled at the knock on the door. "Bet that's our clothes now. I'm bringing them in. I hope they're all right."

"Anything, right now, is going to be great."

Darius took stock in what she said and even agreed. Anything was better than their dirty clothes, or the oversized white robes they were forced to wear. Besides, it was a high priced hotel; the clothes had to be good.

***

Bret turned from the mirror as Darius walked back into the room. "Oh, do we look gay or what?"

"We look like tourists."

Bret checked out her reflection again. "Oh my God."

"Could be worse."

"How?"

Darius walked up to stand beside her and check out his reflection as well. "Okay, it's worse."

Both of them wore khaki thigh-length shorts, slip-on loafers, and green flowered buttoned-down golf-style shirts.

"We're Madge and Marv Miller," Bret said.

"Who?"

"They were this couple in their fifties who constantly went away in their RV when Marv retired early. They dressed alike, and God, they dressed like this. All we need is a camera."

Knock-knock-knock

Darius smiled. "Close."

"Huh?" Bret asked confused.

Darius walked to the door.

Blain stood in the door. "Hey, sorry it took so long."

Darius opened the door wider. "Were you able to get a rental car?"

Blain dangled the key. "Nice outfit."

Bret emerged from the other room.

"Oh, my God." Blain laughed. "You two are the cutest thing."

Bret tilted her head.

"All you need is a camera hanging around your neck," Blain said.

"Okay, okay," Darius held up his hand. "No, matching tourist jokes. It's the only option we had. So tell us."

"Yes." Blain nodded. "I went to the real estate agency like you asked because we have to keep your name out of it. She wasn't really happy that I came by at such an early hour, but when she found out who I was, she pepped up. She took me out to see it."

"And?" Darius asked.

"It's really worth seeing it Darius. It is 'it'."

"Okay, can she meet us?"

Blain shook his head. "Nope. Family picnic. But . . ." he held up another set of keys. "My celebrity status is worth something."

"She gave you the keys?" Bret asked.

"Oh, yeah," Blain answered. "When she saw how interested I was in the property, she was on it. I mean, let's face it; the price tag is high. And when she found out I was willing to pay up front, she got giddy."

The corner of Darius' mouth rose. "Then she hasn't a clue."

Blain shook his head. "Nope. It's not even in the disclosures. It states a barracks style property on 350 acres."

Darius chuckled.

"Wait. Wait." Bret walked up. "If this is the property you have been looking for . . ."

"One of four," Darius corrected. "We believe it is."

"Okay." Bret nodded then continued. "If the real estate agent doesn't know, how do we know for sure this is one of the four urban legend properties?"

Blain smiled. "Like Virginia . . . I saw the floor. I saw the markings."

Darius cocked his brows a few times. "He saw the markings."

Sarcastically, Bret nodded. "Markings. Sweet. How do we know someone didn't mark it for a joke? We don't. So before we hand out three million, let's take a ride out there and see if this is truly the property you say it is and see for ourselves if this is one of the Four Horseman of the Apocalypse complexes."

Darius shrugged. "I'm up for it." He swiped the room key from the table. "Let's go now."

"Me too." Blain jingled al the keys and turned "Let's go. Ready, Bret?"

Bret grabbed her diaper bag. "Ready."

Blain paused by the door. "Okay, if we go out in public with you two, can you not hold hands?"

Bret nudged him as he laughed and all three walked out.

***

The expression on Bret's face would be forever etched in Darius' mind. The gate was weak and flimsy, and they drove up a long dirt driveway. The barrack structure was plain, and as they approached the door a blast of wind hit them smacking them with hot air. It took Bret by surprise. Her eyes rolled slightly, her mouth opened a bit, and she coughed and gagged.

"I ate a bug," she coughed then spit.

"That was weird," Blain said. "Felt like God hit us with a blow dryer."

Bret shook her head. "The world is going to pot, and you think hot air is weird. Try dropping from the sky. Open the door."

Blain removed the box and then unlocked the door.

The barracks were dusty, but not completely empty. Bunk beds were lined up. A few long wooden tables, like something from the forties, were in the middle.

"Oh, yeah, this is a survival place," Bret said sarcastically.

"The markings, Blain," Darius said. "Where are the markings?"

"This way." Blain led them to the back. "It's in the back corner of the office."

They walked across the long rectangular building. At the far end was a short hall. Clearly at the end of the building was a main bathroom. The sun peeked through the windows, lighting the room.

Blain and Darius turned into the office right before the bathroom. Bret did not.

"Bret?" Darius called. "You coming in here."

"I want to check out the old bathrooms. Go on. Look at the markings."

Darius nodded. Bret went straight, he turned with Blain.

"Over here," Blain walked to the file cabinet.

From the other room, echoing, they heard Bret. "This is weird."

"It's a latrine. They pretty much did away with them," Darius answered for her, speaking loudly. "It's a bit of history."

"No, Darius, the wall is off. Why is this room short?" she asked.

Darius looked at Blain. "What is she talking about?"

Blain whispered. "I haven't a clue."

"So strange," Bret said. "Something is behind this wall."

Darius shook his head, and nodded to Blain. "Markings."

"Over here."

Bret called out. "Like anybody cares what I'm discovering."

Darius huffed. "You're discovering a badly designed bathroom."

"Markings." Blain pointed.

To the right of the file cabinet on the concrete floor was an engraved and painted picture, no bigger than four inches, of four horses with a mushroom cloud behind them.

"Wow," Darius crouched down. "This is it. This floor is concrete."

"My thoughts exactly."

"So . . . where's the entrance?"

Bret's voice hollowed some. "What the fuck. This is the weirdest shower stall."

"God!" Darius called out. "It's old, Bret!" he dropped his voice to a whisper. "Jesus Christ."

"Hey, she's amusing herself," Blain said.

"True."

"Where the fuck is the shower head?" she questioned out loud. "I know I'm gonna get wet when I turn it on."

Blain looked at Darius and they both laughed.

"Sorry," Blain snickered. "From what I heard she didn't get turned on."

"Shh." He held his finger to his mouth. "Maybe if she gets wet now, things might change."

"Boy this thing is stuck. It's hard," she said.

They laughed again.

"She's making progress," Darius joked.

"Hopefully," Blain tilted his head. "We may be the only civilization for a while. Virginia is married. Bret's cute . . ."

"If you guys hear me scream, it'll be because I get hit with something slimy!" Bret yelled.

"We're ready!" Darius replied then shook his head at Blain. "Holy shit. I cannot believe you're worrying about getting laid in the future."

"You're not."

"No." He paused. "Besides, I have dibs on Bret."

"What! You can't call dibs on someone. You don't even like her."

"Yeah, I do. Not that way, yet, I don't think. But. It makes sense," Darius said.

"No. Chuck or Bruce make more sense."

"What! No way."

"Let's ask."

"No, you can't . . ."

"Bret!" Blain called. "Can we pull you away from the hard, turning-on task of getting wet?" he snickered.

"What?" Bret came into the office, confused. "What are you talking about?'

"Whatever you're working on there that might make you wet and slimy," Blain said.

"Oh, the shower," Bret replied.

"Yeah, anyhow, hypothetical question for you," Blain said. "End of the world. We for some reason get no other people but us. For a long time. You want to have sex. Which man, out of our group, do you pick?"

"Why are you asking this?" Bret questioned.

Darius nudged him. "See, I told you. She doesn't answer questions about things she doesn't know about."

"I'll have you know I have four children," Bret said.

"Ok, so that's four times you have sex that we can prove. Some people do that in a week," Darius commented.

Bret gasped. "That's wrong. And just so you

know, if I wanted to have sex . . . it wouldn't be with you, Blain." she said.

"Why not?" Blain asked.

"Too young." She faced a smug Darius. "Nor you, it would be too selfish." She exhaled. "I know exactly who I'd pick."

They waited.

"Colin," Bret stated.

"Colin!" Darius snapped. "Oh my God. Why?"

"Well, he's older, mature. Experienced. Probably very unselfish and partner-oriented. And he'd make me laugh."

Darius snickered. "He'd make you laugh all right. I'm not sure he even has a penis anymore."

Bret gasped. "Oh my God, are you rude. I cannot believe you are insulting Colin's penis. Wait until I tell him." She turned and walked out.

Darius laughed. "Let's find the switch to open the passageway."

"Are we sure there's a passageway?" Blain asked.

"Well, this obviously isn't it."

"Guys!" Bret called out.

"Ignore her," Darius instructed. "Look behind the file cabinet."

"OK, check behind that shelf."

Darius agreed.

"Guys!"

"Jesus Christ, Bret!" Darius yelled. "What!"

"I think you should come here."

After a huff, and a wave of his hand to Blain, Darius walked out. He went into the latrine.

"Where are you?"

No answer.

"Bret?" Darius called out.

"Where is she?" Blain asked.

"I don't know." Darius looked left to right. "Bret!"

There was the slightest of squeaks, and the entire tile wall, which looked as if it were a shower area, lowered to the floor.

Bret stood there, hand against the ten by ten foot doorway. "Do you remember the show Let's Make a Deal? Does this remind you of it?" she asked.

"Holy shit." Darius rushed forward. "How did you find this?"

"I turned on the shower to see if it worked," she said. "But it wasn't a shower stall. Check this out." She turned, grabbed the flashlight from her belt and turned it on. "Emergency lighting. Needs batteries." She shined the light to the ceiling. "But check out this ramp. I didn't go down, but it goes down far."

Blain yelled down it. "Hello!"

His voice echoed back.

Darius took the flashlight. The doorway was actually an entranceway to a tunnel; they stood at the top of what seemed to be a long concrete ramp that ran downward. "Let's go," Darius led the way. 'I'm betting the other end of this is big enough for trucks to pass through," he commented as he walked.

How far did they journey? A quarter mile, a half mile? They didn't know, but each step they took drew them deeper underground until the tunnel leveled out.

"Look at this," Darius allowed the beam to reflect off the left and right sides of the wall. "Boxes of food."

"If it's been here that long," Bret said. "I'm not so sure I'll wanna eat it."

Darius laughed. "Me either. Oh, wow." He stopped. "Look ahead."

"Is this for real?" Bret asked.

"Did we really find it?" Blain questioned.

"I believe," Darius illuminated the huge round, vault style door. "This is it."

***

Harry Hart worked for the government. He was also a journalist and novelist. Not many people had heard of him, but Darius had. Harry Hart wrote under the pen name Pat Frank. Pat Frank was synonymous with atomic war stories and survival. His book, Alas Babylon, was always a favorite of Darius, and that book prompted him to locate the out of print, and hard to find over-priced book, How to Survive the H Bomb, by Pat.

Darius remembered when Colin found that book in his room. He chuckled at the outdated tale, but even though some things in the book were outdated, the overall feel and message were not.

In fact, it held true to the situation they faced and could be used as a guidebook. How to Survive the H-Bomb was what prompted Darius to look for the Four Horseman of the Apocalypse complexes.

In the nonfiction book, Pat Frank discusses a privately-funded bomb shelter built in Florida, and designed to house a hundred families.

The bomb shelter was described as self-sufficient, with dorms, a cafeteria, its own water supply, diesel generators, reserve tanks, and so forth.

Catacombs constructed for the survivors of the future.

Darius read about them when he read the book at the age of fifteen and thought no more about it.

Until it snowed one day.

It snowed so hard that the cable was out and Darius decided to clean out the basement to pass time.

It was there he found the book and read it again.

During that reading he read the passages about the Sylvan Shores bomb shelter. But unlike when he was fifteen, the internet provided him the means to research it.

The next day when the cable and internet were back up, he began his research.

He was never able to locate any information about Sylvan Shores, but he found other information. Across the United States there were many government installations built underground, bigger than Sylvan Shores. They were built for thousands, not hundreds. Complete with streets, hospitals, and television rooms.

Two were nearby. In Virginia, there was Mt Weather. It was a well-known bunker for top members of the federal government. The other was at a fancy hotel in West Virginia, a secret installation revealed to the public in the 1990's.

In order for Darius to take a tour of the bunker, he had to book a room.

He did.

It was during his stay and tour that he became more fascinated with the concept of underground cities and shelters. Darius vowed that once he retired he was going to build one.

He spoke to a man who claimed his father worked on the bunker. It was that man who told him about the Four Horseman of the Apocalypse complexes.

His father was called into work on two of them.

Four underground stations, complexes, like the ones the government built. Almost as big, and privately funded.

The four shelters were connected by ownership. Built in the 1970s, those who funded the complexes made a pact to be the new civilization should the world turn to ashes.

Each complex, hidden beneath some sort of diversionary building, bore a symbol on the floor.

Like the one Darius found.

The four were located in the south and southwest. California. New Mexico and two in Texas.

All were built to be self sufficient. Thirty-eight thousand square feet of room. A place to start seedlings. Even a ventilation system designed to be man-run should power fail.

Darius researched these complexes and found no concrete evidence of their existence, only rumors.

Until he stood in one.

It was magnificent.

The hallways were wide and sturdy, big enough to start a transit with golf cart type mobiles. The hospital had a twelve-bed ward. Operating room, and examining room. There was an area for dentistry.

The kitchen was a common area. There were eight latrines and showers, 16 dorm rooms with divider walls. Four recreation rooms and a theater.

It was three levels, at least a hundred feet underground.

The top two floors of the complex were ready for use, the bottom floor, storage or expandability.

The boiler room alone was huge.

Darius chuckled at the bicycles in there, eight of them, that would be peddled to produce energy.

The tour, which was led by the 'You are here' layout plaques on the wall, took two hours.

There wasn't a space they missed, or a room they didn't photograph.

They sat on boxes of chicken noodle soup, taking a break before going topside again.

"Shame," Darius said. "I don't think we can use all this food."

Blain added. "I don't think we should throw it away. It is canned goods. Can't we test it to see if it went bad?"

"We could," Darius said. "At least have it in reserve."

Bret stood. "I can't believe this place. It's huge. It's a building underground. I like the artificial light room, like they have on a sub."

"Me, too. It'll be cool for reading," Darius agreed.

"So, let me ask you a question. Is this like finding the pot of gold for you?" Bret asked. "I mean, you talked about your obsession since reading that book. Is it?"

"Yeah," Darius nodded. "I can't believe this exists and that we're gonna buy it. Tomorrow."

"You never mentioned how," Blain said. "Really, how are we gonna do this."

"Winslow will write out a check." Darius shrugged. "This place is so great."

Bret cleared her throat. "I have a question." She raised her hand. "If it's an ice age, why are we going underground?"

"Because it keeps us safe," Darius answered. "People are not going to be behaving rationally. Do you really want people to know how much survival stuff we have? Being on top of the ground is sending just that message."

"True." Bret ran her hand against the concrete wall. "It's so atomic. Nuclear war-like. Of course," she shrugged, "maybe what we need is a nuclear war. We're already off track. According to all those old sci-fi movies, that would toss back on track again. I love those old movies. We have to remember to get some."

"Stop," Darius held up his hand. "Repeat

what you said."

"We need to remember to get some old movies."

"Back further."

After a moment of confusion, Bret answered. "We need a nuclear war?"

"Bingo." Darius snapped his finger and smiled. "Let's go." He didn't even wait, was down the tunnel, through the vault door and on his way up the ramp by the time Bret and Blain realized he was actually leaving.

20 - A Plan

Colin laughed.

He laughed, said, "Excuse me," then set down the phone on the counter . . . and laughed some more.

Darius' voice was muffled as it carried through the receiver.

Colin didn't hear him. He was too busy laughing.

After a moment, he lifted the phone. "I'm sorry."

"Don't laugh at me."

"It's ridiculous."

"No, it's not."

"Dare-Dare, you want to do what?"

"You heard me," Darius said.

"Yes, I did. I just never thought this would come from you. It's very fifties sci-fi."

"Well, Bret was talking about fifties movies when the idea came to me."

"There you have it, Darius. She thinks this whole thing is a fifties movie. Look at her reaction to Winslow."

"Colin, please. Open your mind."

"I am."

"It could work."

"Based on what?" Colin asked. "What facts do you have to support this?"

"None. It's theory."

"Based on old fifties movies."

Darius sighed. "No."

"You think theoretically you have come up with a way to change things."

"Yes. And don't laugh about it being a theory. We're basing everything we're doing on a theory of what is going to happen to the world."

"No, Dare-Dare, for that we have scientific data. The world is already going to shit. And you want to blow it up."

"No. No. No." Darius was adamant. "I want to create a big enough explosion, at the right speed, right time, right place, so it causes such a disturbance in the magnetic field that it stops the reversal, even reverses it."

"And how big of a bang do you need?"

"I have it calculated. We'd need an explosion that causes about sixteen million gigajoules of energy."

Colin dropped the phone.

"Colin?"

He lifted it back up. "Sixteen million gigajoules. What the fuck, Dare-Dare. Do you know what it would take to produce that energy?"

"Yep. Three trillion, nine-hundred sixty-nine million, nine hundred tons of TNT. Or…3.9 gigatons of nuclear explosions."

"Oh my God, in one area?" Colin asked. "I'm afraid to ask, but do you have a clue how many nuclear warheads it would take to produce that much?"

"Yes."

"I figured as much."

"About fourteen thousand 300 KT bombs. Which is about half the world arsenal, yes, I understand."

"Oh my God."

"But it can be done. The energy . . ."

"Do you mind if I do my own math and work on this?"

"Sure, but...."

"Because," Colin said. "We really can't do anything until you get back. So let me work on this see what I come up with."

"Okay."

"Everything else okay?"

"Oh, yeah, the complex is awesome."

"Deeply set underground?" Colin asked.

"Deep."

"Hmm. Probably would come in handy if your theory is implemented. All right, I'll speak to you later."

"Thank you."

Colin hung up. He looked down to his paper and the figures written. "Half the world arsenal. That's all."

When Darius disconnected his call he turned around in the hotel room to face the stunned expressions of Blain and Bret. "What?" he asked.

Bret tilted her head. "You want to blow up the world to stop the ice age?"

"God, you and Colin are so melodramatic. No. I just want to cause a burp. That's all. Excuse me." He walked from the room.

Blain turned to Bret. "He did say half the world's arsenal right?"

"Yep." Bret nodded.

Blain nodded as well. "He wants to blow up the world."

The Blain Report

It has nearly been four days since the terrorists hit. With the arrest of the terror cell in Mexico that claimed responsibility, things are moving along impressively. Although it is estimated that 65% of all electronic devices will have to be replaced, along with power lines and grids, main grids and terminals have been or are in the process of being replaced, and until the lines are fully up and running, it looks as though they will be channeling energy from New Mexico, Mexico and Louisiana. Officials say by tomorrow morning, Texas should be running at full power. And I'll tell ya, Dan, it can't come too soon for these residents who need air conditioning. Not even the crack of dawn, and already temperatures are already a sweltering 80 degrees. Preparing to head back north, this is Blain Davis....

21 - Dogs

June 18th

"That was brilliant on your part, Mr. Winslow," Colin spoke on the phone as he walked his upstairs hallway. "Please pass on to your attorneys that we were very grateful for their presence with Blain at the closing. Absolutely, I'm sure he can supply you with an autographed picture. Uh huh." He paused in the hallway to check out his reflection in the mirror. "Everything is settled. We plan on moving equipment to the site this week. Virginia and her family."

Colin exhaled, and headed down the steps.

"No, you haven't met her yet. Yes, she's married. You are paying them to live there though. If you think we should we can get security. I don't see any reason for you to go there at this time. We will take you are there with us when the time comes. Yes, sir. I must go. Absolutely, Bruce is there. Have a good day."

Mid descent of the stairs, he paused. Twelve minutes he was on the phone with Winslow. He shook his head, prepared to call Bruce to give him a heads up that he might receive a visitor, but opted against it. Bruce could handle it.

He smelled it, the moment he hit the bottom of the staircase. Cooking. After nearly tripping over the scooter in the hallway, Colin walked to the kitchen. "Morning, girls."

Andi was wiping up coffee spillage by the pot. "You take yours black, right."

"If it was made for me, I take it anyway. Thank you, Andi." Colin accepted the coffee as he took a spot at the breakfast counter. "Ah, my paper."

Casper turned from the stove, "Breakfast is almost done."

"And you made me breakfast?"

"You haven't been around in the mornings, the last few days," Casper said. "And we knew you were home. We want to cook for you. We're really glad you let us stay here while our mom is gone."

Andi added, "We really like it here."

"And I like you kids here, too. Gives the house life. Luke is doing wonderfully learning the equipment. You two are just, sort of, almost, but not quite Suzy homemakers."

Casper said, "We want to do more. You got the new cleaning lady. And it's not fair that you work the labs and stuff and come home and cook. We can cook, you know. Or try."

"Take-out works," Colin said. "But if you want to cook I'm fine with that."

"Good." Casper smiled. "Like I said we made breakfast."

"And it smells…wonderful," Colin paused and looked at the plate set before him. "And this looks like.…"

Andi finished the sentence. "Fried ramen and bacon."

"Ah," Colin nodded. "Fried ramen noodles and bacon. Yummy." He cleared his throat.

"Speaking of which," Casper said, "We used the last two packs for breakfast."

"I just bought the case two days ago." Colin comment. "But then again, that doesn't surprise me. You made ramen noodle sandwiches for lunch yesterday."

"You don't like ramen noodles?" Casper asked.

"I can't say that I have ever eaten ramen noodles until you kids arrived." Colin smiled politely. "But this looks yummy."

He really did. He hesitated before eating, but had the fullest intent to at least try the meal the girls had prepared for him. Fork full of ramen and nearly to his mouth, the door to the basement opened.

"Hey, Dr. Reye, glad you're awake," Luke said as he entered.

"How it going down there, Luke?"

"Good. Good. I think." Luke scratched his head. "Is it like a big problem if there's a red dot on the earth and alarms are going off."

"Um, yes, I believe it is." Colin stood. "Let's go check it out." He stepped away from the breakfast counter, paused, reached out, grabbed his plate and then followed Luke.

***

Virginia's voice piped through the

speakerphone in the makeshift basement lab. "You're the geologist, Colin. Not me."

"Did you get the images?"

"Yes, I did."

"Then I just need you to concur and help me figure this one out."

"It's a hot spot."

"Thank you for that," Colin said. "Fine. You're probably busy with moving."

"Colin, don't get shitty," she said. "I'm just saying it's a hot spot. Whether it's tectonic plate movement or a volcanic eruption underground, I don't know. Did you get in touch with seismologists in the area?"

"I need to pinpoint where it's going to surface. I'll get back to you." He hung up, ran his hand over his chin. "I suck at this computer shit. Okay . . . let's . . ." he pulled up a chair next to Luke. "Let's see if we can watch this bad boy, make a prediction and get in contact with scientists in the area."

"How much time are we talking about?" Luke asked.

Colin shrugged. "I don't even know where this is going. Sort of like that red spot on your chin. We don't know if it will be a blemish, pimple, or a full-blown eruption when it finishes."

"Thanks, dude." Luke touched his chin.

"No problem." Colin returned to the screen. "Earth's acne."

***

It wasn't something that Chuck wanted to deal with. He had just returned home to Johnstown, was working on the Fire Chief story, when he got the call.

It was a blistering call.

Containing the 'f' word in every sentence, Chuck had to pull the phone from his ear.

"Jess, stop," Chuck implored. "You seem to lose the ability to speak English when you're pissed. Why are you screaming at me?"

"Because I was arrested and it's all your fault!" Jesse blasted. "Now you either show up with the key to the fucking house in fifteen minutes or I'm breaking every window and tearing that place apart."

Chuck was confused. "So I'm to assume you're out of jail?"

"Yes! Fifteen minutes!"

"I'm in Johnstown, you asshole!" Chuck blasted back. "Last I heard the speed of sound via automobile wasn't achieved. Two hours. Meet you at Simmons' Coffee."

"One."

"Two!"

"Fine!"

Chuck grunted. "And you shouldn't have trespassed. See you at noon." He hung up and gathered his bearings. Perhaps he shouldn't have given in to Jesse's intimidation tactics. But for Bret's sake, and the kids, he wasn't going to put it past Jesse to do as he threatened. If anyone could calm Jesse or be the peacekeeper, Chuck could. After all, if Jesse did get arrested, it was in a sense Chuck's fault. After he and Colin picked up the kids, he gave the elderly woman across the street twenty bucks to watch the house and call the cops if anyone showed up.

She obviously did her job. That was, of course, if that was what Jesse was arrested for. Attempt to break and enter, Chuck figured, but wouldn't have to wait long to find out.

It wasn't what he expected to see. Perhaps it was the dedication to his friendship with Bret that caused the sickening, disgusted stir in his stomach when he saw Kyomi.

The petite woman looked no older than sixteen. She dressed in the old-style tradition of her native land of Japan. She bowed her head as she sat at the table with Jesse.

"Bout time." Jesse barked.

"I'm sure you kept busy. Who's your friend?" Chuck asked.

"Kyomi, this is Chuck."

Chuck held out his hand.

Kyomi nodded.

"Hmm." Chuck sat down. "So what's up? Why are you so irate?"

"I fucking told you I was arrested."

"Look. It's just with Bret out of town and the kids at a relative's . . ." Chuck held up his hand. "I didn't want to take chances with the house. I didn't think you'd be by."

"What are you talking about?"

"The reason you got arrested," Chuck said. "You went to the house and tried to get in."

"Yeah. But that wasn't why I was arrested. Old lady Helen hit me with the broom and threatened the cops. I wasn't taking a chance since I just got out."

"Jesse, why did you get arrested and how is it my fault?"

"Insurance fraud," Jesse mumbled.

Chuck grabbed his ear. "I'm sorry. I didn't hear that."

"I said . . . insurance fraud."

"How . . . uh . . ." Chuck closed his eyes. "How?"

"I tried to cash in Bret's life insurance policy."

"You asshole, she's not dead!" Chuck blasted.

"I know."

"And you still tried to cash it in?"

"Well . . . yeah. You guys weren't letting anyone know she was alive."

"Exactly, moron. We weren't letting anyone know she was alive. But we weren't saying that she was dead."

"Isn't that the same difference?"

"No!"

"Still. It's your fault."

"Okay. Okay." Chuck sat back. "How is it my fault?"

"Did you tell the airlines she was alive?"

"Actually," Chuck said. "Blain did. He told

them she wasn't on the flight. We all talked and it was determined that it was going to be too tough not to let them know she and Darius were alive. Blain pulled in his connection. And before the airlines could pin the terrorist connection on them, Colin just smugly told them, 'You know as well as I do it wasn't a terror attack. Dr. Cobb was just prepared.' So, how is this my fault? I had nothing to do with it, except sit in on the telephone meeting."

"You knew and didn't tell me."

"Why would I?"

"In case I collected the insurance money."

"Which you shouldn't have done, but tried to do. Knowing full well she was alive. That is fraud. How did they bust you, Jess? When the airlines wouldn't confirm her death?"

"No," Jesse said. "You called the insurance guy."

The corner of Chuck's mouth rose in a smile. "That wasn't me. That was Colin. He had the keen foresight to know you'd go after that policy. And he called the insurance company."

"Why would he do that? I am the beneficiary."

"Yeah, but you know what? For how long? He was protecting his interest in Bret."

"Why does he have an interest in Bret?"

"Why is it any of your business?" Chuck asked as he stood. "Now if that's all, I've got to go."

"I want in the house."

"Then you have to wait."

"No, I won't wait. I want my tools."

"Then you should have thought of them before you left Bret for the mail order virgin teenage Geisha girl wannabe. Have some tact, Jess, and wait until she gets home."

"Fine." Jesse huffed. "But I want in that house for my tools the second she gets back."

"I'll see that she lets you in the house. Have a good day." Chuck turned. He didn't let Jesse see his snide smile. Bret would surely let him in the house. As for his tools, he'd have to see Bruce about them, because last Chuck heard, he brought them off of Bret at a really discounted price.

***

They were on their way back home. Their cell phones were charged and in good shape. They estimated it would take an entire twenty-four hours, if not more, to get back to Pittsburgh. But with three of them driving it would go by quickly.

Three of them.

Blaine was hitching a ride back with them. He convinced his editor that he had an exclusive to the miracle survivor story of Darius and Bret.

The news center paid for the SUV and the expenses of the trip.

The vehicle was decked out, the best possible ride home. They needed comfort after their ordeal.

They would need the time to come up with the story and so forth.

They took off by six in the morning, and Bret

covered that driving. They stopped just before noon.

"Up ahead," Bret announced. "Sign for a small town."

Both sleeping men mumbled, so Bret took the exit. Of course, the exit didn't lead directly to the town; she had to make a turn.

No big deal.

She could tell by the name and of course the sign announcing two-thousand-something population, that Hooks, Texas was going to be small-town charming.

It was. Perhaps farm-small town charming.

One of those corn towers greeted them at the gas station and souvenir shop. The shop and restaurant had signs miles up the road.

From the dusty windshield Bret could see the small town. A one-stoplight place, a single street, both sides with shops. It was set about 100 yards from the Old Farm Market boasting of Texas BBQ.

"Whew, it's hot." Bret declared. "The air isn't even working."

Darius sat up with a 'huh' as she pulled into the parking lot. "Where are we?"

"I thought we'd stop for food," Bret said. "Take a break."

Darius looked at his watch. "Wow, it's late." He reached around to the back seat. "You up?" he asked Blain.

"Yeah." Blaine stretched. "Whoa, look at this place. It's great."

"Yeah, it is." Bret crinkled her brow. "It's

awfully quiet and dead though. I don't see a car or a person."

"It's too hot," Darius said. "They're all staying in the air conditioning." He reached for the car door. "Ready?"

Bret nodded and opened her door. All three stepped out.

Blain grunted. "God! It's hot." He pulled out his phone. "Hey you two, go ahead. I see a money machine down there. And I think I see a sign that says espresso."

Darius squinted. "Yeah, it does. Good eyes."

"Eagle eyes when it comes to espresso."

"I love coffee," Bret said, "But not even I want a coffee now."

Blain fluttered his lips. "Nothing better than an iced espresso. Go on in, I'll be right back."

Bret and Darius nodded and headed to the long wooden porch of the brown, log-style building. They watched Blaine, with his phone, move down the street toward town.

No sooner did Darius reach for the door, it swung open.

"Holy shit, get in here!" the elderly man yanked Bret inside. "We saw you pull up. Wondered what the hey was taking you so long out there."

At first Bret looked at Darius then to the room full of people standing there.

Everyone watched them. Staring. Some people huddled, some sniffled.

Curiously, Darius glanced at Bret. "Are they looking at us like this because we're strangers?"

Before Bret could answer, the elderly man huffed. "No! For crying out loud. Didn't you listen to the radio? Did the state police stop ya coming in on the road?"

Bret shook her head.

The elderly man whined. "Figures, they abandoned us. Maybe they're getting backup. Well, you two come on in, it might be a long wait. Make yourselves at home."

"Wait for what?" Darius asked.

"Until it's safe. It's not safe out there," the man said.

Darius asked. "Because of the heat?"

"The heat? No." the man shook his head. "Can heat do that?" He pointed out the window.

Darius and Bret moved closer to see.

Off to the side of the porch, not far from where they parked the car, were two bodies. Both bloodied, both a mangled mess. Limbs scattered about, blood formed a pool.

"Not safe for a second." The man repeated. "Last three people who tried to leave met that fate."

At the same time, Darius and Bret looked at each other and spoke out in concern, "Blain."

Blain didn't walk fast, nor did he pay attention. One hand wiped the sweat on the back of his neck; the other hand held his phone.

He was sending text messages.

He wasn't a pro at it. Good, semi-fast, but not

one of those pros who could walk and type while never looking at the phone pad.

His phone allotted 160 characters. His message was long. He spoke of the heat, the trip, and the return shortly. It was to a girl he had met at a karaoke bar in Pittsburgh. He didn't think he'd hear back from her, but was glad she sent a message. When was she returning?

Mid-walk down the street he heard banging, or rather knocking. It sounded like hands against a window. Blain paused, looked up and to his right. Inside the hardware store there were four people, banging on the window to get his attention. They were saying something, waving for him to go in.

Blain smiled. Waved, and held up a finger stating he'd be back.

He felt important. Oftentimes when he was in small towns such as Hooks, people would recognize him from the news and he'd be treated like some big celebrity. He always made time for his fans. Without him and their faithfulness to his reports, he wouldn't be the star reporter he was.

He kept walking, chuckling as they pounded insistently at him.

"Gotta love it," he said to himself, with a shake of his head and a laugh.

Growl.

He heard, paused, thought nothing of it, and hit the 'send' button.

Growl.

What the heck was that, he wondered. He flipped the phone closed, put it in his pocket, heard the soft growling again, and just as he looked up to check out the noise, he heard someone call his name.

"Blain!"

Darius? Blain turned around. "Oh, hey." He lifted his hand in a wave and halted midway when he saw Darius and Bret at the end of the street. *Why does Darius have a shotgun?*

"What's going on?" Blain shouted.

"Get inside now!" Darius replied.

"What?" Blain walked toward Darius.

Growl. It was louder. More than one. The second he saw Bret spin on her heels and run back to the farmer's market, Blain slowly peered over his shoulder.

'Holy fuck!' blasted through his mind when he saw the pack of dogs. All breeds, shapes and sizes, all of them in a row, snarling, jaws dripping a thick white saliva.

Whether or not it was a good idea, Blain ran. But he made the mistake of not thinking. Pulling a 'horror chick-flick' move, he didn't think to run into the building two feet away; he ran toward Darius.

"What are you doing?" Darius yelled.

The moment Blain took off the dogs went from snarling to barking and they pursued.

Darius raised the shotgun and quickly moved closer.

Nine. There were nine dogs. The second the first one leapt toward Blain, Darius fired.

With a yelp it flew back. Taking a few charging steps forward, Darius pumped the chamber of the shotgun, and fired again.

Down went a second dog.

He didn't hesitate. It was like a video game. About the fifth dog that he shot, the others seemed to get the message and ran off.

"Oh my god. Oh shit." Blain grabbed his chest and hyperventilated, trying to catch his breath. "Where did you learn to shoot like that?"

"In the Army. I was a marksman. Plus I hunt."

"You, the ecological guy? You hunt."

"One must help keep the delicate balance of nature." Darius shrugged then opened the weapon, reached into his chest pocket and began to load it. "Fucking people, man."

"What? They were dogs."

"No, they're fucking hiding from the dogs. This is a farm town in Texas." He snapped the gun closed. "One would think everyone in this town is a certified NRA member." He pumped the chamber. "Why are they hiding from the dogs? Why are they not just shooting them?"

"You think maybe because it's their dogs?"

Darius looked at him.

"Seriously, the dogs are coming from somewhere. Bet the people in this town own them and just don't want to shoot their own pets, even if they have gone mad."

"But why?"

"But why won't they shoot their mad dog?"

"No, why are they going mad?" Darius looked out. "Doesn't make sense. Rabies. Heat. I don't see any more. But I'm sure they'll be back."

"Where'd ya get the gun?"

With a twitch of his head, Darius indicated back. "Restaurant had it. That's why I don't get them not shooting the dogs. Let's head back."

"Sounds good. They don't have alcohol in there, do they?"

"Probably do."

"Good," Blain said as he took a step forward. "I can use a . . ."

Yap.

Blain paused then finished. "Drink."

Both he and Darius cocked an eyebrow and exchange curious looks when they heard it.

The high-pitched yapping. Yap-yap-yap.

They turned around to see, at high speed, a Chihuahua racing their way. Before either of them could react, the vicious barking little animal jumped up at Blain and plunged its needle point fangs into his legs.

Blain screamed. He shook his leg trying to shake off the dog who didn't just latch on, but rather gnawed at his flesh.

Like a field goal kicker, Darius shot out his foot, nailing the Chihuahua. The dog flew back, landed and rolled.

Darius raised his gun.

"Wait. You aren't gonna . . ."

Bang.

He blasted the little dog with the shot gun. Like a water balloon a burst of blood and flesh exploded.

Darius whistled. "That was a good shot if I do say so myself." He pumped the chamber and looked over. Blain was on the ground. Blood oozed from his leg. "Oh, shit, we better get you some help."

Nodding with a wince, Blain reached up and took Darius' hand.

***

"Let me get this straight," Colin said, speaking to Darius on the phone. "You are in Texas. You stop at a diner. There are people screaming at you to get in, three dead bodies and the cause of it all was dogs?"

"Yeah, can you believe that?" Darius said. "Nothing was on the news."

"Not that I heard. I'll check. Were they wild dogs?"

"No, domestic dogs and I think they were rabid," Darius said. "Just from the behavior and salvia."

Colin paused to think.

"Still there?"

"Sounds very Stephen King-like."

"Tell me about it."

"You think there's a connection with our plant anomalies and this incident?"

"I'd like to say yeah," Darius said. "But I can't see it. I can see the heat causing them to go mad, but rabies?"

"It's possible that a rabbit or bat bit one of the dogs, and they spread it."

"Possible."

"So back to the story. There were all kinds of

311

breeds?"

"Yes."

"And even though you played canine Rambo, our Blain was still attacked…by a Chihuahua."

"Yes."

Colin snickered. "Sorry."

"No, I laughed too until I realized."

"He has rabies," Colin said.

"Bingo. Or should be treated as such."

"Did you bring the dog with you to the hospital?"

"No, I shot it with a shotgun."

"Twelve, twenty, or twenty-eight gauge?"

"Twelve. Remington. Classic 870. It was sweet."

"You shot a Chihuahua with a Remington twelve-gauge shotgun."

"Yep."

"I see why you didn't bring the dog to the hospital. How is Blain?" Colin asked.

"In pain. He has to stay for a week, so we're gonna have to head home."

"Trip delayed approximately?"

"Half day. Okay, I'm going back inside the hospital to get Bret. Are the kids okay?"

Colin chuckled.

"What? What is so funny?"

"So domesticated you are," Colin said. "Actually if you need some pointers on being a step parent.…"

"Ha, ha, ha. Last Bret talked to the kids, I heard they were prepping for you to have that position."

"Hmm, yes, quite the honor. We're headed to the drive-in tonight."

"You're...you're taking Bret's kids to the drive in?"

"Me and Chuck, yes."

"That sucks."

"What sucks, Dare-Dare?"

"You're prepping to be their step father."

"No, more like...grandfather. Have a good one." Colin hung up. He peered through the sliding glass doors to the girls as they swam in the pool, making sure they were okay. They were. He returned to his blue grocery store bags, but hesitated in unpacking the things he purchased to take to the drive-in. Walking to the basement door, he opened it.

"Luke?" Colin called down. "Any news or word on the ticker about mad dogs attacking in Texas?"

"Nope."

"Thanks." He closed the basement door, chalked up the dog incident to just that, an isolated, unrelated incident, and he returned to preparing for the night.

***

Like the bat phone, Colin had a red phone installed at the bunker. Bruce called it a bunker even though it wasn't underground, more so because they had to bunk down until the mayhem ended once the ice age started.

Bruce worked there every day, twelve hours a

day. Just he and Bobby.

He had just set down the red phone and stared at it, tapping his fingers on the resting receiver.

"Something wrong?" Bobby asked.

"Um, no." Bruce shook his head.

"What did Dr. Reye want on the bat phone?"

"He just wanted to invite us to the drive-in tonight."

"The drive-in? We haven't been to the drive-in since I was twelve."

"I know."

"What's playing?" Bobby asked.

"Classic night. Dracula, Frankenstein versus the Wolf Man and Night of the Living Dead."

"That's a fuckin' sweet combo. All black and white at the drive-in."

"That's what I thought," Bruce said.

"I think we should go."

Bruce nodded. "That's what I thought. I'll call him back and tell him to hold a space for us. Should be fun.."

"I would think . . ." The echoing voice called out. "Fun should not be a word you'd be using when faced with the world's extinction."

After a squint of his eyes through the dirty room, Bruce focused in on Winslow, whose wheelchair was being pushed by a tall thin man in a suit.

"Excuse me, sir." Bruce walked toward Winslow. "This is private property."

"I'm Mr. Winslow," Winslow said. "Barry, push me closer. You must be Mr. Weiss." He extended out his hand.

"Mr. Winslow," Bruce shook it. "Heard much about you. Glad to meet you in person."

"What is fun?" Winslow asked.

"Oh." Bruce waved out his hand. "I was discussing with my son, Bobby, here, that the drive-in is having a classic night. We may go."

"Classic night?" Winslow asked. "As in classic films?"

"Yep," Bruce nodded. "One of which is Night of the Living Dead."

"Sounds fun."

Bruce smiled. "That's what I said. You ought to join us."

"I may."

"So what brings you here?"

"I just wanted to check the progress and see how things were going." Winslow looked around. "Will I have private quarters? What I have witnessed, people are in groups of four."

"You'll have your own quarters," Bruce said.

"And who is building the transportation?" Winslow asked.

Bruce pointed to Bobby. "My son's working on it now. I'll be helping him in a bit."

"Hmm," Winslow rubbed his chin. "You both must be very educated men to be able to do that."

"Well . . ." Bruce tiled his head. "Bobby here is more educated that I am."

"I see." Winslow turned toward Bobby. "Are you finding this difficult?"

"Nah," Bobby replied. "Been doing it for so long it's second nature."

"Really. Wow. I'm impressed. Did you work

315

for NASA?"

"Ex . . . excuse me?" Bobby said.

"NASA," Winslow stated. "If you've been doing it for that long, I just guessed you worked for NASA. Can I see it? I have never had a close-up look at a space ship."

"A . . ." Before Bobby could answer, Bruce cleared his throat to silence him.

"The transportation is delicate," Bruce aid. "Mind if I call Dr. Reye about that?"

"Go right ahead," Winslow said.

"Dad," Bobby whispered. "A spaceship?"

After waving off his son, Bruce walked to the bat phone.

***

Not that Bret knew what she was looking at, exactly. She had an idea, reflecting back to her grandmother being in the hospital with an infection. It was nearly as bad.

Blain lay in the hospital bed, which was tilted. Intravenous pumped drugs and saline through him; a vital signs monitor beeped every so often to announce that it worked.

His leg, swollen three times its size, was packed in ice.

He was not conscious.

A single knock on the open archway drew Bret's attention from Blain.

"There you are," Darius said, slipping through the curtain.

"They moved him quickly," Bret said. "He went from the ER, to a room, to Intensive Care in four hours."

"Hmm." Darius rubbed his chain. "Probably a precaution."

"Then why didn't they move him here right away?"

Darius shrugged.

"Four hours."

"Speaking of which, it's actually been five." Darius looked at his watch. "Ready to take off?"

"Excuse me?"

"Are you ready to go? We lost a lot of time. We need to hit the road."

"You can't possibly be serious, can you? His vitals are low. He's not responding. Fever high. The doctor was in here and said his white blood count was astronomically and frighteningly low. I don't know what that means, but still."

"It means he has a toxin in his body. Infection. Maybe meningitis."

"Uh!"

Darius winced.

"He's dying."

"He's not dying."

"He's dying from a Chihuahua bite."

Darius snickered.

Bret pointed a finger. "Stop it."

"What, Bret?" Darius asked. "He's in a hospital. Stabilized . . ." he looked down to Blain. "Sort of. In good hands."

"Have you any compassion at all?"

"What do you want us to do?"

"I think we should stay until we know he's stabilized, at the very least until his mother gets here tomorrow morning."

Darius sighed out. "You realize everyone is going to the drive-in tonight."

Bret just stared at him and blinked.

"Not like we'd make it or anything."

"I can't believe you."

"Fine. Fine." Darius tossed out his hands. "I'll get us a room. But the second he's stable, we're gone. I'll be back."

Bret nodded. After Darius scuffed his feet on his way out, she turned to face the bed. Her hand rested on the railing. "Until you stabilize." Her eyes shifted from the monitor back to Blain. "Why do I feel that's not gonna happen?"

***

It was an institution in Pittsburgh. Originally, and not many people knew it, the drive-in showed pornographic films until the mid-eighties. But it was last of the breed and Colin actually debated on opening up his own drive-in one day.

One main screen and three small ones, a concession stand with adequate food, and a semi-clean bathroom. In the later years they added a secondary concession stand, but Colin always preferred to go to the main screen.

The kids were excited. He stopped for a Starbucks on the way there, got some chicken from the chicken place, and vowed to buy everything else there, especially the popcorn. When Andi suggested they pop some, Colin was adamant about saying no. There was nothing like the bad popcorn dripping with movie theater butter. They had to get the corn there.

Colin didn't think much about it. Actually, when he was waiting in line to pull up to the paying booth at the drive in, he recognized the man. He knew he saw him at Winslow's house and often with Winslow. The late twenty-something man in a suit, named Guy, had an earpiece and looked like a CIA agent more than a drive-in security man.

He thought to himself as he approached and recognized him that, that was life. The poor young man had to moonlight at the drive in-to make extra money.

Colin waved a simple wave over the steering wheel, and Guy gave a nod.

"Know him?" Chuck asked.

"He's a Winslow security employee."

"There you have it," Chuck said. "Rich guys don't pay their man anymore than anyone else. Probably less."

"Probably," Colin looked sideways at Chuck as he lit up. "You smoke like a chimney. How many packs a day to you go through?"

Chuck shrugged. "Who knows? Who cares. It's not what's gonna kill me anyhow."

"Well, you'll have to cut down. I can't see the cigarette market surviving."

Chuck fluttered his lips. "I could buy cartons of cartons and my own tobacco plants."

Colin snickered.

"Dr. Reye." Andi tapped him on the shoulder. "Did you make the Winslow person mad?"

"No, why?" Colin replied.

Andi pointed. "He's going to the booth now and pointing to you."

"That he is. I wonder what's up." Colin pulled up to the booth. "Five please," he told the lady.

"Sir, your tickets are taken care of." She pointed to Guy.

"Wow. Thanks." Colin smiled. He raised his eyes to the mirror. "Guess we didn't piss him off. How nice of him."

Pulling forward Guy asked him to stop.

Colin did and wound the window. "Thank you for the tickets."

"You're welcome," Guy said. "Mr. Winslow paid for them. Pull down to the third row. You can park anywhere there."

"You mean the row conveniently empty with the barrage of security men?" Colin asked.

"Yes, sir. Mr. Winslow rented the entire row for tonight for you and your guests."

"Wow, that's remarkable. I'll have to thank Mr. Winslow."

"You also have an open account at the concession stand."

Chuck whistled. "Now that's sweet."

Guy smiled. "Have a good evening."

With a nod, Colin thanked him and drove forward. "How fortunate is this. An entire row. No annoying babies parked next to us. Call Bruce and tell him."

"Got it." Chuck pulled out his phone. "Man, Winslow likes you."

"Yes, I do make that impression."

"And free concession food."

"Why do I get the feeling you'll take full advantage of that."

Chuck smiled as he dialed the phone, and Colin pulled down to center of the third row.

They were the big drive-in celebrities. People kept staring at the people whose few cars took up the entire row.

Bobby used that to his advantage, giving that flirty 'up' of his chin when a girl walked by.

Chuck huffed when he saw him doing that. Munching on popcorn, he shook his head as Bobby passed, and at Winslow who was in his wheelchair with a portable air conditioning unit by him.

"What is your problem?" Colin dipped into Chuck's popcorn bag.

"How is Bobby going to make it without a woman in the shelter?"

"I would say Bobby is trying to solve that problem."

"How about Winslow with his air conditioning?"

"He wants to be cool," Colin said.

"Unreal. People are pissed at us."

"Why?"

"We took the whole row."

"Nonsense, they're jealous."

"It just doesn't seem right," Chuck said. "Not having a packed row."

"Chuck." Colin turned completely to him. 'In the car you bitched because you hated being packed in. We aren't packed in. You're still bitching. Think of this as a pre-bonding exercise for the apocalypse."

"I don't know if I can get along with these people."

"Can you get along with anyone?"

"Not really," Chuck shrugged.

"Then perhaps like Bobby who is on a mission to have a sex partner in the shelter, then you should be on a mission to learn to tolerate people."

"Why would I do that?"

"Because it's going to be tough enough to keep your sanity without people driving you nuts." Colin reached toward the bag.

"I'm not worried about it, because I don't plan on making it to that phase. I want a hot dog." Chuck walked away.

Mid-reach for popcorn, Colin grabbed air. But he also realized he grabbed on to something else, the possibility that perhaps Chuck was on a different agenda.

***

Darius grunted.

Bret moaned.

322

Each time he cried out, she called out some explicit word. Back and forth.

"Yes, yes, yes." Bret cheered with excitement.

"No, no, I...have to get...." grunt. "Fuck." Darius blurted in frustration.

"Well, you didn't have to throw the controller," Bret reached for the game control.

"I didn't throw it. I dropped it hard in my frustration. I thought I was going to finish that level."

"I did, too."

"But you're glad I didn't."

"Hell, yeah, I want to win."

"So competitive. Take your turn." Darius stood up from the floor where he played the game with Bret. "Want another drink?"

"Um...yeah." Bret focused on the game. A zombie battle appeared on her screen. "I don't know how you made it through this level."

"Don't collect weapons, just kill them. Scotch?" He walked to the mini bar.

"Yeah, please. But let's not get drunk, in case the hospital calls."

"Why would they call?" He asked.

"For Blain."

"They aren't going to call."

"He wasn't...shit...doing good when we left."

"He's fine. Quite worrying so much."

"That isn't very considerate of you to say."

"Why do you do that?" Darius asked, tossing out the tiny bottles.

"I don't know."

"You know…we do have to finish that invitation list."

"I refuse." Bret's arms soared to the left as her fingers clicked. "You're being ridiculous about the gynecologist."

"Bret." Darius sat on the floor behind her. "Yes, we have to invite doctors into our shelter. But why do we need a specialist."

"Because we women need that. If we are a new civilization in a complicated world, we need a doctor who knows babies and birth. Not someone who is general. Besides, it doesn't…fuck, you're breaking my concentration."

"Just making conversation."

"Distracting me. We'll work on the list after…." Bret grunted.

"You're doing good."

"Thanks."

"Besides, I can't wait to hear Colin's thoughts on the gynecologist."

"He'll think you're wrong."

"Doubt it. Colin wouldn't want to be like you and build a new world of liberals."

Darius heaved out a huff. "Bret! Why do you insist I'm a liberal. I'm neither."

"You fight like one."

"Oh, I do not. Colin fights like one."

"He does not. He doesn't even fight. Besides, Colin is as right as they get."

"True." Darius shrugged. "Is that why you'd pick him?"

"What?" Bret was focused even closer on the

game.

"Is that why you said you'd pick him as your partner in the aftermath."

Bret chuckled, then immediately groaned when her player died. "Son of a bitch." She set down the control, looked at Darius and took the drink he extended. "No. I said 'Colin' because you guys were mentioning everyone else but him. I thought it would send you into a tail spin. Thank you," she said regarding her drink.

"So you wouldn't be with Colin?"

"No. But why is this important?"

"Because it is important. If everything happens as we predict, there's not going to be many people left in this world. There's going to be us and any other pockets that make up a survival plan. We will be responsible for starting things over."

"So you want to secure a bed partner?"

"It's not just that...."

"I have to tell you I can't believe you and Blain discuss whether or not I'd put out in the apocalyptic world." Bret sipped her drink.

"You heard that?"

"Yes, and I know I'm the big joke. But let me tell you something Dare-Dare. This thing about me not putting out for Jess? It wasn't me. Okay? I just got used to not doing it and I didn't want to because it was a hassle and aggravation. Jess had problems." She nodded. "That's why he picked a fucking virgin. She didn't know how it's supposed to be."

Darius laughed.

"Besides, you probably know how naive eighteen- and nineteen-year-old girls are and how easy they are to bed."

"Don't have a clue."

"You're a college professor. They don't throw themselves at you? I mean . . . you're pretty hot."

Darius lowered his head in a blush. "I guess they do. I don't bother. That's my job. Plus, that's too young."

Bret raised her glass. "That's good to hear. But, you realize that would be one reason I could never date you in the civilized world."

"I thought it would be because we fight all the time."

"That, too." Bret winked. "But I'm very jealous. I wouldn't be able to handle those girls throwing themselves at you."

"It's a matter of trust."

"Yeah, but it's also a matter of someone throwing themselves at your guy."

"If you're so jealous how did you not know Jess was having an affair?" he asked.

"He had that problem. I figured he'd be too embarrassed to chance it with a woman." Bret downed her drink. "I don't want to discuss this." She stood up and walked to the bar.

"I'm sorry. You're still upset and hurt. I . . ."

"No, that's not it. I'm fine. Really I am. It was just a blow to my ego, that's all. But . . ." she raised the tiny bottle. "With all the people we're inviting into the shelter, maybe I'll get my self-confidence back. I see your point about having a partner. And I'm not talking about a sex partner."

"A companion."

Bret nodded and returned to the floor. "Someone to lean on, depend on, talk to. That one person in the shelter that you have an alliance with that no one can touch."

"Someone that no matter what happens is there. Your life partner. A strong couple can make it through anything as long as they have each other."

"Exactly. Plus, it doesn't hurt to build the morality back up in the new world. Marriage. Commitment. Start things out right again."

"Amen to that," Darius lifted his glass.

"Wow, so conservative."

"There you go again."

Bret snickered. "It gets you going. And Darius, I really feel that once we get all the invitees into the shelter, you won't have a problem finding someone."

"I don't want that."

"Ex . . . excuse me?" Bret asked. "I'm confused. I thought you just said . . ."

"Oh, I want a partner. A 'wife' if you must in the old world. Hell, I wanted a wife in the current world. I always wanted someone to come home to. Share my music. But I don't want the hassle of having to worry about dating, or connecting, then you break up and have to find someone else. Under those conditions head games are bad. We'll all be living too close to each other for partner-swapping."

"What choice do you have?"

"Form it now," Darius said.

"You mean find someone before we go into the shelter. Before the world goes to shit."

"Yep." Darius nodded. "Find someone who will be as committed as me to making it work. A bond before everything happens."

"That's a good idea," Bret said.

"I want . . . I want to form that with you, Bret."

Bret hesitated and paused her glass before her lips. "Me?"

Darius nodded.

"Darius, you don't like me like that. You said so."

"You heard that?"

"Yep."

"Well, I lied." He winked. "I actually am attracted to you, Bret. And I think you and I, if we set our minds to it, can form a fantastic partnership going into this thing."

"We fight all the time."

"No," Darius corrected. "We bicker. And that will keep us strong. We've been together for days, slept in the same room."

"You saw me naked."

Darius smiled. "That, too. And at any time did it feel unnatural?"

"Not at all."

"We click. At least on the friendship part." He finished his drink. "I want you to think about it."

"You're not worried that we'll get in there and suddenly you'll find someone better."

"Nope. Not at all. I'm a pretty dedicated person, Bret. You're pretty cool. I can see when this thing happens, where we'll be, and you know, I can see me only having eyes for you."

"Oh my God, was that sweet." Bret smiled.

"I'm a nice guy."

"And hot." Bret took a drink. "I'll be pretty lucky in the apocalypse. Smart, hot, and talented. Colin played me your CD. You're good."

"Thanks. So you want to?" he asked, pouring a drink.

"Well, we do have the friendship part down. All we have to worry about is will we click sexually."

"Bret, I don't claim to be all that in the bedroom. But if all you say about your ex-husband's problems are true, I'm not worried. I'll be a fucking stud."

Her lips fluttered in an immediately sloppy, hard laugh, one that knocked her back. "I can't believe you just said that."

"Neither can I. I'm a little tipsy. But in control. That was a good line."

"It was." Bret sighed out. "So let's do it."

"Partnership?" Darius brought his drink to his mouth making his way back to Bret.

"Sex."

Darius choked.

"What? You don't want to?'

"Are you serious?"

"Yes, very. Might as well see if we click all the way around before we both make the final decision."

"This just doesn't sound like you. And I'm judging this on the person I got to know. Not your

Virgin Mary reputation."

Bret laughed. "It's not like me. But you know what? You and I have been under some extenuating circumstances. I feel close to you. I haven't . . . I haven't in a while. I'd really like to right now feel that closeness. And I think . . . if you want, I think you'd like that too."

Darius pulled his mouth to one side.

"You're a scientist. Think of it as an experiment."

He couldn't help it. He chuckled and set down his drink.

"You aren't attracted to me in that way?"

"Oh, quite the contrary." He brought himself down to the floor. He reached out and took her drink, softening his voice. "I saw you naked, remember?" After setting her drink on the TV stand, he trailed his index finger through the opening of her v-neck shirt.

"Look at you being the seducer."

"You initiated it."

"I did. Didn't I?" Bret smiled as Darius raised his eyes to her. "So you like what you saw?"

"Oh, yeah." Two fingers, three, he felt the skin on her chest, lightly trailing in circles. "You said it's been a while since you . . ." He cleared his throat. "How long?"

"Long. Very long. You?" she asked, her eyes meeting his.

"Very long."

"Kiss me."

"You got it." Darius brought his hand up, sliding it behind her neck. Then pulling her closer, he leaned into her and smiled widely before he granted her request.

***

The hotel was going to have a billing field day. They called for room service before they closed for the night for more mini bottles of scotch and food.

Nine tiny empty bottles were scattered in and around the garbage can. The video game controllers lay where they left them on the floor by the television. The game was, in fact, still on pause, with Darius in the lead and three levels ahead of Bret.

It took a while. A good half hour of timid kissing, then another drink, more intense kissing, followed by teenage-style making out, until the adult in them brought them to the bed.

Bret was on her stomach. She cradled the phone between her ear and shoulder as she reached for a fry from the plate on the night stand next to the bed. She'd reach, dip into the ketchup, then bite.

"Sorry, Colin, I didn't realize it was three in the morning there."

"We're not sleeping yet. Everyone is still wound up from Night of the Living Dead," Colin said.

"So it was a good time."

"Absolutely, the Winslow treatment was

second to none. Speaking of treatment. How is Blain?"

Bret giggled.

"That's funny?" he asked.

"Um . . . no. Not funny. He's still the same. No better, no worse. I laughed because . . . Darius was doing something." Bret declined to tell him that Darius was playing with her back, lightly tickling it with his fingers and lips.

"Do I want to know?"

Bret giggled again.

"Are you two drunk?"

"We've been drinking," she answered.

"Then I probably don't want to know."

Darius breathed out, laying on his side next to Bret, "Time's up." He grabbed the phone.

"Hey!" she defended.

"Hey, Colin. We are really in the middle of something. She'll have to call you back in the morning."

"She called me, Darius, I didn't call her."

"I know. I gave her five minutes."

"Oh my God." Colin explained.

"What?"

"You did."

"I did what?" Darius asked.

"You have gone and taken advantage of her vulnerable state."

Darius crinkled a brow that Colin could not see. He shook his head, watching Bret nonchalantly eat the fries as she lay on her stomach. "She is so not vulnerable."

"You did. You male vixen."

Darius laughed. "Stop."

"Such a slut."

"Colin, stop."

"You not her."

"I am not," Darius continued his laughing. "I gotta go."

"Dare-Dare, I don't think her emotionally-scarred children are ready for a middle aged rock star wannabe for a stepfather."

"I am not a middle aged rock star wanna be."

"Country, sorry, I stand corrected."

Darius cleared his throat. "Better."

"Dare-Dare, in all seriousness. Do you really think this was a good idea?"

Without hesitation, Darius answered. "Yes, yes, I do."

Pause.

"So do I. Have a good night."

Over Bret, Darius extended his arm and hung up the phone. In returning, he brought his lips to her back again. "You have a great back."

"That's because it's strong from people always being on it."

He chuckled. "That was good. But seriously . . . ." He took hold of her hip and tucking his hand, rolled her onto her side. He scooted her closer.

Bret rolled to her back.

He kissed her and smiled "You taste like ketchup."

Bret bit her lip. "Sorry."

He shook his head. "No, I'm joking. But . . . seriously . . . . ." Just as he leaned closer to her, the phone began to ring.

Bret pulled back. "Phone."

"Let it go," Darius tried kissing her.

"It could be important. It might be about Blain." Rolling to her side, Bret retrieved the phone before the fourth ring. "Hello." A pause. "Yes it is." Another pause. "We'll be right there."

Immediately, she slid from the bed.

"What's wrong?" Darius asked. "What happened?"

"We need to get dressed and get going. Blain took a turn for the worse."

Surprised, Darius sat up. "From a dog bite?"

"They don't think he's going to make it through the night. They want someone there."

"Holy shit." Flinging, the covers from him, Darius, like Bret, rushed to get dressed.

22 - Jump

June 20th

It wasn't supposed to happen.

It wasn't rabies, even though they were able to trace a case to bats in Texas. It was meningitis that raged through Blain, causing his fever to spike out of control, his body to convulse, and his young life to end so quickly.

I wasn't supposed to happen.

It didn't take Darius and Bret long to get to the hospital, but it wouldn't have mattered if they had the ability to fly there. They were too late.

"We're sorry, he's gone," the nurse informed them as they raced down the hall. "He went fast."

Bret turned into Darius for support and there he held her as she cried for a man who had become a friend and a huge part of the survival plan.

They stayed until his mother arrived so they were there for the news.

Another day lost in their journey home, but this was for a good reason.

There was little more they could do but return home, and they did at first light.

***

"I'm not liking this," Virginia stated matter-of-factly, sitting at the console station in Colin's home. "I've been following it for a week now."

"I don't like it either," Luke said.

Virginia looked at him. "Do you know what it is?"

"Hot spot." Luke shrugged. "Hasn't changed, hasn't moved."

Virginia held out her hand toward Luke while speaking to Colin. "There you have it. He's sixteen and he doesn't like it."

"There you have it," Colin said. "He's sixteen. What does he know?"

"Dude," Luke defended. "I've been researching on the internet."

Colin rubbed his chin. "If it was going to do anything, it would have, right?"

"I study the sun. You study the earth. You tell me." Virginia said. "Look, it's not growing, but I feel it's getting more intense." She ran her finger over the screen to the point of the hot spot which seemed to be in the corner of Missouri, Tennessee, Arkansas and Kentucky, heading straight up the Kentucky border.

Colin swished his mouth side to side. "Maybe I'm just not thinking correctly today. A lot is on my mind."

"Blain?" Virginia asked.

Colin nodded. "I have to make arrangements for all of us to travel to the funeral, if plausible. I have Bret's ex ape calling every two hours wanting in the house. Chuck . . . Chuck well I can't figure him out. He's been very anti lately."

"Chuck is always anti," Luke said.

"Well, now is not the time for him to be anti. We have a survival plan to work out. Yesterday we were trying to speak about the invitees to the shelter. He didn't care." Colin sighed. "I feel the catastrophic events are something he's been waiting for."

Virginia spoke softly. "He lost his life. His wife and kids. He just needs something to live for. Right now, this is the perfect way to see his kids again."

"Swell." Colin said. "We just need every mind, every body right now, and with enthusiasm."

"What else?" Virginia asked. "Get it all out."

Colin shook his head. "I just did. I just have a lot on my mind and every day that goes by is a day closer to the news getting out. Once that happens, our preparations and stocking are going to get difficult. Thank God, Winslow is doing his share."

"You mean with the enemy?" Virginia asked.

"And some. He called this morning to tell me he bought out the Giant Eagle Warehouse. Giant Eagle is jumping for joy, and I suppose their suppliers are, too. Don't ask me how he pulled it off."

"Don't forget that old book store on 51," Luke said.

"Yes, that too," Colin replied. "Food and knowledge."

"Now we need medical," Virginia commented.

"We need everyone together," Colin said, "so we can have one big meeting and get our shit together and moving."

"I agree. When does Darius get back?" Virginia asked.

"This evening." Colin looked at the watch.

Virginia sat back. Her eyes moved to the computer and to the hot spot. "What route is he taking home?"

Colin's eyes hit the screen. "That route that leads to the hot spot . . . ."

Virginia exhaled loudly.

"What are you thinking?" Colin asked.

"I don't know . . . call me superstitious, but . . . okay. Think about it. Almost every single big event that has happened has evolved either Darius, Bret, or both. The ants, roaches, birds, radiation, EMP, dog attacks . . . ."

Colin snickered. "Are you saying there's something about those two that causes these things to happen?"

"Absolutely not, no." Virginia said. "I'm just saying that these two . . . well, they have bad luck with these events. And if anything is going to happen with this hot spot, wouldn't it just be their luck that it happens the second they cross into the hot spot at the Arkansas-Tennessee border?"

"Good God, you're probably right." He handed her his phone.

"What?" she asked.

"You call them. If I do, they'll laugh."

338

Virginia flipped open the phone.

***

Darius spotted it in the window. They were pulling through the small town to get something to eat, and he had to pull over and buy it.

He justified the purchase as a need.

He hadn't played his guitar in a week, and he was going through withdrawal.

His whole mood lifted, and that was helpful considering the gloom that hung over his head with Blain's death. So with his new guitar from the hock shop, he and Bret picked up some sandwiches and followed the advice of the clerk who said there was a nice clearing just outside of town.

They'd have to go back through town to get to the highway, but it didn't matter. It was a nice diversion.

He played the entire time they were stopped. Played, ate, spoke, but never did the guitar leave his lap.

"This is so sweet. The action is phenomenal," Darius said of the acoustic guitar. "Fuckin' vintage and I can't believe they had this in a small, no-name hock shop."

"You don't believe what the guy said, do you?" Bret asked. "It wasn't Elvis'."

"You don't know, Bret. It could be. Did you see the price tag on this?"

"Um, yeah, three grand." She shook her head

with a whistle. "That is one of the reasons we'd not be a good couple in the world if it wasn't ending."

"What are you talking about?" Darius asked with a chuckle.

"Your spending habits." Bret bagged their garbage.

He fluttered his lips. "You think I spend this much normally? Nah. What do I have to lose? Put it on the credit card, I don't have to pay it back." After a shrug, he put his guitar in the case.

"Yeah, but aren't you on the 'save the world' thing. You have a theory."

He nodded. "Yeah, I do. But the world is still going to shit."

"What do you mean?"

"I mean even if my plan would work, there's still going to be chaos and destruction. I can't release my theory until everyone knows what's going on. And even then . . . Hell, you know the size of the blast I wanna set off. We're talking dust and clouds that will block out the sun and cause a mini ice age for two years. Not to mention, there could be a radiation danger." He stopped when he saw her mouth agape. He pushed up on her chin. "Don't say why bother. It's a lesser of the two evils thing." He crouched down closer to her. "And even if the world wasn't going to go to shit, even if my theory caused no chaos or damage, I think you're wrong."

"About what?"

Darius dropped his voice to a whisper. "I think we'd be very good couple in any situation."

Darius kissed her. "I'm really glad we decided to do this, Bret. I really like you. You're a really good person."

"I'm glad we did this, too."

"Ready?" Darius stood and extended his hand to her.

"Yep." Bret took his hand and stood.

After grabbing his guitar and the garbage they headed to the car.

Immediately after stepping from the shade, Bret fanned herself. "Whew. Does it feel like it got hotter to you?"

"Actually, yeah it does." He opened the car door for her, and chuckled when she grunted about the heat. He tossed his guitar in the back.

"Open the windows. God."

Darius laughed, turned the ignition and wound down all the windows.

"Air."

"Bret. Give it a second."

"It's so hot."

"It's weird."

"You're phone's beeping."

"Shit, we left it in the car. Hope it wasn't important." Darius reached down to the floor and grabbed the phone next to the gear shift. "Christ, it must be. Twenty-five missed calls."

"How long were we out there?"

"Forty minutes tops."

"Who called?"

"Colin, Virginia, Luke. . . ."

"Oh my God, I hope the kids are okay."

He held up a finger and dialed. "We'll find

out."

Colin answered. "Where have you been?"

"Are the kids okay?" Darius asked.

"Yes, they're fine," Colin answered.

"So what's up?" Darius asked. "Why is everyone calling?" He put the truck in reverse and backed out.

"Worried," Colin answered. "Virginia's been tracking a hot spot that Luke found. It hasn't moved. We think it's getting intense."

"Uh huh, and that has what to do with me?" Darius asked.

"Are you in Tennessee?"

"Heading to Indiana."

"That's where it is," Colin said. "We just figured since the bugs hit where you were, and the EMP, and the dogs . . ."

Darius finished the sentence. "That our luck would have it strike us here, too?"

"Bingo."

"Nothing to report. It is hot here, but just hot."

"Good. Good to hear. Let us know if you see anything or hear anything."

"Will do."

"Have a safe trip."

Darius disconnected the call and turned into the town.

"What's going on? Everything okay?" Bret asked.

"Yeah, just a hot spot in this area."

"Hence the comment about the heat."

Darius nodded. He then smiled. "Check this

342

out, Bret." He pulled up to a stoplight. "He thought we have bad luck with natural phenomena. Like if something was going to happen it would happen because we're here."

"Oh, my God, that's funny."

"Yeah, I thought so . . ." Darius paused in his reach to turn down the fan. "Why are all these people running?"

Bret shifted left to right in her seat. "I don't . . . oh, shit, Darius. Look at the trees."

Brown.

As if the change of seasons were occurring instantaneously before their eyes, the leaves on the streets, and the trees themselves, turned dark brown. Almost burning. The leaves dropped to the ground and burst into flame.

Wooden structures began to smolder, and people dropped. The second their bodies hit the ground smoke emerged.

"Green." Darius said.

"What?"

"Green. There." He pointed. "This is just a spot. We have to get . . ."

Pop.

The SUV jolted as the first tire exploded, then the second.

Bret screamed.

The third and fourth went as well.

Darius hit the gas.

"What are you doing? We can't ride on rims."

"No, we can't, but we certainly can't sit still."

Bret grabbed hold of the bar over her door as he sped forward

"We have to keep moving, to keep cool. I thought I saw . . . yes!"

"What?"

"Tracks."

"Huh?"

Darius didn't answer. He hit the gas harder and turned the wheel to the left. The SUV jolted heavily, and Bret shrieked as they pulled onto the railroad tracks.

"Oh, my God, oh my God." Bret chanted fast, nervously, and out of breath.

"We're good. We're good. See those trees up there. See the green."

"Yes."

"That's our destination. Not far. Not long. That means it's not a hot spot there."

"What if a train comes?" Bret asked.

"There won't be a train."

A long, loud whistle blew.

Bret looked at Darius and screamed.

"Quit screaming."

"Train!" Bret pointed ahead. The sight of the locomotive rippled through the heat. "Train!"

"I see."

"Get off the tracks!"

"I can't." Darius said. "We're stuck."

Another scream.

"Quit!"

"We're gonna die."

"We're not gonna die. We can beat it to the trees."

"Then what?" she asked.

"Jump."

"Jump?"

"Jump."

"No!"

Darius grabbed her hand. "Listen to me. Get a hold yourself."

Bret kept her eyes forward. Her words fast. Hyperventilating. "The train. The train. The train."

"Stop." He ordered. "Get a hold. Grab the door. Get ready."

"Darius...."

"Listen to me. When I say, 'now', you jump. Hands over your head, leap sideways, not feet first. Got it?"

"I can't . . ."

"Yeah, you can. You have to." He grabbed her hand, brought it to his mouth and kissed it. "Ready?"

"No."

He eyed the approaching train, then the trees. "We'll beat it. We'll beat it."

"Darius," her voice inched up.

"Grab the door. Open it some."

"I'm scared."

"Me, too."

"Oh my God."

Darius, reached for his door, one hand on the wheel. "Almost . . ."

Bret watched the train as the air rushed through her open door.

The train neared.

Faster.

The trees wilted less. Darius' sign, he hit the brakes.

345

"What are you doing!" She blasted.

"Slowing us."

The wheels screeched loudly, the train blasted its warning whistle, along with diligently trying to stop. Sparks seared up on all ends of the vehicle.

"Now!" Darius ordered. Bret screamed and opened the door wider. Darius heard and felt the 'whoosh' of air. He saw, through the corner of his eyes, Bret leaping from the car, and then he, too, jumped.

It was close.

He landed and rolled at the same time the whistle of the train screamed out, seconds before the 'smash' of the locomotive into the SUV.

The grass was brownish-green, but not dead and burning. The momentum of the roll carried him down the grade, and Darius stopped with a grunt. He was dizzy and off balance as he tried to stand. He coughed out a mouthful of dirt and dropped to his knees, watching the train roll by.

"Bret!" he called out, standing. "Bret!"

The train noise was too loud. Aside from moving, the conductor was trying to stop it. The air brakes cried out louder than Darius ever could. There was no way she'd hear him. Up in the distance, on his side of the tracks, the smashed SUV had rolled off the tracks as well.

He stumbled to a stand, moved toward the tracks and closer to the train. "Come on, come on," he beckoned, watching to his left for the end of the train. It moved slowly, too slowly. "Bret!"

Darius grew antsy. Almost there. Tired of waiting, Darius raced toward the end of the train, and as soon as it cleared him he ran over the tracks, calling out for Bret as he did.

He lost sense of distance.

How far had he rolled? Which way? They had slowed down some.

"Bret!"

After crossing, he headed back in the other direction, his mind still racing. It couldn't have been that far. A hundred feet, maybe?

Had it not been for the diaper bag, he would have called out again. But he spotted the bag Bret had not been without since they jumped from the plane.

He saw the diaper bag and then he saw Bret, lying in the grass thirty feet from the tracks.

The train finally came to a halt as Darius ran as fast as his feet would carry him.

He slid down the small grade, landing by Bret.

She wasn't moving.

"You guys okay!" a male voice called out in the distance. "Anyone hurt!"

Hands shaking, Darius reached down to Bret. She was on her side. "Bret." He called out. Bret didn't respond. His hand slid to her throat.

A pulse.

Darius sighed out.

He could see the blood trickle from her nose, an abrasion, along with a deep gash on her head. "Bret, answer me."

Nothing.

"Do you need help!" the man hollered again.

Scooting closer to Bret, Darius cocked his

head to find the direction of the man. He was a speck in his vision, but making his way closer. 'Yes!" Darius yelled. "Call for 911! Hurry!" He watched the man turn, and then Darius focused again on Bret.

Still non-responsive and bleeding.

He huddled as close to her as he could, whispering to her to just hang on, while waiting for what would seem like an eternity for help to arrive.

23 - Memories

She woke up twice. But nothing coherent came from her, nor did she respond. But after ten hours the doctors said that there was no sign of swelling, and that was a good sign.

Just before midnight, Bret began to stir again, mumbling words. And when she woke up asking for water and an aspirin, Darius placed a call to Colin.

He and the girls returned to the hospital where Darius and Luke hadn't left Bret's side.

She looked better than when he had left, and Colin conveyed that to Darius as they stood outside her hospital room. He peeked in; the girls were on one side of the bed.

"I have to tell you, Dare-Dare. I've never seen you so worried about anything. Hell, when we couldn't find your mother you weren't this worried."

"I am worried. Or was," Darius said. "I really am into her, Colin. I am. This past week . . . it did a lot for me. I didn't realize our connection, but it's there. I don't want to lose that."

"I'm glad for you. And , , . she seems fine. Actually . . . happy." He took another peek inside.

"Since there was no brain damage," Darius said, "they have her looped up on pain killers for the headache."

"A loopy Bret." Colin smiled. "This should be

fun. Let's go speak to her." Laying a leading hand on Darius' back, Colin brought them in the room.

"We're back," Colin announced.

Darius took his seat next to the bed and reclaimed Bret's hand.

Bret snickered.

"What's so funny?" Darius asked.

Almost giggly, she answered. "You're holding my hand."

"I want to."

"That is so nice." She groggily smiled.

"Yeah, well, right now I want to be nice. I feel like this is all my fault."

"Oh, my God, no," Bret's words were slurred. "Dare-Dare, if it wasn't for your quick thinking and plotting, I'd be dead. I'm fine. Just a bump."

Colin asked. "How is that bump?"

"Good. I don't feel really bad now. They gave me drugs. How long was I out?"

Darius replied, "About ten hours."

"Wow, they got here fast," Bret said.

It took Colin a moment, then with an 'up' of his chin and facial revelation of what she meant, he said, "No. No. You're in Pittsburgh. When Winslow found out about the accident he had you flown up here."

"That was nice of him," Bret said.

"Yes it was," said Colin. "We need you here. Need you to recover, because we have a lot of work to do."

Darius brought her hand to his lips. "But you get well first. I'm gonna help with whatever you need, okay?"

350

The corner of Bret's mouth raised in a smile. "Man, you are being way nice. You won't mind if I take the help?"

Darius shook his head.

Bret snickered. "You kissed my hand. Did you see that, Colin?"

"Yes, you'll have that with him," Colin said. "Anyway. Get well. You'll stay at my house. That asshole of an ex-husband of yours is hounding us, but we'll take care of that. Then it's stocking, planning, and getting our shelter list together."

Bret nodded. "But we have to get the shelter. Plan another trip down there, maybe?"

Colin smiled. "What . . ." he paused. "It's done. Bought."

"In ten hours?" Bret asked surprised. "Wow, you guys work fast. Fly me up here, buy the shelter . . . ."

"Bret." Colin held up a finger halting her. "What is the last thing you remember?"

"Right before the accident," she replied. "I remember. . . " she inhaled. "The rush of the wind. Staring out into the open space and jumping."

Colin nodded.

Bret continued, "From the plane. Boy, I'll tell you I was afraid that chute wouldn't open. But . . ." She shrugged. "It obviously did, I just landed wrong."

"The last thing you remember is jumping from the plane?" Colin asked.

"Yes, that was how I hurt my head, right?" Bret asked then looked at Darius. "Why did you loosen your grip on my hand?"

"Sorry," Darius grabbed held again. "Bret, are you sure that's the last thing you remember?"

"Yes."

"Think."

Bret closed her eyes. "Yeah, that's it. Why?"

"Because . . ." Darius looked up to Colin, the girls, Luke, and back to Bret. "That was . . . that was a week ago."

"I . . . I . . . lost a week?" Bret asked. "How?"

Colin shrugged slightly then shook his head. "I'm sure the doctor will tell you. And I'm sure what you lost will come back. It's the head injury. Then again . . ." he looked at Darius. "There's a chance it may never come back."

"A whole week?" Bret closed her eyes and exhaled. "Well, I can look at it this way. Aside from getting the shelter, it's only a week, right? I mean, I couldn't have missed that much, right?"

No answer.

"Right?"

"Excuse me." Darius stood up.

"Colin?" Bret asked.

After holding up a finger, Colin stepped outside where Darius was waiting in the hallway.

"Dare-Dare."

"She doesn't remember. She doesn't know about Blain. She doesn't . . . she doesn't remember."

"Maybe she will," Colin said.

"What if she doesn't?"

"Then you tell her."

"Ha," Darius released an emotional chuckle. "Oh, sure, I'll just go tell her. Hey, Bret, in that week, Blain died from meningitis and you and I became lovers."

Colin cringed. "You're right, that won't be easy to tell her. But if you do, and she doesn't remember you can tell her it was incredible and she called you a stallion."

"This isn't funny."

"It's not that big of a deal," Colin said "Don't worry about it. Just tell her when the time is right. Give her time for it all to come back and if it doesn't, tell her. Dare-Dare, she's already excited about the prospect of you holding her hand. Something is inside of her, trust me."

Darius nodded.

"If not, and she's what you want, you have to win her back."

Another nod from Darius.

"But for now. We just need to concentrate on her getting better, and us getting everything in order and on track. Because the way things are looking with this Earth," Colin said. "It's not going to be long before everything goes to shit."

24 - Happenings

July 22^(nd)

"I feel like Laverne and Shirley," Bret made the off-the-wall comment, causing Darius to glance up at her with a half-smile.

They sat on Colin's living room floor, stacks upon stacks of books surrounding them.

She continued, "You know the one episode where they won the shopping spree?"

"No," Darius said.

"Yeah, and they tried so hard the only thing they ended up getting for free was a box of Moon Pies, or something like that. Remember?"

"No, not at all."

"Really? Wow."

"Actually, I never saw Laverne and Shirley."

"Oh, my God, not even in reruns? Didn't you have a television?"

"Oh, sure." Darius examined a book. "I just wasn't a TV watcher. Where are you putting the useful fiction?"

"What genre?"

"Science."

"Here." Bret took the book and set it aside to a stack. "I started a new stack for sex books."

Darius laughed. "Really."

"Oh, sure, we may need them. Especially this one." She held up a title.

Darius looked. "<u>Sex in the Senior Years</u>."

She nodded. "It's good to know I may finally get to enjoy sex when I'm older."

"As opposed to now."

"Is that a dig about my ex-husband cheating?"

"No." he shook his head. "I was just gonna say, you seem to enjoy it now."

Bret laughed.

"What is so funny?"

"You." She shook her head. "You know you almost had me with that 'we slept together' tale you told me."

"We did, Bret. We committed to each other."

She giggled. "Sure. Chuck said that next thing you'll tell me is I peed in the woods."

"You did."

Again, she laughed.

Darius tossed up his hands. "Why is it so hard to believe?"

"Because . . . I don't remember it and . . . it's you."

"Okay." Darius brought his knees up.

"You're hot. Why would you want me?"

After a nod of his head Darius leaned to Bret. "You know, I think you're a fantastic woman," he whispered. "And even more so over this past month as I got to know you and like even more who you are. Plus . . ." He bit his bottom lip, leaning closer. "I can't wait until you break down, give back in to me. Cause I think you're pretty hot."

Another giggle. "Stop,"

"Nope." He leaned in for a kiss.

The clearing of the throat caused them to jolt apart in surprise.

Darius looked up to Colin. "This close, Colin. I was this close to finally getting her to kiss me again."

"Just like you, Dare-Dare." Colin said. "She is barely well and you are taking advantage of her vulnerable state. Like last time."

"Thanks, you're not helping," Darius said.

Colin laughed.

So did Bert. "You guys are funny."

"So is this," Colin handed her an envelope. "The attorney dropped these off. Signed, sealed, and filed. Divorce papers."

"Sweet." Bret smiled. "Hey, Dare-Dare, thanks for paying for these. You didn't have to."

"I want you divorced," Darius said. "We're committed." He dropped his voice to a mumble. "Whether you remember or not."

Colin said, "I don't see the point. He'll probably die anyhow when the world ends."

"Just in case," Darius shrugged.

"I heard from Virginia," Colin said. "All settled in the shelter. Kids are loving it. They started the seedlings and her husband installed the fake light for sunlight."

Darius gave a 'thumbs up'. "Ironically…." He showed a book. "Getting the Most out of the Sun."

Colin scoffed. "The sun is our enemy right now; it started the war. Bret, good to see you moving about. How's the head?"

Bret nodded. "Good. I feel good. We were at the warehouse this morning doing inventory for the trucks that are moving out to the shelter tomorrow. I feel so guilty that you guys were busy and I was sick."

"I was worried," Colin pointed out, "after the head injury and then last week you had that stomach flu."

"That was weird. One minute I'm sick, the next I'm fine. I haven't thrown up like that since . . . since . . . ." Bret paused.

"Another memory lapse?" Darius asked.

"No, no." She quickly correctly. "Since I had food poisoning. Which was another episode of Laverne and Shirley."

"I loved that show," Colin said. "How about the one where they won the shopping spree?"

Bret peeped a shriek. "Yes! I was just talking about that. Darius didn't know."

"Darius didn't watch television."

Darius winked. "See, I told you."

Bret's hand paused as she grabbed another book. She lifted it and slowly gazed at the title.

"You all right?" Colin asked.

"Um, yeah. Yeah." Bret nodded, cradling the book to her chest. "Just thinking."

"Well, can I steal that thinking phase and put both of you on pause from sorting books?" Colin asked. "I want to go over the invitee list, tweak it so it's ready to send out when the news breaks."

"Are we sure it's gonna happen?" Bret asked. "I mean, nothing has happened in some time."

Darius nodded. "Calm before the storm."

"The big storm," Colin added. "Kitchen? Ready?" he pointed.

Darius stood up. "Yep." He held his hand down to Bret. "Coming?"

"In . . . in a second. I want to do something first."

"Okay." Darius ran his hand over her head as he followed Colin.

Bret watched over her shoulder until they were out of sight. Slowly she pulled the book from her chest. She glanced at the title once more, exhaled slowly through her parted lips, and closed her eyes. "Oh, boy."

***

On both sides of Colin's front door were two windows, both narrow and floor length. A white curtain graced both windows for privacy.

When Andi heard the 'clunk' from outside, she peered out her window and raced out. First she knocked on the bathroom door stating to her mother, 'we have trouble', then she ran down the steps, pulled one curtain to the side and peeked out the window.

"We have trouble," she said and ran to the kitchen. "We have trouble."

Darius was seated at the counter with Colin. He turned around. "Is that why you're running?"

"We have trouble." She pointed backwards.

Colin nodded to Darius. "We have trouble."

The door bell rang.

"Is that the trouble?" Darius asked.

Andi nodded and her eyes widened when there was a pounding at the door.

Darius stood up and walked by her. "Who is it?"

"Jesse."

Darius picked up speed.

"Where is she?" Jesse demanded.

What he didn't see was Bret sneaking back up the stairs, nor Colin sneaking in to watch the events.

It took Darius a moment to respond; his eyes shifted to the Japanese girl who stood ten paces behind the man.

"Where?" Jesse asked again.

"She's busy," Darius said. "I'll tell her you stopped by." He started to close the door.

Jesse held out his hand, stopping it. "You know I've been patient. I've been put in jail, waited until she got back, waited until her head healed and this flu. But if she's well enough to serve me with fucking divorce . . ."

"Hey!" Darius blasted. "Watch your mouth! And Bret didn't get those together, I did. She only signed them. So if you'll excuse us."

"Why are you getting her divorce papers?"

"None of your goddamn business." Darius said. "Now, I told you I'd let her know you stopped by."

"I want in the house. No one's ever there. The locks are changed."

"No one lives there, Jess. They moved in here. The house is for sale, or did you miss the big sign on the front lawn?"

Jesse growled. "I want my tools and I want in that house."

"Well, go to the house. But there're no tools there."

"What?" Jesse asked, head tilted.

"There're no tools there. I emptied that house last week."

"Where are my tools?"

Darius shrugged. "Gone. Sold, I think. Yeah. She sold them. Fifty bucks." He widened his eyes. "Sorry."

Darius saw it, the red in Jesse's neck, the heaving of his shoulders and the heavy breath that preceded the second growl. He stepped back when he saw Jesse charge forward.

There were two sounds that emanated immediately upon Jesse's storming entrance into Colin's house.

Thud and pop.

The first occurred when Darius hooked his own leg into Jesse's, stumbling the big man and careening him face forward to the floor. That was the thud.

The second came when, with a quick jolt and a snap of his free leg, Darius dislocated Jesse's knee.

Colin cringed.

"Mom!" Andi cried out.

Jesse screamed in pain and Kyomi rushed in.

"No. No." She bent down to Jesse. "You

bwoke his weg."

Darius rolled his eyes. "I didn't bweak his weg. I popped his joint. Excuse me." He walked to the stairs. "Colin, call the police."

Colin showed him the open phone and winked. "I'm already on it. Where are you going?"

"To tell her she can stop hiding." Darius ascended the stairs.

***

"You didn't help much," Chuck pulled out his chair in the dining room. Seated at the table already were Colin, Darius, and Bruce. "Shoot." He stopped. "I need a drink." He walked over to the bar in the dining room. "Colin, may I?"

"Be my guest," Colin said.

"Anyhow," Chuck continued. "You didn't make matters any better for her. Jesse will just heal and come back."

"Ask me if I care," Darius said. "Let him come back."

"Nice flowers," Chuck indicated the arrangement as he took his seat.

"Winslow sent those for Bret," Colin said. "Speaking of which, where is she?"

"She said she had to go to the store," Darius answered. "I offered to drive her, but she wanted to go alone. She's been gone a while now."

"I hope she's okay." Colin interjected. "She still seems a bit off."

Chuck fluttered his lips. "And she's gonna lose her job."

"Do . . . do you ever have anything positive to say?" Colin asked. "I'm wondering."

"Not really," Chuck replied. "And not often if I do."

Bruce smiled and shook his head. 'I have known Chuck for a few years. Never heard him say too much nice at all."

"How's this?" Chuck asked. "I think you're a nice guy, Bruce."

"Thanks, Chuck." Bruce nodded.

"Why don't we start?" Colin suggested. "I'm sure Bret won't mind."

"Sorry!" Bret called from the kitchen. The sound of the patio doors shutting was heard and she emerged into the dining room. "Sorry. I didn't mean to be gone so long. I didn't miss anything, did I?"

Colin shook his head. "Just Chuck being miserable."

"What else is new?" She walked to behind Chuck and gave him a hug.

"How are you feeling?" Chuck asked.

"Good. Good." Bret answered and walked to the chair Darius pulled out for her.

"Thanks," Bret sat down.

Colin asked, "Want something to drink?"

"No, I got my latte," she held up her cup, "which I really shouldn't be drinking."

"Why's that?" Colin asked.

Bret stumbled. "I . . . um . . . I'm addicted and with the world ending soon, I should break that addiction."

"Ah, yes." Colin pulled forth a notepad.

"Okay. Let's begin. I figured let's perfect the list then we will find the individuals to match the job areas we want filled."

Bret leaned into Darius and whispered. "I have to talk to you."

"About what?" Darius whispered back.

"Just about something serious."

"You wanna talk now?"

"Later. But make time."

"Absolutely, just let me . . ."

Colin cleared his throat loudly. "Something you want to share?"

Bret shook her head "No, we're good. Sorry."

"As I was saying," Colin continued. "We need to perfect the list. What professions we are looking to invite. What percentage. I am sure we all have to tweak our own private lists of who we want to come into the shelter. We have the obvious like doctors, farmers, teachers . . . but we need to tweak. We need to think about what professions would be needed to make civilization run, just not the obvious. We're good with our supplies. Although I am certain, that when we get our invitees and experts together that they will look at our supply list and add to it. That's okay; hopefully, we'll be able to get the resources before it's too late. Yes, Bret."

Bret lowered her hand. "Can we have a gynecologist?"

"We went through this." Colin said.

"No, we didn't."

"Yes, we did. When you were in . . ."

Darius cleared his throat. "She doesn't

remember that time. And we did go through it, Bret. We opted against it."

"Why? We need one for the women and for any future babies that are born. We need a doctor to specialize in women. They will be our precious commodity."

"But any doctor will do," Darius said. "I hate having this argument again."

"No, not any doctor will do and I don't recall having this argument," Bret said.

"This is ridiculous," Darius saw her mouth open. "And don't give me that line, are you a woman."

Bret's mouth closed. "How did you know I was going to say that?"

"You said it before."

"Well how did the argument end before?" Bret asked.

"We had sex," Darius replied.

Chuck coughed.

Bruce laughed. "Man, you guys are killing me with this tale you keep telling Bret." He nudged Bret.

Bret grabbed Chuck's drink and downed it. "One won't hurt." She handed it back.

Chuck looked at his glass. "It's a joke, Bret. Stop buying it."

Bret nodded.

"Can we continue?" Colin asked. "Anyhow, let's hold off on the gynecologist argument for now. Back to this. I want to compile a list. The after we get the professions we need, then we can find the people. I don't want to invite a single person until things have progressed to the point that the invitees will have no problem believing our plan and wanting to join."

Bruce asked. "Are we sure things are going to happen? It's been quiet."

"That's what I said," Bret spoke. "Too quiet."

"Exactly," Colin said. "And that's what worries me. Something will happen, something big and soon. And when it does, word is going to get out and watch all hell break loose."

"What kind of event?" Chuck asked.

"Big," Darius answered. "I don't know what kind. But it will be big."

"Big enough to make people stop and see that the world's in trouble?" Chuck asked, and then sat back in his chair. "I can't fathom what kind of event that would be."

At that moment Andi rushed breathlessly into the room. "Hurry up. Hurry, you have to see the television." She flew back out and no one hesitated in following.

"Holy shit," was the first comment and that emerged from Colin. "Turn up the volume, Andi."

Bret moved closer to Darius as they all huddled around the television.

"Are we at war?" Chuck asked.

"It's Paris." Ando pointed. "Look, the Eiffel tower. It's warped."

"Heat of about one thousand degrees Fahrenheit," the newsman reported. "The area is still too hot to get a close shot. What you are seeing now is shot with a long zoom lens."

They were at a loss over what had occurred.

Paris in flames? It wasn't ablaze, it was smoldering.

The newsman continued, "About fifty miles north of Paris and extends south on a path ten miles wide, two hundred miles long. Everything in its path is . . ." he was somber. "Gone. Just . . . gone. Hundreds of thousands dead, more missing. There is zero power from London to Singapore. This is not just a sad day for Europe but a devastating day for the world, the most unprecedented and the single biggest catastrophic occurrence in the history of modern man."

Frustrated, Bret asked, "What happened?"

"You are seeing shots now of Paris, France," the newscaster reported. "If you are just tuning in, About thirty minutes ago, a solar explosion, or as some call it, solar flare, breached through our atmosphere. Though scientists report having monitored the 'X' flare, they also state that it wasn't expected to reach earth. It did. What's next? What is next?"

After the newsman's word, Darius looked at Colin. "Didn't we see this coming?" Darius asked. "We didn't see this action brewing? How did we miss it?"

"Other side of the sun, perhaps?" Colin shrugged. "I don't know." Colin shook his head and then faced Chuck. "You asked about what kind of event. This is it. This . . .s it. As far as the news breaking? Things are about to change." He released the heavy breath he held and turned toward the television. "From this moment on, everything will be different."

DARK AND GRAY

Reye Journal

July 24th

The aftermath of the Paris Flare will leave a vision of pain in the minds of all forever. The fires still smolder and experts estimate they will continue to burn for another six months. Six months? That, alone, could actually propel Europe into a mini ice age.

Thus far an estimated 600,000 are dead, close to a million missing. No doubt this incident is a wakeup call to the ecological and geographical fields.

In fact, an emergency scientific summit has been called in New York. This is planned to occur within the next week or so. The news not yet public was disclosed on the science boards by a couple of colleagues who were invited.

A cache of minds will try to determine what in God's name has been occurring naturally to this planet. Many, I believe, already know. It just has to get to the phase of believing.

I have yet to be invited, not that I would on my own. So, with the help of Virginia and Darius we are preparing to take our findings to Dr. Jeffers, who will be attending. Hopefully when I find him and show him our research, he will review it with an open mind. Somehow I doubt that.

25 - Learning Truths

July 25th

Martin Myers never planned his life to turn out the way it did. In his mind, even as a young boy, he watched his parents and envisioned for himself a similar future.

He'd be like his father, a professor at a local college, with a degree in some field of science, because Martin loved science, even as a kid.

He'd have a perfect wife, two kids, and a house with a fence. And maybe even a dog, because studies showed that an animal or pet in a house made for a happier family.

His wife didn't have to be the picture of beauty externally, but internally she would be the supportive being every man needed.

That was his plan.

The wife and marriage topped of his list of things he wanted most. He saw the happiness in his parents' marriage and wanted to emulate that in his own life.

But that was youthful thinking.

Everything started out that way. He met Janet in high school and married her his second year of college.

Money was tight, so they moved in with his parents while Martin went to school.

Janet and his mother had this fighting thing. Figuring it was typical mother-in law, daughter-in-law bullshit, he just tried to remain neutral, wanting not to disturb the balance of relationship with either woman.

His mother warned Janet was no good, was up to something.

Yeah. Yeah.

Janet warned his mother was overbearing and jealous.

Yeah. Yeah.

His father said it was an estrogen imbalance in the household.

Bingo.

Then he found out his mother was right. The day before graduation, just as Martin was getting ready to move into the teaching phase of his life, Janet left him for someone else. Someone older.

Martin was crushed.

Degree in Molecular Biology in hand, Martin decided he was going to pursue another passion. Something that would make him study and concentrate only on school. He could get his personal life back on track, after he graduated, so he thought.

He found a drive for virology and planned to further his studies, possibly be a research doctor.

Two years into that with failing grades, at twenty-four years old, his parents were killed in a car accident and Martin had nothing.

An Army recruiter found him on a bridge one night readying to take his life.

Driving by the recruiter saw him, stopped,

and hung out on the edge and talked to him.

The rest was history.

Life saved.

With a degree he was able to get into Officer's Candidate School, and Martin focused from that moment on, on building a career.

At the age of forty-nine he received his first star as a general. One year later, he celebrated his fiftieth birthday on the banks of Thailand monitoring the Avian Flu situation.

Shared world knowledge of outbreaks is often minimal. Out of fear, many countries don't release information about outbreaks. That's why he was in the hotspot: To watch, to border control, to check reports of bird flu within the communities and investigate. If the report was viable, he would monitor and let the US government know.

Although many believed the world's end if delivered by plague would begin in Africa, Martin knew better; so did the World Health Organization.

The next pandemic, if any, would without a doubt begin on the heavily populated continent of Asia.

Martin was there.

He loved his appointment, His first real Theater of Operation. He weeded through the rumor mills of the nearby villages and found many facts.

The women often brought him homemade treats, and often farmers brought him their daughters to examine for marriage.

He found it funny.

Unfortunately he was only there for eight months. In fact, he was watching the news on a live blog regarding the Paris flare when he heard the helicopter approach.

A military bird that he wasn't expecting.

He wasn't even in uniform. The uniform often intimidated the nearby villagers, and they trusted him more in civilian clothes.

In the distance the chopper stopped, and after peering out his office window, Martin watched the blades slow and the door open.

He closed out his Internet connection and walked from his office.

It was hot. Grabbing the handkerchief from his back pocket, he wiped the sweat from his neck and approached the bird, stopping at a distance.

The Captain of the bird opened the side door, and out stepped a three-star general.

Martin stood taller, his eyes shifting to the captain as he removed bags from the back of the helicopter.

The general approached.

It was General Hemming. Martin knew him from the Pentagon.

"General Hemming, sir." Martin greeted him with a respectable salute.

After returning the salute, General Grant Hemming shook his hand. "Martin."

"This is a surprise visit," Martin said.

"It's an emergency visit, Martin. I'm here to relieve you."

"Sir?" Martin asked confused.

"I can't tell you more than that. You just need

to pack your gear and be on that bird in 30 minutes."

"But, sir. There's so much to show you . . . ."

"I'm sure your chain of command knows enough to inform me. Besides," Grant winked. "You're a phone call away. Good luck. You better start packing. But first, get me in contact with . . ." he pulled a notepad forth, "Sgt. Major Blackwell."

Blackwell was his right-hand man. Martin nodded at the order. "Right away. This way." He held out his hand. "Sir, do you at least know where I'm going?"

Grant did not, or at least was not at liberty to say.

The only way to find out was to pack up and go. And that was what Martin did.

***

Four satellite dishes were erected in the open field forty feet behind the barrack-style structure in Texas.

The heat had subsided some, and Virginia was hopeful the temperatures would continue to drop. The air conditioning worked below in the shelter, but she had no designs to stay down there the entire time.

An air conditioning unit for the ground floor was due to arrive in the afternoon. It couldn't be soon enough. Amazing how she was able to get a local chain store to come to the property and erect a security fence around the perimeter in two days, but an air conditioning unit?

The wind blew her auburn hair, tossing the curls. Usually it wasn't that curly, but it was too hot and she had little ambition to straighten it.

Returning from the satellite dishes, she waved to one of the six security men she had hired to watch the property. Did they wonder what was going on out there? What she was doing?

She was grateful that the problem with dish four was only a small wind-blown bundle that landed on it. Virginia didn't want to take a chance on missing another geological event, like the solar flare. It wasn't that she missed it; it happened so fast, by the time the sun turned her way, the flare had shot.

There was no preliminary data to alert them. And that frightened her, more than she cared to admit. If it happened once, it could happen again. Only the next time it might not be the other side of the world.

Inside, her husband Rob was sweeping the floor.

"Kids spilled some cereal," he said.

Virginia smiled.

"All fixed?"

"Just a spur. Did Sears call about the air unit?"

"Oh, yeah." He said brightly, placed the push broom against the wall and walked to her. "They'll be here shortly."

"Thank God."

He ran his finger down the trickle of sweat on

her neck. "Not much longer."

"Where are the kids?"

"Watching TV in the other room."

The other room, Virginia thought. She looked around the barracks-style building. She didn't know why it was; it wasn't small, but the separated walls, the living and eating area in one room, the hot dusty air, it made her think of the Depression. That made her think how much life wouldn't be different from that when all went to hell.

"Something wrong?" Rob asked.

"Just concerned. The Paris flare just has me concerned. What if we stop seeing signs? What if things just start happening without warning, what if . . ."

"What if." Rob silenced her. "Then there's nothing you can do about it."

"I just worry about the kids, you know."

He nodded.

Virginia sighed out. "All right, I'm off. Heading down to the bunker. Find me when Sears shows up?"

"You got it."

Virginia started to walk away.

"What are you working on? You need me to help?"

"Data. Collecting data to send to Colin."

"He wants in that conference badly, huh?"

"Yeah, but I don't think they'll let him."

"Why's that?"

"Colin will deliver the truth. They'll know it's the truth. If he goes to the conference, the truth is public. I don't think the conference is about finding out what to do," Virginia said. "I think the conference is keeping the real truth from the public." She planted a soft kiss to his cheek, wiped her hand across where her lips pressed, then walked away.

***

Luke was print boy and find boy, Colin's designated working partner, as Bret was Darius'. Luke was in charge of printing up the data that Virginia sent, while looking for details on the first portion of the list they had composed of Invitees.

"I appreciate this Dr. Jeffers," Colin said on the phone. "I was going to send you all my data . . . ."

"Well, Dr. Reye, part of the reason I placed all of you together in quarantine was to see what you would do. You didn't disappoint me."

"Thank you."

"What about Dr. Cobb."

"He's working on his own way to get to the conference."

"Two of you trying in two different directions?" Jeffers asked.

"Yes, one of us is bound to succeed. I feel . . . hold on." He slid the phone from his mouth and pointed to the list in front of Luke. "See what you can find on him."

"But that's three more."

"Jump ahead," Colin winked.

Luke shrugged and began to type.

"Anyhow . . . ." Colin returned to Jeffers. "How hard is it going to be to get to speak at the conference?"

"Hard. Slots are filled. If I agree with what you have to present, I can present it."

"What do you have?"

"Theories. Not much."

"Our theories have some data as back-up," Colin said and winced at Luke's disclaimer.

"To be honest, it would be a lot easier to get you to speak if you had a viable solution or resolution."

"To stop what I think is going to happen?" Colin asked almost with a snicker.

"Yes."

"Dude," Luke smoothed out. "Check this shit out. I made a typo . . . ."

Just as Colin was about to 'shush' Luke, he peered down.

Luke continued. "An extra 'A', and this shit came up. Oh, well." He reached his hand for the mouse.

Colin stopped him, grabbing his hand. "Not so fast," he told Luke and moved closer to the screen. "Dr. Jeffers, let me call you back. I may have an idea." Blindly he hung up the phone. He gave a pleased pat on the head to an oblivious Luke, and then he took in the inadvertent search engine results that were, to Colin, more of a blessing than a mistake brought on by a typo.

***

Today I talk to him. Today I talk to him. Bret stated it in her mind over and over. She had run through exactly what she would tell Darius and how she would do so.

She had just finished the current inventory of medical supplies when she received the phone call from him stating he was on his way back.

It actually was perfect timing. The kids weren't home, Luke was monitoring, Colin was off doing something he deemed 'crucial'. A quiet house.

Until Darius arrived.

He called out her name with little kid enthusiasm, running about the house looking for her.

Coming out of the bedroom, Bret was not only greeted with his call, but Darius. She jumped.

"You are not going to believe this." Darius grabbed her shoulders. "Oh, wait. Here." He extended a bouquet of flowers to her. "For you."

"You got me flowers." Bret smiled quirkily at them. Purple daisies. "Can I ask why?"

"One, because I'm celebrating and sharing my good news with you. Two, I thought maybe they'd jar your memory. Someone told me that a picture or a symbol can do that."

"Purple daisies?"

"Well, yeah. We saw purple flowers when we had lunch in the field before the accident. You loved them." He watched her expression. It was lost. "No? Okay. Anyhow, my news. I tried to call Colin but he's not around."

"What? What happened?"

Proudly, Darius pulled his shoulders back. "I'm speaking at the conference."

"No." Bret said in shock.

Darius nodded. "I'm gonna get my chance to speak, give my theory and my idea for stopping it."

"You mean the blowing up the world theory."

Darius bobbed his head. "In short. I have a nuclear physicist who will be working with me to tweak it."

"I am really happy for you."

"Wait until Colin hears. Of course, he'll come too."

"Well, how . . . how did you manage this?"

Darius fluttered his lips. "Check this out. Winslow. He's buddies with the congressman heading this up. He called him, said he may want to hear what I have to say, the congressman said he'd slot me in."

Bret smiled. "That's great news."

"It is."

"So bad news isn't something you want to hear."

"Who broke my guitar?" Darius asked.

"Huh?"

"My guitar. Who broke it?"

"Why would you assume that? Is it broken?"

"You tell me. That's the only bad news I can think of."

"I doubt that. Come here." She called him in

the bedroom. "I need to talk to you."

"What's wrong?"

"I need you to be straight with me. One hundred percent honest."

Darius nodded.

Bret continued, "Were you serious about us being in a relationship? That we committed?"

"Absolutely, why would I lie?"

Bret shrugged. "I don't know. Colin does that shit. And we . . . we slept together."

"Yeah, a couple times. Well, twice," Darius replied. "Why, what's up?"

"Oh, Darius, you aren't going to believe . . ."

A knock at the door interrupted them.

"Mom," Luke poked his head in. "I'm looking for . . . never mind. There he is."

"What's up, Luke?" Darius asked. "Can this wait? We're talking."

Luke shrugged. "I guess. You have a visitor."

"Can you tell them I'll be done in a minute?"

Luke nodded. "Sure thing." He turned to leave.

"Wait, Luke," Darius called out. "Who is it?"

"You mom." Luke walked out.

***

How many times had Bret heard Colin mention that she reminded him of Darius' mother.

When the news came that Grace was downstairs, Bret was more excited than Darius. She wanted to meet the woman Colin spoke of and

Darius hadn't seen in eight months.

Darius was less enthused.

'Wow, really?' was his reaction, but Bret insisted they place their talk on hold and go down immediately.

They did.

She had never seen a picture at all. Darius rarely talked about his mother. They probably talked extensively about her on the week she'd lost.

That would be her luck.

Almost bashful she walked down the stairs directly behind Darius. Did Grace see her pause? Bret did just as she reached the next to the last step.

Grace was looking at the photograph table in the foyer, and turned around.

"Dare-Dare!" she belted, reaching out her arms.

Grace was not what Bret expected. After all, according to Colin she was a lot like Bret.

Grace was not Bret.

The woman in the foyer certainly did not match the mental picture Bret derived of someone who dated the distinguished Colin Reye and raised the snobbish Darius Cobb.

She was a younger mother. With Darius pushing forty, one would think Grace was gray and seasoned.

She was seasoned all right. Bret just didn't know which way. Grace was a young mother from what Bret had learned.

First thing Bret noticed was the volume of her

voice and the hick accent that was just a hint raspy from years of cigarette smoking or yelling.

The next thing she noticed was her jeans. They were tight, like jeans that were worn in the eighties or nineties. A thin belt more for decoration than 'holding them up' and a tight blue blouse tucked in.

She wasn't a thin woman or heavy; she was about average. Bret figured at one time she was thin. But what surprised Bret was her height. She was a good inch over Darius' five foot eight frame. Of course, that could have been her hair, which was bleached blonde, teased and big.

She tried to make it small.

Grace was attractive and wore full make-up. Her nails were long and manicured.

She looked more like Darius' big sister than mother.

"This . . . this is a shock," Darius stepped back; running his fingers through his hair. "Wow."

"Well, I told you . . . when was it I talked to you?" She tapped her finger on her lips. "Gosh, had to be what a month ago."

"Probably like four."

She waved out her hand. "Who keeps track of time? We don't on the rodeo circuit, I tell you. One city to the next." She exhaled. "Ain't you gonna invite me in?"

"Absolutely," Darius held out a hand then reached for the door.

"No, no. Wait. That starving boy is fetching my bags."

"Starving boy?" Darius asked.

"The thin one. Luke." She smiled. "And who is this?" she walked toward Bret. "Is this the filly Colin was telling me about?"

"How do you do? I'm Bret." Bret held out her hand.

"Oh, stop. You get a hug." She brought Bret in for an embrace. "You're marrying my son, now aren't you? That's what Colin said."

"Mom. When did you speak to Colin?" Darius asked.

"Yesterday. He invited me in."

"Why didn't you call me?" Darius asked.

"I would if you answered yer phone. I tried. Then I finally got a hold of Colin. He said something about you skydiving and hanging out in Texas. Then you and your fiancé came back to Pittsburgh. I got held up in New Mexico. But when I spoke to Colin yesterday, telling him I'm ready to come off the road, he said come on in. And here I am. Wow. Colin certainly has done good for himself."

Luke walked in the door with arms full of bags. "Where do you want these?'

"Oh, just put them there till we figure out where I'm sleeping. Thank you."

Luke nodded, set down the bags and headed down the hall. "I'm gonna go work on the tracking."

"Have a cheeseburger!" Grace called out. "How nice is that boy. He your son?" she asked Bret.

"Yes, he is."

"Don't he eat?"

Bret chuckled. "Actually, he does."

Grace winked. "Mind if I give it a try fattening him up?"

"Go right ahead."

"Time out." Darius made a 'T' with his hand. "How long are you staying?"

"Dontcha want me to stay?" Grace asked.

"That's not what I said. I asked how long?"

"For good, for a while." Grace shrugged. "Colin said to move right in. We're all one big happy family and he has lots of rooms."

"Rooms. But they aren't all bedrooms."

"Welp, he told me that, too," Grace said. "He told me that it's high tail time you and Bret shared a room anyhow." She smiled at Bret. "Little advice, try on the shoe first."

"Oh my God." Darius closed his eyes.

"What?" Grace asked surprised. "Just givin' advice."

"Did you break up with Chad?"

Grace laughed. 'Three years ago. I've been seeing Ron. He was the comedian and crowd charger for the rodeo."

"A clown."

Grace smiled and nodded. "We broke up. Said I was too serious about all the stuff going on. And I told him. If anyone knows it's my boy. He's the earth genius." She winked again and nodded. "And I ain't no genius. Don't pretend to be. But hell, something is going on. All this hot shit. Bird attacks. Bugs. Planes dropping. Volcanoes erupting. Hell on fury it's the book of Revelation . . . I told this to Colin. He said absolutely. We'll discuss it when you arrive. I'm here."

"Colin told you it was the book of Revelation?" Darius asked.

"He said it was something like that and something big was on the horizon. I want to be with you guys now."

Bret stepped forward. "Well, we're glad you're here."

Darius hummed out a 'hmm'.

Grace shot him a look.

"Did you fly in?" Bret asked.

"Oh, I drove. Pickup is beat to hell and back though."

"Then you must be tired. Come on in; I was about to fix lunch."

"Got any Jack?" Grace asked.

Darius looked at his watch. "It's one o'clock."

"How does that song go? It's five o'clock somewhere."

Darius forcibly chuckled and it showed.

"When's Colin getting back? I can't wait to see him. Since we're all gonna be one big happy family."

"Mom," Darius said with a snicker. "Colin is being polite. I hope you aren't planning a reunion. I mean, it's been fifteen years. You're staying here, great. But I'm sure he's moved on emotionally."

The door opened and Colin walked it. "Good lord, I'd recognize that fanny anywhere. To die for."

Grace smiled at Darius. "You were saying?"

***

Darius was on the phone. Outside with everyone else, but he was on the phone.

Underneath the umbrella-sheltered table, he sat with Bret. He spoke while her focus was on everyone else. The kids were swimming and Colin cooking on the grill, while Grace teetered between Colin and the pool. Jumping in, doing belly splashes and being loud.

Darius rubbed his temple.

Bret snickered watching him.

"Just . . just don't worry about it," Darius said. "Blue is normal. Watch for red. Thanks." He flipped his phone closed.

"Chuck?" Bret asked.

Darius nodded. "He hasn't a clue what he's doing. It's not his forte. I feel bad."

"Then why don't you go in the house and downstairs and help him. Or do the work?"

"I can't. I promised Colin two hours out here."

"Family time."

Darius grumbled.

"Darius."

"No, the world is falling apart and we're having a picnic. Bret, have you seen the news?"

"I try not to. It's depressing."

"Hell, yeah," Darius said. "Paris, the dead . . . ."

"It's depressing, Darius."

388

"I know. I just have so much on my mind. So much work. I have to get ready for this conference, and now…now she's here."

"She?"

A loud splash erupted from the pool and the kids screamed in joy.

"She," Darius reiterated. "I didn't expect her to show up."

"She's your mother."

"I know, and I love her. It's that she drives me nuts. And now, she's trying to rekindle with Colin, a man she hasn't been with in fifteen years. Insane."

"She surprised me," Bret said.

"How so?"

Bret glanced over to Grace. "I don't know. I expected different. She's so . . . so . . . ."

"Trailer park?" Darius asked.

"Oh my God, I can't believe you just said that."

"What? She is. Is it awful of me to say that nowhere in my apocalypse survival plan, did I envision my mother in my new civilization."

"Yeah, that's awful."

With a grunt, Darius rubbed his eyes. "And then . . . then my plan with you went out the window."

"What do you mean?"

"Bret, I thought we were going to be a team. A partnership. A commitment. I saw us going into the end of the world as a couple. When you have someone on your side, someone beside you, you can get through anything."

"Darius, I don't know what transpired in that week or so we were alone. I don't know how we went from friends to making a commitment. We must have been through a lot."

"We were."

"But I do know that during this last month, I can see why we made that decision. And do you know how many times in the past month I just wanted to give in and say, let's hook up?"

"Why didn't you?" he asked.

"I was afraid that the moment I made my move that was the moment you'd say, 'Ha! Gotcha'."

Darius rolled his eyes. "I told you it wasn't a joke."

"I believe it now," Bret said.

"So what does this mean?" Darius asked. "You and I are gonna be committed?"

"We already are," Bret folded her hands on the table. "I'm pregnant."

26 - Preparing the Future

Martin was able to shower when he arrived on the air craft carrier but wasn't given that much time. He was shuffled for sixteen hours straight.

From the carrier, to a plane, to Hawaii, then straight to Washington, DC.

No one knew anything nor told him anything.

He figured he was in some sort of trouble when a car arrived at the airport and took him away at high speed.

Washington. The Pentagon.

A police escort.

It was when the woman in the car handed him his uniform that he realized he wasn't in trouble.

He changed in the car, which was difficult.

Never did he expect the car to pull up to the White House.

Again, escorted without answers.

He was brought to the Joint Chiefs meeting room, where three other generals greeted him, along with the Secretary of State and Chief of Staff.

What was going on?

He almost hated to ask.

The President walked in.

Like everyone else he stood.

President David Greene was wearing a presidential tee shirt and jeans. Carrying a folder he nodded to the men and instructed, "Be seated."

But before Greene took his seat, he shook hands with Martin. "General Myers."

"Mr. President, it is an honor."

Greene half-smiled and sat down. "You may not think that when you hear why you're here."

'Uh-oh' wouldn't have been the professional response, so Martin just nodded and took his seat.

"I'll make this brief," Greene said. "Then everyone else can fill you in and get you situated."

"Yes, sir."

"You're aware of the Paris flare, obviously."

"Yes, sir."

"Are you aware of the other events that have taken place globally, General?"

"The events, sir?"

"Geological events," Karnes said. "Bird problems, earthquakes, tectonic plate shifts. A volcano in freaking Albany, New York."

"Yes, sir. I am."

"Are you aware that there is going to be a global summit regarding these changes and what we can do to prevent further catastrophes?"

Martin cleared his throat before speaking. "Yes, sir. I was not aware that a solution was being sought. I was just aware as most of the public is that the summit is to determine what is happening."

"Correct, but if we can change something we will. I doubt it. And by the way you cleared your throat and hesitated, you doubt it too."

"If it's geological, then how can it be changed?"

Greene nodded. "This is obviously a chain of events leading to something big. We're planning on the worst case scenario and on something big. Right now we have initiated a survival program which my Chief of Staff will fill you in on once I leave. We don't know exactly what this is leading to. Our scientists speculate, other scientists speculate. What we are hoping to accomplish with the summit is to bring all the great minds together, all the speculation together and make one determination."

"Yes, sir."

"The big one is the finale. Excuse my language, but a lot of our top minds believe shit is gonna hit the fan globally until then. You are here to one, be at the conference, listen and report. Two, be in charge of a command center that will monitor the global happenings via our troops and stations around the world. You will keep track of these happenings. Some of these can lead to national security."

"Allow me to clarify?" Martin asked.

The president nodded.

"You're talking about a command center to monitor everything. And I'm only to oversee this and report."

"We may need to send troops. Things may happen in our own country. You'll work closely with FEMA for troop support. This will be removed from the state hands for now and placed into your hands. This will now be a matter of national interest. You'll start immediately."

"May I ask, sir, with many much more

qualified people available, why I was chosen? I mean this is an honor. But I've only just begun my first Theater of Operation."

"Yes you have," Karnes responded. "And I don't mind you asking why I chose you to monitor and command a situation as big as this. Yes, you are correct. There are many more qualified. But you, General, are the best one for this job. I chose you personally, and chose you not just because of your determination, record and skill. But on this . . . ." he opened a folder and lifted from it a huge bound manuscript. "Did you not write this thesis in college?"

The manuscript slid his way and Martin looked at the typed title.

Greene read the title out loud. "A Thesis by Martin Myers. Monitoring the Global Events on the Path to the Next Extinction-Level Event." The president smiled. "Long title."

Martin nodded.

"Do you realize, General, twenty-six years ago you wrote about a lot of possible events that have already occurred?"

"Yes, sir."

"You theorize on a lot of different scenarios," Karnes said. "Your research is phenomenal."

"I enjoyed writing that."

"And it shows. Good reading. Good work. You don't need to ask again why you're the best one for the job or why you were chosen. This speaks for itself." The president stood up. "Good luck."

As Greene left the office as abruptly as he

entered, even standing, Martin's eyes kept going to his thesis. How he dismissed it when he wrote it and thought no more about it.

There it was again. His past was his future.

***

The Paris flare triggered an electromagnetic pulse, which in turn blacked out most of Europe. The widespread power outage caused a martial law to go into effect in the countries afflicted. Panic and chaos, along with violence, ensued. An immediate exodus began out of London.

Chuck was enthralled by the news. He watched it all the time. Every moment he could, down to watching it on his phone.

He wanted to go to Europe, but the Johnstown paper didn't have the funds to send him.

Besides, the fires still smoldered and no one was able to get close to Paris at all.

Like a forest fire raging out of control, experts gathered to figure out a way to put out the fires.

The focus in the United States was on the conference. Like with everything, things returned to normal after a day or two. When the commercials came back into the news programs, people returned to their lives.

Chuck would have rather been watching the television.

Even though he was fortunate enough to be privileged to scientific knowledge, he wanted to hear what everyone else had to say.

He was still in shock over the news of Bret's pregnancy and how Darius and Colin weren't lying to her about their relationship. He didn't know what shocked him more, Bret and Darius or the fact that Bret actually had sex.

The last thing he wanted to do was go out. But he did. He finished his story about the Siamese twin dogs and headed down to the West Virginia-Pennsylvania border to meet Bret.

She was already there holding a table at the Hub-a-Nub Saloon.

Perhaps Chuck should have known by the name what to expect. But he came right from the dog interview and hadn't thought much about it.

Country music twanged loudly on the jukebox. The all-wood atmosphere really aided it in making it a country music bar. An old-fashioned bar, with a pool table, juke box, and round tables for sitting that enhanced the feel. A small dance floor separated the small stage with a tree of three spotlights.

"Tell me again why I'm here." Chuck kissed Bret on the cheek.

"Darius is playing a set tonight."

"He couldn't play in Pittsburgh?" Chuck asked.

"He needs a country feel."

"Great. I am so out of place here," Chuck said. "I am a black man, in a suit, in a hick bar."

Bret snickered. "The suit is too much."

"I just came from work. But it's not the suit, Bret. I'm the only black man here."

"You won't be for long, Bobby is coming."

"Bobby doesn't know he's black. So I'll still be the only black man."

"That's because it's country music. How many black people do you know listen to country music."

Chuck shrugged.

"Bobby does," Bret said.

"As I said before he doesn't know he's black." He paused. "So Bruce and Bobby are coming?"

Bret nodded. "Along with Colin and Grace. They should be here any second."

"What's up with Darius' mother?"

"What do you mean? She's very nice."

"Yeah, but so uncouth."

"That's terrible"

"It's the truth," Chuck said. "Of course, she'll love it here." He ran his shoe across the peanut shells. "Look at this floor."

"It's atmosphere."

"It's unclean. Where is Darius?"

"He's back stage talking to the bar owner."

"He's not gonna come out and sing wearing shit-kicker boots, a fringe shirt, and a cowboy hat, is he?"

"No." Bret chuckled.

"I'd have to laugh if he did. Possibly make fun."

"That's better than bitching."

"I do that well."

"You do."

"How are you feeling?" Chuck asked.

"Good."

"Any memories?"

"Not of sex with Darius."

"So you are having memories."

Bret bit her lip.

"What?"

"Okay, it's not a memory, it's an impression."

"An impression."

Bret nodded. "A feeling."

"So how do you know it's memory related?"

"Because I know how Blain died."

"Continue."

"I keep having nightmares, and I can't explain it. It's the same nightmare, and this dream has actually sparked a phobia in me. I worry about it all the time."

"What? Jumping from planes? Trains?"

"Chihuahuas."

Chuck coughed. "Chihuahuas?"

"Yeah, why is that?"

Chuck laughed. "Ask Darius."

"Do you know?"

"Ask Darius. I need a drink." He started to laugh again, standing. "Do you want one?"

"I'm pregnant."

"Have a glass of wine. It's good for your uterus."

"Okay." She shrugged and watched Chuck. She jumped at the kiss to her cheek. "Look at you spreading affection."

"I like it," Darius sat down. "Where's Chuck going?"

"Getting us a drink."

"Me and him."

"No, him and me."

"You can't drink. You're pregnant," Darius said.

"Chuck said wine is good for my uterus."

"What does Chuck know?"

"More about pregnancy than you. He had two kids. Plus, I had kids, I drank with Luke. Wine."

"Look at Luke."

"Hey . . . ."

Colin, who had arrived, interceded, "Luke is a fine boy who is well on his way to being the next great scientific mind of our world. Of course . . ." Colin pulled out a chair. "There's not going to be much competition."

"Where's Grace?" Bret asked.

"At the bar getting drinks. She said she wanted to go speak to the token black man." Colin chuckled.

Darius said. "Colin, Chuck is getting her wine. Tell her she can't drink."

"Sure she can. Wine is good for the uterus."

Bret smiled smugly and held out her hand. "There you have it."

Darius grunted. "I have to go play."

"Wait." She grabbed his arm. "Before you go. Chuck said you'd know. Why am I having nightmares about Chihuahuas?"

The corner of Darius' mouth raised in a smile and he walked away.

Bret's mouth dropped open.

"Don't worry about it." Colin patted her hand. "He probably doesn't want you to remember."

"I want to. I want to know why I am having

the dream."

"What's the dream?"

"Just this Chihuahua yapping viciously. I'm scared in the dream then all of a sudden I see blood."

"Hmm," Colin nodded. "Makes sense."

"Then please tell me."

He grabbed her hand. "Only if you promise not to let it disturb you."

"I promise."

Colin took a deep breath. "When you were on that plane, a woman had a dog, a Chihuahua. You managed to save it, Bret. You tucked it in your arms when you jumped from the plane."

"Ah." She smiled. "That was nice of me."

"Yes. But then you were lost in the woods without food and Darius roasted it over an open fire."

Bret shrieked.

"Sorry."

"Did I . . . did I eat it?" She asked.

"You were starving . . . ."

Bret shrieked again.

"Darius said you ate more than him."

Bret covered her mouth. Her stomach turned. "I think I'm gonna be sick."

Chuck returned and set the wine down. "What's wrong?"

Colin replied, "I was just explaining the Chihuahua story and why she could be having nightmares."

"Oh, yeah. That's a great story. I don't get the nightmares, though." Chuck said. "I mean Darius said you loved every second of it."

At that point Bret, hand tightly over her mouth, raced way.

Darius saw and came to the table. "What's wrong with Bret?"

Colin answered. "Well I told her about the Chihuahua and how you blew it up. Way to go, Dare-Dare, you have now made her vomit."

"Great. Just great. The head-injury-Bret gets sick, while the pre-head-injury-Bret sang my praises."

"Why don't you remind her when she gets back how much she worshiped your quick thinking and survivor skills?"

"You know what? I will. I'll remind her. Thanks. Gotta play." Darius returned to the stage and picked up the guitar.

Colin grinned arrogantly.

Curious upon seeing his expression, Chuck asked. "What is so funny?"

All but in a full blown gloating mode, Colin shook his head. 'If you only knew."

***

It was about two in the morning when Martin arrived at the Arizona site. It was project constructed in the late nineteen nineties in the event of meteor impact. Construction stopped shortly after the war on terror began and it wasn't continued

Until that moment.

Multitudes of trucks were present going in

and out of the Cavarness project. Martin's headquarters were a command center constructed in the side of the mountain.

He was taken to his room first where he left his belongings and then to the project command center.

The project was named GEP, Global Extinction Project. It still wasn't a complete setup, but a technician there said the monitoring staff would be arriving at dawn and the equipment, though probably needing tweaking, would be operational by noon.

Where to even begin?

Not only was Martin in charge of monitoring the events, he was in charge of overseeing the survival project as well. The specs for the survival city were left on Martin's bed.

After taking a quick tour of the facility and realizing he'd need to tour it again after he had some rest, he went to his room.

A bottle of bourbon was left on his night stand and he poured himself a shot's worth to sip.

He kicked back on his bed, drink in hand and flipped open the construction plans.

A lot of what was amended was what he had suggested was needed in his thesis.

He was high seventy percent of the time he wrote that thesis; he chuckled at that thought, remembering his youth and how he believed marijuana opened his mind more.

Now the product of a stoned young man was being used as a guidance tool for a national project.

Even laying on his bed, in the command center, encased in the GEP, Martin didn't understand the whys of it all.

Perhaps the president was just trying to get a grip on all that was going to happen.

It was obvious he was trying to ensure that an extinction event would not take place.

Martin knew a survival city wasn't needed to ensure the human race would go on. A general, running operations in some mountain, was obsolete in the final stages of survival. The human race was self-equipped with a survival mechanism. No matter what, no matter how, government project or not, the will to live would supersede the cause to die, and when it was all said and done, there would be people left to carry on.

27 - Making Points

July 28th

He didn't realize it, but when Sgt. Mann felt the breeze hit him, he needed it. He closed his eyes and basked in the four-second glory. For a second, a split second, it chilled the sweat on his brow and he had relief.

Stationed in Germany, Sgt. Mann and his family were moved to the United Kingdom when the United States committed some of its European-based soldiers to border and watering hole patrols.

Sgt. Mann worked both.

He was glad that power was restored to the western portion of the UK, but that brought in more refugees. The influx was under way, but where to send the people was the question.

Cruise ships were being used to house refugees, and Sgt. Mann couldn't help but think those people had it best.

Water, cool air.

The heat wave was stifling, and sitting in idling cars didn't help.

The refugees were all from France. Survivors of the Paris flare were traveling into Calais and taking the ferry through the Strait of Dover into the UK.

They were coming by the thousands. Extra ferries were added, but that still didn't help the wait.

There was no power in France, and in the heat wave it proved to be too much.

Although the Paris flare destroyed Paris, France, it scorched much of the countryside in the process.

A surveillance plane flying over the outskirts of Paris could see bodies where they dropped from the oxygen being sucked out of the air.

But that wasn't what was officially posted on the Apocalypse blog ring started by some fiction writer. People would post what they saw or experienced on the blog ring, and people like Sgt. Mann's wife would read it faithfully.

There were things he believed to be true, and other things he didn't think could hold water.

Water.

He hoped he was on the watering hole duty the next day.

The shortage of fresh water coupled with the heat wave caused the UK to establish watering holes where people went and got cooled off. It was recommended to visit them at sundown.

Being on watering hole duty meant being in the water.

It was better than standing in line, checking cars.

Where did they come from, where were they going, check their papers, etc . . . .

Sgt. Mann was just about ready to return from his ten-minute break. He called his wife whom had hadn't seen since they arrived.

"Paris had rain today," she told him. "It rained hard."

"All that smoke, bound to cause something."

"Yeah, now it's steam. It put out a lot of fires, they say. And they think they'll be able to get in and rescue. God, it feels good to have internet and television back.'

He said 'I bet', spoke a bit more about their daughter, informed her he'd be seeing her soon, and returned to his break.

He held new orders in his hand, orders that came via a note.

He was to report any incident out of the norm, no matter how small it seemed, if it was not of the norm, he was to email the incident details to General Myers at Project GEP.

Sgt. Mann wasn't sure of what the GEP stood for, nor did he really care. He just wanted to do his job.

What constituted out of the ordinary was a wide open field. After all, the thought of refugees pouring into London wasn't ordinary.

The United Kingdom freely opened its borders to refugees. This not only put the citizens on high alert for terror, it made the citizens angry.

How many protestors had they arrested for throwing things at the refugees?

Walking back to his post, Mann watched two more cars being moved from the line. The smart people shut off their ignitions and stood outside.

"Thanks," the young British soldier said to Mann, when he was relieved. "Just in time, too."

"What do you mean?" Mann asked.

"See that long line?" He motioned his head upward.

"Jesus," Mann commented, the line of congested traffic had no ending.

"Ten-ten ferries. Three of them. Those folks are not gonna be happy or smell very good."

Mann gave a curious look.

"Poor povvies been waiting for three days to get the ferry."

"Great."

"Good luck mate," the soldier smiled and moved out.

Mann waved the next car through. He was one of fifteen soldiers working the lines. He asked his typical questions, checked the paper work and moved them through. He gave them the informational pamphlet provided by the government. Where they should go, what they could do to be more comfortable.

Five cars later, the line from the ten-ten ferry began to arrive.

The window wound down.

Mann caught with the air conditioned air a whiff of a putrid order, held back a cringe. "Where you coming from?" he asked the driver. An older man. The car held only his wife and children, no belongings.

"Paris." He answered, sounding nasal.

"Paperwork." Mann requested.

The wife handed the paper as she coughed.

"Thank you." Mann reviewed it. After asking a few more questions, he allowed the car to pass.

Next.

The car was packed, people sitting on people. The driver intermittently coughed and sniffled during the processing. Sgt. Mann stepped back. The last thing he needed was to catch a summer cold.

Mann wished him luck, told him to take care of himself, and waved the next car forward.

It wasn't until the car after that arrived that it struck him. Five cars in a row. All the passengers were exhibiting cold symptoms. Maybe it was his imagination, he didn't know. But no sooner did the sixth car pull forward, and the woman driver had dark circles around her eyes and coughed, than Mann stepped back. He told the car to hold on, and while pulling forward the barricade horse, called for a replacement.

"What's going on?" asked the soldier.

"Hold this line while I find Major James," Sgt. Mann said and sought out the commander of the border operation.

He was in his tent on the phone. When he saw Mann he waved him in. The call ended quickly, and he asked what was up. He saw the stoppage of the line.

"It might be me being paranoid, but I halted the sixth car. Five cars in a row had sick people in it. Colds, you know. When the fifth car went through it finally rang to me. But when the sixth arrived . . . ."

"Your point?" the Major asked.

"My point is these are all refugees who were on a ferry together and waited together for two days. Maybe it's my imagination, or maybe they have something, I don't know. We weren't told to look for illness but . . ."

The Major held up his hand and walked from the tent. Mann watched him. He pleasantly approached the stopped car at Mann's line, then walked to the next line. He asked that soldier some questions and moved to the next.

The Major then made his way to his commanding officer, and whistles blew shortly after that.

Barricades were immediately set up. People honked, got out of their cars, screamed and yelled. Major James, uninhibited, walked back to the tank.

"I'm not a doctor,' he said. "But you brought up a valid point. Thank you, Sergeant." And he picked up the phone.

It wasn't long after that orders were given to seal off the border. No one was allowed to pass. Gasmasks were mandatory, and until the health ministry arrived, the soldiers were to walk the line of cars and check each and every passenger for signs of illness. If they contained the ill, they were to yellow flag the car.

Mann ran out of flags. Of all the cars he checked, not one contained a well environment.

***

Darius wanted to kill his mother. Not that sleeping in the same bed with Bret didn't have its perks, but if he had to listen to her throw up one more time he was going to scream.

And she didn't do it quietly. She was loud, as if every ounce of her insides were painfully searing upward.

He dreaded the thought of being in the birthing room.

From the desk in the bedroom Darius looked up to a sound of up-chucking.

He was working on mathematical equations. He thought if he got up early, Bret would sleep.

Another upheaval, this one not productive.

There she goes, he thought. Nothing in her stomach. He looked at his watch. She had four more minute of the dry heaves.

Math problem. Work . . . .

Up heave.

He dropped his pencil. "Bret, can you do that more quietly?"

Silence.

Darius smiled.

The door to the bathroom flew open. "Fuck you, Darius."

"What?" he said shocked.

Bret shoved a cracker in her mouth. "I got sick before, but never like this."

"You were never this old before when you got pregnant."

She gasped and choked, needing a drink of water.

"Your body . . ."

"Are you saying I'm old?"

"Older. Older. I'm saying you're older than you were when you gave birth before. Thirteen years make a difference."

"So does bad sperm."

He turned in his chair, laughing. "Did you just say bad sperm?'

"Yes." Bret plopped on the bed, shoving another cracker in her mouth.

"So this is my fault."

"Yes."

"Well, tell me how it's my fault, so I can fix it and make you either stop throwing up or put a mute button on you."

"Like you vomit quietly?" she asked.

"Yes." He nodded.

"Prove it."

"What?"

"Prove it."

"How am I gonna prove I vomit quietly."

"Take a dose of ipecac."

"Huh!" Darius laughed. "You're out of your mind."

"So now I'm loud, old and crazy."

"I give up," Darius said.

"So you're not gonna argue. You're gonna agree that you think I'm loud, old, and crazy."

"Yes."

Another gasp, Bret grabbed her crackers and stormed from the room.

When the door slammed, Darius smiled. "Ah, silence." And went back to work.

***

Seventeen thousand bunk mattresses arrived at the GEP complex about the same time as the email from a Stephanie Mann. Stephanie, the wife of a soldier working the borders in London, emailed Martin at her husband's request because he couldn't leave the lines.

'Some sort of illness has broken out amongst the ferry refuges from France. Thousands ill. Suspected diphtheria or typhoid,' the email said. She went on to explain who she was and where her husband was posted guard.

Down the chain of command, they were determining what to do with the mattresses that arrived four days earlier than they should have, while Martin was tracing the email, trying to determine if indeed Ms. Mann was correct in her information.

First he called her. She told him that her husband placed a call to her. Then Martin got hold of the post and spoke directly to Sgt. Mann. Sgt. Mann confirmed he had seen the illnesses, he was currently required to wear a respirator, and the health ministry was there.

Outbreaks were to be expected, especially with refugees and dealing with large-scale major catastrophes.

Martin was surprised he hadn't heard of illness sooner. Into the new computer program, he logged the location and marked it as a biologic occurrence.

He needed a cigarette, and while he could go to his office and smoke in the compound, he opted for fresh air, even though it took time to walk outside. Keeping his cellular phone with him, Martin made his way from the mountainside compound.

Lighting his smoke, he stepped out into the bright sun. He probably wouldn't have thought twice about it had he not received the email from Stephanie Mann.

"No, you go on," the construction supervisor said to one of his crew. "Get some rest. Get well."

After a long hit, Martin exhaled and walked over to the supervisor. "Everything okay with your man?"

"Yeah. Yeah, just a bit of a cold that got him down."

Martin nodded. "Anyone else sick on the crew."

"No, not at all, General."

Paranoia, Martin thought. He guessed he was just paranoid after hearing about the thousands ill in London. Walking back over to his smoking spot, Martin brought his hand to his mouth. It was as he was about to take a hit of his cigarette that he saw it perched on his index finger.

Usually a bug on him would cause him to shuck his hand or smash the insect, but not this one. Not yet.

Moving more into the sun, Martin brought his hand closer. Sure enough, it was the type of insect he suspected.

What baffled him was the fact, that this particular insect wasn't usually prevalent after June. And that worried Martin. Most people wouldn't think twice about the insect. Most people wouldn't know. It wasn't just the matter of it being the insect oddly prevalent, the insect made something else prevalent.

He stared at the insect, the flea, or rather, Siphonaptera which perched arrogantly upon his skin. Bold, ready to attack, bite, take in some blood. Martin wouldn't allow that, especially knowing that the Siphonaptera was the number one carrier and cause of the bubonic plague.

***

He didn't look like a scientist, and Darius figured he'd have to do something about that before they went to the conference; Darius needed Mark Pyle to be there. He had never met someone with so much knowledge of nuclear science.

But those at the conference would and could be somewhat ignorant of scientific knowledge, considering most were congressman.

Mark Pyle sounded as if he went to the Luke School of Linguistics, using words like, 'dude', 'whoa', 'sweet', and 'snap'.

He wasn't a young man, but he wasn't old either; maybe thirty, a boy genius, accelerated through his schooling. His hair was rock star long. Not eighties rock star; it was shoulder length, dark. He was thin. Any more weight loss and he'd look like an addict.

Darius had a week to add weight to him.

And the tattoos. Of course he didn't have normal tattoos. He had Einstein equations all over him.

"What about a PowerPoint demonstration?"

Darius asked, overlooking Mark's laptop.

"PowerPoint?"

"It's a program that . . ."

"Dude, I know PowerPoint," Mark said, "but why?"

"We need something effective."

"I can make effective," Mark stated. "Seriously. I can."

"But the Army really likes its PowerPoint, so I would assume so would Congress."

"If we do Flash or a mini-movie." Mark nodded and winked. "It can hit home. Add a little background soundtrack."

Darius smiled. "From Armageddon, maybe?"

"Yeah. We'll take shots from my simulation."

"You have a simulation program?"

"Sort of, it's almost finished. Will be tomorrow."

"Excellent." Darius clenched his fist, excitedly.

"Dude, wait until you see the results. I'll show the ice age, the blasts, the stopping, you name it."

"Can you show what will happen if we let the magnetic reversals continue?"

Mark nodded. "Absolutely."

"This is going to be so cool. Are you . . . are you sure we can't be more effective using PowerPoint?"

"More effective than a movie with a soundtrack." Mark fanned out his hand. "Imagine the faces when they see the facts, hear the strong background music, then see . . . the destruction.

They may puke."

Across the room, Bret's voice entered the room. "Oh my God, are you talking about cholera?"

After shifting his eyes to Mark, Darius looked up. "What are you talking about?"

"Cholera," Bret answered. "You're talking about what's sweeping Europe, right?"

Mark looked up inquisitively. "Cholera is sweeping Europe?"

Nonchalantly, Darius nodded. "Yeah, and typhoid, and . . . um . . . ." he snapped his fingers. "What the fuck did they just discover a couple hours ago?"

Aghast, Bret answered, "Diphtheria."

Another snap of his fingers and Darius nodded. "Yeah, diphtheria."

"God, you're so insensitive," Bret said.

"How am I being insensitive?" Darius asked.

Smugly Bret imitated Darius, and snapped her fingers dramatically. "What's that disease? Oh, yeah, diphtheria."

"It doesn't affect me," Darius claimed.

"It might. What if . . ."

"Bret, sweetie, I'm busy," Darius said.

Bret gasped. "Remind me not to come to you the next time I'm fearful that something is wrong with me."

"What?" Darius asked. "Is something wrong?"

"I think I have cholera," Bret said.

Darius stared, nodded once, said, 'Uh huh,' exhaled and looked down to the computer.

"You dick."

Mark laughed.

"Bret, you're pregnant," Darius said. "You don't have cholera. If you're fearful, call the doctor."

"I will."

"Let me know what he says." Darius chuckled when she stormed out.

Mark snickered. "Congrats on the baby."

"Thanks. I can't wait."

"Check this out," Mark said. "I made a mini-presentation for the day of the ice age coming. See what you think." He clicked the mouse and the movie window opened up.

The music began to play, softly. Then the words read. 'Fifty thousand years ago, the earth went silent.'

The music stopped and a howling wind eerily echoed though the speakers.

Darius grinned. "Oh this is good. Really good."

"Has impact, huh?" Mark asked.

"Fucking right. We're gonna blow them away."

Darius watched with excitement, snickering and grinning over the grizzly computerized image of the world freezing over.

The second the movie stopped, Colin announced his presence with a verbal, "Knock-knock."

Darius rose from his leaning position. "Oh hey, Colin. How's everything."

"Good. Got a pizza. Want some?" Colin

asked.

"Yeah, in a second," Darius answered "Hey, you know Mark."

"Mark." Colin waved. 'You're gonna get a haircut for the conference, right."

"Ponytail," Mark replied.

Colin shrugged. "Works. Where's Bret?"

Darius answered, "Calling the doctor to see if she has cholera."

Colin nodded. "Shall I feed into this psychotic hypochondriac episode or shall I ease it?"

Darius took a moment to think, tapping his finger on his lip. "Feed it."

"You got it." Colin grinned. "What are you guys watching on the screen?"

Mark replied, "A demo I came up with for our conference presentation."

"Is it PowerPoint?" Colin asked.

"No," Mark said. "Flash."

"Should use PowerPoint. Everyone uses PowerPoint. It's effective to some people." Colin smiled and walked away.

Both Darius and Mark stared at the doorway.

"More effective than a Flash?" Mark asked then fluttered his lips. "Yeah, right."

Darius waved out his hand. "What does he know? Show me that again before our pizza." He leaned over Mark's shoulder and basked one more time in the feeling of doom he received from watching Mark's demo.

28 - Permanent changes

Such a tiny insect invoked so much thought, consuming Martin's mind. For some reason he just couldn't separate himself and the work at hand from the sick worker and the flea. The placement of the bunks didn't help.

It made him think of sick people.

He had immediately contacted Sgt. Mann, asking him for pictures of the ill. Although Sgt. Mann didn't question him, there was a tone in his voice that stated he didn't understand why.

After all, Martin wasn't a doctor. If he himself were a sergeant in the field, he'd question in his mind why some general wanted to see pictures of the ill. Especially since throngs of medical personal were on it.

But he said he'd comply, and within an hour of the requisition, Martin received numerous pictures via the phone.

Were the pictures useless? Or was Martin just looking for something that wasn't there?

He would download, look at the each small picture and wait for the next.

Each small photo, blurry, bred nothing. It didn't breed the images his mind was certain would be there.

He'd get a picture, then a text. "More?" the text would read.

Martin would respond with, 'send another.'

419

Then came picture 14.

Just as Martin was about to label that useless, he stopped.

He pulled the phone closer to his eyes; it looked like it...but he couldn't be sure.

Beep.

Mann's text. "More?"

"One more," Martine responded. "Same patient closer on the neck."

Phone closed, Martin tapped his finger impatiently waiting. He saw on the digital screen a message was incoming.

With a musical tone it arrived.

Martin flipped open his phone and smiled.

Perhaps he shouldn't have been smiling, but the fifteenth picture confirmed what he believed. He wasn't insane. Texting Mann that no more pictures were needed at the time, Martin hooked his phone to the computer and downloaded the images.

He enlarged and zoomed in. The pictures weren't crystal clear nor professional images, but they were good enough.

Image on the screen, Martin leaned forward, finger to his temple, thumb to his chin and stared.

Had the medical professionals really missed it or did they know and were only covering up?

Surely they tested, right?

He couldn't be sure. Nothing on the news said anything about it. Nor did his reports and by what he witnessed, he was correct and it needed confirmation.

Confirmed by an official in the field. The

conference was in a few days and the information was valuable.

It made sense. It made perfect sense. Why wouldn't it be happening out of season?

The ill woman lay on a cot, patient 34576. The picture was close to her neck. The tell-tale signs of blackening and swelling were there. Surely they weren't missed. If someone like Martin saw it, surely a doctor did.

He picked up the phone and dialed.

The United States had WHO and CDC specialists on site. Martin phoned them. It took a while to get hold of the doctor, and Martin was met with ridicule. Laughs that weren't masked or hidden.

But despite it all, Martin convinced the WHO doctor to appease him, to just double-check patient 34576. Because Martin was certain that the epidemic in Europe wasn't cholera, but rather the bubonic plague.

***

The finishing touches of the bunker were being applied, and it was the first time in a long time Bret had entered the building. Chuck had been there more frequently, but in the last two weeks, progress had escalated.

All floors were done.

The bunker was designed to hold up to 18 people, but would preferably hold 12. Food was brought in along with wood supplies and a water system.

It would house those staying behind. The invitees, hopefully, would be in the Texas shelter by the initial onset of the final occurrences.

"Wow," Bret spoke upon walking onto the main floor. "It's so dark, though."

Bruce pointed to the windows. "From the outside you can't tell they are blocked. But for insulation purposes, they need to be sealed. It's removable, though."

Chuck asked. "Even with the sun as a source of heat?"

Bruce shook his head. "It's gonna be gray. Plus the glass won't hold back that cold. It's gonna get cold for a spell."

"Enough wood?" Chuck asked.

"Hopefully." Bruce smiled. "We can always start burning things."

"Will the water supplies freeze?" Chuck questioned.

"Nope. The third floor is insulated and the water tanks covered. The pipes run right next to the heating ducts. We're good."

Bret took in the huge loft-style main floor. Divider walls separated sleeping areas for four. A bathroom was built and the kitchen and living area wide open. It was lit by small hanging lights. And even though the sunlight seemed to be an issue for her, after all a week or two without sunlight . . . Bruce assured her that should the temperature be okay Colin said they could unblock a window for more light.

Doing a clockwise turn she spotted it. With the voices of Chuck and Bruce fading, she made her way to the door that she thought was a closet. Stepping out into it, she saw that it was a long hall the width of the building. Against the wall were hanging glass cases six feet tall, three feet wide. They were empty.

"Bruce?" she called out.

A moment later, "Yeah." Bruce stepped through.

"What are these?" She pointed.

And when Bruce answered her, the summer heat that had consumed the building disappeared and a chill went thought her system.

A reality chill.

"Cases for the suits," he replied.

Bret looked at his with question.

"Arctic suits. Like the astronauts would wear."

She envisioned herself in a parka or cute little snow gear. Arctic suit? Envisioning herself in that would be envisioning a world she was not ready to face.

***

It wasn't that the air was cool, but it felt it as the warm breeze swept over the layer of sweat on Virginia's brow.

She had taken the laptop outdoors and was regretting every minute of it.

Her life's work was beating down on her. The

sun, its heat unbearable. But then again, Virginia wasn't really working outside. She was chatting online with her newfound friend from Singapore, Lin.

Lin was a sun watcher, and they were relaying data back and forth. Sharing rather, finding what the other wasn't getting.

Virginia was quite impressed with Lin's data from Singapore Solar Research Center.

The sun's activity was up to the second.

And she thought her equipment was second to none.

Lin had shared with her that his organization believed the sun was going to act up for a period of 60 days. Unpredictable as to the extent, but act up, meaning there would be more solar flares, perhaps even one like the Paris flare.

They were watching.

Virginia asked if they saw it coming. Lin told her looking back, they saw the beginnings of it, but excused it as small sun spots.

However, Lin and his people didn't believe that any more would occur. They didn't think a magnetic reversal was coming. In fact, they had a representative heading to the conference to warn about the sun.

The sun was the culprit. The culprit would behave in a few months time, then all would be back to normal.

Virginia didn't believe that. But she didn't push the issue.

They were actually talking on line about children, when Lin suddenly changed his typing tone.

"Can you access the data now?" Lin asked

"Laptop is older, would take a while."

"Go to your other station," Lin requested. "I'm sending you data."

Virginia agreed, informing him it would take about fifteen minutes. The journey to the lab in the complex was long.

She didn't even shut down the laptop. She carried it into the upper level of the building and inhaled the blast of cooler air.

"Everything okay?" Rob asked her.

"Yeah, yeah," Virginia nodded. "Kids fine?"

Rob indicated to the kids playing video games.

Virginia chuckled "I have to run down to the lab."

"You're not gonna be there for hours again are you? You lose track of time."

"I shouldn't be. But send RJ down if I am."

She darted a kiss to his cheek and went her way.

The fact that Lin was sending her information and his change of tone told her more about the urgency than he did.

The data came though and Virginia viewed it.

"OK," she typed. "What am I looking at? It's normal."

"See those three sunspots in the grid?" he asked.

"Small. Yes."

"Are you watching them?"

"Sun spots are spots. They aren't gonna do

anything in a minute they...." Virginia paused. "Are they moving?"

He replied. "Yes. Circle. Disappear. Reappear."

"Is this what you noted before the Paris flare?"

"Yes," he typed. "As you can see. Sunspots. We thought nothing of them. They'd reappear. By the day of the flare they were this size and in a matter of two hours they grew."

"Did you notify anyone?"

"Absolutely, it took two hours to notify someone. At that point, the flare formed and expelled."

"So you knew it was heading to earth."

"And we knew it was big. We hoped the atmosphere would break it. But . . . ."

"Did you have a destination?"

"Yes. We did. Unfortunately, we only had a two-hour window there, as well."

"Do you think this is the same?" she questioned.

"Absolutely, if this plays out the same. We will watch this happen for three days. They will do the same pattern until flare day. And then they will grow and expel a flare."

"Can we guess where?"

"Not precisely, I can go through the data, guess the area."

"Please do."

"But Gin." He wrote. "The area will be too big. By the time we have more of a precise location there will be no time to do anything. The warning window will be the two hour time frame the flare takes to reach earth."

"Actually a little bit more. We'll have the data when the flare forms."

"We will watch this one. This will help us learn even more should it happen a third time. Right now, let me work on an estimated impact site should a flare form."

Virginia typed a simple letter 'k' and exhaled.

Was it possible that another flare like the Paris flare was likely to occur? It was frightening because they didn't know where or when. They suspected it would happen in a few days, its size unknown.

There was no concrete proof. That was why they didn't see the Paris flare coming. It didn't form normally. It removed any predictability.

It could hit anywhere.

That notion took Virginia's breath away.

***

Bret was talking. Darius knew that, but his mind was elsewhere, actually on a lot. He was going between checking his things that were packed for the conference, eavesdropping on Colin's call, and trying to peek at the data Colin was going to present at the conference.

Data and info he would not share with Darius. Too good, Colin claimed.

'So in the hall is a huge case, did you know that?" Bret asked.

"Uh huh," Darius answered. A box. A briefcase, a portfolio folder. That had to be where Colin had the info.

"Will there be enough suits?"

"Yes," Darius replied. Eyes shifting to Colin on the phone. *What? What was that? Make a mental note. He asked Virginia the location.*

"It really is decked out. Sounds like it will work," Bret said.

"Yes." Darius made a face, squinting in thought. *Why wouldn't Colin share his info?* Every scientist was presenting the problem, the outcome, and their potential solution. Obviously if Colin was getting to speak, his presentation was going to be different. What was it?

"Then Bruce showed me the cool way to heat the place."

"Uh huh." Snap to Colin. Another mental note: Who was Lin? He didn't recognize the name.

"Did you pack enough underwear?"

"Uh . . . " Darius paused. "I'm going for two days. How much underwear do I need to pack?"

"So you were listening."

"Of course."

"I just didn't think you were. You kept saying uh huh."

"Bret. Dear." Darius laid his hands on her shoulder. "I'm just busy and preoccupied. It's a long drive to New York."

Across the room Colin said, "Goodbye," and hung up the phone. This caused Darius to immediately switch his attention.

"What happened?" Darius asked.

"Seems Virginia's newfound friend in Singapore, who works for the solar research center, has found a pattern."

"What are you talking about? Pattern?"

"To the expulsion of a big flare."

Darius scoffed. "That's absurd. We've had one. How can there be a pattern?"

"He's seeing the sun do the same odd thing it did before the last one."

Calmly, Darius nodded. "Hmm. Does he think they'll be another big flare?"

Bret gasped.

Darius reached over and covered her mouth.

Colin lowered Darius' hand. "Yes. In a few days."

"After the conference."

"Yes. He's estimating Asia."

"So if it's true, and the sun is misbehaving, it could be the same location on the sun?"

"Could be."

"Well, at least it's Asia."

"Which surprises me. With the way you and Bret are, I'm surprised it doesn't strike Pittsburgh."

"Better the other side of the world."

Again, Bret gasped. "You are so rude."

"Bret, would you prefer it to be here?"

"Um, no."

"My point."

Colin said, "I'll make mention of it at the conference."

"Along with your other findings."

"Yes," Colin nodded. "Were you trying to peek?"

"Yes."

Colin laughed. "Darius. You'll present with your rock star and I'll present with my scientists."

"My rock star *is* a scientist."

"Without PowerPoint."

"Our demonstration is awesome."

"But it's not PowerPoint," Colin said with a nod.

Bret intervened. "I keep seeing scenes from the movie Armageddon in my head, where all these scientists present ridiculous solutions."

Colin smiled. "Me, too, and ridiculous presentations that are over the edge."

Darius tilted his head. "Why won't you share?"

"Because it's good. It doesn't need drama."

Bret nodded. "It is good."

Darius turned to her. "You know his plan?"

"Yes."

"You didn't tell me."

"You didn't ask and Colin doesn't want you to know."

Darius blinked a few times. "You think this is good for a relationship? We need to be open and honest."

A chuckle from Colin, "Then why haven't you been honest about the Chihuahua?"

"I give up. Fine." Darius tossed his hands outward. "Share your info. I'll hear it then. But mine will be more effective."

"Than mine?"

430

"Yes."

"They'll never take you serious."

"Ha!" Darius blasted. "How do you figure?"

"Darius, you want to blow up the world. You want to show how it will be done and why through a movie-trailer style presentation complete with soundtrack."

"And what's wrong with that?"

"It's not my solution and it's not my style of presentation."

"And yours is?"

Colin smiled arrogantly. "PowerPoint." He laid a hand on Darius' shoulder as he passed by. "Now pack, I have to get ready. And bring enough underwear."

After shaking his head, Darius looked at Bret. She nodded with a 'see, I told you' look.

"What?" he asked.

"Nothing."

Pause.

Bret inhaled. "Do you think you should have used PowerPoint?"

Darius said nothing; he just walked out.

***

Martin was perplexed, an adjective not readily used to describe him. Rarely, if ever, did he allow himself to get to the point where he would scratch his head and say, 'I'm confused.'

He was there . . . almost.

When they gave him all the information

431

regarding the GEP, he knew it wasn't a light day's reading. It wasn't a nifty brochure of frequently asked questions. It was bound manuscript after bound manuscript.

Someone put an awful lot of time into getting it together.

A complete staff.

He read 'book one' which was vital to the basic aspect of the project and Martin's responsibilities. But book two said the how's and why's of it all.

Martin's role as monitor was minimized, in his opinion. He would be more than that. An overseer, yes, of something much bigger.

The GEP was much more than a monitoring station, monitoring events that unfolded globally.

It was just what its name said, the Global Extinction Project.

The US government knew something big was going to occur. They had theories, but just didn't know the exact details.

They knew and suspected because of the global changes that multitudes of catastrophes would take place.

Again, they didn't know the exact details.

That was the reason for the conference. All the great minds together, saying what they think is going to happen, and presenting their proof of it. Then all the great minds that listened would determine who was right and who had the best proposal for a solution.

That was the reason Martin was invited. Because he too had that theory. Unfortunately, it was written many years early

But the government had a backup. GEP.

A way to ensure that man would survive.

Taken from the pages or screen of some sci-fi movie, the GEP complex would eventually house the surviving generation.

Yes, there would be others who implemented survival structures, but the GEP was going further.

Greenhouses indoors, medical facilities, staff, everything.

No matter what catastrophe, wind, water, earth, fire, cold, the GEP complex was being shielded and reinforced to handle it, to withstand all elements. That was unless, of course, a meteor dropped from the sky and landed on the complex.

When Martin looked at the plans, he saw some futuristic world.

He knew something was being constructed. It was assumed he was aware of the 'what', but he hadn't gotten to that page of the book yet. When he did, he nodded to himself. It made sense. At least what the workers were doing.

But after the construction, even though the mountain was somewhat hidden, the other aspect being built was not and how long would that be shielded from the public?

A huge, clear plastic, reinforced dome was being built. Estimated time of completion, 45 days with two thousand men. It would extend high, two hundred feet, encircle a two-mile radius and seal against the western side of the mountain. The only way in was through the other end of the mountain.

The dome city. Tiny houses were being

constructed. People would live in a controlled environment and watch the world outside go to ruin.

Three quarters of a million people would reside in the complex and dome city, a third of which were military and other professionals invited.

The rest would be by selection.

That was where Martin had a problem. Not the 'lottery' so much as the rules behind it.

And when those rules were released, he suspected that an uproar wouldn't occur until the lottery selection. Then all hell would break loose. How could it not? It wasn't fair.

The lottery was going to preserve life, yes. But Martin saw it as a means to also destroy life.

Didn't matter. It was just another disaster in a long string of catastrophes waiting to happen.

A string of events that Martin had to witness and document.

29 - Biblical

August 2nd

"Without a doubt a major geological event is underway. While authorities do not believe this will last much longer, in order for them to paint a complete picture of what is happening, they are asking for assistance from the general public, urging citizens to report any phenomenon, big or small...."

Colin reached over and shut off the car radio. "Urging citizens. Ah, yes, every Joe will be calling in."

Darius slumped in the passenger's seat and shrugged. "You never know."

"What gets me is the public is not dumb. The average fifth grader knows something big is happening."

"Average fifth grader is smarter than most adults."

"True."

"Well, this conference should be a way to keep peace and calm. Unless of course they release that the world is going to shit."

"I think they'll release information, but I think, to keep chaos to a minimum, they'll downplay it," Darius said.

"Hopefully they'll find a solution, no matter what it is, that will change the outcome or prevent so much destruction and loss of life."

"Or stop it."

"You can't stop it, Darius."

Darius chuckled. Yes, you can. I have a way."

"Ah, yes, let's blow up the world."

"You'll see...." Darius then mumbled, "If we ever get to the conference."

"Excuse me?" Colin shifted his eyes and looked at Darius. "Are we remarking about my driving?"

"Yes."

"That's right, Mr. 100 in a fifty-five zone."

"I wanted to get there."

"Yes, well, you got us pulled over."

Darius wave out his hand.

"The officer not only pulled you over and wrote you a ticket, but he took your license as well."

"Minor detail."

"And could you remove your feet from the dashboard?"

With a grunt, Darius dropped his feet. "I'm bored."

"Let's talk."

"Okay. Tell me about your plan."

"I'd rather listen to Nancy Newscast nullify the apocalypse."

"Fine." Darius reached over and turn on the radio.

"Fine." Colin turned up the volume.

***

Armando was a fruit picker before he crossed over the border from Mexico to the United States with his family and sought American citizenship. That was nearly twenty years earlier when his English was not so good. But now he spoke fluently and rarely did people ask him to repeat.

He was married for a while, but that didn't work out. Nor did it breed children. It was the divorce that caused him to seek the real American Dream and migrate from Texas to Nevada to work in a casino.

He wanted to be a pit manager but was told that took years. So he started at the bottom. After two years he made it to the floor. He worked the nightshift cleaning ashtrays, but it was a good-paying job that afforded him the opportunity to meet lots of interesting people.

That was how he met Tony.

A year before Tony was losing on the slots, and he asked Armando what would be a good machine. Armando shrugged and pointed to another one.

Little did he know Tony would hit the progressive jackpot and give Armando ten thousand dollars.

Armando used that to move the rest of his family to America.

But he and Tony stayed friends.

It was Tony who got a call from his cousin in the Army. His cousin was working on some secret project and gave Tony a direct line to contact him if anything weird occurred, mainly because a lot of things were going to get buried by the news.

This special line was different from the number they were giving on the networks . . . .

Something big was happening, and the special project was part of it.

Tony told Armando this and Armando said he'd keep an eye out for it, although he wasn't quite so sure what could possibly constitute a weird occurrence.

He had just finished the phone call with Tony and prepared to go to sleep. The morning sun was already bright, and Armando closed the shades and turned up the air conditioning. Even the air didn't seem to cool down his small home.

The temperature outside had risen to 100 and it wasn't even eight a.m.

He pulled down his bed sheets, changed his clothes and headed to the bathroom. He was so tired his legs were wobbly, and a full bladder didn't help.

It as one of those times for a 'sit down' urination.

After sitting and spreading his legs slightly so gravity could take effect, Armando released.

He sighed out with the rush of water that came from his organ, a steady full stream. Perhaps that was why the 'splashing' caught his attention. He blinked and worried. Had his urine become thick? Did he have a blood clot; something thick was in his urine to cause the abnormal water sound.

With that thought, the last dribble coming out, Armando prepared to lift and look.

Before he could, just behind his testicle sack a searing, sharp pain radiated into him and Armando sprang up, screaming at the top of his lungs. Excruciatingly, Armando reached down, and he saw it, the long brown snake attached to his testicles. Before he could reach it, he dropped to his knees. The agony had become paralyzing and just as he hit the floor, the snake released its grip and slithered away.

Armando didn't see where it went. He curled up into a fetal position and tightened his entire body. Within seconds, everything turned black and he passed out.

***

Martin had a late start to his day. Usually he was on the computer before seven thirty Mountain Time.

But on this day he slept late, having been up until nearly the crack of dawn. He retrieved a cup of coffee and perched himself in front of his laptop.

After he opened his email program, saw a connection, then sipped his coffee and swiveled his chair, not paying attention.

He checked the stacks of paper he had to review, not thinking much about how long it was taking for his email to download.

When the bell sounded, he returned to his computer and nearly spat forth his coffee.

Over three hundred emails.

There had to be a spam error. Opening his inbox, he saw the darkened messages, but he also saw something else: A similar subject message to them all. Even though they were all from different people, some civilian email address, some military, they all had one word in common.

Snakes.

Snakes? Martin thought. What could be going on with snakes that so many people felt the urge to email him? In addition, how bad could it be?

***

The linoleum reflected the cool temperature of the bathroom. Air conditioning blasting, Armando woke feeling the cold. Lying on the bathroom floor, he moved his right leg and felt two things: Excruciating pain that radiated up his thigh and to his stomach, and dampness. He was able to move a little to look down.

A small pool of blood formed by his legs, but not much, that was a good sign, but his testicles had swollen at least five times their normal size.

The painful cramp continued, and as Armando came to a bit more, the fog lifted and he started to feel everything.

The tingling in his hands, the tremor to his body. Moving an inch made him want to vomit.

He shook so badly and was so cold that he knew he had a fever. He couldn't even recall what type of snake it was that had latched on and bitten him. But he knew one thing; he needed help.

His phone was in his bedroom, not far away. If he could just stand or even crawl there.

Arm extending, Armando reached for the tub, and levered himself.

More pain.

Pulling on his inner strength, he managed to weakly stand.

His legs wobbled and felt as if they were asleep. He hoped that it was only the way he had lay, and not the effects of the bite.

Standing wasn't much better, the pain was like a knife and each step was worse.

His vision was cloudy and the room spun.

The phone. He had to get the phone.

Holding on to the wall for support, Armando inched his way to his bedroom.

The phone sat on his bed, and he spotted his salvation.

The front door was unlocked. Call for help, and then collapse to the bed. Surely something was amiss with his health. Surely the snake was poisonous.

He reached for the phone when he heard the screaming outside.

Not just one person screaming, but many. What was going on? His window was directly behind his bed. No sooner did his arm reach for the blind, he heard the screeching of tires, followed by one crash, then another.

Sirens.

Eye shifting to the alarm clock, Armando

noticed the time.

He had been passed out for more than an hour.

Audible pandemonium flowed to him, and with his forefinger and thumb, he parted the blinds.

Armando gasped.

The phone toppled from his hand.

People ran amuck, arms flailing, legs kicking. From them snakes hung, clinging with their fangs; some had slithered up their bodies.

They ran, but to where? Covering everything, every inch of grass and pavement, were snakes. Black, brown, green. Snakes.

Like thick, black tar that rained from the roofs.

Still not understanding where the people were running, Armando praised the safety of his home.

But that was short-lived.

No sooner did he sigh out in the thought of his household sanctuary, he heard the loud orchestra of hissing.

Slowly he turned from the window to see that he was no better off than those outside.

Snakes had taken over his room.

***

The whisper was so soft it was barely heard. But Darius knew what Colin said.

"Snakes?"

"Snakes," Darius replied, showing him the

442

text message.

Immediately Colin's eyes shifted forward, even though he leaned sideways in his stadium-style seat.

Forward to the presentation on the floor.

They sat in the back of the auditorium in Washington. The first speaker was at the table on the floor before the panel of experts.

He didn't look at the experts; he looked at the speaker.

Not ten minutes earlier, he and Darius were making fun of the speaker.

Doodling notes.

Poking fun at how the presenter was going to present his solution.

It was going to be interesting, considering he believed it was God's end.

God's end.

If that were true, then there really wasn't a solution and the presenter was wasting the time of everyone in the room.

But the text from Bret to Darius saying 'Snakes invaded Las Vegas' caused a bit of a cringe in Colin.

It was biblical.

And it didn't take long for the 'snake' news to reach the panel.

He only hoped that the snakes weren't going to be a deciding point for the panel. If they decided it was all God's end, then they would take no precautions.

And that wasn't good.

Something had to be done. Colin hoped it was

his idea. He was certain it would work.

And he wasn't that far from the time to present his report.

He shifted his eyes back to Darius who was in a teenage texting frenzy with Bret.

Then Colin listened, watched the panel for what worked, what piqued their attention, and Colin learned more on what he should do.

30 - Failure

What was he like beforehand? Martin wondered as he peered through the observation window of the sick bay. Inside the medical room a man, estimated swollen twice his normal size, lay laboring in his breathing. A nurse in a biohazard suit took his blood.

Carefully. Martin saw her apprehension, even through the window.

The nurse wasn't experienced in it.

Martin wasn't ready to fly immediately to the special facility in Nevada. But when it rained snakes or rather, the ground erupted with snakes, he had to go. As the observer. Despite how much he had to get ready.

The events unfolding in the world were making people antsy. He had hoped the conference would settle things. But with odd things like the snakes, people would panic. Put pressure on the system.

God help everything if it got out that the world was faced with extinction.

What was he like? Martin wondered again.

"He's one of many," the male voice spoke from behind him.

In the glass, Martin caught the reflection of Ben King, chief virologist on board.

Martin turned around. "Excuse me?"

"He's one of many. Anyone that was bit, got this."

Shaking his head slowly, Martin mustered up

a confused look. "How? Why? Are there unknown viruses carried by snakes?"

"There are many viruses that snakes carry, but none to my knowledge that they transmit. Hantavirus they help to control. This is showing signs of this, but it's different."

"What is God's name?"

"Exactly," Ben said. "Exactly."

Martin wanted to scoff. Was Ben getting religious? Was he joining the masses on the Book of Revelation train?

"Nature's going crazy." Ben said. "New viruses were born every day before all this insanity. Now the heated temperature is just a fertile ground for them."

"Is he going to die?" Martin asked.

"Looks like Armando Gonzales, at the rate his vitals are dropping, will not make it through the night. We have about ten percent of the people bitten that are recovering."

"Everyone bitten is infected?"

Martin nodded. "Ten percent beat it."

"Holy shit, a ninety percent fatality."

"Good news . . ."

"Good news?"

"Good news, we don't think it's airborne. It's a level four though. And contained."

At that Martin did scoff. Contained? He turned and looked at Armando in the bed. How in the world could Ben declare the virus contained? Maybe in that one incident. But if the snakes in Nevada carried it, then chances are others did too. And maybe it wasn't just limited to snakes.

That thought scared Martin.

***

Grace yammered in the background while Bret tried to talk on the phone to Virginia. But it was a fitting topic that Darius' mother brought up.

Food.

She was preaching to the kids that they were too thin and had to learn to eat other foods besides ramen noodles.

Bret didn't want to be the one to break it to Grace that they had in storage 3200 packs of ramen noodles, if not more.

"Rob's on the phone with the company now," Virginia said. "Do we know why?"

"All I know is Colin ordered the rest of the warehouse emptied and the supplies will be en route to you by midnight."

"Can we trust the drivers?"

"What do you mean?"

"Everything is going to shit; can we trust the drivers to get us our food and water, or at least the rest of it?"

"Absolutely," Bret assured. "Bruce got the drivers, all fifteen of them. That should be the last of the trips."

"Good. Good. Rob said it'll take him forever to keep up with the stock that arrived."

"At least we're ahead of the game."

"All that's left is the personal effects."

"Which we really don't need if it came down to a rush move," Bret said.

447

Virginia sighed out heavily. It carried over the phone. "I feel tense. I'm glad we decided to move everything here now instead of in September like originally planned."

"It costs a lot to do so, but . . . I agree."

"With this conference, and snakes, people are gonna panic. It's only a matter of time before hoarding laws go into effect and bottled water will be ten bucks a bottle."

"If we stick with the seventy or so people as planned, we'll be good until the seedlings take hold."

"Invites?" Virginia asked.

"Colin said not yet. They are ready to go. One mass email."

"I guess we don't want it to get out what we're doing or . . ." she paused.

Over the phone Bret heard it, a series of beeps. "What's that?"

"Shit. It's my friend Lin sending me an emergency signal."

"Lin? Why?"

"I think we have another flare."

***

When the word gigaton was spoken by Darius, there was a gasp amongst the scientists, and even though the senator covered the microphone, it was very evident he didn't understand. That simple word was more reaction than the complete silence following his mini-

448

movie.

"What the heck is he talking about?" the senator asked.

A whisper in his ear, and the senator's eyes widened.

He balked and Senator Harrington asked his advisor, "How much is that?

Immediately, papers shuffled as if every scientist in the world was trying to figure out the equation.

Darius leaned into the microphone, "That would be three trillion, nine-hundred sixty-nine million, nine hundred tons of TNT or about fourteen thousand 300 KT bombs. Which is about half the world's arsenal."

"You're serious. Half the world's arsenal? Do you realize how big of a hole that would cause?"

"They," Darius corrected. "I want to set them off at opposite ends of the world. Now I realize that many of my colleagues would argue that such an explosion could ignite a fireball that would rip through the sky and burn out our atmosphere, but I don't believe that to be the case. At most, the negative effects would be a nuclear winter for about 18 months brought on by debris in the atmosphere. We are experiencing a magnetic reversal; the devastation coming our way is nothing compared to that. The ice age to follow is nothing compared to that. We pick the lesser of the evils. Two years of cold with a little radiation."

The senator mouthed the words "A little radiation."

449

Darius continued. "Or a thousand years of frozen tundra. Which most of us wouldn't or shouldn't worry about, because we'd more than likely die before the ice hits."

Senator Harrington cleared his throat. "We have all your research, figures, data, and information. Thank you, Professor Cobb."

Darius turned to Colin, knowing Colin was next.

Colin raised his eyebrows and whispered to Darius as Darius gathered his things, "A little radiation."

Darius shrugged then he and Mark stood.

"Professor Cobb," Senator Harrington spoke up.

Darius paused. "Yes."

"Although we are impressed with your research and presentation, in the future, to drive home a more effective case, you may want to try PowerPoint."

Colin snickered.

Darius shot him a glance and then spoke. "Thank you, Senator. But I don't think that's a problem. Cave men have no need for PowerPoint."

"What do you mean?"

"If we don't do something, there is no technological future. Those who remain will revert to cavemen days. Drawings on the wall, sticks and stones, and uga-uga-uga-chug-a."

The Senator choked out a cough. "Thank you."

A nod and Darius turned to Colin who was

staring. "You're next. Good luck."

"I can tell you, after the lack of PowerPoint and that uga-chugga comment," Colin winked. "You set my stage." He smirked. "Uga-chuga."

Darius watched from his seat as he bit his nails, tiny bites so they lasted.

Colin had them. The attention of everyone in the room.

"High Frequency Active Aural Research Project," Colin explained. "Or HAARP." His PowerPoint display showed on the projection screen as he spoke. "Magnetic reversals are causing massive destruction. Can this be stopped? Although some of my colleagues believe it can be, I do not. The worst destruction will come from the final outcome. We as a people can bounce back from explosions, tidal waves, earthquakes, volcanoes and attacking Chihuahuas...."

Every one chuckled.

Darius shook his head. It wasn't even that funny.

"But man's long-term survival through a millennium of cold, well, we'll survive, but what will we become? We have the technology to prepare, unlike our predecessors. But still that final blow will wipe out most of man's population. People build technology. We need to focus on stopping man's extinction. Can it be? Yes. I believe we can stop the impending ice age."

A flip of the slide showed an underwater volcano.

"Already we've had numerous eruptions

451

underwater. This will not stop. It is estimated that, by the end of the reversal, the underwater volcanoes will have heated the oceans enough to evaporate nearly 22% of the water into the sky, which will come back down . . . dead of winter. Cold."

Switch of the PowerPoint slides.

"Clouds will form. They will do so; I estimate about ten days before they join. When they join, the earth will be covered with one connected giant cloud. The entire earth will be covered with this cloud. I theorize, based on the body of waters, that there will be seven such major storms that will join. Seven eyes. Those areas hit by those will be areas hit the hardest. But make no mistake. Everything north of Virginia will take hundreds and hundreds of years to defrost. Below Virginia, we'll see some balmy temperatures of about sixty degrees. Below the equator, warmth. But those higher temps will only occur after six months. People will flock south. But it will be six months in below-freezing temperatures. Food will run out, water." Colin shrugged.

Colin paced,

"Back to the hardest hit areas. I predict snow; three feet an hour will fall until we'll get about two hundred feet. Instead of high speed winds like a hurricane, we will have arctic blasts that will freeze everything instantly. You have two choices. Move everyone south, or end it as it begins. As I stated there will be seven major storms that will begin to form. That's where the HAARP comes in. Located in Alaska, this research project, though not tested, theoretically is designed to shoot a gigawatt of energy into the atmosphere. I have spoken with the HAARP people and they believe that my theory will work. I propose that when these seven storms begin to form, we use the HAARP as a beam to break up each cloud. We'll still have a storm, but nowhere near the intensity of the pending one. Plus, the HAARP will heat up the atmosphere enough to halt any global freezing."

The PowerPoint ended.

Colin smiled. "Now, I'll take any questions."

Of course, he'd get questions, Darius figured, and he got them with enthusiasm. Sinking back in his chair, Darius had to admit that Colin's idea was a good one.

He also had to admit that, after hearing Colin, the committee more than likely wouldn't choose him.

In the midst of the question and answer session, Colin paused. He actually held up his hand to the committee and lifted his palm computer.

"Gentleman, we have a situation," Colin said. "My people have figured out how to determine if another flare like the one that hit Paris will hit again."

Senator Harrington leaned forward. "We did too. It is highly unlikely, our experts say."

"Well then let's hope your experts are right. Because mine have just informed me that two are on their way. They'll arrive at earth in approximately 6 hours."

"Two?" The senator asked. "Where?"

"Eastern Asia, mostly isolated."

"And the other?"

Colin sighed out. "Los Angeles."

31 - News Out

August 6ᵗʰ

As with any other huge news event, the dual flares that careened into Earth, hours apart, was all there was on the news.

The events had just started taking commercial breaks.

The flare that hit Asia caused minimal damage and loss of life.

But the one that hit Los Angeles.…

It took eight hours to arrive.

Freeways were jammed.

Experts advised those who could not get out of down to get as far below as they could.

Problem was a lot of oxygen was removed from the air.

Hundreds of thousands died instantly. The bright side of it all were hundreds of thousands were still below ground.

Bret intently watched the news and the Moses Project that was beginning, where authorities were leading people out of the subways via the sewers.

They couldn't even go near the surface; fires still raged and the temperature was unbearable.

Not like the heat wave wasn't enough.

Virginia and Lin were tapped by the government to watch for more flares since they nailed it.

One thing was for sure. Not only did the flares change the face of LA and Asia, they changed the face of everything.

There was no doubt now that an extinction level event was to take place. The conference ended. The president declared martial law, and hoarding laws went into effect immediately.

There was a freeze on prices, and it was a crime to charge more. Details of the national survivor lottery would be told as it grew closer to the time, if it was needed. After all, they were going to try to stop the big event. What they'd attempt to do wasn't released.

Bret was grateful they had finished gathering their supplies and stock. Winslow sent fifteen men to the complex for security and hired Bruce as head.

He and Bobby would head down there first thing the next morning.

"Bret?" Bruce called for her attention with a snap of his fingers.

Eyes trailing from the television, Bret summed up an apologetic look. "Sorry. They were giving a body count."

Bruce reached out and shut off the television.

As if she were an addict and someone took away her drug, Bret immediately started worrying about what she was going to miss.

"I'm not gonna see you for a month," Bruce said. "At least. When does Darius plan on making the trip?"

"They expect the underwater volcanoes to peak early September."

"Storm?"

"Mid." She shrugged. "But then it'll be some time before the storm hits."

"Do you think it will be an easy trip down south at that point?"

"Why wouldn't it be?"

"Once people figure out an ice age is coming, that's where they are gonna head. Down south."

"Ok. But they haven't released that information."

"Officially. The internet is talking about it."

"Bruce, I really believe that most people are gonna think this plan will work. If they use Darius' plan . . . ."

"To blow up the world."

"Yeah."

"They aren't gonna use Darius' plan. There's a lottery, you know. The government is . . ."

Bret sighed out. "What are you worried about? We'll be going down south."

"At some point, the government is gonna stop the migration."

Bret snickered. "Don't be silly. Why would they do that?"

"Where are they gonna put 400 million people? Because that's the estimate Colin came up with that we would need to move south."

"We have our own place to go. Winslow has a plane.…"

"What if air traffic is suspended?"

"Why are you concerned?"

"I think you should come down now," Bruce said. "You and the kids. No one is heading south yet. It's not only gonna get crazy now in this world, but the closer to the event the worse things are gonna get. I'd feel much better if you guys just came down now."

'You know we can't. That would mean moving everything and losing days' worth of work. At this point in the monitoring it can't be afforded."

"Then let me take the kids."

Bret stared seriously at Bruce. "You're really concerned."

Bruce replied with a matching stare.

"As well as he should be," Colin said upon entering the house.

Darius walked in behind him.

"Did you hear the news?" Colin asked. "I think they just announced it."

"Aw," Bret gasped out in a whine. "Something happened. He shut my TV off." Bret reached for the television.

Bruce stopped her. "Why don't you tell us what's going on?"

Colin held out his hand for them to have a seat on the couch.

When they did, he spoke.

Darius took a seat next to Bret, kissing her on the cheek. "You okay?"

Bret nodded.

"We were held to confidentiality at the conference until they released the news," Colin said. "But, the news of the impending ice age is out, and, as you know, so is the lottery information. They have also decided which plan they are going with. The scientific advisory board has picked the best defense against the impending ice age."

Darius added. "Ice age. Not reversals."

"Yes, Dare-Dare," Colin said. "We are well aware they aren't going with your plan."

Bret spoke, "By the look on your face, they aren't going with yours either?"

Colin shook his head. "No. Scheduled for September 9th. They are going to watch the rise in temperatures of the ocean. They estimate that's a good time. And before the storm clouds form . . . they are going to use nuclear weapons to break off ice shelves, dumping the ice into the oceans in an attempt to cool the oceans and replenish the lost water."

Bruce crinkled his face. "That's a joke, right."

"Nope." Colin replied. "They think it'll work."

"But . . . you'll get steam."

With a smug smile, Colin gave a single nod. "And that, my friend, won't stop the impending ice age; that will hurry it along. The sudden change in temperature will cause a drastic switch in currents and storms of gigantic proportions. Left naturally, we would have had time to plan. With this . . . the storms will form within hours and be full force in three days.

"The lottery is planned for September 3rd. The individuals selected to go will be detained immediately in a local facility. If the Tundra Plan, that's what they are calling it, if it fails and as hypothetically I foresee, the storm clouds form, they will move the individuals to the GEP."

"Detained immediately?" Bret asked. "How can they do that?"

Colin handed Bret sheets of paper. "We were fortunate enough to get the lottery. It's selective. One-third will be chosen by profession, one-third by age, one-third randomly. Scary part is, it doesn't include families, it's individuals and it's mandatory."

"Married couples too?" Bret questions.

"Being married is the only fortunate thing. If you are selected, and you are married, your spouse goes. The only exception to the mandatory rule is if you are selected and you have minor children. Since the children are not permitted or included, that is the only exception."

Darius added. "But a child can be chosen and go without his parents."

Colin correctly. "Only if the child is twelve years old or older. Younger children will not be drawn."

Bruce held up his hand. "Hold on. They're gonna separate families."

"It's for survival and assurance that the human race will go on," Colin answered.

"But how can they mathematically calculate that?" Bruce asked. "They pick 900 thousand people on September 3rd. What if a large chunk is married?

"Oh, my friend," Colin stated, "the lottery is done. We just only find out those selected on the 3rd. Trust me, they did their math. That is why they'll be able to implement the immediate detaining of them. They'll know who to get and where to get them from. And although we have to stay up north as long as possible, I think we have our leave date. The lottery and detaining will be all day. People are going to wait. I say we leave for Texas on the third, because after that, it'll be a madhouse going south."

"No," Bruce turned sharp. "Bret, pack up now. Pack the kids up now. Let me take them with me before the insanity begins."

"Why?" she asked.

"The lottery. The insanity."

Bret waved out her hand. "What are the chances of being chosen? Slim. You go, get ready for us and the invitees. I'm sure many of them will come early." She shifted down to the couch. "Darius, you're being quiet. What do you think?"

After a shrug of his shoulders, Darius exhaled, and clapped his hands together once. "I think the plan to stop the ice age is stupid."

Colin widened his eyes. "There you have it, an educated response."

"I also agree with Colin," Darius continued. "It's going to throw us into an ice age, and the storms it creates will be far worse than what nature will create. I think people are gonna all hope to be picked for the lottery. That's why they are picking at nine the morning until midnight. So people will hold on until the last moment. Then they're gonna go nuts. Nuts. We're fortunate to have a flight out of here. We should leave on the third in the middle of it all. But, Bret, I think you and the kids should go now."

Her mouth moved but no words emerged.

Darius shook his head. "It'll be dangerous after the lottery."

"What about you?"

"I'll come down with Colin on the third."

"Then no. I stay, the kids stay. We all go down together. We have you guys in our lives. We are a family," Bret said. "We stay and go as a family."

In his typically sarcastic way, Colin interjected. "For as love noble as that is . . ."

"No." Bret cut him off. "We stay. We were in together from the get-go, and now we wade through every storm and we do it together."

32 - Lottery

*September 3rd*

It wasn't even the break of day, and already the lottery had started. Martin monitored the problems that began with the first detaining.

The president issued a speech the night before stating, "We aren't deliberately trying to separate families, we are, however, deliberately trying to ensure man's survival."

Martin knew well ahead of time the moment the first name of a child was drawn, and the moment that child was taken from his or her family, chaos would begin in earnest.

Not that chaos hadn't already started.

The snake attacks set fire to a wave of viral infections that claimed, in one month's time, 15,000 people. Even that paled in comparison to the revived bubonic plague that swept Europe.

Chaos.

Though there weren't any other sun problems, solar flares or EMP hits, the last two flares caused panic.

And chaos.

The heat wave was showing no signs of letting up, and the news of the ice age seemed like a rumor instead of fact. But Martin knew, he knew, the oceans had begun to evaporate, the temperature rose, and it was just a matter of weeks before the air temperatures plummeted.

Nature.

Chaos.

Many of the southern states issued border patrols to stop the pending migration of people.

The only way to drive or fly in was to have your papers authorized by the government ahead of time that you did indeed have a destination down south. A place to go . . . .

Louisiana was a free state. They stated they would let anyone in and set up refugee camps.

Although traffic to the south wasn't as predominant as Martin expected, he guessed after the lottery it would be worse.

People were waiting for their number to be called.

The word 'fire' over the radio caught Martin's attention. A soldier was reporting that a mob had formed and they were burning things. His CO gave the order to use gas.

With the intervention of monitors, Martin felt as if he could see the world.

On one end of the huge monitor board, he could see the preparation for the dome city.

The place where the lottery winners would be moved after they left the local detaining centers.

Martin didn't like the idea of moving the detainees at the last minute, but in an odd way it made sense. It kept people from following the transport. And the longer they waited to move them, the more likely that those who were not chosen would find a survival place or somewhere to go. And leave the detainees in peace.

Plus, the time gave them a chance to hope that the Tundra Plan would succeed, and then the GEP would be moot. The world would be saved.

Martin was doubtful of that.

However . . . the domed city filled Martin with hope. It would work. Of course, they would be buried in snow for three months, but after that it would work. It was basic needs but needs would be met.

Man would live, survive and go on.

An estimated 750,000 people would be brought to the GEP project, or rather chosen. Martin figured 20% if not more wouldn't show and would die, or run away.

Even with half that many, man's extinction was almost guaranteed.

Left. Right.

Good. Bad.

Dome city. Greenhouses. Workers completing projects.

Rioting. Destroyed cities streets.

Left. Right.

Chaos. Peace.

Martin knew, pretty soon, if the Tundra Plan didn't work, there would be a difference between the left and right monitors. It would all be the same.

Quiet.

***

Empty

Bret had been to the doctor's office once

before, and it was packed, but not on this visit.

Not only was the office empty, but so was the clinic, the parking lot . . . the streets on the way there.

Like some sort of sci-fi movie, the streets were barren and papers flew about.

She lay on the table in the examining room, giggling.

Her shirt was lifted some, cold ultrasound 'goo' on her belly, while Darius used the Doppler to listen for a heartbeat.

"There." He smiled.

Swish-swish. Swish-Swish.

"No matter how many times you hear it, it still sounds weird."

"I wonder if Doctor Beck will let us keep this."

"Be my guest," he said as the door closed.

Darius grinned. "Hey, doc."

He gave an 'up' motion of his chin. "Did you get a beats per minute."

"One fifty." Darius replied.

"Good. Good." Dr. Beck, an older man, late sixties, sat on a stool and rolled toward them. "You can take that and the gel. One less thing for me to pack. And as you can see . . . ." He indicted to the near empty exam room. "What I wanted to send, I sent."

Darius handed him a folder. "There're your travel papers for you and your family. Lease agreement approved by the government. Virginia said your cartons arrived. But I have to stress no more than one big bag and one small bag on the plane."

"Absolutely," Dr. Beck said. "My wife and I are very grateful for this chance. Glad to be a part."

"Glad to have you."

Bret interjected. "Oh, me too."

Dr. Beck smiled. "How are the others finding the facility?"

Nodding, Darius answered as he stood and grabbed a paper towel. "Good. Some of the little kids have made the back hall into a bike center." He wiped off Bret's stomach as he continued speaking, "But they need to play. Keep in mind, this is the last plane we have going down there. It takes off at three. Be at the old Clairton Airstrip by 2."

"I'll assume we have to show these papers?" he asked.

"Yes. We didn't have any problems the last two flights. Government is ready for us. Hopefully, they'll have an agent there. They'll check our documentation and we'll take off."

"Why did you wait so long?" He questioned.

"Data. We wanted to be up to date on everything."

"Darius is lost," Bret said, sitting up and sliding from the table. "His equipment shipped down yesterday. My sons Luke and Perry went down to set it up."

"The girls?"

Darius shook his head. "Authorities wouldn't let them travel without Bret. We tried. But they're only thirteen. She could have signed over guardianship, but no one was going down that we trusted for that honor."

"And I didn't want to go." Bret added, shifting her eyes to Darius.

Dr. Beck nodded. "Understandable."

"Well." Darius exhaled, handed Bret the 'goo' bottle, and tucked the wires neatly around the fetal heart monitor. "We'll be seeing you shortly."

Dr. Beck looked at his watch. "Six hours."

"Six hours." Darius extended his hand.

As did Bret.

After another smile and nods goodbye, Bret and Darius left the office.

She paused in the waiting room before they left.

"What's wrong?"

Her eyes shifted to the magazine rack. The empty waiting room, once full of life. With a shiver of what was impending and slight worry, she grabbed a handful of baby magazines.

"You're stealing?"

"Well. You never know."

With a grunt and chuckle, Darius led her out.

***

Admittedly, it was Mother Nature's great diversion.

When the lottery was announced, people assumed that their names would be scrolled across a television screen or a phone call would come. But that was not the case. They were pre-selected

468

and drawn, so when it was time, an armed escort came to their door. No warning. Ten minutes, pack a bag.

Cell phone service was shut down nationwide. The only number that anyone could dial was 911.

Just as he predicted in his thesis twenty-six years early, every phase was occurring, although Martin didn't foresee the emergence of past viruses, the solar flares, the EMP's, earthquakes, all of them.

The sun finally settled down and it was time for Earth to give its last hurrah.

Final signs. Once the volcanoes started erupting, Martin knew it was just a matter of time before the storm started forming for the ice age.

Four underwater volcanoes in the Pacific erupted, but they weren.t the diversion.

The eruption or pending eruption of Mt. Rainer was.

Two volcanoes in Hawaii were ready to blow as well.

All Martin could think about was the dust and smoke joining the evaporated oceans in the atmosphere, evaporations that were growing by the day.

No wonder he found it as no surprise when the government moved up the Tundra Project by three days.

Three days. Which meant they would know shortly after if it worked. Which also meant, the lottery winners would be transported shortly after.

He only hoped that if it failed, the lottery winners could be moved to the GEP faster than the storm would move in.

***

Jovial, joking, sarcastic Colin had lost all inspiration to smile or crack a joke. He dreaded it. The moment that Darius and Bret walked into the house. He dreaded it.

Never in his entire life, with all his accomplishments, had he felt like such a failure.

No words of consolation were helping, despite what Grace said. His black eye was only a war wound of his valiant and failed effort.

Casper's tears were like salt on a wound.

The sound of the car pulling into the driveway was like a gunshot.

Grace turned from the window. "They're here."

Colin swallowed and took a deep breath. He stepped from the living room into the foyer and waited. He wanted to be there facing them when they walked in.

The door opened.

Colin's stomach dropped.

God, they were laughing. All smiles.

But they stopped. Did they know? Was it that evident on his face?

"What's wrong" Darius asked.

Colin choked. The words wouldn't emerge. He watched Bret's eyes shift to the sound of Casper's sob.

"What?" Bret asked.

With an extended hand, he handed a sheet of

paper to Bret. "Cell phones are off. I couldn't call you. Darius didn't take the satellite phone. There was no way to inform you."

A quiet scream emerged from Bret as her eyes skimmed the paper.

"What is that?" Darius looked.

"Information on what to do. Where to go," Colin answered. "I tried. I tried, good God, I tried."

The magazines fell from Bret's arms and she turned into Darius. He embraced her.

"She was picked," Colin said. "They came and took Andi."

***

The letter simply stated that: "Your child has been selected for the Country Survival Lottery. As the parent of this minor child, it is your right to visitation while he or she is in the detainment facility. Visiting hours are . . ."

To Bret it was blah, blah, blah and a blur.

In the city of Pittsburgh, 146 people were chosen for the lottery. There were three facilities. Bret and Darius went to them all. The first one didn't have her, nor did the second. She had been moved to the smallest detainment center. Housing only eight of the 146, Andi was in a small abandoned office building that had been speedily redone to hold the occupants.

After all, they were expected to fly out to the GEP complex within a day or two of the Tundra Plan failing, if it failed.

A military truck and a Jeep were parked outside. The office building was set in a large parking lot on a small winding road off the main drag of Rt. 8.

The detainees were hidden for their own safety, the whereabouts given only to the parents of a minor child.

Andi was the only minor child in Pittsburgh chosen to go.

How many times did Bret pray to hit the lottery?

This was not the lottery she intended on hitting.

She was worried, but not too much. After all, it was her daughter. She would just go pick her up.

The Captain in charge seemed nice enough and sympathetic, but he still said, "Sorry."

"What do you mean you can't release her? I'm her mother. That's her birth certificate, my license . . . ."

He held up his hand. "I understand. But the lottery is mandatory, meaning she has to go. Ma'am, this is the world's survival. This is vital. Now you can visit up until we take her. Visiting hours are . . ."

"I know what the visiting hours are." Bret snapped.

"Who's in charge?" Darius asked. "Someone above you maybe. Who can we go to about this lottery?"

"Sir, I can give you the list of people you can call. But they estimated 75,000 children 12 – 17 have been chosen to go. So there are 100,000 parents, just like you right now."

"Can you get me that information?" Darius asked.

Almost as if he was ready, he reached back to his desk and handed Darius the sheet. "All the way to the President. As I said, you can visit up until we take her. We'll even inform you so you can say goodbye. But I've been advised to advise you that if we're moving her to the survival city, then things are bad and you should plan to go somewhere else than up here."

Bret wanted to say, 'no shit you moron, we spent eight million dollars preparing for our survival'. But she didn't. She asked to see her daughter.

Andi had been crying. Her brown eyes were red, her lips puffy. There was a nice soldier with her trying to calm her, but it didn't help.

"I don't wanna go, Mommy. Don't let them take me. Please."

Andi's tears caused Bret's tears and all she could do was hold her daughter for the two hours she was permitted. Hold her and promise her that if it was the last thing she did, she would get Andi out.

Darius immediately went to work on those calls. He was fortunate enough to have a satellite phone, but he was getting voice mails. But not a machine passed him without him leaving a message. And with each message of "I need some help' he left, he'd shift his eyes to Bret. Trying to convey confidence. Trying to convey to her 'we'll fix this.' Darius had to be confident; he had to try everything he could, because the look on Bret's face said no less than she was counting on him.

***

The last phone call Colin received from Darius, Darius didn't sound happy, but he did say, "Pack the car; we'll meet you at the airport."

That was encouraging.

Until they showed up.

Without Andi.

Bret had been crying and sank into the embrace Grace offered.

"I'm sorry," Colin said.

Darius shook his head. "We're not done fighting yet. I figure we have three days until the Tundra and a couple after that before they move her."

"You're staying up here?" Colin asked.

"What choice do I have?" Darius asked.

"Then I can't go, Dare-Dare. I can't. I'll stay here with you. Stay and fight to get that girl back. There are weapons and tranquilizer guns at the bunker. Bruce has it loaded. We'll pull a mission. We'll steal her, we'll . . ." He silenced at Darius' shaking head.

"I have no intention of not doing everything I can, even if it means pulling an attack on the detainment center to get her back. Hell, there're only four guards there. But . . . you go."

"No," Colin said, strongly. "I will not leave you. If that storm hits we have the bunker, we'll be good. We built that bunker should we need to weather out the storm. We will need...."

Again, Darius shook his head. "You can't. We need you for something else."

From Grace's embrace, Bret stepped forward. "I signed over guardianship to you for Casper."

"You're . . . you're staying here with Darius?" Colin asked.

"It's my daughter, Colin. We're gonna fight every battle to get her back. But if we get stranded up here, I want to know that my other children are gonna be fine. I trust you, Colin, with my children. I need you to be there, so I can be sure that they'll be fine."

"Bret . . ."

She stepped to him, grabbing his hand, whispering. "If something should happen to me, I know my kids will be loved and protected. Please do this for me."

Colin swallowed the lump in his throat, nodded and embraced her. Then he embraced Darius.

He was frightened for them. He knew. He knew that the Tundra wouldn't work and knew that there was no way, if that storm came, that Darius and Bret would make it down south. Not at least until the storm was over.

He gained his composure and stepped back. "Keep the satellite phones charged," He ordered. "That is our only means of communication. We may lose them for a spell if the storm hits, but after that, they'll be back."

Darius nodded.

"Dare-Dare, that storm is gonna be bad. We'll find a way to get you guys. Okay?"

Darius forced a closed-mouth smile.

"Your one means of monitoring the storm will go out for a spell, too. But after that, you'll be back," Colin said. "Once the Tundra fails, once the current shifts, move your ass to the bunker. Got that? Do not leave without the special vehicles. You don't want to get stranded if it hits fast and with a vengeance."

"Colin, I know." Darius paused. "I . . . know."

Out on the runway, the final thirty people lined up to board the plane, each turning over their papers to the government official. The goodbyes were hard. Bret hugged Casper as if it were the last time she would see her. But they didn't have too much time. Rain clouds were forming. She watched Casper walk, holding Colin's hand, until she disappeared into the plane.

Casper looked back, waving the whole time.

The last to board should have been the first, but he wasn't. Winslow was wheeled and stopped at Darius and Bret.

"Well, so much for riding in a spaceship," he said.

That made Bret smile. "Yeah."

"Ice age, huh?" he whistled. "Well, at least we're prepared up here." He reached out his hand, grabbing Bret's. Cold and wrinkled as it was, it was a warm touch that went though her body. "I got two helicopter pilots down there, waiting for adventure. But they'd like to see the new north frozen over. We'll get you guys. We'll get you. I promise."

Confident, Darius said. "It won't get to that point, Mr. Winslow. Your pilot will have to come and get us before the storm hits."

"Then we'll do that." His hand slipped from Bret's. "See you soon."

Bret closed her eyes.

Darius placed his arm over her shoulder and pulled her close. "We will see them again. I promise you."

"I know." She inhaled deeply and shivered. "I just want to get Andi."

"We will." Darius turned Bret to face him. "We will get her." He paused, and he and Bret both watched the plane begin to taxi. A finger to her cheek, he turned her head to him. "We will get her…at any and all cost."

33 - Rescue

September 8th

The day before had been Labor Day, and people had celebrated. Many people began to prepare for the move back north.

The increasingly cloudy skies began to break up, showing a bit of the sun. A sun that wreaked so much havoc peeked through.

A good bit of the population went south after the lottery. Cities were increasingly barren, and the government said that the best place to be on Labor Day was a refugee camp.

The President, like many other world leaders, delivered a hopeful speech to the population, encouraging them to keep the roadways clear and to hold off on returning north, just as a precaution, for two more days.

People didn't listen. Although no one crossed back over the freeze line, they patiently crowded the highways back north.

A bit of Martin, though happy, was irritated because he pegged the Tundra project all wrong. How could science, the actual science of it have been so far off?

It worked? It really worked?

For two days.

Operation Move, the act of moving the detainees to the GEP, would take 12 hours.

Those in detainment centers were already given their instructions, home location, and so forth. Over half of the lottery winners were already at the GEP.

Martin was in charge of giving the order to implement Operation Move.

And he did so without hesitation at 4:30 in the morning, staring at a weather image, just after receiving the news that a tornado blasted through a line of congested traffic on 1-95.

A line of traffic where people camped out waiting to return north. Cars were tossed about like toys.

Unlike originally thought in the short span afterwards, Tundra did not work.

The order was given.

***

Darius couldn't distinguish exactly which sound woke him at 8:36 a.m, the thunder or the phone. Both occurred at the same time. He sat up in bed, as did Bret.

The room illuminated with a bright flashing light that seemed to be in perfect time with the pulsing light on the satellite phone.

Bret immediate jumped from bed.

"Hello." Darius answered the phone, eye shifting about the room. He reached for the bed light . . . no electricity.

"Operation Move has been invoked. The transport arrives in one hour if you want to come and say goodbye."

After a 'thank you' and a 'fuck', Darius hung up. "They're leaving."

At the parted drapes, Bret turned around. "I'm ready."

"Me, too."

For days they had been trying every channel to get Andi from the detainment center. Every legal channel. They failed. They took advantage of the three visiting times a day to see her, assure her, and Darius got to know each and every soldier that guarded the center.

Well, enough to be secure that one of them would call and let him know when the move was to take place.

Darius and Bret had prepared everything, moving things to the bunker, having the Humvees available, and staying at a hotel near the detainment center.

A little fifteen-room motor lodge, where the owner gave them the room for free and simply told them 'lock up when you leave.'

It was after eight in the morning, yet the sky was as black as night. Lightning ripped across the sky sideways as clouds swirled about.

What had happened?

After visiting hours the night before, they were hopeful.

The sky was crystal clear and he and Bret sat outside, taking in the cool weather and looking at the stars.

What had happened?

The satellite phone rang as they finished backing the Humvees. Darius nodded to Bret to get in, as he closed the hatch, and secured his weapon.

The wind whipped about, and he knew if he wanted to hear any of the call he'd have to get in the car.

Tossing in his weapon, Darius answered the phone as he slid into the Humvee.

"Dare-Dare. Have you gotten Andi?" Colin asked.

"On our way now," Darius answered. "They're moving her to the transport. A helicopter will land and take them. But the wind has picked up . . . ."

"Well, pull a Rambo if you must."

"I plan on it, Colin, I plan on it." He began to drive.

"Do it fast, Dare-Dare."

"What happened, Colin?"

"Exactly what we thought would happen. Satellite images are more frightening than I ever thought. We're gonna lose communication with you. But know this, you have two hours."

Instinctively Darius' foot wanted to hit the brakes. "Two hours?"

Bret peeped out. "Two hours."

"The storm isn't even lowered yet. Two hours it will start. Once it does, expect hail the size of baseballs, winds at hurricane speed, and flooding. That's all before the temperatures drop and the snow begins."

"Got it."

"Get to the bunker, Dare-Dare."

A crash of thunder, flash of lightning and the

rain began. It fell instantaneously and hard. Darius turned on the wipers. "We'll get there; somehow I think we have less than two hours."

"Then don't take a chance on . . ."

Nothing.

Dead air.

A rush of static and nothing.

Darius handed Bret the phone. "Lost the connection." He gave a squeeze to her hand.

She looked at him with a concerned face, Her lips pouting before she spoke. "We'll get her, right? We're gonna get her."

Darius shifted his eyes to his gun, then up to Bret. He winked and smiled. "I have every faith. We'll get her."

***

Colin slid the satellite phone slowly from his ear to his chin. His back to everyone, he felt a hand touch upon his shoulder and grip, a grip that could only be from Grace.

Taking a breath, he turned around.

Not a word was spoken to him but he could see it in their faces. Grace, Virginia, Luke, Perry, Casper . . . .

A sniff, clearing of throat, Colin spoke. "We lost connection. The storm must be moving in."

"What was the last thing that was said?" Grace asked.

"They were moving Andi. He was going to do what it took."

"Even storm the detainment center?"

"If that's what it takes."

Grace stepped back. "He could be shot."

Calmly, matter-of-factly, Colin replied. "Could, yes."

Luke pointed to the radar. "He's gonna have to get her, Dr. Reye. From this, can they fly them out of there?"

Colin looked at the screen. "This storm is huge. I don't know."

"How long will this last?" Luke questioned further.

"From start to finish . . . a week, maybe more. It's gonna be a while for this baby to dump all that it's supposed to." He looked Virginia. "What's it like topside?"

"Just getting overcast. A few flurries."

Colin drew everyone's attention to the images of the storms. "See this . . . this . . . and this . . . ." he pointed to three different systems. "These three alone will cover the continent of North America. With eyes on the east coast. Canada and Midwest. We're gonna get the tail of all of them, but we should be spared the worst. Maybe get twenty, twenty-five feet of snow."

"Good Lord," Grace gasped out. "If we're getting that much, how much will they get?"

"More, much more," Colin replied.

Virginia interjected. "Up to four or five times more."

Casper asked. "When will we know if they're okay, if they got my sister?"

"I'll keep trying. Every second I can, we'll try to get through. But it may not be until the majority of this passes. And by the looks of things . . . ." Colin pointed to the screen. "That may be a while. Right now we just hope and pray."

***

Flash!

Crash!

The lightning was blinding and the thunder vibrated the Humvee just before it swerved.

"What's going on?" Bret asked panicked.

"Wind gust." Darius answered. "We're ok."

Bret leaned forward. "Helicopter's there. Please don't let her be on that."

"They can't fly that, Bret. They can't." Darius pulled to the facility, hitting the brakes and sliding. "Let's go." He reached down for his weapon.

The light flickered just above the front door of the detainment facility, and two soldiers were posted out front, which led Darius to believe two more plus the Captain was inside.

He seemed to forget that Bret was with him; at least that was the way he moved, rushing, with his weapon under his long black coat.

He approached the soldier. "Hey, Gus."

"Dr. Cobb, they're getting her ready. Just on time. You look like the Matrix guys."

"Yeah, that was the plan," Darius said. "We both do."

Gus chuckled, a younger soldier not even a sergeant yet. "You do."

484

"We're sorry, Gus," Darius said.

"For?"

Out from under his coat, Darius swung his shot gun and aimed it at Gus. "We came to take our daughter."

Gus raised his hands and before the other soldier could react, Bret had her weapon on him.

Darius gave a nudge. "Let's go get her."

***

The rain and thunder was muffled slightly the second they stepped through the door. Darius' assessment was slightly off. Six people lined the hallway, Andi first. They had a single bag at their feet. Where were the other two? The Captain?

Darius shifted his eyes.

"Mommy!" Andi cried out and raced to Bret.

"Keep your aim, Bret," Darius ordered.

"Dr. Cobb," Gus tried to be reasonable. "Come on. Put the gun down."

"I'm not hurting anyone, Gus. Just taking the girl. You people can go back to what you were doing."

Gus, shotgun nearly against him, tilted his head Darius' way and whispered. "You know I ain't gonna stop you, Dr. Cobb."

Darius replied in a whisper. "And you know I'm not going to shoot you."

Gus nodded.

Another motion of his head and Darius said to Bret, "Back it up, Bret, slowly, and take Andi to

485

the car."

From a side office door, the First Sgt. emerged. He paused a split second then pulled his revolver. "Hold it!"

Darius kept his aim on Gus. "John, I just want our kid. That's all. Bret, keep going."

"Dr. Cobb, I can't let you do that."

"You don't have anything to lose. Just let her go with us."

"Again, I can't let you take her."

What? What was he looking at? Darius wondered. Then he heard Bret and Andi scream.

Darius couldn't turn around. He couldn't take a chance on his weapon being confiscated.

Gus whispered. "They got her."

Darius clenched his jaws. The missing soldier. That's where he was. Behind them.

John stepped closer, aiming. "I'll shoot you. Put down the weapon, say goodbye to your daughter and just go. Go to safety."

"I can't do that, John." Darius said. A blast of thunder and the rain fell harder, making it louder in the hallway. "Let me take her. I can't let you put her on the chopper. Did you see it out there? It's getting worse by the minute."

"Put down the weapon now!" John ordered.

"The big one's here," Darius stayed firm. "Where are you going, John? Huh? You load these people on the bird. Where are you and your men going? To the survivor city?"

He heard a whispering 'no', from Gus. And Darius chuckled. "You mean you and your men have to find a place to...."

"Put down your fuckin' weapon, Darius!" John blasted.

"No!" Darius held firm.

"I know you love this girl. I know her mother loves this girl. But for God's sake," John pleaded. "This is her survival. She's being taken to a safe place! She will live. She will survive this! Your love for her should make you let her go. Isn't that what you want? For her to live!"

"Yes, that's what we want, that's why we're taking her!"

"And do what!" John spoke loudly to be heard over the pouring rain and moved in toward Darius. "Die in this storm! The government has a survival city. A place for her to go. Grow old. Live! A safe haven! Do you have a better plan?"

With a connection of eye contact to John, Darius cocked a crooked smile.

***

"Where exactly is this place?" John asked, leaning between the front seats.

Darius lifted his eyes from the rain-soaked windshield to John. "Not far, just on the outskirts of downtown. Which is good. Water's rising. I can feel it."

Gus was positioned in the turret of the Humvee. Not just because he wanted that demented experience of the mega-storm, but also it was helping Darius with navigation. The skies were dark and the amount of water unbelievable.

Darius lifted the radio. "Gus, you sure you

don't want to come in."

"Nah, I'm good. Over."

Another shift of his eyes to John. John smiled with a shake of his head and sat back.

The Humvee was hot and crowded. John, Gus, and another soldier named Peter joined Darius. The fourth solder said he had to find his family.

Six people were to board the chopper for the GEP. Only three of them did. The other three, like the soldiers, opted for the bunker . . . .

John's eyes locked on Darius in the after seconds of being informed about the Bunker, Texas. Not that Darius said much. Just that, "Hey, we've been prepping for nearly six months. We've put over eight million into our survival. We got a safe holding place here in Pittsburgh, and a final survival city in Texas."

For some reason that information pushed a release button and Andi ran into Bret's arms.

"Wait a second," a woman named Lucy spoke up. "Darius Cobb. You spoke at the conference. You wanted to blow up the world."

Darius cringed.

Harris, a businessman who still looked the part, spoke up. 'Hell, if he has a place, I want to go there instead of that chopper."

"I'm gonna assume by the look on your face, John," Darius said, "we're taking her."

"Go." John nodded. "Go. Be safe."

"Take her to the Humvee," Darius told Bret.

'Thank you, John," Bret whimpered out.

Darius shouldered his weapon. "Now who

else is coming."

It was quiet in the Humvee except for the pounding rain, and Darius reflected on the rescue moment. They went there for Andi. There were supposed to be only the three. Now they had nine additional. The bunker was ready for that, equipped for that, and while the Humvee was crowded, it was worth it.

Admittedly, Darius was relieved that people had joined them. Not that he couldn't handle the storm and take care of Bret and Andi, but an old saying, 'safety in numbers,' held true in the situation they faced. Darius had the numbers.

Hands were needed for hunkering down at the bunker and for the eventual trip with the second Humvee going south. Now he had five additional men for that. It would work and be better.

The storm was just the beginning. Just the literal tip of the long series of icebergs ahead.

***

Even though the Bunker was safely located away from the three rivers, there was still about two feet of water when they arrived.

The hindrance of the storm slowed their journey, and by the time they crossed the bridge, the downtown area of Pittsburgh had already flooded. The rivers had risen, as Darius estimated, nine feet.

The initial scary portion of the freak lightning had passed, and the blackened skies turned dark gray, affording some visibility.

The brightest spot of the day was the continuous saying of the word 'Dude' from Gus.

Dude, when they arrived.

Dude, when he saw the outside of the building was just a cover for what was built.

Dude, when they drove the Humvees up to the fourth floor via the interior ramps, around the stockpiles of firewood and generators.

Dude, when Darius told them that, once the snow started to build, they'd erect a ramp and drive up to the next level, until they could drive up no further.

John explained to his men their duties. And they worked with Darius to learn.

The others were situated on the home floor, second to top level. Bret assigned sleeping areas and informed them of 'the plan' while Darius took John to the floor below.

The lab.

The generator powered up, but they'd have to conserve that. John assigned Gus to the furnace. Fire it up.

The Bunker was already getting warm.

But not for long.

"Temperature's dropping," John informed. "We're at 12 degrees now."

"Expect it to get colder, really cold," Darius said. "It was sixty last night."

Pete peered out the only open section of window on that floor. "Looks like the water stopped rising," he said. "Looks like the water's freezing."

"It is." Darius clicked on the keyboard and turned the monitor to John. "This is where we are."

"Storms still to the east and north of us. It looks like we're only on the outskirts."

Darius nodded. "Yeah, so can you imagine when it rolls in?"

John whistled. 'I don't want to. Bad?"

"Yep. Once it starts, then we switch into hunker down mode."

"It's quiet out there now. Calm before the real storm."

Darius only nodded with a facial expression that stated, 'you aren't kidding."

"Hey, guys," Pete called out. "Sarge. We might want to hit that hunker phase." He pointed to the window. "Here comes the snow."

34 - Buried

September 12th

The tiny window on the community floor was the only peek outside that Andi had. She watched out the window so much, that man named Harrison kept telling her she was going to get snow blindness.

She guessed he had a point. After all, every time she turned away everything looked green. So she put on sunglasses, even though there was no sun.

It was still snowing, and she watched the tracks from the Humvees fast disappear behind the falling snow, snow that was still accumulating after four days.

Her question of whether or not you'd sink if you walked on the snow was answered when the Humvees moved up one more level.

Darius told her that he didn't foresee the snow reaching much higher, maybe another fifteen feet.

Fifteen feet.

Andi laughed when she heard that. The grown-ups were talking about how lucky they were that the snow hadn't hit a hundred feet yet. But it was close. Darius stated he thought it would surpass a hundred and fifty.

But did any of them realize how much was buried beneath the snow they already had.

492

Telephone poles were buried. Any building that wasn't more than seven stories wasn't seen. The only tracks in the snow were those made by Darius. And those fast disappeared.

The world looked wide, white, and flat. The snow made everything even.

It wasn't even playing snow. Darius told her that it was layered. Ice, snow, ice, snow. Hard like an ice skating rink and the temperature hadn't risen above minus thirty. There went that old science theory that it could get too cold to snow.

As she traced circles in the window condensation, Andi imagined the feel of being off from school. Like a snow day. It was quiet and boring. She couldn't take another movie or book.

She'd rather sit at the window and watch the world vanish beneath the layers of snow and ice.

***

Martin tried to contain his composure and not laugh when he heard one of the monitoring soldiers' comment that the dome city looked like a big snow titty.

The comment wasn't intended for his ears and the young solider apologized. Martin shook his head but didn't let on that he found it amusing.

In fact, he had to agree.

The dome was completely covered in ice. Snow covered all around the circumference and everything but the top was white. The top, Martin supposed was warm enough to melt the snow, giving the appearance of a nipple.

The first two days were hell and that alone should have melted the ice.

If, indeed, emotion could generate the energy to do so.

People panicked, cried, screamed, fought. The minor children brought without parents were distraught. Thank God, they had counselors, but there weren't enough.

There weren't enough arms to hug the children. Well, there were but there weren't enough adults who cared to hug the children.

To Martin that was a crime. They were the entire surviving race.

As the storm blew in, outsiders formed a riot and tried to break in.

How they found the GEP, he didn't know.

But since the snow started to fall, things outside quieted.

People . . . froze to death.

After the initial panic, people calmed, but they didn't adjust. They weren't accepting the new living arrangements, the new laws.

899,788 people were supposed to occupy the GEP, a good number of them due to arrive on Operation Move day. Close to 27,000 never arrived.

They either ran or crashed in the storm.

It wasn't bad for percentages.

But that was still 27,000 people who weren't there.

The satellite images showed no sign of the storm letting up, not for a few days.

Martin guessed that once the snow stopped falling and the sun peeked through a little bit, those things would calm down and the residents would soon begin to adjust and live.

Of that, Martin hoped. He truly hoped.

***

"Nothing yet," was the common response Colin often gave. Every time someone saw him, they'd ask. "Have you contacted Darius?"

"Not yet."

Even Colin was surprised he hadn't made contact yet. Then again, the storm was still strong and lingering where Darius resided.

The best he could do was keep trying to get through, keep trying to get a signal, and stay busy.

For the first two days he did inventory and devised, with a mathematician, rations.

He played video games with Casper and Luke, listened to Perry play guitar, and never sat quietly for too long.

When he did, he worried. Even though he had every faith that Darius not only rescued Andi but had secured their safety in the Bunker, there was still a chance.

And Colin didn't want to consider that, so he kept his mind busy any way that he could.

35 - Better Days

September 25th

Colin dreamt.

He dreamt of sunshine and popsicles. Warm weather and his backyard. The Fourth of July was prominent on his mind, more so the last one and that's what he dreamt.

Although subconsciously he knew he was cold, because someone in his dream kept saying, turn the air conditioning down.

But the dream was nice.

Darius. The kids. Grace.

The kids splashed in the pool while Colin grilled hot dogs.

Laughter.

Lots of it.

The whisper of his name in this dream caused him to awake and he sat up. He had fallen asleep at his desk chair.

So much time had passed. Too much. He hadn't reached Darius and the pilot said the weather was still too unpredictable to fly.

Colin was ready. On a whim to go to Pittsburgh with the pilot to see.

He had to visit the bunker.

He had to know.

They went through phases. First hopefulness, then hopelessness.

Twenty-some days with no word. No break in

the weather to try to reach them. How much snow was dumped up north?

He stretched in his chair and looked at the clock. 5:00 a.m. Another day. Another day of drudging through, planning for a future and worrying about Darius and Bret. Another day of facing Bret's kids and not having an answer.

Feeding the 44 people in the shelter and keeping spirits up.

He had become the leader against what he wanted.

A knock.

A knock at the door started Colin.

He assumed it was Casper. She had been suffering from nightmares lately, waking her and making her cry.

Colin did his best to assure her, but how well did he do when he himself was seeking assurance.

"Colin," Virginia called out softly.

"Yes." Colin, cracking voice replied.

The door opened.

At first, she was a mere shadow against the hall light. But then as she emerged, Colin saw she was smiling. He stood.

"What's going on?"

She sighed out heavily then grinned. "The storm broke."

***

They found an old movie and watched it, taking them into the late hours, and then Darius and Bret found a quiet corner and made love.

Being alone was difficult and they knew once they arrived down in Texas, they'd have a bit more privacy.

The tiny two-room quartered-off room that Darius deemed his and Bret's was sounding like a castle after two weeks in the Bunker.

The temperature had risen to just above zero, and they were able to unblock windows.

The two spotlights on top of the bunker were the only light. No stars, no moon, total blackness.

Morning would break soon, another gray dismal day.

Cuddled under a down blanket together in a large comfy chair, Bret and Darius both stared out the tiny lab window at the reflection of the spotlights on the snow. A small lantern added romantic lighting.

"One time," Darius said in a whisper, his lips close to Bret's ear as her back snuggled against his chest. "Colin and I went hunting. A huge storm hit. Huge. We were stranded for four days. This reminds me of that only more severe."

Bret chuckled. "Do you think animals survived?"

"Yeah. Many died. But, yeah, they found a way. Trust me they found a way. I believe they are equipped with an instinct to prepare, like us. They uh, stood more of a chance than people."

"How many died, Darius?"

Darius shrugged. "I know so many were buried trying to make it back north, and those who went south. God, Bret, I don't want to think about it."

"They'll survive."

"Yep. At any cost. But I can tell you, they're on their own."

"The President?"

"The President is running the new civilization at the GEP complex, wherever that is."

Bret inhaled deeply. "We'll be fine, though, right."

"Yeah, we'll be fine," Darius said. "And we'll make it south, eventually. We have enough food and water here for months. Months. By then, things should warm up down south."

"To forty."

"Yeah," Darius chuckled. "Maybe."

His head cocked to the sounded of running footsteps. Both he and Bret sat up, bringing the covers over them.

The door opened.

"Mom!" Andi burst in.

"What's wrong?" Bret asked.

Darius saw everyone in the hall. "Andi?"

Andi extended the satellite phone. "It's Dr. Reye."

***

The ringing of the phone woke everyone, an odd sound not heard in weeks. For as much as Colin had worried, those in the bunker did as well. Were their counterparts down south alive? Was there really a survival city in Texas?

All that was answered with the ringing of the

phone.

"My God, Darius, am I proud of you," Colin spoke with enthusiasm over the speaker. "You did it. You got that little girl. Did I tell you how excited I was to get a ring, and then when she answered . . ."

"Yes, yes, you did."

Bret spoke up. "How are my kids?"

"Great," Colin replied. "Doing well. Missing you. You folks are good?"

The group answered.

"I'll take that as a yes," Colin said. "How much snow did you get?"

"More than we thought," Darius took the reins of speaking. "We got worried a few days ago when we moved the Humvee to this floor. But the snow never rose higher. We can actually walk right outside from the window."

"That's amazing."

"But we're safe, warm, getting along. Not too bored."

"Hmm. Yes. As I overheard you are still finding time to take advantage of Bret to feign off boredom."

Off speakerphone, Darius, with an embarrassed smile, grabbed the phone and lifted it. "Thank you for that."

"You're welcome for that. In all seriousness, I am so glad you're fine."

"Did you expect we wouldn't be?"

"Not at all. What's the temperature?" Colin asked.

"Zero. There?"

"A balmy 36."

"Above freezing?" Darius questioned with enthusiasm. "That's great."

"And encouraging, yes. Now tell me something encouraging. When do you think we'll see you?"

Darius looked about the faces in the room, then to the window. He knew the journey was going to be tough, long, and well planned out. "Soon, Colin. Soon."

***

Colin hung up the phone and admittedly wanted to dance a jig right there in his office/room.

But Virginia and the pilot were the only ones there. Casper and Luke went to spread the good news.

"I'm very happy for you, Colin," Virginia said. "You have to feel relieved."

"I do. I do. I'll be one hundred percent relieved once they arrive."

"When will that be?"

"Who knows? He has to wait until weather conditions permit. Where they won't use too much fuel to stay warm."

"Do they have enough?"

"They have the two tanks on top of the Humvees. They should have just enough."

The pilot finally spoke. "How many folks are there?"

"Nine," Colin replied.

"If they can get to Kentucky I can fly there. I looked at the map."

"That's excellent."

"Yep." He nodded. "But we got one problem."

"What's that?"

"The chopper is in the hanger. The hanger is buried, right along with us under twenty-five feet of snow."

"Yes, that does present a problem." Colin rubbed his chin and smiled. "Good thing I thought ahead."

***

Sun? Was that sun? The moment Martin received the 'pass it on' chain message, he looked at the monitor, and then had to see for himself.

He made his way from the interior of the mountain out into dome city.

Sure enough, people were cheering, wearing sunglasses, and dancing.

The sun was peeking through and the cloud-spotted sky was turning blue.

Martin smiled.

It was a new day and somewhat a new beginning. That was reiterated when he received a radio call from the President.

He led them to the GEP; he put it together, now Martin had another mission. He had to come up with a plan that would lead them to the future.

36 - Uncovered

October 9th

No way did Colin expect over twenty feet of snow, but he didn't rule it out. That was why he had that machinery in the west tunnel, a Bobcat and a tunnel digger. With a blade nine feet round, the machine would dig a circular hole eight feet in diameter, but it took a while. Through snow and ice, they made it a mere twenty feet a day. The barricade wall they put up at the tunnel kept the snow packed in.

It took five days to get outside, creating a tunnel of ice and snow all the way topside.

Then they had to dig out the hanger.

Colin knew or rather guessed the odds of Darius and the crew arriving before the chopper was dug out were great. That was until he kept getting calls that they got lost. Fearful that Darius wouldn't find the complex, they unearthed the flag pole and secured that on top of the hanger. The signal.

Two days earlier, he had a frustrating conversation with Darius.

"You're not Moses, yes, I know," Colin said. "And I understand there are no roads or streets signs."

"It's fucking frozen tundra out here. We've nearly hit a building."

They relied on navigation and compasses.

No visuals. N0 landmarks.

"We think we're in Louisiana. We think," Darius said the day before. "What now?"

The best Colin could do was tell him go to the ocean and make a right.

That was the last time he heard from Darius. The check-in calls were thereafter made by a youthful sounding man named Gus.

Colin had just finished a cup of chicken soup when he got the radio call that they hit earth.

Which meant they'd finally dug out the hanger.

Sucking in that last drop, he donned his coat and made his way from the complex to the tunnel hall.

He heard it before he arrived.

That distinctive sound that was common over the last several days.

Laughter.

Whoosh!

Children's screams.

As he got to the snow tunnel, he stopped. He knew it was coming, he heard it and waited.

Sure enough, full speed on a plastic sled came a young boy named Marcus, nine and fully padded in a snow suit. He screamed with delight as he not only rode down the ice, but also slid onto the concrete floor another fifteen feet before he rolled off another ten.

"You okay?" Colin asked.

"Oh, yeah, I'm fine." He stood up.

"Did you ice up my walking path?"

"Um , , , no."

"Um no." Colin shook his head "I'm sure I'm gonna break a hip, thank you."

Grabbing the snow pole Colin embarked up the ice tunnel staying left on the gravel laid for traction.

Before reaching the top, Colin placed on his sunglasses to battle the bright sun.

It felt warmer, and it was. Pushing forty, he knew it wouldn't be too long, maybe a month, before the snow was melted all together.

Then the snow-slide ride would turn into a water slide.

"Dr. Reye!" He heard the call of his name as he emerged.

The workers who were actually scientists and not men who dug ditches were standing above a hole.

They'd made tons of progress.

Colin smiled as he reached the edge. "You can reach it."

"Yeah!" The pilot shouted from below. "Now I can scan the sky if she starts."

Just about ready to embark down the ladder, Colin stopped. He heard the beeping. Continuously. A jolt hit his stomach and he turned.

Closing in were the two Humvees.

"Dare-Dare," he whispered. It had been a month, and Colin ran.

Filled with glee and enthusiasm, Colin didn't stop until he met up with the Humvees and they stopped.

His heart raced when Bret and Darius along

with Andi stepped out.

"My God." Colin rushed them.

"Turn right at the ocean," Darius shook his head and embraced Colin. "Good to see you."

Colin didn't want to let go. But he did, embracing Bret then Andi before meeting the others.

So few people. And he knew they ran across no one on their journey.

Colin grinned ear to ear, a smile that was frozen by the emotions and the cold.

It didn't matter that the world faced extinction, that it was frozen over, that very few were left.

What mattered to Colin was the very few left. He knew they were safe and that they would survive and thrive.

37 - Defrost

Four Years Later…

A thousand years of ice. That's what was predicted, and that was true. If a line was drawn center across the United States, chances were, without greenhouse resources, it would be like the North Pole. Uninhabitable.

Martin knew that.

When given the task to plan, he did just that.

The greenhouses in the dome city were flourishing. As soon as one month post-storm, people could venture outside for fresh air, but not for long.

But his plan would take certain conditions. And at three years post-storm, the conditions started to ripen.

It was time to implement.

Temperatures down south had stabilized.

Communication with the third world and countries below the equator were minimal. Hurricanes, volcanoes and tsunamis took their toll in the last hours of the Storm.

But in New Mexico and in parts of Texas it had leveled at sixty five. It was time to venture out and start planning.

Small farming towns were rebuilt, and preparations for new farmland were made.

The livestock that was moved in the GEP

were being transported to the farms.

The dome city couldn't exist anymore. They had close to a million people and they had to find them homes.

They had close to a year or more to do so.

According to Dr. Colin Reye, the discovery that the shifting weather was causing fast glacier movements and the face of the earth was going to geologically change, including the mountain that housed dome city.

That eventually would move and spread.

Colin made communications with Martin via continuous radio transmissions. They had been in communication since six months post The Storm.

He was finally going to meet him.

In the northwest part of Texas, a town would hold 30,000 people.

Crews were there finishing up. It was one of twenty sites they were preparing.

When he heard Dr. Reye had arrived, Martin anxiously stopped what he was doing to find him.

Colin was wearing a pair of tan pants and a golf shirt. He looked ready for spring.

"Dr. Reye." Martin extended his hand.

"General Myers, it is a pleasure." A firm happy grip from Colin, and he took off his sunglasses. "This is my grandson, Luke."

Luke, a tall young man, greeted Martin.

"Pleasure," Martin said.

"Luke has that data for you to look at. It's quite captivating," Colin said. "Disturbing but expected. It's been his project. Not mine."

"Then, Luke, I owe you our gratitude. You

saved a million lives over your discovery."

Humbled, Luke shook his head. "You would have signs, sir. But I have to thank my stepfather; he was the one that got me interested in this aspect. And I focused on it."

Colin interjected. "Young Luke theorized it and he and my son, as you know, made several trips up here to measure."

Martin nodded. "Speaking of which, where is Dr. Cobb? I was looking forward to meeting him."

"Unfortunately he can't make it. Fortunately it is for a good reason," Colin explained. "His wife is giving birth as we speak."

"Wonderful news."

"Yes," Colin smiled. "With all the children that they have I'm glad we've ventured out into the neighboring town."

"How's that working?"

"Good. The surviving locals were minimal. Not many survivors. So we're adjusting. It looks as you are doing well."

Martin exhaled. "On schedule. Thank God. It's a new beginning. Everything seems so fresh. The air, the earth."

"It does. It has to be a new beginning," Colin spoke as he took it all in. "We're all still stuck in the past. We have to look ahead or we'll never move forward."

"The world was going to pot when this happened," Martin said. "Maybe this ice age was a fresh start we needed."

After a short stare, Colin winked with a nod. "Maybe."

EPILOGUE

Year 3325

Joshua wanted to extinguish the night light. Put out the flame for the evening. He was tired. His old hands ached from sculpting. But there was a buzz. News had spread throughout the village that the village journeymen that headed north, explorers had uncovered what they believed was the mythical city of Gep, buried in the northern mountain range. They sent back a messenger and would be back soon.

They found it. They found evidence.

Suddenly everyone was excited at this discovery. The ancient city that many believed was just a fable did exist.

Joshua didn't buy it.

He was eighty-nine years old, his father had lived even longer, and so did his father; not once had anyone ever uncovered any indication of an ancient city, Nor of the advanced civilization that was said to exist thousands of years earlier.

Yet everyone searched. Everyone always searched. Someone always found something. A pot, a bowl, bones. But nothing ever was conclusive.

Ready to set on his bench, he heard the call of his name.

"Grandfather?"

Ah, Daniel. The worst of them all. The most anxious. Joshua headed to the other room to check on him. Daniel lay on his bed. A bed that was like a cot.

"Yes, what is it now?" Joshua asked as he knelt by the boy's head.

"Have they returned? It's been four days. I heard they were almost here."

Joshua ran his hand over the six-year-old's hair. "Daniel, it's not true. Don't get your hopes up. Since I was your age, I was hearing news of the lost city."

"But they found it."

"Everyone always finds it."

His innocent eyes peered up. "You don't think it's real?"

"If an advanced civilization existed, surely we would have their means. If the myths of their destruction were true, would we not have found ruins somewhere?"

Daniel nodded.

"God has made us the way we are. We live peaceful and simply. How much more advanced, Daniel, can we get?"

"The stories say that had things that ran without fire."

"Nonsense."

"That they had ways to speak to people through the air."

Joshua laughed. "And if that was possible, do you think we would have rid ourselves of that ability? No. Now . . . sleep , , , ," He stopped and his head cocked at the sound of horses.

Daniel sprung up in bed. "They're back."

There was a commotion in the street.

'Find the elder, find Elder Joshua!" someone shouted.

No sooner did Joshua hear that, a knock came at his door.

"Elder. Come quickly."

Daniel scurried from the bed. Joshua would move as fast as he could

When he made it outside, a mob had gathered around the four returning journeymen.

"Clear way for the Elder!"

Donald broke free of the crowd. He bowed his head to Joshua.

Joshua felt the touch of his grandson holding his arm. "What is it?"

"We found it, elder. We found it. The ancient City of Gep. We found the sign, Monroe has it."

Joshua cocked back. Yet he still didn't believe.

"And . . . we found the bible. It was sealed in a bag in a case with other items. It is ancient as time. A bible that dictates exactly what happened. Written by a God. Fire. Disease. They had leaders and Gods. I had to know. I was very careful. I did not ruin it. I've read it on the journey back. Forgive me for doing so before you." He said as he extended the thick red book, perfectly preserved, a hard cover engraved with gold lettering. "I am full of knowledge and await questions."

"Forgiven." With nervous old hands, Joshua took the book. It was in a sense fragile. He lost his breath. Frightened he lifted the pages, the multitudes of pages. Words filled each page. He had never seen anything like it. Their books were bound with wire, string. The covers for their books were leather and the words burned on them. Not etched in gold.

People cheered in the background. But Joshua focused on the book.

"Grandfather," Daniel tugged his sleeve. "What is it? Is it really their bible?"

"I . . . I don't know." Joshua looked at Donald. "You say this outlines what happened to their world?"

"Yes, Elder, yes. It tells of disease and fire from the sky, the hand of God."

"Grandfather? May I see?" Daniel asked.

Still shaking and stunned, Joshua lowered the book to Daniel. "It is documentation from an ancient civilization."

Daniel gasped out as his tiny fingers traced the words. "What does this say, Grandfather?"

"Their bible and God's name," Joshua replied, and then read the title. "*The Stand* by Stephen King."

Made in the USA
Monee, IL
15 February 2023

27907642R00298